Slaying
The
DRAGON

Book One in the Deception Duet

T.K. Leigh

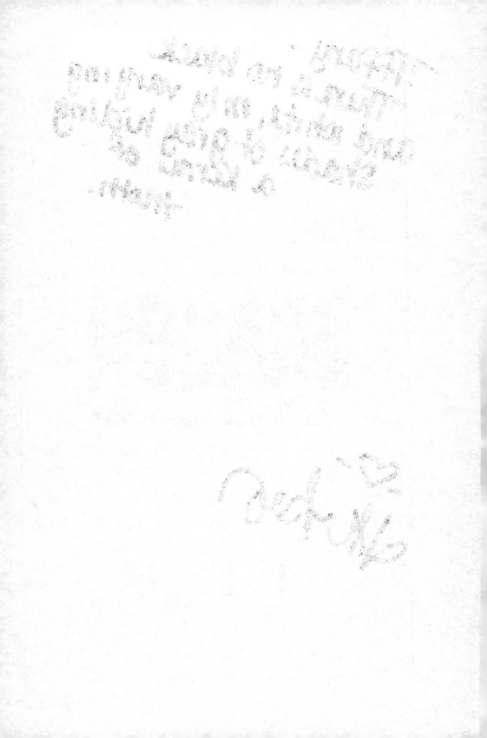

SLAYING THE DRAGON

Published by Carpe Per Diem, Inc / Tracy Kellam, 25852 McBean Parkway # 806, Santa Clarita, CA 91355

Edited by Kim Young, Kim's Editing Services

Cover Design: Cat Head Biscuit, Inc., Santa Clarita, CA

Front Cover Image Copyright 2015 Denis Mirinov

Back Cover Image Copyright 2015 Wallenrock

Used under license from Shutterstock.com

ISBN: 0990739937
ISBN-13: 978-0-99073993-7

To Stan and little #Tinkerbump... The irony is not lost on me.

Slaying The Dragon: /slang/ A common literary motif used in fairytales whereby a dragon held a young princess hostage. Many would try to slay the beast, but none would prevail... Until a handsome young knight came on the scene and defied the odds, rescuing the princess from her prison. Today, the phrase has been broadened to mean overcoming a seemingly insurmountable obstacle, either internal or external.

We all have dragons that need slaying...
What's yours?

Chapter One

Ghost

Mackenzie

BREATHE, I TOLD MYSELF, using my trembling hands to lift the parking brake on my Mercedes convertible. I stared at the two-story cream-colored stucco house, ghosts of what was for a brief period of time dancing in my mind. It had been a week since I ordered Tyler to let me go, leaving him alone and heartbroken on the streets of Boston.

But not as heartbroken as I was.

I had so many questions...questions I desperately needed answers to. Despite his lies, I still woke up each morning with an emptiness in my heart because another day had passed that I didn't get to feel his skin on mine, his lips brushing mine, his heart beating in time with mine.

I didn't want to feel this way anymore.

I needed to wash my life of his existence so I could return to the old Mackenzie, the one who maintained complete control over her feelings, but I knew I couldn't do that until I finally confronted him and said the things I needed to say. Only then could I finally move on and forget about Tyler Burnham.

Walking up the cobblestone driveway on unsteady legs, I tried to focus on simply putting one foot in front of the other. If I thought of anything else – why Tyler lied to

1

me, why he used me, why he didn't come after me even when I told him to let me go – I would lose the small amount of nerve I finally had. I had driven to this same house every day since I had gotten back to South Padre. Each time, I sat in my car, never having the courage to walk those fifty steps up to the front door. I had walked fifty steps countless times, but nothing seemed as daunting and insurmountable as the path that lay before me today.

I didn't know what I hoped to get out of finally confronting Tyler. Closure? Answers? *The truth?* Maybe I just wanted to look into his eyes and see that it was real for him, like he had begged me to believe. My brain never wanted to see him again, but my heart wanted it to be real because, for that brief moment in time, it was so real for me.

Step one, I thought to myself, my hands growing clammy as I timidly began the short journey that seemed akin to mounting the tallest peak. My eyes fell on Tyler's Bronco parked beside his Jaguar and the memories began to pour in. Memories I had tried to suppress. Even though our two-week romance was short in the grand scheme of things, it felt as if it lasted so much longer, our connection stronger than any I'd ever had with another human.

A breeze blew my dark hair in front of my face as I ran my finger against the metal of the Bronco, dust settling on my skin. I stopped in my tracks, recalling the first time I sat in this very car. I had been shocked he would drive a Bronco, throwing all my preconceived notions of the ridiculously wealthy and handsome Tyler Burnham out the window. He was worth more than the operating budget of several small countries, yet he drove around in a vintage Bronco with an engine that made an obnoxious amount of noise. That was one of the things that had attracted me to him, and it was one of the things I missed. I missed never knowing what each day would bring with him in my life. I actually missed the unexpected, even though it had brought me nothing but grief and regret.

My hand resting on the hood of the Bronco, I closed my eyes, wishing I could turn back the clock and return to that first lunch date, every little detail still ingrained in my memory. It had been unseasonably hot and humid for the middle of March, and I was a bundle of nerves as Tyler led me to his car. His hand had lingered on the small of my back, sending an electrifying tingle through me. I had done everything I could to remain the poised woman I wanted him to think I was. In reality, I couldn't remember ever being as nervous in the presence of a member of the opposite sex as I was around Tyler.

He had done everything right, making it impossible for me to imagine my life without him. He had become my lightning strike, just as he had sworn I was his. But lightning burns, and with each day that had passed since I learned the truth, I welcomed back another piece of my heart. Soon, it would be whole again, the wall around it rebuilt, and my life would go back to the way it was.

Soon, I would forget the sound of his voice, his musky scent, his dominating presence.

Soon, I would no longer be haunted with the memory of his arms wrapped around me, shielding me from the demons of my past.

Soon, he would just be another reminder of why life was better when planned.

Approaching the front door, I lost the few nerves I had and spun around quickly, ready to bolt. My chest heaved, a sick feeling settling in my stomach. Swallowing hard, I took a moment and leaned on the railing. I had no idea why I was as terrified as I was. I had been through much more challenging situations – losing my first love to what I thought was mental illness, burying my mother, losing my father – but I was petrified of what awaited me on the other side of that door.

Maybe I was scared to learn the truth. Maybe I was scared to learn I had put my faith and trust in another human and my instincts had faltered...again. Maybe it was because I didn't want to be faced with the reminder that life was better if I kept my heart guarded. Maybe it was because Tyler had done what no man had ever done before... He made me *feel*. Maybe it was because once he opened that door and I finally got the closure I needed, this chapter in my life would come to an end. Maybe it was because I wasn't ready to say goodbye, despite what my brain was telling me.

Turning back around, I composed myself, drawing in a deep breath. My arm seemed to weigh a ton as I raised it and rang the doorbell. The sound of a dog barking echoed, followed by approaching footsteps. Shifting from foot to foot, I fidgeted with the hem of my dress, tugging at it. My jaw tightened as I braced myself for the impending conversation.

Everything seemed to play in slow motion as the door opened and a built man with short dark hair stared back at me. He wore a black t-shirt and cargo pants, his breathtaking smile able to light up a room. But instead of striking green eyes, the eyes that gazed back at me were blue and foreign.

"Mackenzie," he said in a way that gave off the impression we had met before, although I couldn't place him for the life of me. I combed through my memory for how we could have known each other. He couldn't have been more than thirty-five, his jaw square and distinguished. His cheekbones were defined, his brow strong. Months ago, he was exactly the type of guy I'd

4

spend a week with before he returned home to wherever he came, but I'd remember him. There was only one explanation that made sense, and my blood began to boil once again.

"So you're working with Tyler, too, aren't you?!" I asked with ice in my voice.

He scrunched his eyebrows, clearly taken aback. "Tyler? Tyler who? What are you talking about, Mackenzie?"

"I don't know who the hell you are or what you're doing here, but if this is another one of his mind games, you can tell him I'm not amused. Better yet," I said, pushing into the foyer, "I'll tell him myself. Where is he?"

"Where is who?" he asked, his voice soft, almost concerned.

"Tyler!" I exclaimed, becoming irritated. I strode down the hallway, peeking my head into each room for any sign of him. His large waterfront house was exactly as I remembered – the furniture modern, the art lacking personality. I should have known something was amiss when I first saw his décor. It was frigid, cold, and heartless, just like Tyler.

"There is no one named Tyler here," the man insisted, following me as I tore through the house.

Refusing to believe his words, I ignored him. "Tyler!" I shouted, throwing open door after door, only to be met with emptiness. "Eli?" I choked out, my voice strained. There was no sign of either of them. Worse, there was no indication they had ever been here.

Feeling my world spin out of control, desperation took over and I ran toward the back door. "He must be on his boat," I muttered to myself, feeling a pair of confused eyes on me as I bolted down the stairs toward the back gate leading to the dock. I pulled on it, but it was locked.

"Mackenzie, I know things have been hectic for you,

what with the opening of the restaurant and the eighty-hour work weeks…"

I reeled around and met his sympathetic eyes. "How do you know who I am?"

"It's me," he said, urging me to recognize him. I prayed this was all a dream and I would wake up, open my eyes, and see Tyler standing in front of me. "Jeremiah. I own a club on the island. You reached out to me for advice about opening up your own place several months ago."

"But how do I remember this house? And I *know* I've been on that yacht." I gestured toward the beautiful vessel anchored behind me, certain I had spent one of the best nights of my life on it just a few weeks ago.

"You've been here," he said. "Hell, last fall, you were here at least once a week to pick my brain."

"I was?" I asked, my breathing growing more ragged. I searched my brain for a memory of this man, but it just wouldn't come. The last six months seemed to be a puzzle. Nothing of significance stood out in my mind…except meeting Tyler Burnham. And I was certain I had met him and that he lived here.

All the blood rushed from my face and I couldn't help but feel as if the world was giving out from beneath me.

"Hey, hey," he soothed, rushing toward me as I struggled to maintain my balance. "Let me call someone for you." He placed his arm around my waist in an attempt to usher me back into the house.

The feel of his flesh on mine scalded me, setting me off. "Don't touch me!" I bellowed, pushing him away. "And stop with the games! It's not funny! Tell me where he is!"

"I'm not playing any games," he insisted. "This is my house. I've lived here for years with my partner. There's no one named Tyler here."

Frantic, I pulled my phone out of my pocket and

flipped through it, searching for proof I wasn't crazy. "We met a few weeks ago! I just got back from Boston, where he's from!"

"Then why are you *here*?" he asked, his gaze narrowed as he studied me with concern.

"Because he lives here!" I exclaimed. "Don't you see?!" I continued searching my phone, my chin quivering as I scanned through photo after photo of me in Boston, on the waterfront, in the Commons, in the North End, eating oysters... But where Tyler was once in those photos, there was nothing. It was as if he had been erased.

The air was thick as I tried to make sense of it all. I was living in some sort of alternate reality. I prayed I would wake up and everything would turn out to have simply been a nightmare, that Tyler didn't just date me to gather information about my father. I had always relied on what I knew to be real and true, and I thought Tyler was. Now, I felt as if I couldn't trust any of my senses. Not sight, not sound, not touch...and I certainly couldn't trust my heart.

Staring at the yacht on which I thought Tyler and I had spent our "one night", I slowly turned around, my head fuzzy.

"Are you sure there's no one I can call for you?" the man asked once more.

I raised my head and stared into his blue eyes, wishing I could see proof this was all part of some fucked up plan to mess with my memory, but they were stone cold, impenetrable.

Sighing, I shook my head. "No. I'm sorry," I apologized flatly, my voice barely audible. "You're right. I've been working too much. I must have..." I fought back the lump in my throat. "My mistake."

My expression void of any emotion, I climbed the steps

and walked back down the hallway, a lone tear falling down my cheek. I didn't think I could ever feel any more pain than I did after learning the truth of who Tyler was and what he wanted from me, but I was wrong. *This* was the worst pain imaginable.

In a daze, I couldn't remember getting in my car and driving back to my condo. All I could remember was questioning what was real and what wasn't. Things I thought I touched and saw were now being presented to me as fake. It made me begin to question everything else in my life, too.

Pulling my Mercedes into its usual spot, I ran into the building, ignoring Paul's attempt to introduce me to the new security guard as I dashed into an open elevator. When it finally stopped at my floor, I couldn't get to my condo fast enough, holding out one last ounce of hope that there would be some proof of Tyler's existence within the four walls of my home…a home I was certain he had invaded so fully for a short time.

I ran to my kitchen, pulling open drawer after drawer, hoping to come across some lasting remnant of our time together, but I came up empty. Everything was how it was before I had met him. My silverware was just as I liked it. All my cooking utensils were in their precise location. There was barely a particle of dust on the counter, let alone a piece of Tyler's hair. The vases containing the flowers he had sent me after opening night of my restaurant had mysteriously disappeared, if they had been there at all.

Feeling the walls closing in around me, I grabbed my cell phone and searched the contacts. I pressed the entry for Tyler, my heart racing as I waited for it to begin ringing. But it never did. All I received on the other end was a message that the phone number was no longer in service. My chin began to quiver as I hung up and tried

Eli's number, only to get the same message.

Screaming in frustration, I threw my phone on the ground, the screen shattering from the impact, and ran down the hallway into the master bedroom. I flung open the chest where I kept my father's Victoria Cross, along with all the other keepsakes, recalling that I had placed the card Tyler sent with the extravagant flowers in it. As I rummaged through, the card was nowhere.

I let out a loud sob, starting to believe I had imagined it all. It was the only explanation that made sense. The realization was overwhelming and I darted into the master bathroom, heaving into the toilet, wishing Tyler was there to trace a pattern across my back and chase away my demons, just as I thought he had done for a short but remarkable time.

~~~~~~~~~~

AS THE WEEKS WORE on, I continued searching everywhere for some sort of proof that Tyler Burnham was real, but I found nothing. Not one piece of tangible proof he had entered my life in a whirlwind and flipped it upside down. There was nothing left, other than my memories…which I couldn't help but question.

It was as if every trace of his time on South Padre had been erased.

All but one…

Chapter Two
Kernel Of Truth

Mackenzie

THE SOUND OF SEAGULLS and laughter surrounded me as I sat on the sandy beach, trying to make sense of everything. I raised my eyes and stared at a seemingly peaceful ocean, a few boats bobbing up and down in the distance. This island was supposed to feel like paradise, like an escape, but it didn't. Not anymore. All I felt when I looked at the calm water, the sun shining and warming everything on that Memorial Day at the end of May, was a raging storm, a ship about to sink. My surroundings were mocking me, reminding me that my life would never be the same again. The truth was, it hadn't been the same since I met Tyler.

I should have been crying, but tears refused to fall. I should have felt *something*. *Anything*. Anger. Hatred. Resentment. Fear. Confusion. But I felt nothing. Ever since the day I had gone over to what I thought to be Tyler's house to see someone else living there, I shut down even more than I already had. I was a shell, a ghost of a woman going through the motions of living when I was really dead inside.

I closed my eyes, trying to remind myself of a happier time, hoping that would bring forward some sort of emotion. It was like trying to jump-start a battery that was long dead. Nothing worked. I was empty, my heart no longer able to feel.

I wanted to scream, but no noise ever came from my throat. I now knew why Catholics feared purgatory. I was there. I was a lifeless soul forced to walk among the land of the living. I wanted to make it all go away, to forget the beautiful, touching moments I shared with Tyler. The thrill of his kisses. The passion in his eyes. The fire in his touch. I was still tortured by all those things, sentenced to live the past two months in a constant nightmare because I was foolish enough to love him.

A small child, who couldn't have been more than two years old, ran in front of me, his parents trying to catch up. The glee in his laughter struck me as I watched the happy family enjoying their vacation. The mother playfully grabbed the little boy, swinging him around and around, his squeals echoing and calling to a side of me I didn't know existed. A tear escaped my eye and trickled down my cheek, cooling the fire that had been burning inside me. Then another tear fell. And another. And another.

The dam broke and, for the first time in months, I felt something. I lowered the iron fortress I had erected around my heart and stopped pretending I was okay, pretending what Tyler did hadn't destroyed me. It wasn't his deception that shattered me. It was my love for him, then and now. In my heart, I knew he was real, that we experienced a love so perfect, which made everything so much harder. My heart ached for him. My skin craved his touch. My body longed to be held in his arms. The arms that would always remind me of dancing, full metal jackets, and *Truth or Dare*.

He had tainted something so beautiful, so pure, so fucking perfect. His love was toxic and I needed to purge it from my system through my cleansing sobs. I had bottled it all up for months and it felt therapeutic to

11

finally let it out. With each tear, I was letting go of another piece of him. His smile. His green eyes. His husky voice that swore he loved me. His words begging me to spend the rest of my life with him. They were all leaving me and, once my tears stopped, I vowed to never cry because of him again.

I had no idea how long I sat there with my head buried in my knees, my cries ravaging my short and slender body, but I didn't care. It didn't matter that people could have been laughing and pointing at the poor pathetic girl who gave everything to a man who used her, then tried to cover his tracks and make her think she imagined him. I needed this. Maybe then I could finally be over him.

I *needed* to be over him.

I wouldn't let him ruin my life anymore.

A warm presence approached from behind and two arms enveloped me. I sighed, molding my body into Brayden's. He was exactly what I needed right now. I needed his smile, his laugh, his compassion. I needed his reassurance that I was strong enough to get through this. That this wouldn't break me. That I could rewind the clock and forget all about Tyler Burnham.

Pulling at the crisp gray shirt underneath his black suit, I drenched him with my tears, and he simply continued to comfort me, not saying a word. He knew me well enough to know I didn't want to talk. Not yet. He was the only man in my life who always gave me exactly what I needed when I needed it. He had always been true and honest. He never had an ulterior motive. His love was pure and untainted.

"It's about time you started acting like a human again," he soothed, breaking the silence between us. He rocked me gently, running his fingers up and down my back. "You can't keep pretending what's been going on didn't affect you, baby girl. It's obvious it did. It's okay to show your emotions once in a while. It's okay to show you're not impenetrable."

I nodded slightly and clung to him as if holding him was the only way to keep my world together. He and Jenna had prodded me for an explanation about why I ran out on Tyler, but I didn't know what to tell them. I couldn't tell them the truth. Instead, I maintained that I wasn't ready to talk about it, but that I found out he wasn't the man I thought he was, which had a sliver of truth.

"How did you know I'd be here?" I pulled back and stared at his kind face, his blue eyes sparkling as he gazed at me with all the tenderness and understanding I needed from him at that moment.

"Call it my gut instinct. I went to the restaurant and Jenna said you had an appointment this morning, then never showed up afterwards. That doesn't exactly sound like the Mackenzie we all know and love, so I had a feeling something must be wrong. I was on my way to the condo and noticed your car on the side of the road here."

I wiped at my cheeks, taking a deep breath to settle my cries.

"Want to tell me what's wrong?" he asked, almost guarded at how I would react.

"What *isn't* wrong?" I scoffed. "I still go back and forth, boo," I confessed, leaning my head on his shoulder. I picked up some shells in front of me and began tracing patterns in the warm sand. "Sometimes I feel like I'm losing my mind, that something in my brain snapped and I made it all up." Lifting my gaze, I stared at the ocean waves, hoping they would calm me as they used to. "The only people who assured me I didn't imagine any of it were you and Jenna. If I didn't have you swearing it was real, that *he* was real, I probably would have checked myself into the loony bin at this point." I glanced at him,

13

seeing him studying my every move, almost as if he was ready for me to freak out at any second.

Returning my eyes to the sand in front of me, I softly asked, "Do you know I still go by his house every day?"

Biting his lip, he nodded. "I figured."

"I don't know why." I shrugged, fighting back the new tears brimming in my eyes. "Part of me wants to think all of this has just been one giant nightmare, that I'll wake up and everything will be like it used to be. What would you think if you were me? If, a week later, you decided to be the bigger person and try to talk things over, but you find someone completely different living in Tyler's house, trying to convince you he's lived there for years? It's as if someone wants me to feel like I'm losing my mind. As if they want me to question whether any of it's real. No matter how many times you and Jenna have told me it *was* real, I still had my doubts. My brain was yelling at me that it couldn't be real. I had no physical proof it was. My heart didn't want to believe it, though, and that's been the only thing that's kept me going. In my heart, I just knew it had to be real." Meeting his gaze, I studied his gentle face, his eyes brimming with the same pain I felt.

Taking a deep breath, my voice quivered. "But there's no doubt anymore." I pulled the black-and-white image I had been staring at most of the day out of my purse and handed it to Brayden.

He glimpsed at the photo, then shot his wide eyes to me, questioning.

"You're going to be an uncle, boo." I covered my mouth, my breath catching at the words. Until that moment, it hadn't sunk in. Even after the doctor confirmed what over a dozen pregnancy tests already had, I didn't think it was real. Finally speaking those words surrounded me with the truth amidst a lifetime of lies.

Brayden's expression momentarily grew grim before he replaced it with a cheerful smile I was certain was for my benefit. "Uncle Boo... I like the sound of that." He pulled me to him once more and planted a soft kiss on my temple.

A thousand thoughts ran through my mind, the most pressing of which being how the hell I was going to afford this. Since most of my money was tied up in the restaurant, I had allowed my health insurance to lapse. The doctor visit itself was going to cost me a small fortune. I knew Brayden would offer to help, as he always did; however, at some point, I was going to have to find the man who had become a ghost...Tyler.

"Mack, I know you probably don't want to, but you need to talk about what you're going to do." He released his hold on me, forcing me to stare into his eyes.

"What do you mean?"

"You *know* what I mean," he insisted, raising his eyebrows at me once more. "He has a right to know. I'm assuming it's his..."

I nodded. "But how am I supposed to tell him? It's like he's dropped off the face of the earth! His cell is disconnected, and so is Eli's! Every time I've called his company's office, I get nowhere! Hell, maybe I *am* losing my mind. Maybe I did imagine him. Maybe it's someone else's kid! Right now, I just..." My chin wavering, I squeaked out, "I'm barely holding it together here, Brayden."

Tears began to stream down my face again. There was a hollow feeling in my chest as I struggled to come to terms with the reality that would soon be my life, that I was carrying the baby of a man who wounded me, then disappeared. I would be forced to stare into my baby's eyes every day and be reminded of how stupid and naïve

I had been.

"Shhh, baby girl," Brayden soothed, comforting me in his embrace. He kissed the top of my head, brushing my hair back just like my mother used to all those years ago.

"I'm stuck and it's all my fault."

"Mack, baby, it takes two to tango. He's just as responsible as you so don't you *dare* put all the blame on your shoulders. He could have easily slipped on a rubber and you wouldn't be faced with this."

I shook my head. "I told him it was okay. I was so stupid and caught up in the moment. I wasn't thinking straight. Now I'm knocked up, carrying the baby of a man I can't even think about without breaking down." I turned to him and stared into his eyes, finally allowing myself to voice my true emotions instead of bottling them up. "How am I supposed to get through this?"

"Mackenzie," Brayden started, "you are one of the toughest females I've ever had the privilege of knowing. You have so much life, so much strength. You'll get through this just like you've gotten through everything else over the past few years. With Jenna and me by your side." Enclosing my hand in his, he gave me a sincere look. "You know, you have options and I will fully support you, no matter your decision."

Taking a deep breath, I briefly closed my eyes. "I love how you'll back me, no matter what."

"Why wouldn't I? I don't have a vagina or uterus. I'm certainly not going to try to tell you what to do with yours."

I giggled at Brayden's words, thankful he always had a way to lighten the tension. "I know. As much as I hate the idea of having his baby, it's also part of me." I held my hand over my stomach. "I can't... I'm keeping it. I'm sure there's going to be moments down the road where I may regret this decision, especially when I'm trying to do all of this on my own—"

"You won't be on your own," Brayden interrupted. "In the past eight years, when have you *ever* had to do anything alone? I'll be there. Hell, if I need to, I'll move back into your condo and help out."

"You don't need to," I objected. "You have your own life you need to live."

"I know, but you're my soul mate," he explained, caressing my hand. "I love you, Mack, and I will *always* do whatever you need." He beamed, placing his hand over my stomach. "And this kid, well... He'll be the most spoiled baby ever. Come on! Every kid needs a fantastic gay uncle who has no problem spending a ridiculous amount of money buying him Prada diapers!"

"I'm fairly certain there's a law against shitting in anything with a designer label."

He scrunched his nose at me. "Possibly, but it still doesn't mean that the newest addition to our family deserves anything but the best. And that's exactly what he'll get."

"What if it's a girl?"

"Trust me. It's a boy. I have a knack for knowing these things." He winked and placed a tender kiss on my cheek. For the first time since leaving my doctor's office earlier, I actually felt as if I could get through this, that I didn't need Tyler to be a good mom to the baby growing inside me.

I relaxed into Brayden's arms, wanting to live in that moment for as long as possible. I was calm, the demons that had been haunting me absent. Brayden gave me a sense of stability and comfort that had been lacking from my life.

"You loved him, didn't you?" he commented softly.

"I did, but it wasn't real."

"What makes you say that? I saw the way he looked at

you. I don't care how good you are. You can't fake that."

"He lied to me, boo."

Running his fingers up and down my back, he said, "I think he was truthful with you where it mattered. Nothing dishonest comes from love. We may hurt those we love, but we often think we're doing right by them. We tend to lie to those we care about to protect them."

"There's no black and white, only varying shades of gray hiding a kernel of truth," I murmured, remembering my father's words when he asked me to pretend as if he were dead. I had done so to protect him, to keep him safe. Did Tyler keep the truth of who he was and what he was doing for the same reason? And what was his kernel of truth?

His words from that day back in Boston, begging me to believe his love for me was real, replayed in my head, his remorse-filled eyes flashing through my memory. A look of realization washed over me and I snapped my eyes toward Brayden's.

A knowing smile on his face, he continued, "Like I said, you can fake a lot of things, Mackenzie, but you can't fake being in love. There's your kernel of truth."

Chapter Three
Nothing

Tyler

THE AIR WAS DRY and dusty as I sat in the passenger seat of the all-terrain vehicle Eli expertly navigated through the barren desert of Sudan on a hot June day. The heat was unbearable, but at least I had all my limbs, which was more than could be said of many of the refugees seeking safety from South Sudan at the camp my brother's company had been sponsoring for the past several years. The path that led me to this point in my life was an odd one, but I needed to be here.

It had been over three months since I watched Mackenzie walk out of my life, but the look on her face when she found out the truth continued to haunt me, finding me no matter where I went. Every woman I saw had that same exact expression in her eyes. Men glared at me with a look of disgust, as if knowing I had destroyed the most precious gift there was...love. My betrayal and deception tormented me, reminding me I would never be worthy of anyone's love again, especially Mackenzie's. Regardless, I wasn't giving up. I simply needed to do something to prove I had a heart...that I was someone worth taking a risk for...that I was someone worth forgiving despite the heartache I caused. But I needed to learn to forgive myself first, and I hoped that by protecting some of the most vulnerable people I had ever met would put me on the right path.

However, that didn't make me miss her any less. I missed her smile. Her voice. Her soul. Her heart. Her love. I was a coward. Even though I had limited access to a satellite phone and a computer here in the middle of nowhere, I hadn't called or emailed her, following my brother's orders to refrain from contacting her for security reasons. Even if I could contact her, nothing I said would ever tell her what she wanted to hear, what she *deserved* to hear. Instead, I kept a journal of all the things I wanted to say to her, hopeful she would be able to read it one day and see that she didn't escape my thoughts once over the months of our separation.

Carrying the guilt of the failed mission that would always haunt me, I tried to find peace in my work, in my new mission, but that day continued to repeat in my mind like a horrible movie.

An excruciating lump formed in my throat as I watched a flash of dark hair scramble from the elevator of my brother's building and bolt through the revolving doors, exiting onto the busy Boston street. I was foolish to think I could keep the truth from her. She was bound to find out, but I didn't want it to be like this. I wasn't cut out for betraying people, no matter the reason. Months ago, I thought this was the perfect assignment for me. I hadn't cared about a woman since Melanie, but Mackenzie had spoken to my heart and I fell for her hard and fast.

I darted after her, knowing it was now or never. I needed to make my move. I needed to prove to her that it wasn't an act, that it was so fucking real for me, that she truly was my lightning strike. Catching up to her with ease, I reached for her arm and spun her around. Her eyes grew wide, her mouth agape. Her chin quivered and I saw the hurt on her face, but I felt that spark and I knew she did, too.

Pinning her against the brick wall, I covered her mouth with mine. *She pushed against me at first, her fists slamming into my chest.*

"Go ahead!" *I bellowed.* "Fight me. I want you to!"

I earned everything she could do to me, but even when I was covered with bruises and scars, it still wouldn't compare to the scar I had caused her heart. Mine would heal. I doubted hers would.

"I want you to hurt me. I deserve it! Cut me. Kill me. My heart won't beat without you!"

Tears running down our faces, I pressed my lips against hers. After a brief struggle, she finally relented and melted into me. She combed her fingers through my hair, tugging at me, drawing me closer. Fire smoldered within as she moaned. A heat came off her body and I knew she couldn't deny the attraction. Love like this didn't happen twice. This was as real as anything I had ever experienced in my life.

I pulled back and rested my forehead against hers. A sigh escaped her lips and I grew hopeful we would make it through this, that our love for each other was stronger than the mountain of lies on which it was built. Her gaze softened and she cupped my cheek in her hand. All I ever needed was to feel her skin on mine. It was perfect. It was exhilarating. It was my home. She *was my home.*

Instantly, her back grew rigid and she pushed against my chest. Stumbling back, I flung my eyes open, watching in bewilderment as she ran down the street.

"You stay away from me, Tyler!" *she howled, signaling for a cab.* "I can't... I'm not going to let you hurt me again!"

"I won't!" *I yelled, chasing after her. My chest tightened as I tried to make sense of the drastic turn. It was almost as if her brain was battling with her heart, which I knew was true. She had been doing that since we started our whirlwind relationship.*

"There's no possible way you won't!" *she exclaimed, wiping at the tears pouring down her face.* "Every time I look at you, at your eyes, I'll always wonder whether it's real."

A cab pulled up to the corner and she opened the door, about to get in.

"Please, Mackenzie..." My mouth was dry, a pained stare on my face as I pleaded with her.

"I should never have trusted my heart," she said quietly. "The heart is impulsive and can't be reasoned with."

"Tell me what you want from me!"

"You really want to know?" she quivered, narrowing her eyes at me.

"Yes! Just tell me." I swallowed hard. "Whatever it is, I'll do it."

She paused, studying me, and my heart raced in anticipation.

"If you really care about me, if you really want to prove to me that it was real for you..." She stared long and hard into my eyes, the pain I caused covering her face, her eyes, her entire being. "You'll let me go."

I remained mute as I absorbed her words, a weight crushing my chest.

"Do you understand what I'm saying?" she asked, sobs overtaking her, and I knew those words were just as difficult for her to say as they were for me to hear. "Please," she begged. "You need to let me go."

"I don't know if I can," I whispered, brushing my thumb under her eye. "I love you, Serafina."

"No. There is no Serafina. There's no Mackenzie. There's nothing left to love." She stood on her toes and planted a soft kiss on my cheek, her body trembling. "Goodbye, Tyler. Enjoy the lonely." She slid into the back seat of the cab and slammed the door.

An ache in my throat, I watched the yellow cab disappear down Atlantic Avenue. I was at a crossroads. Do I grab my car and follow Mackenzie wherever she was going, thus ignoring her pleas that I let her go? Or do I let her leave, proving to her that it was real for me? No matter my choice, it wasn't going to lessen the damage I had done.

Retreating to the building, I ran into the elevator, frantically pressing the button for the garage. I jumped into my car and peeled onto Atlantic Avenue. As I tried to merge onto the freeway toward the airport, traffic was at a standstill and I slammed on my brakes. Craning my head, I saw a five car pile-up that must have happened no more than a minute beforehand, blocking all the lanes. I couldn't help but think that someone was trying to keep me from getting to Mackenzie. Maybe I wasn't meant to approach her yet. Maybe the best thing for me to do was give her space, like she asked.

Fishing my cell phone out of my pocket, I ignored dozens of missed calls from my brother and pressed Eli's number.

"Tyler, what's wrong? Your brother just called and is flipping out."

"She knows," I said quietly.

There was a long pause before Eli spoke again, his voice soft and sympathetic. "I'm sorry, Ty. Is there anything—"

"Actually, yes," I interrupted, trying to mask the heartache in my voice. "That's why I'm calling. Are you at the office?"

"Yes."

"Run Mackenzie's credit cards. And her friends', as well. See if you can find any information about where she is. I'm stuck in traffic trying to get to the airport. I need to know if she's even headed that way, or whether I should turn around and try one of the train stations instead."

"I'm on it," he said and I could hear him typing away at his laptop. "What are you going to do?"

"I don't know," I responded dejectedly, my shoulders deflating as I impatiently waited for traffic to begin moving. "She can't trust me. No matter what assurances I tried to give her, none of it mattered."

"Do you blame her?" he asked, his voice guarded.

"No," I sighed. "I'd probably think the same thing if I were in her shoes. She told me the only way she'll know it was real is for me to do the one thing I don't think I'm ready to do."

"And what's that?"

"Let her go."

The line was silent, and the sound of honking horns echoed around me, as if that would clear the accident quicker.

"Tyler, don't you think that maybe it's..." He stopped short.

"*What?*"

"*I've got a hit,*" *he explained in an excited tone.* "*Just ten minutes ago, there was a purchase on Brayden Weller's credit card for a flight from Boston to Brownsville, connecting out of Dallas. Better hurry. The flight leaves in less than an hour.*"

"*I'm stuck in the Callahan tunnel. Traffic is at a standstill.*"

"*Do you want me to hop on the subway?*" *Eli asked.* "*I could try to stop her.*"

I felt as if the universe was conspiring against me. "*No, but thanks, Eli. I'll just wait it out and hope I can get there in time. I don't want her to think we're chasing her.*"

"*You got it. Keep me updated.*"

I hung up and tossed my phone in the cup holder of the SUV. The only thing keeping me moving forward was the possibility that Mackenzie's flight was delayed.

An hour later, I finally pulled into the parking garage at the airport and bolted for the terminal. Adrenaline coursed through me as I searched the departures board for her flight. A heaviness set in my limbs when I saw it had just left. In a daze, I shuffled from the terminal, unable to think clearly.

I didn't even know how I ended up there, but I found myself parking just off Storrow Drive by Boston University. As if on autopilot, I headed toward the Charles River, my legs carrying me to the boathouse where Melanie had breathed her last breath. I didn't know what I hoped to gain from visiting this place. Maybe I hoped to find some sort of clarity in a world that seemed to turn on its head overnight.

As I sat down on a bench by the boathouse, I felt a lump in my pocket and pulled out a small black velvet box, flipping it open to stare at the ring I intended to give Mackenzie today. The sun reflected on it, causing the three-carat diamond to glimmer. I hated that I never got the chance to see it on her finger.

I had no idea how long I sat there, staring at the ring, when I heard a familiar voice.

"*I had a feeling you'd be here.*"

I snapped the box closed and turned my head. Meeting a pair of dark eyes, a forced smile crossed my face.

"Hey, Ma," *I uttered.*

"Hey, baby. How are you holding up?"

I shrugged, shoving the black box in my pocket and hiding my face.

"Tyler..." *She sat beside me on the bench as I stared at the gentle waves of the river.* "You can't hide from your mother."

"I hurt her, Ma." *I returned my eyes to hers, feeling all her compassion, understanding, and love envelope me from that one look, despite the fact she probably disapproved of my actions.*

"You did. She has every right to be upset with you. It takes ages to learn to trust someone, but only one lie to ruin it."

Tears formed in my eyes and I struggled to reel in my emotions. "I ruined it."

"Maybe," *she said.* "Maybe not. What did she say?"

"To let her go," *I replied, barely able to speak the words.*

"And did you?"

I nodded. "She got in a cab and I couldn't get to her in time."

"That's not what I meant, and you know it. Tell me. Did you let her go?"

I shook my head. "She's a part of me, Ma. But she said the only way for me to prove I do love her and all of my feelings are real was to let her go."

She nodded. "Then give her some time."

I shot my head up, surprised she wasn't urging me to go after her. "Really?"

"Trust me, baby. If she wants you to let her go, all she probably wants is some time to herself and to be with her friends. She wants to cry on their shoulders and commiserate about what an asshole you are. Let her have this time. If you want any shot at winning her back, you'll give her exactly what she wants. Right now, that's a life without any reminders of what she considers to be her biggest mistake... You."

I opened my mouth, wanting to argue that letting her go wasn't an option, but she held up her hand. *"Don't worry. It'll all work out."*

"I don't know if I can stay away," I admitted. *"I've seen her every day for the past six months. I—"*

"Tyler, sometimes, we need to give those we love space to work out their feelings, and I'm not talking about months or even weeks. Right now, she's upset and confused. Her world's been torn apart. She needs to put the pieces back together, but she can't do that with you in her life. Not yet, anyway. Give her space to find her life. Eventually, she'll find her love. She'll find the truth amidst the lies. But you need to give her time."

I gazed ahead as runners jogged along the promenade path, considering my mother's words. Sighing, I turned to her. *"How do you always seem to have all the answers?"*

"Because I'm old, baby." She smiled at me, the wrinkles around her eyes showing. *"Do you know how many mistakes I've made in my life?"*

"No."

"Well, I've made enough that I can speak to you from experience. Trust me. The best thing you can do is give her time. Then you can go to her and beg forgiveness with the most ridiculously expensive jewelry money can buy." She nudged me and I laughed at her attempt to bring me out of my sour mood. *"She'll come around."*

"I hope you're right."

"I'm your mother." She winked, a sparkle in her eyes. *"I'm always right."* Her jovial expression turned serious once more as she grabbed my hands in hers. *"Go back to your routine, Tyler. It's gotten you through tough spots in the past. Do it again. It will give you the clarity you need right now."*

A loud throat clearing sounded and we snapped our heads up to see Alexander standing off to the side. I could see guilt hidden beneath his tough exterior. Even though he should have been upset at the failed mission, it was readily apparent he wasn't there as the head of the security company, about to berate me regarding what happened. He was there as my brother.

"Well," my mother said, placing her hand on my leg. *"I think you boys need to have a bit of a chat. I love you, Tyler, baby."* She planted a soft kiss on my temple and, for an instant, I wanted to think everything would be okay, that it would all work out.

A group of cyclists flew by as she got up from the bench and strode to Alexander. He bent his almost six-and-a-half foot frame down to allow my mother to place a kiss on his cheek and she whispered something in his ear. I couldn't hear what, but I knew she had to be giving him a piece of her mind.

She retreated from us and Alexander approached me with a shrunken stature, exhaling as he sat next to me on the bench. He placed his forearms on his legs and stared at the river. An awkward silence passed as we both sat contemplating everything. The sun had begun to set over the city, a chill in the spring air. Runners were out getting some exercise, people were walking their dogs... The world continued to spin even though it felt like I was stuck in that moment when Mackenzie learned the truth.

"Ty, I need to talk to you about something," Alexander finally said.

The timbre of his voice gave me pause. I glanced to him, observing him run his hands through his dark hair, his shoulders slumping in defeat.

"What is it?"

He turned his eyes to meet mine and I braced myself for what he was about to tell me, unsure of whether I could deal with any more bad news. *"You can't go back,"* he said softly.

"I'm not. Not yet, anyway. I'll give her some time and—"

"No, Tyler," he interrupted, his voice firm. *"It's not safe—"*

"And it is for Mackenzie?" I responded, my voice incredulous. *"What about Charlie? What if he figures it out and goes after—"*

"We need to cease all contact for everybody's protection, including hers."

"Why?"

He rubbed his temples. I could sense the wheels turning in his head, debating whether to tell me the truth or simply something to

27

appease me for the moment. *"Please, Tyler, I need you to trust me. I've worked special ops long enough to know when something isn't right and, at this moment, there is something severely fucked up going on. I called our agency handler to give him a status report on the mission."*

"Yeah...?"

"According to his secretary, he's been missing for a week. I couldn't get any more information out of her, but I have a feeling in my gut that it's related to this case. He made his last contact with her on the same day Charlie made headlines for being wanted for all those murders. Based on everything you've been telling me, I can't help but think there may be a connection between the two, that there's something bigger at play here than we've been led to believe. I have a bad feeling my agency handler's been compromised. It's only a matter of time until they turn to you."

"Who?" I asked, my heart racing.

"I have no idea. It could be anyone. Maybe someone who was worried word would get out that Mackenzie's father possibly had nothing to do with everything of which he's been accused. I'm sure that's the reason you refused to tell me his location the other night."

I shot my eyes to his, shock washing over me. *"How did you know?"*

"It was pretty obvious, Ty. I know all your tells. I knew you were covering for him and, well... I get it. But if I'm right, and I have a feeling I am, your connection to Mackenzie could potentially make you a sitting duck. If they think you have even the slightest inkling someone other than Galloway is to blame, I don't need to spell out what they'll do. I need you to disappear."

"What? I can't–"

"Just one month. That's all I'm going to ask of you. I need time to comb through the intel you gathered and find out what's really going on here. I have a new assignment for you anyway. One that's more of a humanitarian project. No lies. No betrayal. Just helping people who desperately need it."

"But what about Mackenzie?"

28

"Nothing will happen to her, Tyler. I promise you. I made a few arrangements and will have eyes on her around the clock."

I shook my head, confused. "But what about you? You were involved in this assignment, too. What if someone comes after you?"

"Don't worry about me. It's my job to worry about you."

"Why?"

He shrugged. "You're my brother, Ty, and I love you." He met my eyes. "Plus, I promised Dad years ago I would always watch out for you. That's why I need you to leave. Eli, too. I need you to go somewhere else so I know nothing will happen. Like I said, if our agency handler has been compromised, your life could be at risk. This is me fulfilling my promise to Dad."

I stared ahead at the Charles River, my mother's advice to give Mackenzie some space echoing in my head. I hated the idea of abandoning her, leaving her vulnerable to anyone who wanted to do her harm, but if there was one thing I knew about my brother, it was that he kept his promises. If he vowed to watch out for and protect Mackenzie, I knew he would take that oath as serious as he took the oath he pledged to his country all those years ago.

"Do you swear you won't let anything happen to her?" I asked, my eyes fierce.

"I give you my word, Ty," he assured me, conviction in his voice. "She'll be better protected than the president. I've sent my best team down there to ensure it."

Absorbing his words, I sighed, running my hands through my hair. "When do I leave?"

"You okay?" Eli asked, cutting through my thoughts about how one month had turned into three. So much time had passed, the rift between myself and Mackenzie had widened. I wondered if I even crossed her mind anymore. I couldn't forget her if I wanted to. Her existence was permanently etched on my heart...on my soul.

"Yeah. I'm good."

Eli glanced at me briefly before returning his eyes to the road. "Liar."

"I said I'm good. I didn't say I was fantastic. Just let me be good for a minute."

He shook his head and clenched his jaw, taking his foot off the gas as he approached a guard shack at the entryway of the refugee camp. We nodded a greeting to one of the security company's employees and were granted access. Driving the outskirts of what had become my home, we navigated past rows and rows of white tents.

This experience had been humbling for me. These people had nothing to their names. Due to civil war and political unrest, they had been forced out of their homes, the massacre of thousands upon thousands of their people causing them to seek asylum. When they left, many of them lost their families, their lives, their identities. The refugees spanned all age groups. I didn't know how any of the older people in the camp coped with the fact they would never see their home again. The only thing that got me through each day was knowing that, with every passing hour, I was that much closer to finally being home. These people didn't have that luxury.

The past few months weren't without hardships, despite how much I believed in what I was doing. When I first arrived here, I wondered how long I would last out in the stagnant desert heat. But when I stepped out of the tiny tent that had become my home and a little African boy, who couldn't have been more than six or seven, his right arm missing from his elbow down, came up to me and asked if I was here to help, nothing else mattered. I wasn't here to betray or deceive anyone. I was here to make a difference, to protect these people, to ensure they had access to everything I had taken for granted my entire life...food, water, education, clothing, medical aid.

They would have it all and then some. Working this assignment made me proud of my family's company. Despite the numerous questionable operations it had been involved in, the humanitarian missions it sponsored outweighed all of that. Seeing women playing with their children, not worrying about whether today would be the day they could no longer outrun the enemy, made it all worth it.

"What did your brother say?" Eli asked, pulling up to the administration building.

We had just spent the better part of the day traveling to and from the only communications center within a hundred miles. Infrastructure in this country left much to be desired, and internet and phones were practically non-existent. I did have a satellite phone; however, it tended to be sketchy at best and completely useless most of the time. My only means of somewhat reliable communication with the outside world was through a weekly visit to a command center located three hours away. It was during this time that I tried to check in with Alexander.

"Not much. He still has Martin and his team keeping an eye on Mackenzie. He's yet to see any viable threat from Charlie or anyone else, but he's ordering everyone to maintain their post. He must feel guilty. Why else would he send his right-hand man down to Texas to watch over her? That must count for something." I wanted to believe my brother was a good person, that he was trying to make amends for how things had spiraled out of control between us, but there was a nagging I couldn't ignore, especially as the weeks went by and I was told to maintain course.

"And *our* assignment?" Eli asked. "Did you talk to him about whether he's figured out what's really going on with all the shit that went down when your cover was

31

blown? I don't need to remind you by whom."

"He still needs us out here," I responded firmly. "That's all he would say. That, and it's not safe to come back yet."

He gripped the steering wheel and slammed on the brakes. "And you believe him?" he asked through his hard-set jaw.

"I have to," I insisted. "He's my brother. Despite everything else, I need to believe he wouldn't keep me here unless it was necessary. Or else…"

"What? Or else what?" Eli urged, almost begging me to say the words. We had been having this same discussion for the past month. Every week, I had gone to touch base with my brother. And every week, he told me I needed to stay, despite his promise at the start of this assignment that, no matter what, it would only be for a month.

"Or else he's not the man I thought he was," I answered softly. "Who I always looked up to and admired when I was a kid." I shook my head, not wanting to believe the words. "But for now," I continued, maintaining my composure, "I need the routine. I need the comfort of following orders. It's what got me through everything with Melanie. The only way I survived that was because of the discipline the navy gave me. Working for my brother's company is a lot like that. He gave us a mission and I'm going to obey orders. Look around you!" I gestured at the refugees strolling through camp. "These people need us, Eli. They have nothing. If all I do is make one person feel safer, then this is where I belong. Not back home, but here." I opened the door of the ATV and headed toward the large tent structure in front of us.

"Tyler!" Eli shouted, dashing out of the vehicle and catching up to me. Although he was slightly shorter than my six-foot, four-inch frame, he made up for that in build. He kept his dark hair at a sensible length, the discipline he learned in the Marines evident in his appearance. I, however, kept my sun-lightened hair somewhat unkempt. If I remembered to shave once, it was a good week. What did I care? I didn't have anyone to impress.

"Listen, I understand following orders," he continued. "But, at some point, you need to forget about doing what you're told is right and do what's right for *you*. From where I'm standing, you're turning a blind eye to what your brother's doing so you don't have to face your problem. That's what you did with Melanie..."

"What?" I hissed, my green eyes growing wide in shock. Eli had never been one to question following orders. In fact, he had always adhered to a strict code of ethics, but our history predated him working for the security company. I supposed his loyalty to me outweighed that to his job. "I didn't—"

"Yes, you did! You just admitted it! After she died, you ran. You went into the navy so you didn't have to deal with your grief! I get it, Tyler. Believe me. After my father died in the line of duty, I was so fucking angry. I hated that he lost his life to save some sorority girl."

I nodded, remembering that case. It was splashed all over the news. I was a junior in college, and Eli was starting his third year with the Marines when the case that rocked our city for years finally came to a bloody end. Eli's dad was a homicide detective and brought the man responsible for brutally assaulting and murdering over a dozen college females to justice. Sadly, Eli's father sacrificed his life to save that of the man's last victim. Eli had to sit in court nearly every day as he stared at the girl who survived, wondering whether her life was more valuable than his father's.

"I couldn't bear being around town because,

everywhere I went, I was faced with a reminder of what he gave his life for. I ran back to the Marines, even after they offered to give me an honorable discharge to be with my family. You're doing the same thing, Ty! You've never allowed your scars to heal. At some point, it will all become too much and you'll bury yourself in your guilt. That's why you're happy to stay here and help all these people, but not because you genuinely want to. You're trying to bury your guilt in all the good you've been doing, but you can't hide it forever. You can't run away from your mistakes for the rest of your life. You need closure."

"Maybe closure's not in the cards for me," I said softly. "She told me to let her go." I spun away from him. I hadn't had a moment's peace in months. I hadn't been alone in months. And, right now, I wanted to be alone.

"But you *haven't* let her go, Tyler!" he exclaimed, catching up to me. Grabbing my arm, he forced me to stop. "You left to give her space. Three months is a long time to give someone space. Just..." He took a deep breath. "Just think about it and stop punishing yourself. This Tyler..." He gestured to me. "This is not the Tyler I remember. The old Tyler would have fought tooth-and-nail for what he believed in. He wouldn't stand by and allow his brother to order him to stay thousands of miles away, instead of going after the one girl who finally taught you how to be human again."

I sighed. "Carrying my guilt is the only thing that reminds me I'm human," I admitted. "Without it, I'm empty. I'm nothing. I *need* the guilt. It's the only way I can live with the lonely."

Chapter Four

Skeletons

Mackenzie

MY BRAIN WAS SPINNING as I flipped through page after page of a pregnancy book, the words starting to blur together. Since learning I was pregnant nearly two months ago, I got my hands on every book possible, hoping that, with a little bit of guidance, I would be able to get through this on my own. It didn't help. I felt even more lost and confused about how to raise a little human.

I had put on a smile to assure Brayden and Jenna I was handling it, but the truth was, I was scared out of my mind. Cloth or disposable diapers? Bottle feed or breast feed? I was overwhelmed by the amount of books and advice, most of it contradictory. I felt like a fish swimming upstream, everyone else passing by, telling me what was best.

The stack of overdue bills had gradually grown higher and higher as I struggled to rub two pennies together. Every dime went to paying for the bare minimum of doctor appointments I could get away with. I was two months behind on my mortgage, my credit cards were maxed out, and my checking account balance was teetering on being overdrawn on a weekly basis. Jenna and Brayden had offered to help me out countless times, but I refused. I took after my father in that respect. I inherited his Irish stubbornness.

A loud knock on the door sounded, startling me, and I tore my attention away from one of the dozens of pregnancy books Brayden had picked up for me. Raising myself from my lush sofa, I walked through the living area and into the foyer of my ocean-front condo. I checked the peephole to see a man dressed in a messenger uniform standing there. I pulled back the door, praying it wasn't the bank sending notice of foreclosure on my condo. Surely, I'd have to have missed more than two payments, right?

"Mackenzie Delano?" the stout man asked, eyeing the envelope in his hand.

"Yes. That's me."

"Sign here, please." He handed me his scanner and I scribbled on the screen.

"Have a good day, ma'am." He gave me the envelope and I retreated into my condo, plopping down at my kitchen table. I nearly threw the envelope on top of the large pile of unopened bills, but stopped myself.

Intrigued as to the contents, I tore at the tab, letting out a long breath when I saw it wasn't from the bank...or a bill.

As I read the typed letter accompanying a church bulletin, guilt overwhelmed me for having ignored the only family I had left during the past several months.

Dearest Mackenzie,

I hope this letter finds you well. Many days have passed without your attendance at any of our services, including those which have been said to honor your mother. Even though years have gone since her passing, I understand the wound may never heal. But don't carry the burden alone. Allow others to help shoulder it. We have set a celebration of your mother's life at Monday evening mass this coming week. I do hope you will choose to honor her memory, as she so rightly deserves.

Peace be with you, child.

Father Baldwin

Call to me and I will answer you, and will tell you great and hidden things that you have not known. Jeremiah 33:3

I placed the letter on the table and opened the church program, noting a mass to be said in my mother's memory on the day specified in my father's letter. I had purposefully not shown up at each of our pre-arranged meetings over the past few months. I was angry at my father for getting himself into whatever mess he was in. I was angry at my mother for knowing what happened and keeping it from me. I was angry at Tyler for using me to get to my father. But I was mostly angry at myself, if for no other reason than I knew my anger toward other people wouldn't make me feel better.

As my eyes remained glued to the postscript of the letter, I felt something I hadn't in months. Hope. It could have meant nothing, but a small part of me believed my long-term absence from the church made my father reconsider shielding me from the truth of what was going on. I prayed he would come clean with all the secrets so we could go back to having a normal father-daughter relationship...or as normal a relationship as we could.

Folding the letter and bulletin, I hid them in one of my kitchen drawers and spied the time. I groaned, not really feeling like going to our traditional Friday evening girls' night, but I couldn't break from my routine. The last time I strayed from the normalcy of my life, I ended up heartbroken. I needed to find comfort in my routine once more, regardless of how tempting curling up in my bed sounded at the moment.

I made my way down the hallway toward my decent-sized master bedroom, then stripped off the yoga pants and tank top I had put on when I got home from work earlier. June had come and gone too quickly for my liking. It was now the middle of July and I was seventeen weeks pregnant. It seemed as if my stomach had grown overnight. What was just a small bump last week was now more pronounced. My small and slender frame made it even more noticeable, and I knew I couldn't cover it up much longer.

Turning on the shower, I allowed the hot water to wash over me, cleansing me of everything as I tried to clear my mind. All the books I'd been reading told me to maintain a low stress level so my baby didn't become stressed. I couldn't help but think he or she had nothing to be stressed about…no paying bills, running a restaurant, or finding the father of the kid growing inside you. Brayden was right. Tyler needed to know. I just worried he would want to be a part of my baby's life, and I wasn't sure I wanted that because that would make him part of *my* life. I was certain I didn't want that. That was what I tried to convince myself anyway.

After an invigorating shower, I headed toward my closet and picked out a long maxi dress that was tight around my chest, then flowed to my ankles. It was comfortable and hid my stomach. I towel dried my hair and placed a touch of gel in it to tame the waves. Putting a bit of powder on my dark complexion, I then added a hint of blush and some dark eyeliner, giving my hazel eyes a dramatic feel. After applying some pink gloss to my lips, I stepped back and surveyed my five-foot, four-inch frame, satisfied I didn't look how I felt…

Shattered.

Broken.

Lost.

Putting on a smile that masked my true feelings, I rushed down the hallway and was met by a chubby gray cat meowing at me. "Ready for dinner, your majesty?" I asked Meatball. He rubbed against my leg, purring in appreciation. "Okay. Let's get you fed."

I bent down, grabbed his bag of kibble from the cabinet, and poured it in his bowl. Giving him a quick scratch on his tail as he ate, I made my way from the condo, taking the elevator down twelve floors to the lobby.

"Hey, Mackenzie!" Paul, the security guard, said when he saw me emerge. He was in his late fifties or early sixties, and had distinguished gray hair and brilliant blue eyes. He had been retired from the police department for ten years, but he still kept in decent shape, apart from the occasional cheeseburger. He was like a father to me, probably more so than my real dad, who I only got to see once a month at a pre-arranged time and couldn't even tell anyone he was still alive. "How are you feeling?"

"Okay, I suppose. Tired."

He nodded. "I remember those days. Poor Angie was exhausted through all three of her pregnancies."

I groaned. "Don't tell me that. I'm sleeping more than I have in my life, but it's still not enough. I constantly wake up exhausted. Having to give up caffeine hasn't really helped, either."

"You work too hard, sweetie. I see the hours you keep at that restaurant. At some point, you need to start taking better care of yourself."

"I will. I promise." I leaned down and placed a soft kiss on his temple.

"Good. You better get a move on. I'm sure Brayden and Jenna are waiting."

I glanced down at my wrist and checked my watch. "Shit!" I exclaimed when I saw it was quarter after six, bolting from Paul. I was usually the one waiting on them, not the other way around.

"Drive carefully!" Paul yelled.

"I will!" I responded as I dashed out the doors and into the parking lot of the condo building I lived in on the north end of South Padre Island.

The sun was still shining brightly as I took quick steps toward my car. Clicking on the key fob to unlock the door, I was startled by the sound of glass breaking and I swung my head toward the front gate. A chill washed over me when my eyes settled on a dark sedan idling on the street, the driver wearing darkened sunglasses. His expression remained fixed, never looking at me...or anything else, for that matter.

Part of me had hoped the glass breaking was Charlie making an appearance, but he was too smart to do anything that would draw attention to himself. Nearly four months ago, he had disappeared from my life when his photo was splashed all over the news as the only suspect in a rash of murders spanning close to a decade. Murders he claimed he had nothing to do with. I didn't know what to think, although I secretly wanted to believe him. But months had gone by with no communication at all. Not even a phone call on our secret spy line, which was what I named the cell phone he left me the night he disappeared. I worried the worst had happened, that he was silenced forever, leaving me more confused than ever about whether I was simply naïve to want to believe him, given our past, or whether Charlie was another pawn in the bigger picture.

Sighing, I got in behind the wheel of my Mercedes convertible. I knew it was only a matter of time before I had to think about how I was going to afford a bigger car. I certainly couldn't put a baby seat in the back seat of my two-door coupe.

I pulled out onto the main road and, within minutes, arrived at the wine and tapas bar Brayden, Jenna, and I had been going to for our Friday girls' night for the past several years.

I threw the valet my keys, then strode into the restaurant and toward the bar, Jenna and Brayden sitting at the counter.

"There she is!" Brayden exclaimed, spinning on his barstool and facing me. "Come on, Mack. I saved you a seat." He winked.

I glanced around the empty bar, rolling my eyes. "Yeah. Thanks. I don't know what I'd do if you didn't save me *that* seat." I sat down beside him and smiled at Jenna, who was sitting on the other side of him. It was a popular place, but mostly for dinner. The dining room was packed with locals, businessmen, and tourists, but the small little bar remained relatively vacant.

I hung my purse on the hook underneath the counter and my eyes darted to the opposite end of the bar where a mystery man sat one night months ago. His stool was empty, which was exactly how I felt. I had been pretending I was over him and all the lies he told, but I wasn't. I had hoped if I kept saying I was over him, I had moved past him, I didn't need him, I didn't *love* him, it would be okay.

I *needed* it to be okay.

"Hey." Jenna broke into my thoughts and I snapped my head in her direction, meeting her small blue eyes. A gentle smile crossed her face, her pale skin taking on a pinkish hue from spending some time in the sun. "Stop thinking about him. He's not worth it. He could have at least called or something."

Biting my lip, I nodded and struggled to mask my real feelings from my friends, wishing I could convince myself they were right. "I'm fine, guys. I swear. For all I care, he can drop off the face of the earth, which he pretty much did."

"What can I get you?" the bartender interrupted, leaning on the counter. "The usual? Cranberry juice with tonic and a piece of lime?"

"Yes. Thank you."

I sat forward and avoided both Brayden's and Jenna's eyes, knowing they would ask me the same question they asked every Friday. Smiling in appreciation when the short blonde bartender placed my new cocktail of choice in front of me, I took a long drink, missing being able to enjoy a glass of wine.

"So…," Brayden started, his voice cautious.

Exhaling in annoyance, I refused to face them. "Yes, I called again, like I do every Thursday, more so out of obligation than an actual desire to speak with the prick. His phone was still disconnected, and I got the same speech from the same receptionist at his company. That Tyler has no role in the security company."

"How are you doing with all of this?" Jenna asked.

I shrugged. "No better than yesterday, and I'm sure tomorrow will be the same. I'll wake up and go to the gym, spending the entire time worrying about how the hell I'm going to do this on my own. I see parents struggling to raise a baby all the time. The constant diaper changes. The midnight feedings. They're exhausted, but they have each other to lean on for help. I don't have that."

Brayden slammed his fist on the bar. "Have you not been listening to us at *all* the past few months?! How many times do we need to tell you we'll help with anything you need?!"

"I know," I conceded, exhaling and leaning back in my chair. "And I appreciate that, but you guys are both young with your entire lives ahead of you. I hate to saddle you with my problems. I got myself into this mess and I shouldn't count on other people to shoulder the burden."

"Mackenzie Sophia Delano!" Jenna shouted, her voice high-pitched and shrill, taking me by surprise. She was never one to raise her voice at anyone. "Did you ever stop to think it's *not* a burden to us? That we want to help because we care and love you? That we want to be part of this kid's life? So, for crying out loud, stop being a stubborn ass and just let us in!" She took a deep breath, calming herself. Lowering her voice, she met my eyes. "You've been pushing us further and further away since you came back from Boston. Don't let your pain become who you are, Mackenzie. Please."

Her words cut me, leaving me speechless.

"We both love you, Mack," Brayden said softly. "We'll do whatever you need. Hell, I'll even change dirty diapers for you."

I giggled, picturing Brayden's upturned nose the first time he had to follow through on his promise, but he would. He would walk through fire for me. They both would.

"I'm sorry, guys." I grabbed each of their hands in mine. "I know I've been a bit of a bitch lately. I've just always done everything on my own and I hate the thought of—"

"Asking for help isn't a sign of weakness, Mack," Jenna cut in. "It's a sign of someone strong enough to know when she needs a helping hand. We'll start with this." She released her grasp on my hand and reached into her purse, pulling out a card.

"What is this?" I asked, giving them a cautious look as I surveyed the light blue envelope.

"Just open it!" Brayden shouted, bouncing up and down on his barstool, his lips turned up into a sly smile.

Eyeing my two friends, I slid my thumb beneath the flap of the envelope and pulled out a card. Opening it,

43

my jaw dropped. "Guys...," I started.

Brayden held his hand up. "I don't want to hear it."

"But you have student loans to pay back, boo. And Jenna... This is too much." I placed the card back on the bar and pushed it toward them.

"No, it's not," Jenna countered, pushing it back to me. "You need to take care of that baby, which means you need to take care of you, too. I know it's tough with the restaurant just starting up. Richard was supporting us on his income alone before we even started the restaurant, so that money is just an extra bonus for us. I wish it could be that way for you, too. So, please, take the check, deposit it, and pay some of those bills sitting on your kitchen table. It won't cover everything, but at least you'll be able to buy groceries instead of trying to survive on ramen noodles. I'm tired of tricking you into eating healthy meals by 'testing' out new recipes at the restaurant. I'm running out of ideas."

I stared at the check, speechless. "It's just too much. You guys work so hard for your money."

"So do you," Brayden offered. "Consider it years' worth of back rent for letting me crash at your place when I was too drunk to drive back to mine." He winked.

"I'm not going to be able to persuade you otherwise, am I?"

"Not a chance in hell," Jenna said, crossing her arms in front of her chest, a satisfied smile on her face.

"Fine." I shoved the card into my purse and raised myself off the barstool, walking between them and hugging them both. "I love you wholes."

"We love you, too," Brayden soothed. "We're in this together, Mack."

I kissed both their cheeks and slid back into my barstool. Returning my attention to my very boring non-alcoholic drink, I took a sip of the tart cranberry, my eyes catching a news broadcast on the large screen mounted on the wall of the understated bar. Ghosts of my childhood flashed before me and my breath caught. I was unable to make sense of the scene being displayed.

"Can you turn that up, please?" I asked the bartender, my mouth becoming dry.

She finished making a drink and grabbed the remote, raising the volume.

"What is it, Mack?" Jenna asked, her voice heavy with concern.

"I'm not sure," I replied, my tone even. "But I know that house." I gestured with my head to the blonde reporter, her hair perfectly coifed, her makeup heavy, standing in front of a large white colonial. Reading the subtitle saying *Double Homicide Outside Fort Bragg,* I tried to wrap my head around what was going on.

"How do you know that house?" Brayden asked. I could feel his eyes examining me, penetrating my soul, reading all the secrets I could no longer guard.

"I grew up in it," I muttered, the words leaving my mouth before I could stop them. "Nearly every night, I sat in that tree between the two yards with my best friend, Damian, who lived next door." I instantly began to regret that I never tried to find him after I disappeared in the middle of the night all those years ago. I was warned not to because it could put my family's life in jeopardy.

"I thought you grew up in San Antonio," Jenna interjected. She tilted her head, scrunching her eyebrows.

"No." I shook my head. "We moved there when I was ten. Before that, my dad was stationed at Fort Bragg." I had probably already told them too much, but if I couldn't trust my two best friends with the truth of who I was, who could I trust?

"New orders?" Brayden asked.

"Something like that," I agreed, straining to listen to the newscast.

"Tragedy struck this tight-knit neighborhood in Fayetteville, North Carolina, just outside of Fort Bragg early this morning. This is a community of servicemen and women where people watch out for each other, but nothing could have prepared them for the horror they woke up to."

The live broadcast cut to previously shot footage of a medical examiner rolling two gurneys down a driveway I remembered playing hopscotch on, the bodies covered with a sheet, distraught neighbors looking on with sorrow and condolence.

"The decapitated bodies of a married couple in their sixties were found at approximately nine o'clock this morning at the house behind me, which has been vacant for the past several years. A real estate agent stumbled on what is being called a 'horrific, ritualistic killing'. The victims have been identified as Lucian and Emily Sheperd."

A photo of a happy couple surrounded by an extended family appeared on the screen and I gasped, my trembling hand covering my mouth. It had been years, but I'd never forget the woman who was like a second mother to me when I was growing up… Damian's mom. I didn't recognize the man at her elbow. All I knew was it wasn't Damian's father. They must have divorced.

"Emily Sheperd was known as Emily Mills before she married her second husband approximately five years ago. She and her first husband lived in the house next door, but it is unclear whether that has any connection to her and her current husband's murder. The Sheperds, who lived in Raleigh, were scheduled to return from an anniversary trip to the Outer Banks. According to the preliminary medical examiner's report, they suffered blunt force trauma to the

head, leading to the conclusion they were knocked out elsewhere, then brought here and decapitated in the early hours of the morning, their heads found just feet away from the remainder of their bodies. The family has requested privacy during this difficult time.

"Curiously, this neighborhood isn't new to the headlines. Over fifteen years ago, Francis Galloway, a highly-decorated colonel, who lived in this same exact house, died during a gruesome and fiery attack on the U.S. Embassy in Liberia, which cost over sixty people their lives."

A dated photo of my father in his dress uniform flashed on the screen. I could barely recognize him, his face clear of any scars or burns.

"Just hours after the attack, his wife and daughter were reported missing and were never found."

My fears realized, old photos of both my mother and me appeared on the screen, my mother wearing the jeweled cross I had worn nearly every day until I ran from Tyler, leaving it at his house in Boston.

"There were always suspicions of a connection between the two events, although no suspect was ever brought in for questioning and the case has been left unsolved for the past decade-and-a-half."

I could feel both Jenna's and Brayden's eyes on me as they glanced from the television to me. They had been in my bedroom and had seen the portrait that hung above my vanity, the jeweled cross clear for anyone to see. It was such a unique and remarkable piece. There was no way for me to deny who I was anymore.

"Mack...," Brayden began before I hushed him, listening to the broadcast once more.

"The police here feared another unsolved case, but were able to

47

lift hair fibers found at the scene. They were identified as belonging to one Charles Patrick Montgomery, who is on the FBI's Most Wanted list in connection with over a dozen other murders spanning the better part of the past decade."

A photo of Charlie wearing his Ranger beret appeared on the screen, his blue eyes brilliant as he smiled. That was before the madness ate away at him, before he dug into something he shouldn't have…if his version of events could be believed.

"Law enforcement officials have not speculated on the connection between Montgomery and the Sheperds, but an anonymous source informed us that it is believed Mrs. Sheperd's former neighbor, Mr. Galloway, isn't dead, and that he's the one responsible for orchestrating the attack on the U.S. Embassy all those years ago. The source indicated Galloway has teamed up with Montgomery to silence anyone who could possibly be a witness against him. Perhaps Emily Sheperd knew something she shouldn't, considering she was his neighbor during the years in question. The source went so far as to mention that several of the victims Montgomery is accused of murdering were people thought to have been on Galloway's team when he orchestrated the attack on the embassy. Regardless, it goes without saying that Montgomery is a danger and needs to be brought to justice to give this community of patriots the closure they need after this horrific crime."

I sat in silence, feeling the burn of my friends' eyes on me. I kept my gaze trained forward, my heart thumping in my chest, thousands of questions circling in my head. Questions I was certain I would never get the answers to. Questions I wasn't sure I *wanted* the answers to.

"Ummm… Mack?" Brayden said, breaking the silence once the broadcast was over and moved on to a public interest piece on top swimwear for a flattering figure.

"Yes, boo?" I responded, trying to ignore his wide,

disbelieving eyes.

"That's not...? You're not...?" He leaned toward me, lowering his voice. "You're the little girl, aren't you? Because, correct me if I'm wrong, that was your mother. I've seen her portrait thousands of times, Mack. And that cross the woman in the photo was wearing is the cross you wear, and—"

I inhaled quickly, a sudden chill washing over me. Brayden and Jenna noticed my reaction, still eyeing me cautiously, concerned.

"How did they get that photo?" I asked softly. "She didn't get that cross until after we..."

"After you what?" Jenna prodded.

"After we left the church we were hidden away in for nearly two years when we fled North Carolina," I exhaled, feeling a weight lift off my shoulders when the words left my mouth. I hated having to keep such a huge secret from my friends. "But if they showed *that* photo, someone involved in the case knows who my mother was, knows her changed identity. That means they could know who *I* am. No one knows that except for..." I trailed off, glancing down at my stomach.

"Holy shit," Brayden whispered, not taking his eyes off me. Narrowing his gaze, he was able to put all the puzzle pieces together. "That's what Tyler lied to you about, isn't it?"

I took a long sip of my drink, wishing there was alcohol in it. "He was working on an assignment for the security company. That's why he approached me. Not because he liked me, but because it was his job to get close to me. He was only dating me to find out where my father was." I stared at my cocktail, twirling the ice with my straw. "No other reason."

"So what the news said about your father... The source is right, isn't he? Or she? Your father's not dead, is he?" Brayden asked.

I raised my eyes to his and slightly shook my head.

"Fuck..." Brayden and Jenna exhaled in unison, sinking into their barstools.

"So all of this," I began, waving at the television screen displaying the news, "is confusing. Everything's just spiraled out of control since I met Tyler." I lowered my voice. "Then Charlie mysteriously reappeared in my life and I found out he's supposedly systematically killing people and I'm on the list, as is my dad. He has no idea where my dad is and I'm the only one who could lead him there. I just... I don't know which way is up anymore, especially considering Charlie was the sole survivor of the attack on the U.S. Embassy. The news conveniently left that out, probably to make their accusation that he and my father were working together more believable."

My mind was spinning as I kept talking, both Jenna's and Brayden's eyes wide. "Tyler thought Charlie wanted revenge and was going after the people responsible for his family's death, but I don't know..." I sighed. "I just can't help but feel he's being set up. And my father, well... He's not the monster people think he was...or is. I can't believe he's responsible for what they say he is. Maybe Charlie and my dad are both victims of something so much bigger. Maybe they're too close to blowing the lid and that's why my dad had to go into hiding. Now Charlie has been forced into hiding, as well."

"But what about the hair fibers?"

I shook my head. "I can't explain that, but I know Charlie. Maybe I'm naïve, but I want to believe he wouldn't hurt anyone."

Brayden placed his hand on my shoulder, squeezing affectionately. "Mack, I know you always want to see the good in people. I do, too. But you're obviously a target.

Does Charlie know who you really are?"

Taking a deep breath, I nodded. "He said he was looking into something for a friend of a friend when he was working Cryptology and that's why he originally approached me. Then we started dating and, according to him, he didn't care about any of that anymore. However, something happened toward the end of my freshman year and it all went to hell. He was manic, desperate for me to admit who I really was. Looking back, all I can think is that he knew someone was coming for him, that he needed to find my father for some reason, but it was too late. They took him away and locked him in the psych ward, almost like they knew he was close to figuring out what was going on, who was really behind the embassy attack."

"Or maybe he wanted you to lead him to your father, Mack," Jenna offered. "I don't think you should be so quick to trust Charlie. And even if that were the case, if they were worried about Charlie opening his mouth, they must have known who you were, don't you think?"

I sighed. "This is just so complicated and I have no answers. The only person who does is my father, but he's refused to tell me anything about what happened all those years ago. There are so many possible explanations for everything. I have no fucking clue what to believe, who to trust...who I really am," I quivered.

"Do you really think you need to know what your father did or didn't do to know who you are? I know who you are, Mack," Jenna said. "I've known that for years. You're one tough bitch. You have a hard exterior, but you love with your whole heart, although you refuse to show when you've been let down by those you care about. You always put others ahead of yourself. You always push to achieve greatness, and because of that, because of your influence, I'm a better person. Your past, your roots have no bearing on who you are. Maybe everything you've been through has turned you into the woman you are today, and I'm thankful for that because I *love* who you are, Mack, regardless of the skeletons lurking in your closet."

Chapter Five

Second Nature

Mackenzie

THE FLICKER OF THE television was bright against the darkness that surrounded me. I kept replaying the same national newscast I had seen at the bar, now able to recite each word from memory.

How? I kept asking myself.

How did the media connect my mother to the woman she became after we disappeared? Was it someone involved in the investigation? Or was it the anonymous source from whom the reporter was getting her information? I always knew my mother's death wasn't just an accident. Was the source the one who killed her? Or was it someone else? My questions were mounting with each passing moment.

In the pre-dawn hours on Saturday, I lay on the couch and continued to watch the news report. My brain was on overdrive, restless thoughts extinguishing any hope I had for sleep.

As footage played of the paramedics rolling the two gurneys down the driveway of the house I knew so well, the bodies of my former neighbor and her husband mutilated and destroyed beneath those crisp white sheets, something caught my eye.

Fumbling for the remote, I paused the television, backing up a few frames. I squinted at an out-of-focus man briskly walking through the crowd of concerned onlookers. I had seen the rhythm of that gait practically every day my freshman year of college. The brim of his cap was pulled down, obstructing his face, but I knew that strong jaw all too well. Wearing a pair of army fatigues, denoting the office of captain, he blended in. I wondered who he stole them from, and if the man was as unlucky as his other alleged victims. I surveyed the crowd, all eyes focused on the gurneys being loaded into the coroner's van. No one realized the man accused of committing the crime was just inches from them.

I closed my eyes, leaning back onto the couch, and wrapped my arm around Meatball's pudgy body. I didn't want to believe Charlie had been responsible for such a brutal crime, but there he was at the place of a vicious attack attributed to him.

Since March, my life had slowly spiraled into a world I never imagined. Now, not only was I battling my feelings for the man who deceived me, I was faced with the reality that he may have been right about everything...about Charlie...about his motive...about my dad.

A loud chiming noise, foreign and unexpected, reverberated through the walls of my condo. I bolted up, blinking rapidly. Feeling breathless and dizzy, I stared down the narrow corridor to my bedroom, my eyes focused on a cell phone on my chest of drawers. It had only rung once before and, after the recent murders, the timing had me on edge.

Tiptoeing down the hallway, the wood cold on my bare feet, I entered my bedroom and stared at the phone as it began ringing once more. A blocked number flashed on the screen and my hand hovered over it. The rational part of me said to turn the phone off and avoid contact with Charlie at all costs. But that side was at odds with the small part of me that wanted to believe Charlie was a good person, that wanted to remember the gentle, caring man who doted on me, who treasured me...who *loved* me. I simply couldn't forget about *that* Charlie.

Clutching the phone in my hand, the small object felt like it was burning my skin. The sound of my racing heart echoed against the gray walls as I held the small flip phone up to my ear, unsure of whether this was a smart move or incredibly stupid.

"Charlie?" I whispered.

"Kenzie," he breathed, sounding relieved. "Thank god. I thought..." He stopped short, a heavy quiver in his normally even and tempered tone. "I thought they got to you."

"Who's they?" I asked, heading to the windows in my bedroom, the ocean illuminated by the mid-July moon. I didn't know how much longer I could deal with his vague assertions that someone was setting him up.

"I don't know. It could be a they. It could be a he. Hell, for all I know, it could be a she. I have—"

"Really, Charlie?" I interrupted him, my voice shrill. "It seems the only time I hear from you is when you're being accused of committing another murder! That's a whole lot of finger-pointing by one guy who keeps claiming his innocence!"

"Mack!" he exclaimed. "It wasn't me! I'm—"

"I saw you!" I screeched. "You hid your face, but I'd recognize that walk and stature anywhere, Charlie! You were at my old house! You can't deny it!"

"I'm *not* denying I was there," he responded quickly.

"Why were you? What have you been doing this whole time that I haven't heard from you? How many other bodies can I expect to learn about?"

"None, Mack! I swear to you. I've been looking for answers, but trying to stay hidden at the same time. I'm trying to find *something* that can clear my name…and your dad's."

"So you don't think he's guilty, do you?" I asked, no longer denying the truth of who I was.

"No. I don't, but I have no concrete proof to back it up. All I know—"

"What do you remember about the embassy attack?" I asked, suddenly curious about Charlie's side of the story.

"Why do you want to know?"

"Because maybe hearing what you went through will help me figure out what to believe."

"Kenzie," he countered, his voice distressed. "I haven't talked about that day since I was released from the hospital and sent to live with my aunt and uncle."

"Surely you had *someone* you could talk to."

"No," he said. I could hear the despondency in his voice. "I didn't have anyone. My aunt and uncle considered me to be more of a burden and were counting down the days until I turned eighteen. When I wasn't at school, I pretty much stayed locked in my room. If they knew my whereabouts, I'm fairly certain they'd have no problem turning me into the authorities."

"Then talk to me, Charlie," I urged. "I want to know what happened." I leaned back onto the bed, throwing my duvet over my body. Rolling onto my side, I kept the phone glued to my ear in the darkened room, the sound of Charlie's voice and breathing reminding me of all those years ago when we would fall asleep on the phone with each other.

"Every summer," he began, nostalgia in his voice, "we would spend three or four months abroad. Mom was a legal aid attorney. Dad retired from the army and was a political science professor who specialized in African politics, mainly civil wars and international intervention. I thought it was completely normal to spend each summer vacation living in a small tent with my parents and sister, volunteering at whatever refugee or aid camp needed our help. My parents were the most selfless people I knew. The rest of my family always criticized them, saying if they stopped always trying to do for others and took care of their own family, they'd still be here. But that wasn't who they were. They were only happy when they were helping others, hence why my mother worked in the legal aid office even after she had been offered a hefty six figure salary at one of the top law firms in Philadelphia. She didn't care about money. Dad didn't either, although teaching at Princeton was a good career."

I got lost in his story, learning a side of Charlie I never knew…a side he hid from me the entire time we dated. Absorbing his words and listening to the torment in his voice made me wish he had shared this part of himself with me before. I found myself becoming upset he didn't think he could trust me enough, but then I snapped out of it. I had done the same thing. It wasn't intentional or malicious on his part, just like it wasn't on mine.

Over the years, it simply becomes second nature to keep that part of yourself from everyone. One day, you wake up and forget what you're trying to hide. You become a new person, almost a shell of the person you once were. You hide your pain, your heartache, everything. You find a routine and adhere to it because there's less chance of a slip-up, but you never have that connection to another human. To have that, you'd have to share who you really are, and you don't even know who that is. You never get to share your soul with someone else.

I thought I loved Charlie, but I now knew it wasn't love. I had never opened my heart to him because of the secret I was guarding. But Tyler knew who I was and still loved me. That was why the pain of his betrayal hurt more than Charlie's ever could.

"The civil war in Sierra Leone was winding down, but it was still dangerous," Charlie continued, bringing me back from my thoughts. "We were working at a refugee camp in Liberia, trying to help the victims who had barely escaped with their lives. We were getting ready to head back to the states and were staying at the embassy before our departure. There were about a dozen or so families camping out there for the night, cleaning up and finally sleeping on something other than dirt. We were all gathered in a large ballroom, having dinner, when there was a sudden commotion. Embassy staff began running into where we were eating, then I heard a rapid percussive outburst. I had heard something similar to that noise in the movies, but nothing could have prepared me for the echo of nearly a dozen machine guns being fired simultaneously.

"There was screaming, crying, complete strangers holding onto one another. It was chaotic. I had no idea how I had gotten from the table I was sitting at to the center of the room. We were all huddled together, parents trying to hush the sound of their young children's whimpers and cries. I remember being chilled to the core, my entire body trembling. I had no idea what was going on, but I knew I didn't want to die. I was only sixteen. I hadn't even gotten my driver's license yet. I hadn't asked a girl out to prom. Hell, I hadn't even had sex. I hadn't *lived*."

"Charlie, I...," I whispered, feeling his pain, his suffering, his overwhelming panic as if he were reliving that moment all over again.

"Yes?"

I let out a long breath, finally putting together the pieces of Charlie, wishing I had known all of this when we were together. Perhaps things would have ended differently.

"Why didn't you say anything before? When we were together? Maybe—"

"I didn't want to burden you with my past, Kenzie," he explained. "I knew who you were and that you were trying to deal with your own past. The last thing I wanted to do was saddle you with the trauma I was still dealing with."

"I remember you having nightmares." My voice was barely above a whisper as my brain rewound to waking up to Charlie flailing in bed, screaming about being burned. I had always thought it was simply from his time with the army. I never would have guessed it was something bigger...something so much worse.

"My dad saw how scared I was," he said, clearing his throat. "How scared we both were."

"You and your sister?"

"Yeah," he choked out. "Brooke... She was two years younger than I was. She... She didn't make it."

"But you did," I said, trying to encourage him to finish his story.

"I remember my dad wrapping me in his coat, shielding me as a liquid was poured over everyone. A man with a deep, throaty voice was shouting about trust. How without trust, we would all be left burned, scarred...the bond incinerated. I felt a heat unlike anything I had before. It was an inferno, a distinct smell surrounding me, and I knew... That liquid poured over us was gasoline. This sick bastard was burning us alive."

I gasped. Although Tyler had told me bits and pieces about what happened, hearing someone relive it was so much more intense than I could imagine.

"I don't know how, but I remember being pushed from the flames and crawling under the cover of heavy wool or tweed or something. I was fighting for clean air, choking on smoke, my lungs on fire. I remember craving water, something to put out the inferno raging inside me. My vision grew blurry, my legs weak, and I collapsed, praying my death would be quick and painless. Suddenly, an arm grabbed onto mine and I looked up, unable to focus on the face. For years, I searched my memory trying to recreate that face but I couldn't."

"But...," I prodded, able to sense there was more.

"After college, I enlisted and eventually got reassigned to Cryptology. It didn't take me long to realize nothing is what it seems. When a friend of a friend started asking about a girl named Serafina Galloway, I looked up the file. I was hesitant to go any further once I realized who Serafina Galloway really was. The daughter of the man responsible for my family's death... The dragon. Of course, it wasn't public knowledge, but it was fairly well-known within the intelligence community that Colonel Galloway was responsible for orchestrating hundreds of arms deals and the attack on the embassy.

"As I scanned through photo after photo in his file, I noticed something...a black onyx ring on his right hand. I *remembered* that ring. I had clutched onto that hand as I was pulled from the smoke. It was such a unique piece, I knew he had to be the person who rescued me from the fire. I pulled up all the files pertaining to the investigation into Galloway after the embassy attack, then reached out to the agent in charge. He indicated he had the same concerns but his hands were tied. He was told to close the case and keep his findings classified. Apparently, the army didn't want a black mark on its face and wanted to keep Galloway's alleged activities buried. They were all convinced he had died in the attack anyway.

"I contacted other people named in the investigation, but they all gave me the same response...almost to the word. This didn't sit right with me, but I had exhausted all my resources. Then I realized there may be someone else who could help answer some of my questions."

"And who's that?"

He sighed. "Your mother. I went to talk to her."

I closed my eyes, remaining mute.

"It was a few weeks later that she..." He trailed off. "I am *so* sorry, Mackenzie. I can't help but think if I didn't... Someone may have been tipped off that I was looking into Galloway, and maybe they followed me to her. I don't know. It wasn't until the night I was taken away that I realized I was being set up and someone was tasked with silencing your mother, too."

Listening to him speak about those last few weeks reopened old wounds I never allowed to fully heal. But as much as I wanted to blame Charlie for it, like I had done for years, I just couldn't. Not anymore. "What did you talk to her about?" I swallowed hard, trying to hide my unsteady tone.

"The time leading up to the attack on the embassy. Your father. It was during this conversation I realized he was still alive."

"How? I didn't even know he—"

"It was the way she spoke of him," he interrupted. "I've studied human behavior and responses. People respond a certain way when speaking of someone who's no longer with us. Your mother displayed none of those characteristics when speaking of your father. She responded as one may when talking about someone they see on a somewhat routine basis. She spoke of him in the present tense. That usually only happens when someone *just* died. However, at this point, he had allegedly been dead for eight years. Surely, she would have been speaking of him in the past tense. I pushed her to disclose his location and she denied he was alive, just as you did.

A few days later, she called, asking me to meet her at a location several hours out of town. It was the same day I was taken away. The same day she..." His voice grew quiet. "All I can think is someone knew about us and was trying to keep us from helping each other figure out the truth of what really happened all those years ago."

"And what's that?"

He sighed. "I still don't have a fucking clue. I'm trying, Mack, but I'm no closer to finding out who's behind it than I was years ago. All the physical evidence still points—"

"To my father."

"Yeah."

"Maybe he *is* behind it all," I offered. As much as I didn't want to think my father could be capable of committing such a heinous crime, I couldn't disregard what years of investigations had concluded. "I have no idea what evidence there is either way, but I can't help but want to put faith in our criminal justice system."

"Well, you shouldn't, Mack. The decisions made in law enforcement offices across the country...fuck, the *world*...are nothing but power plays done for political gain. It's all about public appearance in the press, making the concerned citizens believe that something's actually being done to put a stop to rampant criminal behavior. So they find someone to pin crimes on..."

"You expect me to believe everyone who is arrested is innocent?" I asked, my voice heavy with disbelief. "I highly doubt that, Charlie."

"I'm not saying that, Mack. I'm just saying that, in high profile cases, ones with a lot of public attention, you have to take everything you learn from the media with a grain of salt. Hell, they think I'm responsible for killing over a dozen people. Their only evidence? A web blog and some phony visitation records. Anyone with decent computer skills could have faked that."

"But why?"

"Maybe because I was getting too close. Maybe because someone figured out I knew who you were and wanted to try to protect you. Until I know the answer, please promise me you'll be safe and will stick close to Tyler."

My breath hitched and I debated how much I should tell Charlie.

"I can't," I whispered. "We... We're not together anymore."

"What? Why? What happened?" His voice was panicked.

I considered telling him everything. How Tyler had only dated me to find my father, just like Charlie had, but it made me seem simple-minded and gullible.

"It just didn't work out between us, Charlie, and that's all I'm going to say about it."

"Shit, Kenzie," he muttered. "If I had known..." There was a heavy pause and I could picture Charlie's strong face, his vibrant blue eyes illuminating his dark features.

"I've been fine, Charlie. It's been over for months now."

"Months? And you didn't tell me?"

"How could I?" I shot back. "I have no way of getting in touch with you!"

"It's a necessity. I'm sorry. I have to do everything I can to make my movements untraceable."

"I'm being careful," I offered in consolation, able to sense his unease. "I'm—"

The sound of sirens blared through the phone, growing louder and louder, and my heart sank in my chest.

"I've got to go," he whispered.

"Wait! Charlie?"

The line went dead.

Chapter Six

Listen

Mackenzie

THE CLOCK ON THE far wall of my bedroom struck eight as the alarm on my phone sounded, but I continued staring at the ceiling. I was at the point of exhaustion where I was wide awake. I wasn't sure if I had actually slept or not. All night long, my eyes were glued to the national news, waiting for a breaking report that Charlie had been apprehended. Since he hung up on me, an unsettled feeling had grown more and more intense, leaving me with more questions than answers, and I needed to do something to ease my restless thoughts. There was only one thing that would give me the peace I needed. My routine.

Swinging my legs to the side of the bed, I padded to my dresser and pulled out some running shorts and a loose-fitting tank top that was no longer quite as loose-fitting. After lacing up my sneakers and eating a banana, I headed out of my condo to get to the gym.

"Have a nice workout, Miss Delano," a formal voice said as I exited the elevator.

I looked over my shoulder to see the new security guard, who started a few months ago, sitting at the desk. He was easily in his early sixties and, from his tone and stature, I could only assume he was retired military. I expected him to start saluting the tenants of the building at any time now.

"Thanks, Wyatt."

As I approached my car and was about to duck into the driver's seat, I saw the same black sedan as the day before idling on the street, the sole occupant keeping his eyes trained forward. I wondered if it had some connection to Charlie. Or maybe it was it someone looking for my father. I immediately grew suspicious and recalled Charlie's words from months ago, urging me to stray from my routine because it made me a predictable and easy target. As much as I cringed at the thought, I knew he was right.

Pulling my iPod out of my bag, I clipped it to my tank top and put in my earbuds, lowering the volume so I could hear the traffic around me. Feeling surprisingly composed with the break in my routine, I threw my bag in my car, locked it, then stored my keys in my pocket.

As I trotted through the parking lot and ran south along the beach, I noticed the dark sedan driving along the main drag of the island in the same direction I was heading. Trying to shake off my paranoia, I took several calming breaths, running through dozens of possible scenarios as to why the sedan that had mysteriously appeared in front of my building had left at the same time I did. I was on alert, perhaps more than necessary. It could have all been a coincidence, but I was beginning to learn there was no such thing.

Running at an easy pace, thanks to my doctor's admonition that I not overexert myself and keep my body temperature low, I basked in the morning sun, the humidity causing sweat to drench my tank top after a mere five minutes. The beach was relatively empty, apart from a few people enjoying a morning walk or jog. A few dogs were chasing balls their owners threw and seagulls were flying overhead, looking for their next meal.

A smile crossed my face and my usually tense shoulders relaxed. It was invigorating to be outside and not in some stuffy gym. After everything with Tyler, I had become diligent to never stray from the safety of my routine, as I had with him. But perhaps a new, better routine was exactly what I needed to give myself a renewed outlook on life. Everywhere else on the island had been tainted with Tyler's presence. My condo. The gym. The tapas bar. The restaurant. They all held memories of him. But the beach held none of that. Out here, I could have the new start I needed and deserved. Out here, I could sever the chains binding me to the lies he fed me to get what he wanted.

What was that anyway? I thought, slowing to a stop as a golden retriever darted past me, chasing after a ball his owner had thrown into the ocean. I closed my eyes, the ghost of Tyler dancing in my mind, replaying a scene I had suppressed the past few months.

"Hurt me! Hate me! I want you to! I deserve it! I deserve everything you can do to me, Mackenzie, but you need to know something... I didn't say anything. When you found me last night at the dedication dinner and I was distant, that's because my brother asked about your father. He asked me if I knew where he was, if you had told me. And you want to know what I said? I said nothing, even after he warned me I could face potential prison time, or worse, if I withheld that information. So you can hate me all you want. You can bleed me dry and I will still bleed for you."

Feeling lightheaded, I lowered myself to the ground, lying on the sand. It was refreshing against my sweat-drenched back, temporarily cooling the heat running through me at the possibility I had been too stubborn to consider all the shades of gray that made up Tyler's lies. Yes, he led me to believe he was genuinely interested in me, but at what point did I become a priority over his job, his mission? Or was his plea to me that day all part of the act? I ran my hand over my face, trying to make sense of it all. I didn't know what to believe anymore, but I knew one thing...

"He really didn't say anything," I mumbled to myself. I told Tyler everything. How I knew my father was still alive. How I knew where he was. How I still saw him on a regular basis at the church I attended when I lived in San Antonio.

He knew exactly how to find my father, yet he was still a free man. Tyler continued to safeguard my secret, regardless of the possible repercussions to his own livelihood. I thought I did what was right, what anyone would do after learning the person they loved wasn't who they said they were. But I was now more confused than ever, wondering whether my obstinacy had cost me the only man who would ever make me swoon.

~~~~~~~~~~

AFTER MAKING THE DECISION to cut my run short, I headed back to my condo to get ready for my day. I went through the usual motions...shower, dress, makeup...but Tyler was on my mind more than usual today. As I was preparing a cup of coffee, I couldn't help but think there was a reason for this.

Lost in my thoughts, I jumped when there was a light knock on the door. My heels clicking as I made my way to the foyer, my heart dropped to the pit of my stomach as I pulled open the door, all the memories of the life I was trying to move past rushing forward.

"Mrs. Burnham...," I said, unable to hide the surprise in my voice as I stared at the petite woman with short platinum hair.

"Please, dear." She took off her large white sunglasses and put them in her purse. "Call me Colleen," she said with a genuine smile.

Nodding and in a daze, I stepped back. "Won't you come in, Colleen?"

Her eyes shot to my stomach as she took in my side view. Today *would* be the day I chose to wear something that showed off my figure, including the baby bump, instead of one of my flowing maxi dresses. The black sheath dress I wore made my stomach rather pronounced.

"I see," she said, walking through the foyer and into the living area.

Nervous about why she was here, I headed toward the kitchen area of my open living space. "Can I get you anything? A coffee? Water?"

"I'm fine, dear."

I nodded, grabbing the cup of coffee that had finished brewing. Adding a bit of sweetener and some milk, I tried to ignore the unsettled thoughts floating through my mind. This was the story of my life. Just when everything seemed to be back on track and I thought I'd get over my past, a reminder of what I had been through would show up on my doorstep. I didn't know how many setbacks a person could possibly endure before it became too much.

I walked to the living room, noticing her eye the stack of bills on my kitchen table, a look of sympathy on her face. I didn't want her empathy. It would just be another reminder of how naïve I was.

"Won't you have a seat?" I gestured to the couch as I sat down in the spot that had always been mine.

"Thank you," she said, sitting down on the opposite end. She glanced to my stomach again, a forlorn expression crossing her face. "Well, you're probably wondering what I'm doing here."

I laughed nervously at the light tone of her voice. "You could say that. In all honesty, I'm scared to know." Raising my cup to my lips, I took a much needed sip of my coffee, despite the fact it was decaffeinated.

"May I ask you a question?"

"Certainly," I replied, my voice guarded. Placing my mug on the coffee table, I braced myself for whatever she was about to ask.

"How far along are you?"

"Seventeen weeks." I glanced at my stomach, placing my hand over it. "Almost eighteen."

"During those almost eighteen weeks, how many times have you tried to get in touch with Tyler?"

"I've lost track," I admitted, trying to swallow the lump in my throat. I didn't want her to see how much her son's actions affected me. "I told him to stay away, but I didn't think he would."

"I know, dear," she said, scooting across the couch and grabbing my hand in hers. The contact was comforting and soothing.

"I started to think I made him up. I went to his house and..." I turned my gaze from her, the memory of that day still fresh, the feeling I was losing my mind resurfacing.

Placing her hand on my shoulder, she said, "I can imagine how difficult it is to see the reminders of him—"

I shot up. "*No!* It's so much more than that. After I was home for a week, I finally stopped being stubborn and decided to go over there to talk to him about everything. You know who answered the door?"

Her eyes narrowed. "Who?" she asked cautiously.

"A man who knew my name, who tried to convince me he had been living in that house for years!" I began pacing in front of her, reliving that day from hell. "It was exactly as I remembered. The décor the same. The cars

70

the same. Hell, anchored out back was the same yacht I remember! I was so confused. I was convinced I imagined everything between us! I searched for some sort of proof that what we had was real, that we *did* know each other, but there was nothing. Photos had been manipulated on my phone so he was no longer in any of them. Not one trace of his existence in my life was left. I couldn't help but think I made it all up! Even after all the assurances my friends had given me that he was real, that he did exist, I still questioned it. Until…"

I stopped in my tracks, my hand settling on my stomach. "Until I found out I was pregnant. This is the only proof I have that I'm not fucking crazy and I hate it. I hate that he lied to me. I hate that he did this to me. But mostly…" I fell onto the couch, finding my way into her nurturing arms. "Mostly I hate that I miss him. I hate that I told him to stay away and he listened. I hate that I can't stop thinking about him. And I hate that I think I still love him, even though I'll never be able to trust him again."

"Shhh," she soothed, kissing the top of my head like my own mother used to do. "It's going to be okay. He went after you, ya know."

I pulled out of her arms and stared at her. "What do you mean?"

"He tried to stop you at the airport, but couldn't get to you in time. Hours later, I found him sitting on a bench along the Charles River. I watched him for a good twenty minutes before I approached him. You know what he was doing the entire time?"

I studied her through the tears in my eyes. "What?" I asked, almost nervous to know the answer, fearful it would cause an overwhelming feeling of regret.

"He was staring at the most beautiful diamond ring I've ever seen."

71

I gasped, the memory of that weekend rushing back. "He asked me to marry him right before the dedication dinner," I whispered. "I said I didn't want a ring..."

"I taught my boys better than that." Colleen smiled, then sobered. "But I must confess, I feel partly responsible for why you haven't heard from him."

"Why is that?" I wiped at the tears on my cheeks.

"I've been where you are. I've been hurt by the one person I thought I loved. I told my own husband to get out and stay out of my life."

"And did he?" I was desperate for advice from someone who'd been where I was and could sympathize with what I was going through.

"He did," she recalled. "He gave me the space I needed in order to realize my life sucked without him."

I laughed at her words.

"At first, Tyler didn't want to give up without a fight, but he decided to give you the space you needed in order for your heart to heal. He took a humanitarian assignment in Sudan that was only supposed to last a few weeks. As far as I know, he's still there, helping refugees have a better life, trying to dampen the pain he's caused you." She grabbed my hands in hers as I fought to control my emotions. "I know Tyler. He's a bit of a lost soul. When he hurts someone, he physically feels that pain. He wears it. He carries it as he would his own. He's probably struggling with his guilt and is taking this time to learn to find meaning in it."

"I still don't understand why he hasn't called or anything."

"And what would you do if he did? Is this really something that could be settled with a simple phone call?"

I shook my head slightly.

"Mackenzie, darling, his absence from your life right

now is giving you space to figure out what you *do* want. Even though he's my son and I will always support him, I also know he hurt you. That's not something which can be easily forgotten. He's working on forgiving himself right now. When he's ready, he'll be back. Just promise me one thing."

"What's that?"

"When Tyler comes back, and he *will* come back for you, keep your heart open." She raised herself from the couch and headed toward the front door.

"But how am I going to believe a word that comes out of his mouth after everything?" I asked, following her.

"Sometimes, Mackenzie," she began, spinning around and grabbing my hands in hers, "the most meaningful thoughts can't be communicated with words. Don't listen to what comes out of his mouth. Listen to his heart. Then you'll know." She enveloped me in her arms once more and planted a soft kiss on my cheek. "Here's my card, dear," she said, pulling a business card out of her purse. "I expect regular updates on my grandbaby." She winked. "Do you know the gender yet?"

"I find out Tuesday."

"Perfect. I'll await your phone call."

She turned and opened the door.

"Colleen, you're not going to tell...?"

"It's not my place to say anything. This is your decision. However, remember how you felt when Tyler kept *his* secret from *you*."

Chapter Seven

Forgiveness

Mackenzie

"HEY, MACK," JENNA SAID as I entered the kitchen of the restaurant later that morning. She was busy playing around with some new recipe. Her apron was covered in batter and frosting, and I could only assume the end result would taste amazing.

"Hey, Jenna. Do I even want to know what you're up to over there?"

She scrunched her nose. "Probably not. But don't worry. You'll be the first to taste it when I'm done!"

Shaking my head and trying not to think about what Jenna's experiments were costing, I made my way through the industrial kitchen, line cooks busy preparing orders for our customers.

The restaurant had been more successful than I could have imagined. Our business plan filled a gap in dining on the island. Instead of simply opening another seafood restaurant because of our proximity to the ocean and fresh fisheries, we strayed from the norm and certainly reaped the benefits. Although the restaurant was packed with a line out the door most nights, we were still in the red, trying to finally make back the substantial amount of money we had put into this place before it opened. After paying the loan, the lease, our staff's salaries, and other overhead, there wasn't much left. I desperately wanted to pay off that loan so Jenna and I could finally start making some money off our dream.

I climbed the stairs and unlocked my office, making my way through the somewhat cluttered space to my desk. It wasn't untidy, but the small area was congested with my desk and loveseat.

I pulled my laptop out and began searching news reports for any more information on the murders of which Charlie was accused. I wanted to believe the story he told me last night, but a nagging voice was reminding me of Charlie's background and the fact he was trained to get people to believe what he wanted them to. Was he just a pawn in a bigger scheme? Or was he simply saying that to get me to fall into his trap again? The more I learned about Charlie and his past, the more confused I was. I wondered whether I would have this problem had Charlie been honest with me from the beginning. His deceitfulness was always in the back of my mind, reminding me I couldn't put all my faith in his words.

My thoughts wandered to Colleen's visit earlier this morning, her words echoing in my mind, beseeching me to give Tyler another chance. How could I possibly forgive a man who had betrayed me? How could I ever trust him when I would always be wondering whether his words were true?

I slammed my laptop closed, groaning. For the past several months, I had been fighting to do everything to forget about Tyler. But a small part of me wanted him to come back, to be near me once more, to promise me everything would be okay...that *we* would be okay.

I buried my head on my desk, the cool metal of my laptop comforting against my forehead. I was frustrated, uncertain, and confused. I wished I could just write Tyler off. I considered whether I'd be able to do just that had I not gotten pregnant by him. Would I still think about him as much as I did? I knew I would. My pregnancy had nothing to do with it. My heart belonged to him and I needed to get it back. If I didn't, I'd never truly be able to move on like I needed to.

"Mack? You okay?" Jenna's soft voice cut through my thoughts and I raised my head to see her standing in the doorway.

"Just thinking."

"About what?" she asked, walking into my office and sitting down on the loveseat, her face eager.

"Just stuff," I said, trying to shrug her off. "It's been a busy morning. And I didn't really sleep well last night..."

"After seeing that newscast about Charlie?" She lowered her voice.

"Yeah, but I don't want to talk about any of that. How's everything going with you?"

She bit her lip, almost considering whether to continue our conversation. Her normally jubilant and carefree attitude faded, replaced with an uneasy aura. I knew I needed to be the same kind of friend to her she had been to me for the past eight years. As much as I wanted to tell her about Colleen's visit and ask her advice on whether I could ever forgive Tyler, I knew Jenna needed to get something off her chest.

"What is it, Jenna? You can tell me." I got up from behind my desk and sat beside her on the loveseat.

She studied me for a brief moment before sighing, leaning back. "It's probably nothing, but I can't stop thinking that..." She trailed off, avoiding my eyes.

"Thinking what?"

Facing me once more, she appeared so small and insecure. "Do you think Richard's cheating on me?"

"What?!" I asked in complete surprise. I didn't know what I expected to be worrying her but it certainly wasn't that. I had never seen another man look at a woman with the amount of devotion and yearning Richard looked at her. If they couldn't make it, I would lose hope for any couple having a chance. "What makes you think that?"

"You'll probably think it's nothing, but all the small things over the past few months have been adding up, culminating this morning. He left early yesterday, claiming he had an emergency at one of his other hotels on the east coast. He assured me he'd be back late last night. When I got home from girls' night, he wasn't there. I was worried something happened to him so I called. It rang a few times and then was sent to voicemail, like he was purposely ignoring my call. I finally got a hold of him this morning and heard a woman's voice in the background. He said he was in the middle of a meeting and things were worse than he was led to believe, but I don't know. Why didn't he just call and tell me?"

"Jenna, I think you're overanalyzing the situation. I know how it is when you're trying to put out the metaphorical fire. Everything else takes a back seat, including personal relationships."

She vehemently shook her head. "No. That's what *you* do, Mack. That's not me. And that's never been Richard, either. At least it wasn't..." She turned her head briefly before returning her gaze to me. "This has been happening more and more. He used to go out of town once a month at most to personally check in on one of his hotels, but now it seems to be a weekly occurrence. It's almost like it's a chore for him to be at home with me." She studied me for several long moments. I could tell she wasn't done with her story yet, so I remained silent. Lowering her eyes, she softly said, "I even hired a private investigator."

"You what?!" I exclaimed, shocked.

She shrugged. "It was about a month ago. I didn't know what else to do!"

"Why didn't you come to me with all this before?"

"I couldn't," she replied. "You've been buried with all your own shit. The last thing I wanted to do was burden you with my problem that may or may not be an actual problem."

"And what did the private investigator find out?"

"Nothing."

"So that's good!"

She shook her head, her motions slow and measured. "No. That's the problem. He found *nothing*. There was no record of Richard's previous marriage or divorce."

"I'm sure there's a reason for that. He's a pretty high profile guy, Jenna. Maybe he didn't want his name splashed all over the media and paid some people to make his marriage simply disappear. Stop thinking the worst of everything and talk to him about this."

"I gave him Richard's ex-wife's name," she continued. Her tone grew frenzied and hurried. "He found out she died in a car accident last spring, right before we met. You don't think…?"

"Jenna," I said, placing my hand on her shoulder. "That's crazy. You're letting your imagination get the better of you. Stop digging into something that's not there. Richard loves you, plain and simple. That's all you need to worry yourself with. And if we *do* find out he's been cheating, he'll wish he never stepped foot on South Padre." I winked, wrapping my arms around her.

She was usually the one to lend me a shoulder to cry on, to bitch and commiserate about whatever was going on in my life. She was never one to appear anything but composed. She appeared so vulnerable now and I hated that I had allowed my best friend to cope with this on her own for the past month. I vowed to never put her through that again. She had always been there for me and I needed to start being here for her, regardless of what was going on in my own life.

"Thanks, Kenzie. I don't know what I'd do without you."

"Ditto," I replied, pulling back as she got up from the couch and headed toward the door to my office. "Hey, Jenna?" I called out as she was about to disappear into the hallway.

"Yeah?" She spun around to face me.

Sighing, I met her eyes. "Do you think I'll ever be able to forgive Tyler for what he's done?"

Her expression softened a bit and she gave me a sincere look. "I don't know if I can answer that for you. You gave your heart to Tyler and it's not easy to get it back. But what I *can* tell you is what you're going through right now won't last forever. With each passing day, you'll think about him a little bit less. You'll get back one more piece of your heart and, one day, you'll wake up and someone else will have taken his place." She bounced down the hall, leaving me alone.

"That's what I'm afraid of," I whispered to the empty room.

Chapter Eight

Through

Mackenzie

"WHAT'S A GUY GOT to do to get a great IPA around here?" a soft voice with a beautiful British accent said as I buzzed around the bar, pouring drinks. I could have just as easily hired additional bartenders, but there was something I loved about being behind the bar. Plus, it helped with our overhead to have me work the bar instead of hiring someone else.

I almost replied with one of my typical snarky comments to get him to leave me alone, but as I spun around to open my mouth, I quickly softened my expression. The man standing in front of me was strikingly handsome. He wore a loose-fitting white linen shirt with the sleeves rolled up, a pair of dark jeans, and flip flops. His sandy hair had a windblown look about it, his forearms muscled and tan.

Smiling, I simply said, "All you have to do is order one." I grabbed a pint glass and poured one of the IPAs from the tap. "Hope you like this one." I put the glass down in front of him. "Harvested and brewed right here in the fine state of Texas."

"I'm starting to think there's a lot to enjoy in Texas."

My ears heated from his stare and I felt my face begin to blush. I hadn't allowed myself to flirt with another man in months, not wanting to put in the effort. I knew this wouldn't go anywhere, but maybe it was exactly what I needed to make me shake off all the memories of Tyler that still found me nearly every day.

"I'm Ellis," he said, reaching his hand across the bar. I grabbed onto it lightly and he raised it to his lips, kissing it softly. The contact on my skin was dull. Even when Tyler wasn't touching me, I was ready to fall apart. My body was always hyper-aware of him...his presence, his caress, his gaze. With this guy, I felt absolutely nothing. No spark. No flame. No lightning. *Nothing.* And it made me long for my mystery man even more, although he was no longer mine.

"Mackenzie," I said, finally snapping out of my daydream.

"It's nice to meet you, Mackenzie."

"Well, I should get going. Lots of customers to get drunk and..." I scanned the area to see the other bartenders had it well under control.

"And...?" He narrowed his dark eyes on me and I shrugged, knowing he had caught me in my excuse to end our conversation. An understanding look crossed his face and he leaned on the counter. "I get it. It's a bit cheeky, isn't it? Trying to pick up a girl at a bar?"

I eyed him. "A bit, especially when you don't even live here."

"What makes you think that?" He smiled, flashing a set of perfectly straight white teeth, made brighter against his tanned skin.

"Call it a hunch. That accent seems to be a dead giveaway that you're not local."

He shrugged. "Or I could have left mother England because of a better business opportunity."

"So which is it?"

"The latter." He winked, and I could have sworn I felt a slight fluttering in my heart.

81

"So what is it that you do, Ellis?" I asked, crossing my arms.

"Oh, a little bit of this. A little bit of that."

I rolled my eyes. "Nice. How about a little bit more detail, though."

"I'm not a criminal or anything, if that's what you're worried about."

"I'm not worried about that. I'm just wondering what it is you do for a living, how you support yourself... See, this is what Americans would refer to as an icebreaker, some sort of conversation to find out about one another."

He studied me briefly. "I'm an applications developer for a company up in Houston."

"And what does that mean?"

"Computer stuff."

"Ah," I said. "So you're a computer geek."

He took a sip of his beer. "More or less, but that's just something I do on the side."

"Oh, really?" I raised my eyebrows and gave him a playful look. "What's your *real* job then?"

"I'm a professional poker player."

"Poker?" I swallowed hard, my voice becoming quiet.

"Yeah. You know. Poker... It's a card game. Placing bets... Going all in..."

Those last words hit me, making it feel as if all the air had been sucked out of the room. This conversation was yet another reminder that moving on wasn't in the cards for me. The sounds of the bar grew muddled and became background noise as I was whisked back to that day.

"I'm a broken man." Tyler leaned his forehead on mine and lovingly caressed my face as we sat in the front seat of my Mercedes, the March sun beating down on us.

"Everyone's broken in one way or another, Tyler."

"Not like me. Some days, I feel like I'm barely hanging on. But I

*haven't since I met you. For the past six years, all I've felt is pain. I
know this sounds crazy but, whenever I'm with you, I find meaning
in that pain."* He held my face in his hands, but I remained
speechless, his impassioned words overwhelming me.

*"So whatever this is and whatever it's going to be, know that I'm
all in, Mackenzie. You have enchanted my heart and, for the first
time in years, I feel alive, even when I'm not with you. I know we
just met and I'll be the first to admit I wasn't expecting to be so
captivated by you."* He took a deep breath. *"But I am. I am
unimaginably bewitched by you. I'm all in, Mackenzie."*

The memory was so vivid, so sharp, as if it was
happening at that moment. I remembered precisely what
he was wearing…a yellow polo shirt and jeans that fit
him perfectly. His green eyes were brilliant but scared.
What I didn't see as I relived this memory was a lack of
sincerity. It covered him, from the way his fiery gaze
burned into me to the way he caressed my skin. Even
early on, I could sense he didn't say those words just to
get information. They were true. I couldn't help but
think about what else was true.

"Mackenzie," Ellis' voice cut through, bringing me out
of my memory. "Where did you go?"

"Sorry. I was just thinking about something." I
grabbed a towel and began to wipe down the counter. "I
need to get back to work. Enjoy your beer, Ellis."

I heard him call my name as I rushed from behind the
bar, through the busy restaurant, and up to my office,
struggling to breathe. Even after all the times I had tried
to convince myself, I knew I wasn't over Tyler Burnham.
I doubted whether I ever would be.

~~~~~~~~~~

THAT NIGHT, I TOSSED and turned for hours, a thousand
thoughts running through my head. I had kept my true

feelings buried for months, forbidden from communicating what was going through my mind to the one person who needed to know. I had let it all fester, but it wasn't until I met another man who seemed to be interested in me that I realized how messed up I still was. I was desperate for closure, to finally tell *him* what I was feeling…even if it fell on deaf ears.

Rummaging through my bag, I grabbed my laptop and booted it up. I typed in the email address I had for Tyler and hovered over the keyboard for what seemed like an eternity, my hands shaking at the prospect of him reading this. I needed him to know how much his lies hurt me. I needed him to feel my pain. I couldn't shoulder it all on my own anymore.

The words I had thought on a daily basis for the past several months filtered from my head to the laptop, the visualization of weeks of pent up feelings therapeutic and soothing the fire within.

I don't even know where to begin. I don't know what to think. I don't know what to do.

Worse, I don't know who I am.

Maybe I never did.

It's past three o'clock in the morning and I can't sleep. I'm exhausted, run down.

Heartbroken.

The fact you lied to me isn't what hurts now. I've stopped feeling the pain from that. It's knowing no one can replace you. It's knowing I'll search for someone else to give my heart to for the rest of my life and never find him.

It's knowing lightning doesn't *strike the same place twice.*

It's knowing you're my turtledove.

It's knowing I'm through.

I met a guy tonight. An attractive, charming man. He made me smile. He made me laugh. He made me forget about everything for a minute.

But I felt nothing…because of you.

I felt no butterflies.

I felt no spark.

I felt no lightning strike.

Because. Of. You.

It's been nearly four months.

One hundred and ten days, to be exact.

When I first met you, I had a feeling you would be the one person who could break down my walls. I knew you'd be the one to make me feel, *something no one has been able to do for years. But I also knew you'd be the one to ruin me. You told me as much. I didn't want to believe it. I didn't want to think something so evil, so hurtful, so ugly could come out of something I thought was so fucking beautiful.*

And that was my love.

I loved *you, Tyler. Unconditionally. Completely. Wholeheartedly.*

But you deceived me. Because of that, I should be over you. Since you've been gone, I've done everything I could to convince myself I don't care about you. That I'm over you. That I hate you. That I despise everything about you.

I should, ya know.

I should hate the way you looked in your tuxedo the night you asked me to marry you.

I should hate the way my name used to roll off your tongue and make me shiver.

I should hate the way you used to snore.

I should hate the way you used to smile at me unlike the way you smiled at anyone else.

I should hate the way you used to wrap your arms around me and make me feel like I finally had a home.

I should hate the way you used to make me laugh.

I should hate the way you used to make me feel alive.

You did everything right. You said exactly what I needed to hear when I needed to hear it. You made me fall in love with you. You took my love from me, and I'll never be able to get it back. I'll never be able to give anyone else all my love. I'll never be able to experience that unmistakable feeling of absolute euphoria just from being around them. For that, I should forget about you.

The truth is, no matter how much I say I'm over you, you're still on my mind.

The truth is, despite it all, I don't hate you.

The truth is, despite it all, you made me feel*, and I'd rather have felt something so fucking intense for you than to never have that memory at all.*

The truth is, despite it all, I still love you. And I always will.

Seeing the words on the screen in front of me made the tears streaming down my cheeks fall with more intensity. My sobs wracked through my body, and I could barely see the screen through my fuzzy vision. Choking on my own cries, I hovered the mouse over the SEND button.

Could I really do this? Could I really send this email? Would it make me feel any better? Would it make the heartache hurt less?

Would he even get it?

Would he even care?

When you hit rock bottom, there's nowhere else to go but up. I was at rock bottom. I was at the lowest of any low I could remember. Since leaving Tyler, there had been a permanent ache in my chest, which had only grown more intense over the days and months with no communication from him.

Realizing I had nothing to lose by sending it, I clicked on the button, the whooshing sound of my email being sent causing me to immediately regret the decision. My heart thumped in my chest and I prayed for a message telling me the email was undeliverable, but that never happened.

The rest of the night, I stayed awake, waiting for an answer.

I didn't know why I expected one.

I didn't know why I hoped for one.

But I did.

I never got one.

Chapter Nine

Second Chances

Tyler

"DROP YOUR ELBOW JUST a little," I instructed a Sudanese boy, who couldn't have been more than ten, as he stood next to a makeshift home plate. "Keep your eye on the ball. Then knock it out of the park."

"Like Fenway Park?" the little boy asked in a thick African accent.

I laughed. "Exactly."

"I'm Babe Ruth then?"

"No. Definitely not. He's a traitor who went to play for the Yankees."

"Boo, Yankees," a chorus of voices sounded around me. I looked up, laughing at how easily they picked up on the rivalry between the Red Sox, my team of choice, and the Yankees. Turning my attention back to the little boy, I said, "You're David Ortiz. Big Papi."

"Okay. Big Papi. I'll hit a big slam."

I chuckled. "Grand slam, but close enough," I said. "Okay, you ready?"

The little boy bent his knees and held the bat as I had taught him, turning his head toward the pitcher's mound. I nodded to Eli and he tossed an easy pitch. I stood back and waited in anticipation, as if this was game seven of the World Series.

Since I had arrived here, I had been teaching a group

of young boys and girls everything I knew about American sports. I occasionally helped in the medical tent, but everything was well under control, so Eli and I spent most of our time playing soccer, basketball, and baseball, my personal favorite. It was challenging, considering many of these young kids had suffered injuries, some requiring amputation, while trying to escape the civil unrest in their home country. But instead of one kid trying to stand out and be better than another, they helped each other, even when they were on different teams. Adults could learn something from watching these kids interact with each other. It was humbling and eye-opening.

The crack of the bat brought me back to the present and I shot up, jumping up and down. "You did it! Run! Run!" I shouted, darting past home plate toward first to show him how to run the bases. "Keep going until I tell you to stop!"

"See! I'm Big Papi!"

I beamed, my smile reaching my eyes. It was the happiest I could remember being for months. Moments like these made me feel as if I had some purpose. "Yes, you are!"

As he rounded the bases, the opposite team cheering along with his own, I glanced at my watch.

Clapping as everyone congratulated the little boy, I gestured to them. "Come on. Bring it in, everyone!" They all ran toward me, throwing their second-hand baseball gloves in a mound. "That's it for today," I said and they all groaned. "We'll pick it up sometime after your classes this week."

"Can we watch a real baseball game one day?" a little girl, who couldn't have been more than eight, asked.

"I'll see what I can do," I said, wishing there was a way for me to share the joy of a live baseball game with these kids. They probably would never be able to savor the smell of popcorn and hot dogs as they listened to the crack of the bat echo through the ballpark, thousands of people cheering. It was one of the things that always excited me, even as I neared my thirties. There was something timeless about sitting in Fenway Park watching the Red Sox play. It was something I believed everyone should experience at least once in their lives. Knowing these kids were lucky to even be alive reinvigorated why I was here, despite the nagging doubt finding me at odd times.

After getting hugs from nearly all the children, Eli and I packed up the equipment and locked it in the storage shed. We hopped in our armored truck and left the refugee camp, beginning the three hour journey to the communications center for my weekly check-in with my brother.

"We missed Fourth of July," Eli commented during our drive.

"It seems like we've missed a lot, doesn't it?"

"Is Griffin still with your mom?"

"Yeah. She loves that dog. I'm sure she's going to have a hard time parting with him when I get back home."

"And when do you think that will be?" Eli asked, never missing an opportunity to convince me it was time we leave, with or without my brother's permission.

I shrugged. "I don't know. I'm not sure I'm ready to walk away now. These kids... I feel like I'd be abandoning them if I just go. Maybe it's been a blessing in disguise that Alexander keeps insisting we stay over here."

"And what about *your* life back home?" Eli countered. "What about your family? Your responsibilities?" He lowered his voice. "What about Mackenzie? Don't you think you're abandoning her?"

90

I sighed. "That ship may have sailed. It's been almost four months. I'm not sure she'll want to see me again. I had a window of opportunity and it's probably closed."

"So you're just going to dismiss her and pretend none of it happened? If you ask me, seems like an easy way out."

"I'm not looking for a way out, Eli," I countered. I turned my head away from him and stared at the barren desert, the vehicle kicking up dust as we drove, but I couldn't ignore the truth in his words. Was giving her space just an excuse to not have to face my problems? I wronged her and the guilt ate away at me. But staring into her eyes again would just remind me that I failed her…and myself.

"I'm doubtful she'll want to see me after everything," I added, my voice low.

"Or maybe she's worried because she doesn't know where you are." I could feel his eyes studying me. "Maybe she needs some sort of closure and your being over here, trying to run from your responsibility, has left her more confused than ever. How would you feel if you were in her shoes? You find out everything you believed was a lie, but the one person who could answer all your questions mysteriously disappears?"

"She's the one who told me to let her go," I explained.

"And you didn't," Eli shot back. "Do you think she was able to let *you* go?"

"I don't know," I said dismissively, the uneasy feeling that had begun to form in the pit of my stomach growing stronger and stronger. Over the past month, something had seemed off to me, but I couldn't put my finger on it. At least once a week, I briefly entertained the notion of disobeying my brother's orders, but that was as far as it had ever gotten. In truth, I liked the bubble I had been living in, regardless of the fact I was all too aware that I was ignoring my duties and responsibilities back home. Over here, it was as if none of my problems would find me, as if I wouldn't have to be faced with a reminder of what I had done.

"At some point, you have to stop running and face this. You both need closure so you can move on with your lives. You owe that much to each other." He paused and lowered his voice. "You owe that much to her."

I closed my eyes and leaned against the window. "She got the closure she needed when she found out who I was...a monster who used her. She deserves to be happy, but that can't be with me. She's probably already moved on and is dating someone else."

"I wouldn't be so sure, Ty."

"What makes you say that?"

He shrugged. "I don't know. It's just a feeling."

I simply nodded, not responding. As much as I wanted to believe Mackenzie hadn't moved on, I knew it would never work out between us. How could she trust me again when, for the short period of time we were together, it was based on duty, an obligation? When it all fell apart, I blindly followed my brother's instructions that I leave the country, at least until any potential threat had been neutralized. I should have picked up the phone or sent an email, despite my brother's warning that I not communicate with her at all. Now, so much time had passed – too much really – I was sure I had ruined any chance that I was still on her mind.

Sighing, I pulled my dog tags out from under my t-shirt and stared at the diamond ring hanging on the chain. It was now a reminder that all actions have consequences, that I didn't deserve to be happy, that I didn't deserve anything except to live with the lonely again, as I had been doing since I watched Mackenzie disappear into the back seat of a taxi. It was the penance

I deserved to pay.

We passed the remainder of the drive in a strained silence. Around mid-afternoon, we finally pulled up to the remote communications center. It was in the middle of nowhere, no other civilization visible. To the outside world, it appeared as a small military base, tall metal walls enclosing the compound, barbed wire surrounding the area, but it was really a CIA outpost we were granted permission to use to communicate with people back home.

Pulling up to a dark gray armored door, Eli punched a secure access code into a keypad and we were granted entry. Eli parked the truck in our usual spot in front of a small white brick building that looked like it had seen better days.

Nodding a greeting to the guard at the front door, I proceeded past him and unlocked what had become my office. Eli waited outside, making small talk with a few of the agents on duty.

I checked the clocks on the wall, seeing it was roughly nine in the morning on Sunday in Boston. Opening up my laptop, I connected to the secure satellite, giving me internet access. I was about to launch a video chat with Alexander when my email caught my eye. I had ignored all my emails, per my brother's instructions, but when I saw the sender of the latest one, there was a lightness in my chest, an unexpected rush of adrenaline coursing through me.

I could hear my brother's voice in my head, urging me to delete it, not to read it. But why? So much time had passed. I doubted anyone would take notice of any communication between us. Just seeing her name forced thousands of feelings I had fought to bury over the past few months to rush to the surface.

I missed her.

God, I missed her.

Her hair. Her smile. Her laugh. Her scent... Cinnamon. It followed me everywhere.

Closing my eyes, I imagined how different things would have been had she not found out, or if I had been truthful with her when I realized I was falling for her. Would she have walked away? Would I still have been shipped across the ocean while my brother attempted to neutralize any threat? Was that really what he was doing? I certainly had my doubts.

A renewed sense of determination washing over me, I opened my eyes. Instead of blindly following orders, as I had been doing since day one of basic training, I did what I believed to be the right thing. I clicked on the email, bracing myself for what it contained.

Her words piercing my soul, bleeding me dry, it felt like all the air had been sucked from the room as I struggled to breathe. I could picture Mackenzie in my head...sitting on her bed, wearing a tight black tank top and boy shorts, what she always slept in, tears soaking her face as she wrote these words to me. I thought I was doing what was right, giving her space so she wouldn't be faced with a constant reminder of her biggest mistake. I was convinced my presence would cause her pain. I never imagined my *absence* caused her even more.

I continued to read her words, the stabbing ache in my heart growing more pronounced, more intense. I had been a coward, justifying my reticence to get in touch with her on the grounds that it wasn't safe to do so, and even if it were, how a simple phone call couldn't fix this.

Nearing the end of her email, a lump formed in my throat as I soaked in the last line, my eyes glossing over those final words. Despite it all, she still loved me. Screw following orders. It was time I followed my heart. This was a second chance for me, and I refused to ruin it.

Printing out the email, I folded it and placed it in the pocket of my shirt, over my heart. A light feeling about me, I was about to launch the video chat session with my brother, then decided against it. He knew me. He would pick up on the fact that something was amiss, that I wasn't being truthful…that I was *happy*. Alexander was good at what he did and I knew he would say something that would make me second-guess my decision to abandon my post and return home.

Disconnecting my laptop, I rummaged through the office, grabbing everything I needed and throwing it into my pack. I opened the door and Eli noticed the crazed look on my face almost immediately.

"Everything okay?"

I shook my head and reached into my pocket, shoving the folded email at him. He started reading, his eyes darting from the email to me and back again. "We're leaving," I said sternly.

"Back to camp?"

"No. We're leaving the country. We're going home. It's time I try to make this right."

"What about your brother's warnings?" he asked smugly, throwing my own excuses back at me.

"None of that matters anymore," I insisted, my voice full of passion as we dashed out of the communications building and into the truck. "The only thing that does is giving Mackenzie what she needs… The truth heard straight from me. If she still turns me away after that, then fine. But she still loves me, Eli. I'm not going to let what we have slip through my fingers. Not again."

I should have done this months ago.

Chapter Ten
The Past

Mackenzie

"ARE YOU SURE YOU don't mind, Brayden?" Standing in his office at the law firm, I stared out the windows and onto the streets of Brownsville, my eyes glued to that same dark sedan that had been tailing me off and on for the past few days.

"Of course not."

"I know I need to get a new car eventually," I said, sauntering back toward his desk. "I can't really fit a baby seat in my little convertible, can I?"

"Don't worry about any of that, Mack. If you need to swap cars with me for a while, I'm fine with it. Believe me. I think James would love cruising around in your convertible." He winked.

"Thanks, boo." I stood on my toes and planted a kiss on his cheek. "You're the best. I'll make sure to fill it with gas."

"Don't even think about it. But if you need gas, here." He reached into his pocket and handed me a stack of bills.

I held my hand up. "Brayden, I don't want your money."

"Well, I don't, either. So if you're not going to use it to fill up *my* car with gas, you can go buy my little nephew some toys or...whatever babies need."

I laughed at how little he knew. Hell, *I* didn't know much more. I had been looking online at all these baby stores and was completely overwhelmed by the sheer magnitude of everything. I didn't know the purpose behind half the stuff. I thought all I'd need would be a stroller, a car seat, and some diapers. I soon found out how wrong I was. For something so small, babies required a ton of stuff.

"I'm serious," he insisted. "You need to start thinking about getting some things for that little guy."

"It could be a girl."

"Whatever," he said, brushing me off. "Let me take you shopping this weekend."

"Brayden, I—"

"If you don't want me to buy you anything, I won't. But you should at least have a registry so people can buy your baby things he's going to need."

I rolled my eyes, sitting in the chair across from him. "Like who? You and Jenna are the only people who give a shit about me."

He glared at me. "That's not true and you know it. Stop with the pity party, Mack. It's getting old." His normally light and buoyant voice turned harsh. My spine straightened and I did a double take.

"What do you—"

"You know damn well what I'm talking about," he shot back. "I get it. You're pissed. You're angry. You're hurt. But don't let what happened between you and Tyler become *who...you...are.*"

I slouched into the lush chair, placing a hand on my stomach. "But it has, and I don't know how to change it."

"You don't have to change who you are, Mack. You know the best revenge, don't you?"

"What's that?" I tilted my head and his eyes softened,

reminding me of the special bond we had that I didn't have with anyone else in my life…Jenna included.

"Living a happy life, Mack. People love you. Your employees. Your friends from college, who you've cut out of your life. You'd be surprised how many people will be at your side to support you if you'd just let them. I know you love the challenge of trying to prove you can overcome any obstacle, but it's okay to let other people do things for you once in a while."

I eyed him, the sincerity in his gaze warming my heart. "Fine. We can go shopping. I know how much you love it." I winked, easing the tension between us.

"You know me so well, baby girl."

Spying the time on the clock behind Brayden, I stood up from the chair and grabbed my purse. "I've got to get going. I'll drop your car off before my doctor's appointment tomorrow, okay?"

"Okay. Call me when you get to wherever you're going."

"I will." I placed one more kiss on his cheek and left his office. Taking the elevator down to the garage beneath the building, I found his mid-size SUV, hoping the change in vehicle would throw off my mysterious tail.

Getting behind the wheel, I checked my rearview mirror as I pulled out of the garage and onto the street, relieved when the dark sedan idling against the curb didn't follow. However, almost immediately, a nondescript gray compact car pulled out from beyond the sedan and came to a stop behind me at a light. I squinted my eyes to see the man driving the car bore a striking resemblance to Wyatt, one of the security guards at my condo building. Was *he* following me, too? I hated that I was paranoid, but I couldn't risk anyone finding out about my father.

A horn sounded, snapping me back to reality, and I

looked up to see the light had turned green. Instead of taking a right, as my turn signal indicated, I pressed my foot to the accelerator and took a quick left, my heart racing in my chest as I waited to see if the car followed. Several anxious miles passed as I constantly looked into my rearview mirror, seeing no sign of it.

Beginning to relax, I pulled up to a stoplight, getting ready to make a left onto the interstate. As the light turned green, I spied the gray car a few yards behind me, Wyatt at the wheel. Irritated, I pulled a U-turn. He swung his car around, as well, tailing me down the street. Swerving into a nearby gas station, I parked Brayden's car, and stormed up the street toward him.

Slowing to a stop on the side of the road, Wyatt quickly opened the driver's side door and looked over his shoulder in a frantic manner. "Get in the car, Mackenzie," he said, his voice grave. He ran around to the rear passenger side and opened the door.

"I don't think so," I scoffed. "Not until you tell me why you're following me."

"I'll tell you after you get in the car!" he ordered in an agitated manner.

"I wasn't born yesterday. There's no way in hell I'm getting in the car of a man who's following me!"

He opened his mouth, but must have noticed something in the distance. Moving swiftly, he covered my mouth with his hand and lifted me up. I struggled against him, my screams muffled as he placed me in the back seat. He slammed the door and ran around to the driver's side, the entire time my mind racing as I attempted to open the door...to no avail.

Once he was situated, he turned around to face me. "*I'm* not following you," he said finally, insinuating someone *was* following me. His expression was soft and compassionate, making him look...human, and not like some former military guy with a stick permanently shoved up his ass.

"Then who is? The guy in the dark sedan that's been parked outside my condo building the past few nights?"

"You mean him?" He gestured up the street and my spine stiffened. I watched the dark sedan pull up next to Brayden's car, the sole occupant getting out. He peered into the SUV, circled it, then paused briefly before looking beneath it.

"Who is he?" I asked, my voice soft as I observed him scanning the area for what I assumed was my location. He fished his phone out of his pocket and made a call. After a brief exchange, he got back into his car and peeled out of the gas station. As he drove by, I crouched in my seat, trying to hide.

"I'm not entirely sure," Wyatt said, "but I'm treating him as a potential threat to your safety."

"Taking your new position a bit seriously, aren't you? Or did Paul not tell you that your job was to simply look out for anything suspicious occurring in the *building*, not follow me to see my friend." I climbed into the passenger seat, hoping the childproof locks were only installed in the back. As I was about to open the door, a strong, calloused hand clutched my arm and I was once again facing Wyatt's concerned gray eyes.

"That's not my real job," he admitted through clenched teeth.

"Then what is?" I hissed.

"That's confidential, ma'am." He released his hold on me. "All you need to know is it's my job to make sure nothing happens to you."

I raised my eyebrows in a somewhat contemptuous manner. For years, I put up with vague declarations that I was in need of protection. I still didn't really know from what.

"I'm twenty-six, almost twenty-seven!" I shouted. "Nothing's happened to me yet. I'd appreciate it if people would finally be honest with me and tell me what the hell is *really* going on. Are you willing to do that?"

"Miss Delano...," he began, his eyes still stern. I knew there was no way I was going to get any information out of him. My guess was he would carry any secret to his death before putting his job in jeopardy. I knew his type. I fell in love with his type...twice.

I threw open the door and walked at a fast clip back toward the gas station.

"If you get in that car," he shouted after me, "you'll lead whomever it is straight to your father. Is that something you're willing to do?"

My breath hitched and I stopped in my tracks, slowly turning around to face him. I craned my neck to stare at him, my mouth agape in shock.

"I told you," he said. "It's my job to protect you. I can only do that if I know everything about you, including who I need to protect you *from*."

"You mean...my father?" I asked in a muted voice, almost too scared to hear his response. I raised my eyes to his and he exhaled, shaking his head.

"No. I don't think he's a threat to *you*."

The way he said it made me think he still considered my father a threat. I tore my gaze from his, not saying anything in response.

"Or should I be concerned?"

"No. My father would never hurt me." He nodded his head. "Or anyone else, for that matter," I added, my eyes fierce.

"Like the sixty-plus people he's accused of killing all those years ago at the embassy in Liberia?" he asked. I could feel the burn of his eyes on me.

"How do you know about that?" I glanced at him,

lowering my voice. "How do you know who I am?"

"I told you. It's my job to know everything about you, including who you really are."

"So you can know everything about me, but I'm not allowed to even know who you're working for? You want to protect me from some unknown threat? Trust is a two-way street, Wyatt," I sneered. "How do I know this isn't some sort of sick, twisted joke?"

I spun on my heels, my irritation loud and clear.

"Did you know Tyler refused to go back to his house after you ran from him?" he shouted.

Stopping abruptly, I inhaled quickly, my eyes growing wide as I turned to look over my shoulder. "I don't know what you're talking about," I hissed.

"Yes, you do," he said, taking slow steps toward me. He stood in front of me, his expression soft. "It was the last Sunday in March. It was foggy in the morning, but it cleared later so when you got into that cab, it was a picture perfect day. But not for Tyler. That was the day he stopped living."

"How do you—"

"That was also the day he found out his own life could be in danger. You see, his brother realized Tyler knew where your father was. I've known Alexander for longer than I care to admit."

I rolled my eyes at the mention of that name, my animosity toward Tyler's brother obvious.

"You may not like some of his decisions, but his main concern has always been his family. Watching out for them. Protecting them."

"So...what? He was an ass to me to make me want to walk out on his brother? To protect him from me?"

"No. Truth be told, until you get to know him, Alexander can be a bit of a cold person."

"His behavior was normal?"

"Yes, ma'am. But your presence certainly took him by surprise. When it all went to hell, he needed to do something to regain control over the situation and protect his brother."

"So he sent him away?"

He nodded. "Tyler didn't want to go, but he reluctantly agreed after making Alexander promise you'd be safe from harm, as well."

I absorbed what Wyatt was telling me. Being angry at Tyler for disappearing was so much easier when I thought he simply used me, then abandoned me, despite what his mother had told me. Now that I knew he was *ordered* to leave, that he did everything to ensure my safety, it softened my resentment.

"When will he be back? And why hasn't he picked up the phone?"

Wyatt's expression hardened once more. "It's not my place to say, ma'am. However, you should know that Mr. Burnham considers your safety to be a top priority."

"What does he know?" I asked, placing a hand on my stomach. An uneasy feeling washed over me at the prospect that Wyatt had been working for Alexander and was communicating with him about me.

"Only what is necessary to successfully complete the assignment, nothing more, ma'am. And nothing of a personal nature," he said, raising his eyebrows.

I let out a sigh of relief. "Thank you, Wyatt."

"It's not my place, ma'am."

I nodded and fidgeted a bit, uncomfortable about the heavy silence. "Well," I said, clearing the air. "I have an appointment I can't miss."

"Right," he replied, escorting me up the block and back to the gas station. As if he knew precisely what he was looking for, he lowered himself to the ground and pulled a flashlight out of his pocket, shining it on the undercarriage of the SUV. "Just as I expected," he commented, reaching underneath the car. After a few seconds, he raised himself.

"What is it?" I asked.

"GPS tracker," he said. "Government-issue, too. Identical to the one I pulled off your convertible this morning. It looks like our friend stuck it beneath Mr. Weller's car so he could track your whereabouts."

"Government-issue?" I asked. I didn't know what was worse...an unknown entity keeping tabs on me or a federal agent. "Why didn't you remove it?"

"Because if I keep the tracker on, I can lead him straight to me and find out who he is and what he wants."

"Do you think he's looking for my father, too?"

"It would appear that way, wouldn't it? Give me your keys. We're switching cars," he said, tossing his keys at me. I reached into my purse and handed him the keys to Brayden's SUV. "You go do what you need to do, but I will check in every hour. Understand?"

A million thoughts circling in my head about who the man in the sedan could possibly be, I remained in a daze as Wyatt walked me to his car and helped me into the driver's seat. With each day that went by, my life was spiraling more and more out of control, ghosts of my past resurfacing. I feared it would only be a matter of time before it all came crumbling down on top of me.

Chapter Eleven

Full Disclosure

Mackenzie

THE SUN WAS SWELTERING when I stepped out of the car several hours later and made my way across the church parking lot, past the main building, and proceeded up the familiar path to the rectory. It had to be over a hundred degrees, the white material of my dress sticking to my skin.

As I approached, I tried to suppress my urge to turn around. I was apprehensive about seeing my father for the first time in over four months. So much had happened, I didn't even know where to start. Between the drama with Charlie, Tyler's deception, and the pregnancy, I had no idea how he was going to react. I prayed he would offer me some sort of guidance about what to do, like my mother would have if she were still alive.

I knocked on the door, fanning myself. It was nearly five in the evening, but the rays of the sun were strong and practically unbearable. The door opened and I felt a momentary relief when a rush of cool air escaped the house. I expected a nun to answer, as was normally the case. Instead, I stared into Father Slattery's tired eyes.

"Good evening, Mackenzie."

"Father Slattery," I said, nodding.

He surveyed my appearance, his eyes settling on my

stomach. Taking a timid step backwards, I pulled at the hem of my dress and stared at my feet. I didn't know what to say. I thought about defending myself, but didn't the church teach forgiveness, not judgment? I couldn't really remember anymore.

"When's the last time you went to confession, Mackenzie?" he asked in the same pacifying voice that calmed me when I was younger.

"It's been a while, Father." I shuffled my feet, staring off into the distance, feeling ashamed.

"I suspected as much. Please, come in."

I shot my eyes to him. "But the mass for my mother… I need to—"

"Some things are more important and can't be handled during a mass," he interrupted, almost trying to tell me something with the way he stared at me, his gaze narrowed. "Please, Mackenzie. Come in." For the first time in nearly fifteen years, I cautiously stepped foot in the rectory.

Being back here made my skin crawl with the memories I had struggled to forget over the years. It looked just as it did during the period of time my mother and I lived in a cramped room. Removed from the only life I had known. Forced into hiding. And why? I still had no definitive answers, only speculation.

"This way, child," Father Slattery instructed, heading down a long, dark hallway and stopping outside a large cherry wood door. Reaching into his pocket, he produced a key and unlocked it, pushing it open.

I stepped into a spacious, dimly lit office, the smell of old books and wood finding its way to my senses. The walls were lined with shelves containing hundreds of hardbound books. In the center of the room sat a large desk, and several chairs were strewn throughout. The windows were covered with blackout curtains, although one was pulled back slightly, allowing a sliver of sunlight to filter into the room. Dust particles danced in the air and I smiled as a memory rushed forward.

"What are those, Daddy?" I had asked my father when I couldn't have been more than three or four.

"Those are angels, mi bichito. *They're just here to check on you."*

I still thought of my father and angels whenever I saw dust particles being illuminated by sunlight.

The sound of the door shutting startled me and I jumped, spinning around to see that Father Slattery was no longer behind me, as I expected him to be. The door knob began to jiggle and I heard the click of a lock.

My heart began racing. I had never questioned Father Slattery's intentions before. He was the one who helped us escape North Carolina, after all. He put his reputation on the line and hid us in this very house for nearly two years. Now I wondered if there was more to it than that.

"Serafina," a voice cracked and I whirled around, my eyes falling on a familiar silhouette sitting in a reading chair by one of the large windows. Confused, I glanced over my shoulder at the locked door. "Please, come sit. There's much to discuss."

I remained speechless, my voice nowhere to be found. Eyeing him guardedly, I hesitantly put one foot in front of the other and sat in the reading chair opposite him, noticing a tray of cheese and crackers set out on a table between us.

"I'd ask if you'd like some wine," he said in the husky voice that once lulled me to sleep, "but I suppose that question is not quite appropriate, is it?"

I looked up, almost expecting to see a disappointed look on my father's time-worn face, but that wasn't the case at all. He actually looked genuinely happy, perhaps even proud of the woman I had become. For years, the only conversations I'd had with this man were when he'd sit behind me in church, not face-to-face, for fear someone would put the pieces together of who we both truly were. Now that we were in the same room and looking into each other's eyes, I didn't want this moment to end.

My eyes scanned my father, trying to imprint everything about him to memory. His face showed signs of his age. His brilliant blue eyes no longer exuded the vitality I remembered growing up. Scars still covered the entire left side of his body, reminding me of the purpose of this visit. I wanted to know precisely how he1` got those burn marks, and whether his side of the story corroborated Charlie's.

"I see you got my letter." He poured wine into one glass and water into another. "I'm sure you have a thousand questions."

"I–"

"But," he interrupted, "this works both ways. Full disclosure from this moment forward. I will tell you everything, Serafina. However, I expect reciprocity from you. I want you to understand where I'm coming from and why things have to be the way they are. But I need to know exactly what's going on in your life. I need to know you're okay, that you'll *be* okay knowing the truth."

"Full disclosure?" I repeated, surveying him. I couldn't help but wonder whether this was a double-edged sword. I had been waiting sixteen years to know who I really was, why my father had been hiding, and why the man I loved felt the need to use me to get information about my father. However, I feared learning the truth may change my perception of everything. Sometimes ignorance was bliss. I just prayed this wasn't one of those situations.

"Yes," he reiterated. "No more secrets. No more lies. Just the truth from this moment forward, regardless of the consequences. You deserve that much." He stared at me, catching my gaze, regret covering his demeanor. I wondered how difficult it must have been for him to keep his existence a secret from me for all those years. I didn't know what to think, but I knew the only way to move forward was to learn to trust my father again. And the only way to do that was to finally learn the truth.

"What about all the talk for years that it wasn't safe for me to know?"

He picked up the knife on the serving tray and sliced a piece of cheese, placing it on a cracker and handing it to me before preparing one for himself. "At the time, I thought that was true. However, things have been brought to my attention, making me think it's no longer safe for you *not* to know."

"How can I be sure you're telling me the truth? I've heard so many stories. I don't know which way is up anymore." I placed the cracker on the plate in front of me, feeling sick to my stomach.

"I wish I had told you everything years ago." He took a deep breath, his shoulders dropping slightly. "If I had, maybe it wouldn't be so difficult for you to trust me now, but there were reasons for it."

Straightening my spine, I strengthened my resolve. I went there for answers and I refused to let my apprehension get in the way of them.

"The embassy fire?" I asked in an even tone.

"Was not me."

"Then who was it? How come you left for Liberia right before it happened? It looks suspicious—"

"Serafina," he interrupted, "I joined the army the day I turned eighteen. I left my house and rode my bike thirteen miles to the nearest recruiting center. My parents didn't want me to go into the army, or any branch, but I had wanted to be a Ranger as long as I could remember and nothing was going to stand in my way. I wanted that Ranger beret and I was lucky enough to spend many years wearing it. I love the army. I love my country. I devoted my life to protecting it, so much so that my superior officers noticed I had a knack for seeing things no one else could. Before I knew it, I was working in Army Counterintelligence. I was thrilled. But my ability to see things no one else could ended up being my downfall."

I scrunched my eyebrows. "How so?"

"I started noticing patterns. Our weapons were being used against us. Our intel was being used against us. Someone on the inside was betraying their own country for profit. For months, maybe years, I tried to find out who, but I was always one step behind whomever it was. Then, one day, I thought I caught a lucky break. I unscrambled an encoded message confirming the U.S. Ambassador to Liberia would turn his head and allow a large stockpile of our weapons to disappear in trade for a substantial amount of diamonds."

"Blood diamonds?"

"Most likely. The civil war in Sierra Leone was winding down, but there was still a great deal of corruption in the area, and Liberia borders Sierra Leone. I was permitted leave to go to Liberia to see if I could stop the arms deal, or at least find out who was behind it all, without causing an international incident. When I got there, I went to the embassy to speak to the ambassador about what was going on, but whoever was behind these deals, whoever the traitor was, beat me to it."

"It was a setup?" I asked, staring at my father's forlorn expression, recalling Charlie's words from just a few days ago.

Swallowing hard, he didn't answer. He simply continued with the story I could sense he had been wanting to share with me for years. His gaze was fixed on the bookcase behind me, as if he were watching a movie of what really happened and was simply narrating it for me.

"I remember walking in the front doors of the embassy, immediately halting in my tracks. There were no staff members at the front desk and the reception area was empty. As I made my way through the entry area, I heard a loud voice giving a speech about a circle of trust." He tore his gaze back to me. "That was something I used to do in the field whenever I had new team members. It was a way to make them remember we had to work as one cohesive unit."

He shook his head, almost like he was frustrated that he didn't see the signs of it being a setup. "I stepped toward the source, trying to keep my presence unknown. The voice grew louder, more impassioned, and my heart dropped to the pit of my stomach as I listened to my own words. I physically felt sick and had to fight back the nausea. This guy took what I said verbatim and was repeating it to a huge room full of frightened people." His lower lip trembled and I could sense he was back in that room on that day.

He avoided my eyes, staring past me once more as the memory washed over him. "The smell of gasoline was overpowering," he said, his voice soft. "I knew it wasn't going to end well, but what could I do? It wouldn't do much good for me to go in shooting. It was twelve against one. The odds were not in my favor. So I did what I thought to be the best tactical decision. I hid my presence in the hopes I could save at least one person, even if it cost me my life.

"As I watched those traitors terrorize their hostages, I mentally began to sort through all the intel I had amassed, wondering what I could have missed. That's when it hit me this was part of the plan all along. This guy wanted me to find everything. He wanted me to go to my superiors to tell them what I found and ask for leave to come here. Then, when word of my trademark fire spread, they would put two and two together and name me as the culprit to this attack, along with all the arms deals I had been investigating. Hell, one of the first things you look for when trying to find the person responsible for a crime is to see who tries to ingrain themselves in the investigation. I had made myself into the perfect suspect."

"So you hid? You abandoned your family? You watched as over sixty people were murdered and did nothing?"

"I didn't do nothing, Serafina!" He ripped off the hat he wore that shielded most of his face. "Do you think this is the result of nothing?!" he bellowed passionately, gesturing to the permanent scars covering the left side of his body. "I tried to save them, but I couldn't! By the time whoever was responsible made his escape, it was too late! The flames were out of control, bodies were on fire! Their screams and shrieks plague my dreams every night! Have you ever smelled burning flesh?!" he exclaimed, tears welling in his eyes.

I stared in shock, shaking my head.

"It's scorched in my memory, Fi! Every day, I'm reminded that I failed to protect people from a monster. *A real life dragon!*" He reached for his glass with shaky hands, the trauma of that day all those years ago still wearing on him.

"I did everything I could," he continued after sipping his wine. "In the end, the only person I could save was a boy who couldn't have been more than sixteen or seventeen. Someone must have shielded him from getting doused with the gasoline. His burns were minor but the smoke got into his lungs. He was barely breathing when I pulled him from the building. When I was about to go back and see if I could rescue anyone else, a convoy of Liberian soldiers pulled up. I knew it was probably cowardly of me to run, to hide from them, but I couldn't risk being detained. At that point, my sole mission was to try to get home to you and your mother. I feared I would be painted as a monster and I couldn't let you think that of me."

"Where did you go?" I asked, still trying to wrap my head around his story. It seemed so unreal, so far-fetched, but it complimented Charlie's version of what happened perfectly. All the puzzle pieces were falling into place.

"I found a church. I didn't know what else to do. I had burns on over fifty percent of my body and was convinced I wasn't going to make it." He reached across the table, squeezing my hand. I took a quick breath at the contact. It had been years since I felt my father's flesh on mine. His hand was scarred, rough, and warm. I choked out a loud sob at the gesture. It was so simple, yet it brought back memories of my life before it all fell apart.

"I wasn't thinking clearly, but I knew I would do anything to try and get a message to your mother that I loved you both. I guess I hoped God would listen and give you that message." Sincerity covered his face as his eyes locked with mine, the turmoil he had been living with over the years evident.

"But he answered my prayers in other ways. The nuns at the church treated my burns as best they could without modern medicine. I kept asking about the boy I pulled from the fire, but I think they thought I was delirious. They drugged me with medication to help with the pain. I half expected to wake up in a detention center, but that never happened. Finally, after several months, they said I was well enough to leave. I had no idea how to repay the debt I owed. These women took me in and cared for me without asking for anything in return. They even lied to the authorities and said they never saw me. I don't know how they knew I wasn't responsible for the tragic fire, but they did."

"How did you get back home?" I asked, engrossed by his story.

"It wasn't easy. I did some things I wasn't proud of. I stole to barter for transport, then spent weeks aboard a cargo ship, trying to get back to you. Every day was torture, never knowing if I'd make it to the end of the day. Finally, we pulled into the Port of Miami and the captain smuggled me ashore. Days later, in the middle of the night, I finally arrived home.

"I sought Father Slattery out and he told me what happened after the attack. How an investigation had been conducted, naming me as the mastermind behind everything, but they didn't pursue any course of action because it was presumed I had died in the fire. Before my trip over there, I had a bad feeling, so I had gone to him and made him promise if anything suspicious happened, he'd do everything to keep you safe until the threat passed. He assured me he had done what I asked, made arrangements for new identities for you both, and that you were well-protected and in hiding. And that was when I had to make the hardest decision of my life."

"What was that?"

"I told him to have your mother tell you I was dead."

"Why?"

"You were only a little girl. I had agents, some specialized in intelligence training, who couldn't always keep a secret. To protect you, I needed you to believe I was dead. I needed you to forget the life you once had. It was the most difficult decision I ever had to make, but my saving grace was the possibility that, one day, I would find out who was responsible for everything and finally come out of hiding."

"Charlie," I said softly.

He looked at me, a confused expression on his face.

"The boy you pulled from the fire was Charlie."

"Charlie?" he asked. "*Your* Charlie?"

I nodded slowly.

"How do you know?"

I knew I couldn't avoid this forever, although reliving those two weeks in March was the last thing I wanted to do. But my father had shared what was arguably one of the most difficult times in his life with me. I needed to do the same.

"Full disclosure," I murmured.

"Yes, Serafina. Full disclosure."

"Well, I suppose I should start at the beginning."

A smile on his face, he said, "That's usually a pretty good place."

I grinned, a feeling of hope washing over me as I shared a moment with my father. This was what a father-daughter relationship was supposed to be like. Sharing our troubles, our triumphs. After sixteen years, I finally had that. So, instead of closing up, I shared a piece of my soul with my father, telling him all about Tyler, the break-ins, Charlie's reappearance, Whitman's murder, Charlie's disappearance, and the day I found out the truth of who Tyler really was.

When I was done, I expected him to want to know more about Charlie, but I was mistaken.

"It's clear you love him very much," he commented.

"Who? Charlie?"

"No, Serafina," he responded quickly. "Tyler."

"I don't love him," I lied. "I was just an asset, nothing

115

more. He used me to find out your location. That's all I was to him."

He spread his arms. "And, yet, I'm still here."

"The fact you're still here doesn't change that."

"I think it does, Serafina," he contested. "I think it proves that, at some point, you switched from being an asset to being something so much more."

I avoided his eyes, trying to ignore the same argument I had made to myself over the past few days. "That still doesn't mean I love him."

"It's normal to be defensive about your feelings. I can imagine how confusing it must be for you. Your mother fought her feelings for me, too, because I was much older than she was, but you can't always control who you fall in love with." He glanced at me with a twinkle in his eye. "You look so much like her. Every time I see you, I see more and more of her in you."

"Do you miss her?" I asked softly.

"Every minute of every day, Serafina," he choked out, his words barely audible.

"How do you get through it? How do you go on breathing when that love has been ripped from you?"

"You go on," he replied, placing his hand over mine, caressing my knuckles. "It's not easy. It's never easy. *Love* isn't easy. But you carry the memory of those happy times with you and those moments remind you of the beauty of life. And you just hope to find that beauty once more. I beg you, Serafina. Don't let your stubbornness deprive yourself of something you deserve."

"And what's that?"

"Love, Serafina. You deserve to feel love."

Chapter Twelve

Good Things

Mackenzie

"SO," I SAID, TAKING the keys to Brayden's SUV from Wyatt as we stood just outside the same gas station as yesterday. "Did it work?"

He paused for a beat before he nodded. "Yes. He followed me."

"Who?"

"His name is Clinton Evers and he is an FBI agent."

"So he *is* a fed," I replied. "What did he want with me? The same as everyone else? To find my father who, according to most of the world, is actually dead?"

"Not exactly, ma'am," he said and I raised my eyebrows.

"Really?"

"Yes. I drove Mr. Weller's car out to Austin and Agent Evers showed up approximately five hours later. I confronted him and asked what he wanted with you. He showed me his badge and indicated he was working a case."

I sighed. "So he *was* after my father."

"No, ma'am. I got him to tell me what he was working on. He said it was off the record. Unofficial. Just him and another agent. One of their colleagues took a leave of absence several months ago and hasn't been heard from since. They believe something's happened to him, that someone's abducted him and are using him for his…unique skills."

"Which would be?"

"Apparently," Wyatt began, eyeing me, "he's one of the most skilled hackers out there. The knowledge he has, in addition to his skills, makes him a powerful weapon in the wrong hands."

"Who is this guy?" I asked, my mind spinning.

He studied me, almost as if gauging whether or not he should tell me. After a protracted pause, he said, "His name is Damian Mills and, if I'm not mistaken, he grew up next door to you when you lived in Fayetteville."

My jaw dropped, not expecting to hear that name. "They think *I* have something to do with his disappearance?" I asked, confused about why they would follow me and put a tracker on my car.

"They do not believe you're responsible. Apparently, they were two of the agents who had arrested Mr. Mills nearly a decade ago when he hacked into the FBI computer system trying to find the location of one Serafina Galloway."

"He was arrested?" Despite my shock at that news, my heart warmed a bit with the knowledge Damian had never forgotten about our friendship, just as I never did.

"It appears so. I've looked into his story and it all checks out. Mr. Mills was given a choice. He could either go to prison or work for the FBI. He chose the latter and has been there for almost a decade. Agent Evers said he and Damian had grown close over the years. He talked about you, your childhood, stuff like that. Then, just a day before he took his mysterious leave of absence, Damian made Evers promise to do everything he could to find you and keep an eye on you if anything ever happened to him. I checked the timeline and this coincides to around the time Mr. Montgomery was named as the man behind all those murders. After months went by, Evers couldn't help but think something is wrong, especially with Damian's mother's recent death."

I absorbed his story. "So they weren't tracking my car to get to my father."

"No, ma'am. They were tracking you to keep an eye on you, as Evers promised Damian he would."

I nodded.

"But I've assured him I have that under control. He won't be bothering you anymore."

I couldn't help but feel slightly deflated at the thought. Agent Evers knew Damian, had worked with him. He may have been the only link I had to him. I wished I had confronted this agent myself. Maybe he would have told me what he was doing and I could ask all the questions I had about the person Damian had grown up to be.

"I'm sorry, Miss Delano. Even though I checked out his story, it's still too risky to have him tailing you. You understand that, right? I've been tasked with your safety, and it's a job I take very seriously. My decisions may be extreme, but I'd rather be safe than sorry...at least until we can neutralize the threat to you."

"Fine," I hissed, feeling as if Wyatt was trying to decide what was best for me without my input. It was like dealing with my father all over again. How many more people would I have to convince I didn't need them to decide what was best for me?

I spun around and jumped into the SUV, trying to focus on my upcoming doctor's appointment instead of the idea that Damian could be in trouble.

~~~~~~~~~~

WHITE WALLS SURROUNDED ME as I surveyed the waiting room, children running around playing or fighting with each other. I felt bad for their mothers, who were trying to wrangle not only the infant in their arms, but two or three older kids, as well. By the look of things, some of these women barely gave their uteruses a break between popping out kids. And this was what women wanted? I didn't get it. I guess I never had that maternal instinct. I never saw myself *wanting* children, but here I was, forced into a situation I never expected.

My eyes shifted to the far corner and I spied a woman with beautiful red hair who couldn't have been much older than I. I was captivated, watching her cradle a newborn swaddled in a blue blanket, rocking him gently. Something about it spoke to me in a way the other puking, screaming, mauling rugrats running carelessly around the waiting room didn't. I saw something strange between the mother and child. I saw a bond. It wasn't just one-way, either. The baby was no more than a month old, but was staring into his mother's eyes as she hummed a song, swaying him.

I placed my hand over my own stomach, excited and nervous about meeting the little person growing inside me. Regardless of this baby's connection to what I still considered to be one of my biggest mistakes, I wanted that same bond with my baby and my heart warmed.

"Mackenzie?" a sweet voice called. I tore my eyes from the young mother and saw a woman dressed in scrubs standing in the doorway leading to the exam rooms. "We're ready for you."

I raised myself from the chair, wondering how much longer it would be until that became difficult, and made my way across the waiting area, dodging toys that had been left on the floor. The nurse gave me a comforting smile as I approached her, but I knew what she was thinking. The first few appointments, they had asked if my husband was going to join me. They stopped asking at my last appointment. Part of me was happy I no longer had to answer that question. The other part of me felt pathetic, stupid…and ashamed.

I went through the usual routine of getting weighed, giving them a urine sample, and having an ultrasound. Every time I looked at that machine, I didn't see my baby. I saw overdue bills. I saw sleepless nights. I saw my world falling apart around me. I knew it was only a matter of time until the bottom dropped.

"Do you want to know the gender?" the ultrasound technician asked enthusiastically, cutting through my growing unease. I snapped my head to her and looked into her vibrant brown eyes. "You're eighteen weeks along, so I can tell you the gender with certainty."

Tearing my eyes from her warm face to the screen, the sound of the little heartbeat echoing in the room, I nodded. "Yes."

She smiled at me. "Congratulations, Mama. It's a boy."

I sighed, letting out a breath. "Brayden will be happy. He's been convinced it's a boy."

"Is that your husband?" she asked, pressing a few buttons on the machine and producing yet another printout to add to my collection.

Shaking my head, I swallowed hard. "No. He's just a friend."

After being assured my baby was developing well and my health was on track, despite their concerns that I hadn't gained as much weight as they would have liked to see, I grabbed my things and proceeded to the desk.

"How can I help you?" the girl asked when she saw me approach.

"I was wondering if you offer any sort of payment plan

for my bills. I know I'm overdue on a bunch of them and I wanted to see if there was a way to pay over time. My name's Mackenzie Delano."

Nodding, she turned to her computer, typing feverishly. She stared at the screen and scrunched her eyebrows. My heart sank in my chest, worried the amount was so much, it wouldn't make a difference anyway.

"You did say Mackenzie Delano, correct?" she asked, turning to me.

"Yes...," I answered cautiously.

"I'm sorry. I don't understand. What exactly do you need to work out?"

"My bill. I have an unpaid balance from my last several appointments. It's at least a few thousand dollars from all the ultrasounds and the testing. I know it doesn't sound like a lot, but I can't pay it all at once. I—"

"You're not showing any unpaid balance, dear," the woman said, interrupting me. "It's showing your bill was just paid on Saturday. There's a note to send a copy of all future bills to a Colleen Burnham in Massachusetts. She has asked to be listed as the guarantor of any and all medical bills."

Confused, moved, and relieved, my mouth fell open. I wanted to pinch myself to make sure this wasn't just a dream. Covering my mouth, I let out a small sob, elated.

"Is that your mother?" the woman asked, a genuine smile on her face.

"No. My baby's grandmother," I replied, placing my hand on my stomach.

"Well, your baby is very lucky." She returned her eyes back to the computer screen. "We have you scheduled to come in for your twenty-two week appointment in the middle of August, so we'll see you then," she said, handing me an appointment card.

"Thank you. Thank you so much." I nearly had to restrain myself from leaping over the counter and hugging her. I was overjoyed and wanted to share my good fortune with someone else.

"See you next month."

A grin on my face and a spring in my step, I hopped into my car and made the short drive back home, feeling like a weight had been lifted off my shoulders. Pulling into the parking lot, I was about to swing my car into my assigned spot, only to see it was occupied by an Audi SUV. I cursed under my breath and proceeded toward the back of the lot.

"There she is!" Paul exclaimed as I entered the lobby, irritated.

"Paul, someone else is parked in my spot," I said, my tone annoyed at the inconvenience. "Can you look into it for me, please?"

A mischievous grin crossed his face, his reaction confusing me. "Someone else isn't parked there, Mackenzie."

"Yes, there is. I just tried to park my car and I couldn't."

His smile grew wider. "You're not listening." He opened the desk drawer and handed me an envelope with my name scrawled on it in elegant handwriting. "That's not someone else's car. It's *your* car." He dangled a key fob in front of me.

"Who would give me a car?" The minute the words were out of my mouth, I knew exactly who was responsible. My heart thumping in my chest, I tore open the envelope and pulled out the note.

Mackenzie,

I know you must be so confused about everything right now. Trust me. I know. I've been where you are. You feel as if you, alone, got yourself into your position and you can get through it on your own. You think asking for help is a sign of weakness, but it's not.

My oldest daughter, Carol, was a mistake. She was never supposed to happen, but I am so glad she did. I was young and thought I was invincible. Hell, I was only eighteen. I thought I had my entire life before me. I was the girlfriend of a handsome navy pilot who was about to travel overseas and serve his country in Vietnam. Then I found out I was pregnant and my life changed. We were married almost immediately. Both our parents were rather conservative and didn't want to listen to any backlash about my 'condition', as it was referred to back then.

Thomas was in flight school during this time and missed everything. He never got to come with me to a doctor's appointment. He never got to hear the heartbeat. He never got to feel our baby kick in my stomach. He didn't get to hold my hand when I gave birth.

I felt alone the entire time. I watched as all of my friends went away to college and I remained behind, my stomach growing bigger with every passing day. Some days, I woke up wondering if I would ever see Thomas again. I kept convincing myself he wasn't going to come home to me, that he would disappear into the night and find a new girl, one without a baby. I was so stubborn and desperate to prove to myself and everyone else that I could do this alone, that I didn't need my parents' or anyone else's help.

But the truth is, I did.

I needed them to sit with me at the doctor's office and tell me everything was going to be okay. I needed them to squeal with joy when they placed their hand on my stomach and felt her kick. And, above anything else, I needed them to stay with me while I pushed all seven pounds, six ounces of human out of me. If I didn't admit I couldn't do it alone, I don't think Carol would have had the wonderful childhood she did.

Don't look at any of this as you accepting a handout. That's not what it is. This is simply an old woman with too many zeros in her bank account providing for her family. Regardless of what happens in the future, your baby has my DNA running through him or her, *and I will always make sure he or she has every opportunity available. I will do everything to ensure you have everything you need, whether it be a car suitable for a child, the best medical treatment available, or no longer having to stress about repaying your mortgage or the loan on your restaurant. Those are also taken care of, by the way.*

Please accept what I can give you and don't think twice about it. Pay it forward if and when you can.

Most importantly, take care of yourself and that beautiful baby.

With all my love,
Colleen

I wiped at the tears streaming down my cheeks, my shoulders visibly relaxing.

"What did it say?" Paul asked, eyeing me.

"She bought me a car," I whispered, my heart feeling fuller than I ever thought possible. I wanted to stop time and remember this exact feeling. I wanted to drink in this moment to remind myself that good things did happen. "And she's paying my medical bills, and she paid off my mortgage and the loan on the restaurant."

"Who?"

"Tyler's mom," I choked out through my tears.

"Oh, Kenzie..." He wrapped his arms around me, planting a soft kiss on my temple. "I'm so happy for you. It's about time something went right. You deserve this. Now you can finally take a break from working so hard and take care of yourself for once."

Shaking my head, still in shock, I replied listlessly, "Earlier today, I was happy to find out she covered my medical bills, but this... I don't even know what to think."

He placed his hands on my arms and looked deep into my eyes. "I'll tell you exactly what you should think. You should think that you worked your ass off and you deserve this. You should think that someone upstairs finally listened to your prayers, sweetie. That's all. Now, go up and get some much-needed rest. I love you, but you look like hell." He winked.

Concern washing over my face, I protested. "I need to get changed and go to the restaurant."

"I'm sure they can handle it," he said, his voice soothing. "And if I know Jenna, she'll make you leave the second she sees you anyway. So go. I don't want to see you back down here until tomorrow, got it? And I'm leaving strict orders with the night shift to drag you back to your condo if they see you."

I opened my mouth at his mention of the night shift, tempted to ask him if he knew who Wyatt was really working for. I feared the answer may just upset me, so I suppressed my desire and playfully punched Paul in the arm. "Okay, *Dad*," I said, heading to the elevator. "Can I have friends over, though?"

He smiled, the joy reaching his eyes. "Sure. But no R-rated movies."

"Don't worry. We'll just watch some porn."

"Kenzie!" he exclaimed in exasperation, his face turning red. "I have daughters the same age as you. I don't want to think about–"

"Don't worry, Paul. Women don't like to watch porn. We prefer to read it." I winked and entered the elevator, the sound of his chuckles echoing as the doors closed.

Walking through my condo, everything seemed so different. I no longer glowered at the stack of bills piled high on my kitchen table. I no longer looked at everything I owned as if it had a price tag.

Just as I was about to collapse on my couch and take a minute to fully absorb everything, there was a frantic knocking on my door.

"Mack! It's me! Open up!" Jenna's excited voice sounded. "I know you're in there! Paul said you just got in!"

Grinning, I dragged myself into the foyer and pulled open the door, Jenna nearly tackling me to the ground.

"Is it true?" she exclaimed. "I mean, it's not a joke, is it?"

"What are you talking about?" I asked, already knowing all too well to what she was referring.

"This!" She thrust a letter drawn on official bank letterhead towards me, confirming the note they had issued in exchange for the loan was clear and paid in full. "I mean, that was over a quarter of a million dollars, Mack!"

"I know. She paid it off!" I replied, still in disbelief about the fortunate turn of events.

"Who?"

"Tyler's mom."

"I can't believe this!" she said, pulling me towards the couch and sitting down. "This calls for a celebration. I texted Brayden. He'll be coming over as soon as he gets off work. We'll order a ridiculous amount of pizza and you can drink all the cranberry juice you want! Or Shirley Temples! The sky's the limit!"

I laughed in response. "Let's not get too crazy."

"Oh, we are!" She jumped up from the couch and ran into the kitchen, grabbing a few water bottles out of the refrigerator. "Isn't it nice not to have the stress of money problems anymore?" She returned, handing me one of the bottles.

"It is, but I have to find a way to thank her." I glanced at Jenna. "I think I'm going to fly to Boston tomorrow so I can do that in person."

Jenna's eyes widened and she grabbed my hand. "Are you sure? I mean, do you think you'll be okay? I can talk to the girls at the restaurant to see if they'll be okay and I can come with you."

"No, Jenna," I replied, meeting her sincere blue eyes. I would have been fooling myself if I said I didn't like the idea of her being at my side to help me through what I knew would be a difficult time. "I appreciate the offer, but I need to stop breaking down whenever I'm reminded of him. I had a life before him, and I'll have a life after him. It'll take time to not find pieces of him throughout my life. Hell, I still see him in practically everyone I pass on the street. But I know it'll get easier. I'll probably stop seeing his eyes everywhere, I'll no longer hear his voice in my sleep, and I'll forget what he looks like."

"Is that what you want, Mack?" Jenna asked, giving me a concerned look.

I shrugged. "It may not matter if it's what I want or not. My memories of him will fade and will be replaced with other memories. Maybe happier ones."

"For your sake, I hope there's nothing but happier times ahead, Mack," Jenna commented, leaning back on the couch and flicking on the television. "Life always has a strange way of working out, doesn't it?"

Chapter Thirteen

Love Happens

Mackenzie

IN AWE, I GAZED out the window as the cab drove down a long driveway and up to a three-story colonial in Wellesley, just outside of Boston. The estate was beautiful, the grass a shade of green unlike anything I had ever seen. The driveway was cobblestone and led to a small circle with a breathtaking fountain in front of the house.

Getting out of the cab, I looked up at the brick building, the opulence in front of me making me feel out of place. Nausea settled in the pit of my stomach. I couldn't tell whether it was from the pregnancy or having to be in a house where I would inevitably be faced with reminders of Tyler. I knew I needed to do this, but I couldn't ignore the small voice saying I would regret my decision.

Hesitantly climbing the few steps to the front door, my breath caught when it swung wide open, Colleen's warm smile greeting me before I even had a chance to knock.

"Mackenzie, dear…" She held her arms out to me as if I were her own child.

Dropping my bags, I wrapped my arms around her, squeezing her tight. "Thank you so much," I sobbed into her chest. "You have no idea what it means to me."

"Oh, hush, darling," she replied, rubbing my back.

"You don't have to thank me. I'm the one who should be thanking you for giving me another grandbaby."

"It's a boy," I said through my tears.

Pulling back, she held me at arm's length, gazing at me with the same warmth and devotion my mother used to when she was alive. "A boy!" she exclaimed, hugging me once again. "I'm so happy for you, and I'm even more thrilled that you're here, Mackenzie. Truthfully."

I met her eyes, amazed at her sincerity. For a family who seemed to make a living off deception and lies, she appeared to be so genuine. Apart from getting knocked up, I didn't know what I had done to deserve to have her in my life, but I was glad I did.

"Come on. Let's get you some food. I'm sure you must be tired from traveling all day."

Nodding, I turned to grab the handle on my suitcase and she quickly tore it out of my hand. "Don't even think about it. I've got this. Go on in, dear."

In a daze, I walked through the doorway and into her stunning house. Just past the foyer was a sitting room, the furniture probably costing more than my entire college education. It was formal with a touch of personality. I half expected the house to be museum-like, but it wasn't. It was a house for a family, and I could just picture the fights Tyler and his brother must have gotten into in this house.

The sound of paws clicking on the hardwood floor caught my attention and I looked down, my eyes growing wide as a stubby French bulldog came wobbling toward me, a silly grin on his face.

"Griffin!" I exclaimed, bending down to scratch his head. He barked in response, as he always did when someone said his name. "It's so good to see you, buddy." Panting, he briefly showered my face with kisses before a photo on the mantle in the sitting room caught my eye. I strode to the fireplace, Griffin close on my heels, and picked up the framed photo of a happy family.

"Griffin seems to like you," Colleen commented, approaching me.

"He's a great dog, stinky breath and all."

She laughed. "You've got that right."

"Is this your husband?" I asked, referring to the man in the photo who had those same green eyes as Tyler and his siblings.

"Yes. That's Thomas."

I returned my eyes to the photo, seeing a strong resemblance between the man and his two sons. He was tall and built, having dark hair and an exquisitely handsome and distinguished face. Colleen stood next to him and looked somewhat younger, perhaps in her late forties. In front of them sat a young woman with blonde hair and those trademark green eyes. Carol. She was probably in her late twenties or so. Next to her sat Alexander, a forced smile on his face. He couldn't have been more than fifteen. Beside Alexander sat a child of no more than six. Tyler. He had the biggest grin on his face, his arm slung around his brother's shoulders. From the photo alone, I could sense Tyler looked up to Alexander. I supposed he still did.

"You have a beautiful family," I offered as I returned the photo to the mantle.

She placed her hand on my arm in a consoling manner, obviously noticing I was struggling not to crack. Not only was I pregnant, which caused my emotions to go from one extreme to the other within seconds, but I was still struggling with my feelings about what Tyler did.

"He'll come back," she encouraged. "I promise."

"What if I don't want him to?" I met her eyes. "What if I'm not ready to see him? To forgive him?"

"Mackenzie, sweetie," she sighed, grabbing my hand

131

and pulling me to the ornate white couch where we both sat down. "Forgiveness is a funny thing. Sometimes we don't forgive people because they deserve it. We do so because they *need* it. I saw the guilt and remorse etched on Tyler's face that day in March. It was a look unlike anything I had ever seen on my baby boy's face, even after Melanie..." She glanced down, gently caressing my knuckles and squeezing my hand. "I don't know when he'll be back, but I can tell you this much. Not one day has gone by where you haven't been on his mind. He may seem to have a tough exterior but, inside, he's still a boy who has had his world ripped out from underneath him. His love for you is unlike anything I've ever seen."

"How can you tell?" I asked, my curiosity getting the better of me.

"He's my son. He's part of me. There's not a whole lot of gray when it comes to Tyler."

I laughed, wiping my tears. "I noticed that."

"When he loves, he loves with his entire heart. When he hurts, the pain is excruciating. I'm sure he's spent every day since you left trying to figure out a way to convince you he's worth you taking a risk on him again, despite what happened between you two." She squeezed my hands, the gesture warm and precisely what I needed to assuage my fears. "Now," she continued, her voice returning to its typical frivolity, "you must be starving. Do you like lasagna?"

I beamed at her, nodding.

As I sat watching her prepare dinner, I couldn't help but be reminded of spending time in the kitchen with my own mother. Despite the posh surroundings, everything was so homey and comfortable. Time passed seamlessly as we sat at an informal farmhouse-style kitchen table and she told me stories about Tyler when he was a little boy. I told her about our crazy whirlwind romance that only lasted all of two weeks, but felt like we had known each other for years.

"Time doesn't matter, dear," she offered when I questioned whether he could feel as strongly about me as she insisted he did. "You can be in a relationship for years and feel nothing for the other person, or you can be together for mere weeks and feel something so strong, so beautiful, so perfect, you'd be a fool to walk away just because it hasn't been long enough. Don't let society dictate how long you need to be together. Love doesn't grow. It happens, and you can't control it. If you don't feel it from the beginning, it's not love."

"When did you know with Thomas?" I asked, sipping my water. The smell of garlic and tomatoes made my stomach growl, and I couldn't wait to devour the cheesy deliciousness she had prepared.

"Before he even said a word," she responded, a dreamy glimmer in her eyes. "It was the summer after I graduated high school and I was enjoying my time with friends before we all went our separate ways. I was supposed to be leaving for college in a few months, and some of my friends were heading to teaching or nursing school. Others were hitchhiking their way across the country, trying to get to California. It *was* the sixties, after all."

Her voice was gentle and calm, a warm smile crossing her face as if she were remembering the moment like it was yesterday.

"My girlfriends and I took the train into the city so we could go to the esplanade to listen to the Fourth of July concert and watch the fireworks. At the time, the drinking age was eighteen, so we brought a cooler and a few blankets, found a spot on the grass, and spent our day soaking up the sun. After a few hours, we ran out of beer, so I went in search of a concession stand to buy

133

some more. There was a long line, but I waited, knowing my friends would be disappointed if I returned empty-handed. As I was heading back to them, balancing four beers in my hands, I ran into a very tall, very hard body, crushing the beers between us. It was like it happens in all those cheesy romance movies. Everything was in slow motion as I looked up from my beer-soaked tank top and shorts. I finally knew where the term love-struck came from because it felt as if all the oxygen had been sucked from the atmosphere. When I saw his eyes, the most ferocious butterflies began fluttering in my stomach. The rest of the evening was a blur as I got to know this beautiful man, and I'm fortunate that I got to spend nearly forty years with him."

"That's beautiful," I sighed.

"It wasn't all easy for us. For the first several years, especially after Carol was born, we were barely scraping by. He was over in Vietnam for years, so I was forced to raise Carol without him. When he returned, she was already four. He had missed all of her firsts. After finding out he volunteered to stay in Vietnam after his first tour was over, even after he told me he didn't have a choice, I kicked him out. His lies hurt, Mackenzie, so I know how you feel. But the time apart gave us both an opportunity to realize how much we couldn't survive without each other. We both realized what was important in life. Thomas vowed never to lie to me again. He wanted to be there for all our next baby's firsts, but we were in no position to try again. We were living in a studio apartment, barely making ends meet. I couldn't find a job, even with the college degree I eventually got after having Carol. Employers didn't want to hire me because I had a child. They wanted someone reliable who wouldn't have to miss work because of an ill child. Things were a lot different back then."

"I guess so," I responded, shaking my head. I couldn't imagine what she went through raising a baby while the father was overseas fighting a war.

"Then, one day, he got a letter. He had been trying to get in with the CIA for years, and had been faced with rejection after rejection. Finally, they agreed to see him for an interview. It was a long process but, two years later, we moved to Connecticut, bought a house, and he began working for the agency out of one of the satellite offices. He eventually started his own private security firm and we moved back up here.

"After he passed away, I traveled a lot. It wasn't until my granddaughter was born that I decided to make Massachusetts my home once more and I'm glad I did so I could be around for all of her firsts.

"I guess what I'm trying to say is, even though things may look bleak right now, life has a funny way of working itself out."

"I hope you're right."

"Excuse me, Mrs. Burnham," an imposing man clad in a dark suit interrupted, popping into the kitchen. Based on his stature, I knew he worked for the security company. Maybe he was Colleen's version of Eli.

"Hello, William." She looked away from me and gave him a congenial smile.

"I apologize for interrupting, ma'am, but I have news." He slid an envelope in front of her and she opened it, examining the contents.

I turned my head to allow her to read whatever it was without me trying to look over her shoulder, but I was certainly curious. Instead, I occupied my mind with my surroundings. The kitchen was modern and homey. It opened into a laid-back sitting room with a large screen TV, and I could tell this was where most of the entertaining occurred.

"Thank you, William," Colleen's voice cut through, bringing my attention back to her and the formidable-looking man standing at ease next to her.

"Ma'am." He nodded, retreating from the kitchen.

As if on cue, the stove buzzed, indicating that the lasagna was done. "Perfect." She jumped up from her chair. "Hope you're hungry."

"Are you kidding me?" I responded, rubbing my stomach. "This little guy has a monster appetite."

"Well, he's got Burnham DNA in him. He's going to be a big baby."

"How big was Tyler when he was born?" I asked, almost scared to know the answer.

"Nearly ten pounds. Word of advice, dear," she said, looking over her shoulder as she retrieved the lasagna from the oven. "Don't turn down the epidural."

Chapter Fourteen

Sign

Tyler

THE WHEELS OF THE plane finally touched down at Logan International in Boston after midnight, the end of three very long days of traveling. The drive to the closest airport in Sudan was nearly fifteen hours, then a thirty-hour series of flights back to the States. It was torture. Every minute that passed was another minute Mackenzie believed I was avoiding her. After clearing customs, I debated continuing on down to Texas, but I was exhausted. No commercial flights would be departing for several hours and it would take just as long to get one of the company's jets prepped for flight. I could use a few hours rest for what I knew would be one of my most difficult missions to date – convincing Mackenzie I was someone worth forgiving, that my love for her was real.

"So what's the plan?" Eli asked, helping me carry my bags up the short steps of my house in Beacon Hill.

"Sleep for a few hours, I suppose. Then head back home."

"Home?" He raised his eyebrows.

"Yes. Home. Where Mackenzie is. I'm done being a coward. I'm not going to let my brother dictate what's best for me anymore. For all I know, there may never have been any threat to our safety. Maybe he just made it up to keep me away from her. I don't know, but I'm through being his pawn."

Eli nodded before holding his hand out to me. I grabbed it and he pulled me in, patting my back. "Good for you. I'll do what I can to get a flight plan in place for tomorrow, hopefully without your brother knowing."

I smiled appreciatively at him. "Thanks. Call me with the details."

"Will do," he said, turning from me and hopping back into the cab we had shared from the airport.

Alone once more, I stared at my front door, my chest tightening. I hadn't stepped foot inside this house since the day everything fell apart. I had my mom grab the few things I needed for my trip, too distraught to face the memories I made with Mackenzie within the four walls of the house that, for a brief moment of time, actually felt like a home.

After unlocking the door and disarming the system, I entered the foyer. Everything looked just as I had left it four months ago, but it was all different. Darkness enveloped the house, despite the light that was now flooding through the foyer.

The sound of my shoes hitting the hardwood floor echoed as I walked into the formal sitting room and poured myself a scotch from the wet bar. A strong memory rushed forward and I placed my hands on the counter, trying to steady myself.

"Something about being near you makes my heart race faster than it has in years. And I want this feeling to last for as long as possible, preferably forever. It took meeting you to make me realize I was lost. I was numb for years. I always held out the smallest glimmer of hope someone would come along to make me feel again, just like you did. So, yes, this is my home. Just like South Padre is my home. I'm home as long as I have you. Alaska could be my home. Antarctica, Idaho, a corn field in Nebraska. Fuck. I don't

care where, as long as you're with me. You're my home."

Closing my eyes, I fought against the memory, trying to forget it. The ghost of Mackenzie's spirit surrounded me here, tormenting me. I could almost smell her scent of cinnamon and it broke me more than I thought possible.

I grabbed the scotch and poured more into my glass. My world spinning, I dashed up the stairs, wishing I could find somewhere in my house that hadn't been tainted by my betrayal and deception, but I knew it wasn't possible. It surrounded me, mocking me, reminding me that I didn't deserve her forgiveness.

Hesitating outside the door to my master bedroom, my hand hovered over the handle. A voice urged me to open it, to face my demons, to live with the reminder of what I had done. That was my penance for using Mackenzie.

Tentatively, I turned the knob and pushed the door open. I stood frozen in place as my eyes fell on my bedroom, everything exactly as I remembered, as if it was suspended in time. The bed still had a rumple on the duvet from where Mackenzie had been reading when I came back from picking out her engagement ring. The shadows of her soul, her heart, her love were everywhere, torturing me, reminding me, punishing me.

A low glimmer on the nightstand caught my eye and I went to it. I grew breathless when I saw the jeweled cross she always wore. I picked it up and my eyes scanned the room to see what else had been left behind. Her suitcase was still in the corner. I opened the closet to see the clothes she had brought with her hanging neatly. At the end of the rack was the dress she had worn the night of the dedication dinner. I ran my hand along the lace, Mackenzie's words replaying in my mind.

"I love you for you. I don't care about the man you wanted me to think you were. I know the real Tyler, and I love all the sides of that man. I love the caring side, the controlling side, the side that takes, the side that gives, and the side that loves. And I'm so grateful you opened your heart to love me."

The pain was back. It had never really left, but being faced with reminders of how I destroyed everything was too much and I sank to the ground, throwing back the scotch, her cross scorching my flesh. I needed the burn to dull the rest of the heartache coursing through my veins. I had distanced myself from any physical memories of Mackenzie, but now that I was back in Boston, it all came rushing forward and the remorse was overwhelming. I physically felt it in my throat, in my chest, in my heart.

I reached into the pocket of my jeans and pulled out the email she had sent me, reading it once more. I had lost track of how many times my eyes had read over her words, absorbing them, trying to find the meaning behind them. I put all my hope in the last line... *The truth is, despite it all, I still love you. And I always will.*

I prayed her love was strong enough to give me the forgiveness I needed.

Jumping to my feet, I shoved the email and her cross in my pocket, then dashed down the stairs, grabbing my bags as I rushed out of the house. The city of Boston was quiet and still as my footsteps echoed in the alley behind my house. I unlocked my Mercedes SUV and sped away.

As if on autopilot, I found myself making the drive out to my mother's house. It was the only place I could think of that hadn't been tainted by memories of Mackenzie. Pulling down the long driveway of the house we had lived in most of my teenage years, I continued past the fountain and put the car in park just outside the rear garage. My bag clutched in my hands, I ran up to the front door, trying to be as quiet as possible as I used my key to let myself in. Silence greeted me, the house still. I padded through the foyer, past the formal sitting room, and into the kitchen. Opening the refrigerator, I grabbed a bottle of water, my mouth salivating when I saw my mom had made her famous lasagna for dinner. My stomach immediately began to rumble and I pulled out the casserole dish, cutting out a small portion.

Just as I was retrieving my snack from the microwave, the overhead lights snapped on and I spun around to face the doorway.

"Tyler, baby," my mother whispered almost in relief as she rushed toward me. She enveloped me in her arms and I bent down to match her short height. "You're home." She rocked me, planting a kiss on my cheek. "I'm so glad you're finally here." She hugged me tighter, her arms strong around me.

"Yeah," I said, my loud voice echoing in the kitchen.

She pulled back abruptly, her eyes growing wide. "Shhh, baby. Quiet."

I furrowed my brow, confused about why I had to lower my voice if she was awake. I nearly cringed at the thought that maybe she had an overnight guest. I was more than aware that she had occasionally dated since my dad died over ten years ago, but it still didn't make the thought any more comfortable.

"Sorry, Ma," I said, not wanting confirmation of my suspicions.

"Tyler, there's something—"

I held my hand up. "I don't want to hear it. There are some things better left unsaid."

"What do you—"

"It's okay if you have an overnight guest, Ma," I explained, praying my face wasn't turning a brilliant

141

shade of red. I pulled out a chair from the kitchen table and sat down. "I get it. I just don't want to hear about any of it, okay?"

I avoided her eyes, shoveling the lasagna in my mouth as if I hadn't eaten in days. Truthfully, I hadn't. It had been *months* since I'd had a good meal, having to survive on the limited rations provided to the refugees at the camp. We all ate the same thing, and everything was bland and simple. This lasagna was decadent and filling. Now that I was back home, I couldn't wait to eat my weight in cheese and meat.

"If that's what you wish. If you really don't want me to tell you all about my overnight guest..." She shrugged.

The tone of her voice struck me as odd and I raised my head to see her standing there, arms crossed in front of her chest, a smug look on her face.

"Why would I want to hear about any of that?"

"Suit yourself," she sang, pulling the chair out beside me and sitting down. "I've been expecting you. William stopped by with a copy of your itinerary indicating you'd be flying in tonight."

"How did he know?"

"Do you really need to ask that question?" She paused and I remained silent, knowing how much information our company had access to. "Now, tell me... How are you doing?"

"Good." I avoided her eyes as I swallowed a large bite of lasagna.

"You can fool a lot of people, young man, but I gave birth to you. Tell me how you're *really* doing."

I sighed, leaning back into my chair. I savored the last bite of lasagna, contemplating having seconds. "Shitty," I finally admitted and she nodded in understanding. Her intense dark eyes bored into me, goading me to continue.

"I thought being away from it all was the right thing to

do, like you suggested, but I don't know. I think I was away too long."

"Why didn't you come back sooner?" she inquired, placing her hand on mine.

"I wanted to, but every time I brought it up, Alexander insisted I stay put, claiming I was needed, that he didn't think it was safe for Eli or me to return yet. I'm starting to think he kept me there on purpose to keep me away from..." I trailed off, her name causing a lump to form in my throat.

"Yet, here you are. What happened?" Mom asked.

I snapped my eyes to her. "What do you mean?"

"Well, you're back, aren't you? Why now? Something must have changed for you to disobey your brother's asinine orders. What was it?"

I reached into my pocket and pulled out the folded email, sliding it across the table, eyeing my mom as she unfolded and read it. She had almost the same reaction I did when I first read those sorrowful words. Her chin quivered and her eyes moistened with unshed tears.

When she finally finished absorbing the words on the page, she looked up. "What do you intend on doing?"

"Whatever I have to. I can't go another day without her, Ma." I stood up from the chair and placed my plate in the dishwasher, then began to retreat from the kitchen.

"Where are you going?" she called out.

"To get a few hours' sleep," I said over my shoulder. "Then I need to get back to Texas." I headed out of the kitchen, briskly walking toward the elaborate staircase.

"Tyler, baby," she whispered, running after me in her bathrobe. "Wait..."

I spun around. "What, Ma?"

She searched my eyes. I couldn't help but think she was hiding something from me. "You need to go, I understand that, but do me one favor."

"What is it?"

Her nervous expression softened. "Wait until after breakfast, okay? I need one of your father's frittatas and you're the only one who knows how to make them right."

I planted a kiss on her forehead. "You got it, Ma."

I tiptoed up the stairs, praying I didn't wake my mom's "special friend", and headed down the long corridor to the last door on the left...my old bedroom. I looked across the hall, a low glimmer of light coming from beneath the door of one of the guest bedrooms. Too exhausted to care, I entered my room, closing the door behind me. An unexpected waft of cinnamon washed over me, and I only hoped it was a sign of things to come.

Chapter Fifteen

About A Girl

Tyler

TOO EARLY FOR MY liking, the morning light started to peek through the shutters. I had barely slept since going to bed just a few hours before. The smell of cinnamon haunted my dreams. I felt an intoxicating electricity that now invigorated me with a renewed sense of determination to do everything I could to make Mackenzie mine once more.

Stretching in my bed, I fought the temptation to close my eyes and go back to sleep. It had been months since I had slept on a proper bed and I didn't want to leave the comfort surrounding me. My eyes drooping, I threw my legs over the side of the bed and padded to the en-suite bathroom. After splashing some water on my face, I rummaged through my bag and found some gym shorts and a t-shirt. I tossed them on and laced up my sneakers, heading quietly from my room and out of the house for an early morning run.

Time passed as I escaped into my thoughts, running through thousands of different scenarios as to why our agency contact had disappeared, whether Charlie had any involvement in his disappearance, and whether we were all being played. I wondered if Alexander had made any headway into what was really going on. I had so many questions and was anxious to get back to Texas so I could pick up where I had left off…with the job *and* Mackenzie.

Before I knew it, the sun began to beat down on me with more intensity. When I left my mother's house, the sun was just starting to rise. Now, it was shining brilliantly, and I knew I had probably been gone for a few hours. I circled back toward the house, putting in another few miles, and entered the foyer, hearing voices from the kitchen. Not ready to face Mom and her special overnight guest, I dashed up the stairs and hopped in the shower. After shaving and dressing in a pair of cargo shorts and a light green linen shirt, I found the email I had kept with me since receiving it and placed it in the pocket over my chest…over my heart.

Checking the clock to see that it was nearly ten, I hurried through the remainder of my morning routine. I still needed to cook my mom breakfast, then get to the airport in time for the noon flight Eli had arranged on one of the company jets.

Dashing down the stairs, I entered the kitchen and came to an abrupt stop.

"Alex…," I said nervously when I saw him sitting at the table. I felt like an employee who had been caught in a lie after calling in sick. "What are you doing here?" I sat down opposite him, studying his every move.

"Tyler." He raised himself from his chair, a knowing smirk on his face as he straightened his crisp suit. Heading toward the coffee machine to prepare a cup, his expression remained fixed. "Mom called and asked for a family breakfast this morning. I tried to say I had work to do, but she mentioned you were home, which certainly got my attention."

My eyes narrowed at him, my blood boiling every second I was in his presence. His odd demeanor made it readily apparent he was not happy I was home. I would have rather had him shout at me. I could handle that, but the fake smile, the niceties, the even temper... I just wanted him to get on with it so I could get on with what *I* needed to do.

"I was going to wait until you were settled, but I have a new assignment. You're on a transport to Afghanistan tomorrow at sixteen hundred hours."

I remained quiet as he returned to the table with two cups of coffee, placing one in front of me.

Sitting down, he reached into his laptop bag, retrieved a file, and slid it across the table toward me. "We've opened a shelter for girls who have been the victim of abuse and are at risk of further harm, possibly even death. Honor killings and all that. These girls—"

"Just stop," I interrupted. My voice was soft, my lips barely moving.

He snapped his head up, his green eyes meeting mine. "Ty—"

"No. Enough, Alex!" My voice rose with the anger that was slowly building within me. "I'm not going to be told what to do by you anymore, not when it's readily apparent you only have *your* best interests at heart and no one else's!"

"Where is this coming from?" he asked in an authoritative tone, his Adam's apple bobbing in his throat.

"Oh, you know...," I sneered, standing over him and leaning on the surface of the table. "Just being sent to Sudan for four months, having little to no means of communicating with anyone except you! Whenever I mentioned coming home, you gave me orders to stay on longer, saying I was needed! But I wasn't, Alex! I trusted you and followed your orders, even though I knew I didn't belong there. At first, I refused to believe it. You're my brother. There's no way you'd make me stay just to

147

keep me away. I agreed to a month to let you figure out what was going on, but as time passed, I knew I was wrong about it. I knew I was wrong about *you*. You didn't send me there to keep me safe. You probably never even tried to look into what was going on! You ordered me to stay to keep me from seeing Mackenzie!"

He rolled his eyes. "You don't know what you're talking about." He returned his attention to the folder in front of him. "Now, this shelter has been open for a few months, but there are still threats of—"

"*Bullshit!*" I roared, tearing the file out of his hands and throwing it to the ground. "*Bullshit, Alex!* You're purposely doing this to keep me away from Mackenzie! Of course, it's completely normal for *you* to not feel any guilt about lying to anyone. Hell, be enough of an asshole and they'll learn to love you, right?" I taunted, recalling how Alexander had kept so much information from his wife about their past, it nearly tore them apart. He had lied to her from day one, claiming it was the only way to keep her safe, but he was lucky enough that she learned to look past all of that. "It worked for you and Olivia so why the fuck should anyone else be happy?" Picking up my full coffee mug, I threw it against the wall and charged my brother, trying to tackle him to the floor.

"What the hell do you mean by that?" Alexander asked, placing his hands on my forearms, attempting to free himself from my hold.

"Exactly what I said! You lied to her for months and felt no remorse! What kind of person does that? I'll tell you. A cold-blooded prick who wouldn't know what love was if it slapped him in the face!" Pulling my fist back, I landed a hard blow to his jaw, forcing him to the ground.

Alexander grabbed onto my leg, swiping at my other one with his foot. I lost my balance and, in an instant, he had the upper hand, pinning me against the tile floor.

"I did that because I love her!" he bellowed. "Don't assume you know how I feel about that woman, Tyler!"

"Oh," I groaned out, unrelenting in my assault. "Looks like I hit a soft spot, doesn't it? Now you know how it feels." I raised my knee to kick Alexander in the groin unsuccessfully. My brief stint in the navy was no match for his SEAL training. I wrapped my hands around his thick neck, trying to break his hold. "How would you feel if someone refused to let you see her?!" I grunted, my breathing becoming labored. "I just want to see her! To explain! Stop trying to control—"

"*Boys!*" a shrill voice echoed through the kitchen. "What in God's name do you think you're doing?!"

As if we were two errant children instead of grown men, we quickly released our hold on each other and craned our heads toward the doorway. Our mother was standing there, Olivia and little Melanie close behind.

"Ma…" Alexander scrambled to his feet. I mirrored his movements, brushing my shorts off and trying to make it appear as if I hadn't been trying to kill my brother.

"Don't *Ma* me. I brought you two into this world and I can damn sure take you out of it. Alexander," she scolded, glaring at him, "you're thirty-seven, almost thirty-eight! You're married with a child who's nearly six! Right now, *she's* acting more mature than you are!"

"We were just—"

She held up her hand. He quickly snapped his mouth shut.

"And you, Tyler!" She turned her attention to me and I cowered under her gaze, more scared of her than I ever was of my drill sergeants during basic training. "We haven't seen you in four months and this is how you behave?!"

"Blame Alex," I muttered.

149

Mom shot her head toward Alexander. "Why does he want to blame you?"

Stuffing his hands into his pockets, he shrugged sheepishly. "Because…" He avoided her eyes, not giving her an answer.

"*All right!*" she bellowed, her voice firm.

I cringed. I hadn't heard that tone since I was a small child. It was the voice that always made me stop whatever I was doing and pretend I was the perfect angel she raised me to be. Her nostrils flaring, showing her heavy Irish temper, she stalked toward where we stood and grabbed our hands, yanking us out of the kitchen and into the living room. Alexander and I towered over her by more than a foot, but she always had a way of making us feel slightly terrified.

"Sit!" she ordered. "Alex, you over there." She gestured to one end of the couch. "Tyler, you over there." She nodded toward the other end. "This way, I know you won't kill each other."

Alexander and I quickly obeyed, both of us lowering ourselves onto opposite sides of an oversized cream-colored sectional set against a large window, the sunlight streaming in behind us.

"This has gone on long enough. You two are going to talk, and you're going to talk now." She ran her hand through her nearly white hair. Looking at the ceiling, she took a deep breath and returned her eyes to us, her expression softening. "We should have done this ages ago, but I thought you two would be mature enough to handle it on your own. Apparently, I was wrong."

I crossed my arms in front of my chest and stared straight ahead, not wanting to be the first to speak. I wasn't the one who had been acting unreasonably.

"Olivia, dear," Mom called over her shoulder to the tall, slender brunette. "I think it's best you join us, as well. You seem to make Alexander less of a stubborn ass and more of a rational person. Melanie, sweetie..." She directed her attention to the dark-haired little girl at Olivia's side. "Can you go down to your playroom for a little while and play with your toys? Grandma will buy you a brand new doll if you do what I ask and don't get into any trouble for the next twenty minutes. Can you do that?"

Grinning and showing a few missing teeth, she said, "Okay, Grandma." She was about to head away before she ran toward me and flung her arms around my neck. "I missed you, Uncle Tyler," she whispered softly.

I returned her hug and placed a kiss on her cheek. "I missed you, too, munchkin."

Releasing herself from my grasp, she spun around and bounced toward the stairs leading to the basement, which had been modified into an extravagant playroom of which any child would be jealous.

"Now," Mom said once younger ears were no longer present, "it's time you boys stopped acting childish. Tyler, you've kept everything inside for a while now. Get it out."

"What are you talking about, Ma?" I asked quietly. "I haven't—"

"Bullshit, Tyler. You're still carrying the guilt of what happened to Melanie and it's strained your relationship with your brother...with everyone. I am the last one to ever demean someone for wanting to join the military, but I voiced my opinion with Alexander and I'm sure as hell going to voice it with you. Your reasons were fucking bullshit and cowardly. Instead of learning to cope with losing Melanie, you went into the service." She took a deep breath before softening her expression. "I'm so proud of you." She glanced from me to Alexander. "Of both my boys. Your father was never a great communicator and I fear you both inherited that trait from him. So, please, I'm getting old. I don't want to feel like I'm walking on eggshells around you two."

Alexander narrowed his gaze at me. "What's going on, Ty?" he asked quietly, holding Olivia's hand in his.

I shrugged, trying to ignore the tension building in the room. I had been angry for so long, I didn't know what I was upset over anymore. I tried to go back in my mind to what started the break between my brother and me...losing Melanie. But I didn't feel that pain anymore, and I struggled to find a reason to hold a grudge against him. *He* didn't kill her. He was no more responsible for her death than I was. It all seemed so childish now.

"I know it probably feels like my words don't mean anything," Alexander continued when I didn't respond, "but you have no idea how much losing Melanie hurt all of us. I know how much you loved her, Ty. I thought I had lost my one true love and the pain was excruciating." He looked at Olivia, their eyes meeting. "I'm lucky enough that I didn't lose her." Standing up, he took carefully measured steps toward me and sat down. "But something tells me this isn't all about Melanie...not anymore."

I shook my head. "I loved Melanie, but that feeling is *nothing* compared to what I–"

"Then you need to go to her," Olivia interrupted, standing up. Her heels clicked on the hardwood floor as she walked toward us, Alexander's eyes wide. "Apologize for not going sooner, for having a bit of an overbearing ass for a brother, and for using her and keeping secrets from her in the first place. Trust me. I know exactly what's going through that poor girl's mind right now. She's probably questioning everything in her life, wondering whom she can trust, wondering what's real and what's not. There are few things worth fighting for these days, but I can guarantee you that love is one of them." She sat down next to Alexander and planted a soft kiss on his cheek. "And it's a damn good thing your brother fought for me."

"Olivia," Alexander said, his tone somewhat harsh, "it's not that easy. This woman was an asset, and our agency contact went missing. I didn't know which way was up, so we had to do something to protect everyone involved."

My eyes glued to Alexander, my heart raced in my chest. "What did you do?" I whispered.

He studied me for several long moments before finally speaking. "We gaslighted her."

"What the hell does that even mean?" Mom interjected.

"It means we made her question her reality, made her question whether she had really met Tyler or not. We removed any and all traces of him from her life, even had a few of my agents move into his old house in the off chance she went over there. They were told to use any means necessary to convince her there never was a Tyler Burnham who lived there."

An understanding look crossed my mom's face, as if she had just received the missing piece of a puzzle. "Spies," she mumbled under her breath.

"Why would you *do* something like that?" Olivia demanded, her temper rising.

"So she would think she never met him. His cover had been compromised, so we had to do *something*. Gaslighting is one of the most effective manipulation techniques there is to make the target or asset think what we want them to think...that they never met someone, in this case, Tyler. It's a way to protect his blown cover, which can have drastic consequences to both parties, especially in this case."

"This is absurd!" She raised herself from the couch and glowered at Alexander. "Do you really think she'd believe she never met him? For crying out loud, just let him go to her, regardless that you attempted to 'gaslight' her!" she sneered. "He needs closure! I'm sure Mackenzie does, too! Then you can all move on with your lives. He can stop moping around, you can stop trying to keep him away from home so he doesn't go see her, and things can go back to normal…or as normal as they can be in this family." She plopped back onto the couch and crossed her arms in front of her chest, annoyed.

Silence rang in the living room as we all absorbed Olivia's words. My mom was right. She was the only person who could ever break through my brother's thick skull and make him be the compassionate person we all knew was hiding beneath the layers of his tough exterior.

"Ty," Alexander finally said, clearing his throat. "I hate to admit it, but maybe Olivia's right." He met my eyes and I knew it must have taken a lot for him to accept that. "If I were in your shoes and someone tried to keep me from the woman *I* loved, I'd be pissed." Sighing, he ran his hand through his dark hair. "I'm sorry. About everything. About getting you into this mess, then trying to decide what's best for you without asking what *you* wanted. I've been a shitty brother. I should be supporting you instead of trying to keep you down. If you love her like you say you do, I'm happy for you. If you want to be with her, I'm not going to fight you, but you need to be careful. I've spent months trying to track down our agency contact to see if there was some sort of trail and I've come up empty. I can't help but think there's something suspicious going on and that his disappearance has everything to do with this case. The timing is too perfect."

154

"Have you looked into his family?" I asked.

"Of course," he responded. "He had none. Parents dead. Never married. No children. Hell, I can't even access any of the missions he was a part of. This all makes me believe he had more than just top-level security clearance. So please, promise me you'll think with your head and be extra cautious."

"I will. Promise." I gave him a quick reassuring look before jumping off the couch and bolting from the room.

"Tyler, baby," my mother called out. "Where are you going?"

Beaming, I glanced over my shoulder. "I have to go see about a girl."

I ran toward the staircase, dashing up to the second floor and down the long hallway to pack up my stuff as quickly as possible. As I approached my room, the door opposite mine opened, startling me. I halted in my tracks, my jaw dropping as I stared at the woman standing in the doorway.

Chapter Sixteen

One More Time

Mackenzie

I CHECKED MY REFLECTION in the mirror, my formerly loose-fitting yellow sundress now rather snug. I took a closer look, my eyes vibrant for a change. I felt refreshed and rejuvenated after finally getting some much-needed sleep. Escaping South Padre for a little bit was exactly what I needed to help me cope with what had become my new normal.

Pulling open the guest room door to head downstairs, a rush of a familiar scent found its way to my nose, stirring up memories of that happy, yet heartbreaking time in my life. I raised my head, inhaling quickly when I was met with a pair of striking green eyes.

I whimpered, almost in disbelief. Over the past several months, I had seen him everywhere. I had heard his voice in my dreams, saw his face on every man, smelled his musky scent no matter where I was. I was convinced this was just a dream, too.

"Mackenzie…," Tyler said, surprised, his tone guttural and raspy.

"Is this real?" I felt numb, like I was daydreaming… But this was one daydream I didn't want to wake up from. Closing my eyes, a warmth approached and a finger brushed away the lone tear trickling down my face. A current flowed through me, sparking a sensation that had been absent for the past several months. It was intense, burning, piercing. I fought to contain the thrill I felt from this man's simple touch.

"What are...? How...?" he stammered, and I returned my eyes to his. He glanced at my stomach and I cringed, imagining his bewilderment. "Is it...?"

"I'm sorry. I shouldn't be here." I spun around and dashed toward the bed, frantically throwing my things into my bag. "I get it. It's my fault. I was stupid and—"

"Mackenzie, stop!" his voice thundered, startling me and bringing back so many memories of our short-lived romance.

I filled my lungs, hoping for the strength to get through this when all I wanted to do was crawl in a corner and pretend I didn't exist. I knew this day was inevitable, but I didn't expect to be in this situation so soon. I had made no plan on how to get through it, making me all the more apprehensive about the conversation I knew I could no longer avoid.

"Look at me, Mackenzie," he crooned, his voice tender. I shook my head, refusing to look into his eyes. I needed to remain strong and I knew I would break if I gazed into those eyes that once held so much hope for my own future. "Please. I... I'm such a fuck up."

"You never came for me," I said softly, keeping my back turned to him when I felt him approach behind me. He was so close, there was a buzz in the air from his proximity. "I thought you cared enough that you would."

"You told me not to." He ran his hand down my arm, calming me.

I faced him and saw tears forming behind his eyes. "Since when have you actually listened to what I wanted? No phone call! No email! *Nothing*! I thought I imagined you. I thought I was so desperate to feel *something* for someone that I made you up in my head. I drove through the streets of South Padre every day, Tyler! Every. Fucking. Day! And do you know what I saw?"

"What?"

"You! Whenever I saw a dog, I'd think of you and Griffin. Every boat. Every bar. Every restaurant."

His shoulders dropped and he swallowed hard, his normal confidence lacking. "Mackenzie, I'm..." His voice cracked as he reached out for me.

"*Sorry*. I know." Avoiding his touch, I fell onto the bed, fighting back the lump in my throat. I refused to cry in front of him anymore. He didn't deserve my tears.

"I questioned everything in my life, Tyler," I confessed. "If it weren't for Jenna and Brayden, I would have thought I imagined you. Even with them, there have been days I was convinced I *did* make you up. I was certain if you really did care, you would have come for me. Then a week passed. Then a month. Then another month. And then..." I glanced down at my stomach, my hand resting on it protectively, as if hoping I could keep my baby safe from a world of hurt and pain. "Then I knew you were real, which made your absence hurt even more. I called, Tyler! I called your cell and it was disconnected. I called the security company and they gave me the run-around every time. I missed you so much, I vowed to swallow my pride and admit I made a mistake when I pushed you away, but now..." I shook my head. "It hurts too much to be near you. I can't—"

"You told me the only way to prove it was real was to let you go," he interrupted.

I stared into his eyes, scared to see that the love he had for me no longer covered them.

"But I can't, Mackenzie," he said, his voice wavering. "You're my heart. The air I breathe. My *everything*. I don't care what it takes to prove it was real. That it *is* real. Still. I will beg every day for the rest of my life to make you mine. You can tell me no every day for weeks, months, years. I don't care how long you want to hurt me, to tell me you never want to see me again. I deserve it."

"*Four months*, Tyler!" I exclaimed. "You've been gone for almost four months. Four months where I had to question everything. Four months where, every night, I lay awake, wondering how I was going to explain to the baby growing inside of me where his father is, why he wasn't good enough for his father to love him." I let out a slow breath. "But I got up every day, and every day I didn't hear from you, another brick was built around my heart. Every day, I missed you a little bit less. I thought of you a little bit less. I cried for you a little bit less. I let go of another piece of you. Your eyes. Your lips. Your smile. Your touch. I had to let go of all those things."

"Please, Mackenzie. You have to realize how sorry I am, how much I love you—"

"How can I believe you?" I asked, shooting off the bed and heading to the window. "After everything you did to me, I will always think this is all just another lie, another way for you to get what you need, then toss me out like last week's garbage." I looked back at him and saw how full of regret he was. The pain of my words were etched on every inch of him. Part of me wanted to jump in his arms and forget how much he hurt me, but I couldn't do that. Not anymore.

"The thing is, I can deal with that pain again, but it's not just me I have to worry about now. I can't let you back into my life just for you to leave again. I can't let you hurt my baby—"

"Truth or dare," he interrupted, his voice impassioned as he stalked to me.

"What?" I asked, my eyes widening.

"You heard me, Mackenzie," he countered, narrowing

his gaze at me. "Truth. Or. Dare."

I swallowed hard. "Truth."

"Did you mean this?" he asked, pulling a sheet of paper out of his shirt pocket.

Squinting my eyes, I recognized the email I wrote him and inhaled quickly.

"This...," he said, gesturing to the piece of paper. "Because of this, I drove fifteen hours to the closest airport I could get a flight out of, from one end of Sudan, where I was volunteering at a refugee camp for the past four months, to the other. Then I flew thirty-three hours on a series of three different flights. You want to know why?"

"Why?" I quivered.

"Because of the last line," he admitted. "You said you still love me. You picked truth so please tell me. *Do* you still love me?"

Staring into those green eyes that had haunted my dreams, I let out a loud sob, nodding as my tears washed over me. He pulled me into his body and planted a kiss on my forehead. My emotions overtook me and I drenched his shirt. He held me close, warming me with his embrace.

"I've missed this," he murmured.

I had been craving this feeling for months, needing his arms to assure me everything would work out, that I would finally be over the ache his absence caused my heart. Could everything really be forgiven by a simple "I'm sorry" or "I love you"? They were just words. Meaningless words.

Straightening my spine, I pushed against him, freeing myself from the hold he still had over me. I tore back to the bed and finished throwing all my things in my suitcase, zipping it up.

"Mackenzie, wha–"

"Yes, Tyler. Yes, it's true. I still love you, but that doesn't fix this. You can't just come back into my life and pick up where things left off. As much as I want to forgive you because you need it, I can't do it."

Tears streaming down my face, I rushed out of the room, darting down the stairs and into the foyer.

"Wait, Mackenzie!" Tyler cried out after me. "Tell me what you want me to say and I'll say it! Letting you walk away from me once was the biggest mistake of my life. I won't do it again."

I spun around just as I was about to open the front door. "You *let* me walk away from you?" I hissed, my teeth clenched.

"That's not what I meant." He ran his hands through his dark brown hair and I could see the desperation wash over him. "What I meant to say is all the lies, all of it... I'm so sorry I put you through it. But do you think I regret any of it?" His eyes grew more intense and impassioned, his chest heaving as he poured his heart out to me. "Not for a second."

I glared at him, waiting for him to explain.

"If it wasn't for all the lies, for my assignment, I never would have met you, so I'm not going to say I regret a fucking second of any of it. I don't care what it takes to win back your heart. You can push me away all you want. You can tell me you'll never forgive me, that there will never be an 'us' again, but I will *always* come back for you. A hundred times. A thousand times. I will fight for us until I take my last breath."

He stepped toward me, grabbing my hand in his, caressing my knuckles in such a delicate way that made me want to melt into a puddle.

"Please, Mackenzie..." He leaned toward me, brushing his lips against my forehead, kissing me so delicately, so lightly. "Serafina," he whispered, "tell me what it will take and I'll do it."

Despite everything he had just said, I simply couldn't let him back in. Relationships were based on trust, and Tyler took my trust and used it against me. I couldn't forget that, no matter how much my skin yearned for his touch.

"You want to know what it's going to take?" I asked softly, freeing my hand from his grasp.

He nodded, nervous anticipation radiating through his body as he looked at me with eager eyes.

"It'll take one more time," I murmured, opening the door. Peering over my shoulder, I saw his deflated expression. "It will always take one more time."

Chapter Seventeen

Start Again

Tyler

"DON'T TELL ME YOU'RE giving up," a voice said, startling me. I didn't know how long I had been staring at that closed door, thinking the only thing that mattered had just walked out of my life once more.

"Ma." I spun around. "Did you–"

"I heard enough."

I let out a low sigh, feeling weighed down. "What should I do, Ma? She wouldn't even listen to me!"

A sympathetic look on her face, she approached me and placed her hands on my shoulders, forcing me back around. "You get back out there, Tyler. It's not going to be easy, and I have a feeling this battle certainly won't be won overnight. It's going to take some time. She spent the last several months getting used to her life without you in it. You being back is going to take some adjustment on her part...and yours. You can tell her you're sorry all you want, but your words don't hold any merit, not after what you put her through. Start from the beginning again. Be the Tyler I love. Show her the real you..."

"I *did* show her the real me."

"Then help her get reacquainted with that person."

I nodded and stared out the window of the front door, seeing Mackenzie's trembling frame sitting on the grass.

163

Her head was upturned, staring at the sky. I wished I knew what she was thinking at that moment.

"Go, baby. You've got a lot of work ahead of you. Don't expect a miracle. Get to know her again. Let her know you. Let her fall in love with the new you. I have a feeling she'll come around."

"I hope you're right," I said, leaning down and planting a kiss on her forehead. Taking a deep breath, I placed my unsteady hand on the doorknob and turned it, heading down the steps and onto the grass. My silhouette cast a shadow over Mackenzie, but she remained facing forward. I could tell she was consciously trying to ignore my presence.

"Do you mind if I sit?" I asked in a firm tone, trying to mask my unease.

She craned her neck to look at me and nodded slightly...an ambivalent gesture.

"Thanks." I lowered myself, not sitting too close. Although nothing had really changed between us, there was still an electricity in the air just from being near her. She hadn't turned me down or run away, so I was taking this as a step in the right direction, regardless of how small a step it was.

A few birds chirped, flying in and settling on the fountain, bathing their feathers. The sun was pleasant, and clouds drifted in the sky, reminding me how much I missed being home. In the African desert, the sun was relentless, barely a cloud in sight. The texture in the sky here was beautiful, reminding me of all the times I sat in the backyard with my mother, spying animals in the clouds.

"It's a boy," Mackenzie said, breaking the awkward silence. I snapped my head toward hers and met her eyes. She fidgeted with the hem of her skirt and I could sense her nerves. I felt the same way, although I didn't want her to know it. "I mean, I figure I should tell you since you're the father and all."

"Mackenzie, I—"

She held up her hand, stopping me. "Don't worry, Tyler. I'm not asking you to help. I know this is probably all a bit of a surprise. It took me quite a while to wrap my head around everything. Truth be told, I'm still coming to terms with it, but I don't want you to feel like you have to change your lifestyle or act any differently around me. If you don't want any part of this—"

"What makes you think that?"

She shrugged and avoided my eyes. "I just—"

I reached over and grabbed her hand. She looked at me and a glimmer of hope ran through me when she didn't immediately pull away. "I want to be part of this baby's life. Despite what you want to believe, our son is the result of my love for you, and I will make sure he has everything he needs. The same goes for you. I want to be part of *your* life, too, but I know we have a lot to work through before that can happen. I get it. We know each other, but we don't really *know* each other. I'm willing to start from the beginning again, to find out who you are as a person. I hope you'll give me the chance to at least find out who I am as a person, too. I hope you'll give me the opportunity to prove I'm worth your time, your trust, and maybe your heart."

She nodded and tore her hand from mine, staring forward once again. I expected her to give me a list of reasons why it would never work between us, but that didn't happen. I was hopeful that meant she was willing to give us a second chance, despite it all.

I glanced to her as she gazed out over the perfectly manicured lawn of my mother's house, unable to remember ever being so on edge and nervous around a woman before. I was cognizant of each of my movements, from a flicker of my tongue to a deep breath that could be taken the wrong way.

"Why do I feel like a thirteen-year-old boy who is talking to a girl for the first time?" I joked.

She gradually faced me, a small smile crossing her beautiful lips. Lips I had dreamt of nearly every night since I had been gone. "Did you really not talk to a girl until you were thirteen?" she asked, her voice coy.

I chuckled, relieved the thick tension between us was starting to break.

"I was a bit of a late bloomer, I guess." I smiled, running my hand through my hair.

"What was her name?"

"Who?"

"Your first crush." She looked at me with eager eyes, and hope washed over me that she had taken my words to heart. She was trying to get to know the real me again. She was willing to give me the chance that, just moments ago, I didn't think she'd ever give me. This wasn't forgiveness, but it was a step in the right direction.

"Marcy Brennan. She had the cutest freckles behind her ears. I sat behind her in Math and, whenever she had her hair pulled back, I always stared at them. She forgot her pencil one day and she turned around and asked to borrow one of mine. She had never spoken to me before and I was in shock. I gave her my pencil without even thinking. Too late, I realized I had given her my only one, but I didn't care. I would have given her anything."

She kept her gaze trained on mine, absorbing my story. A light expression crossed her face and her rigid stature relaxed.

"How about you?" I asked in an attempt to keep the conversation going.

"Damian Mills," she answered without hesitating. She pulled a blade of grass out of the lawn and began to tie it

166

in knots. Her eyes grew bright, a slight smile crossing her lips. "I was eight. He moved in next door to us. I remember sitting in a tree that separated our yards when the moving trucks pulled up. Then I saw a boy who appeared to be my age jump out of a car. I thought he was so cute. We became friends, nearly inseparable, and I no longer looked at him that way. Every night, after we were supposed to be asleep, we climbed out of our bedroom windows and met on the limbs of that tree. We just sat there and watched the stars."

"What happened to him?" I asked.

She let out a shallow sigh. "Two years later, it all went to hell and we had to disappear without saying goodbye. I wanted to call him or send him a letter so he knew I was okay, but my mom told me I couldn't because it was too dangerous. As the years went on, I guess finding him seemed to be less of a priority. I mean, I'm still not supposed to tell anyone who I really am, so it's not like I could have called him up and said, 'Hey, it's Fi. Let's go climb a tree.'" She smiled before her expression turned serious. "And now I think he's in trouble."

"What do you mean? You said you haven't talked to him."

"I haven't," she said. "While you were gone, apparently your brother sent one of his guys to keep an eye on me and make sure everything was okay. Well, Wyatt...although I'm pretty sure that's not his real name...noticed a car tailing me and looked into it. It was an FBI agent who works with Damian. He said he's been on a leave of absence from the FBI for nearly four months, but this agent thinks he's missing." She glanced at me as I did the math in my head, noticing my expression. "Exactly. The timing fits all this craziness a bit too perfectly. It could just be a coincidence, but if his FBI buddy thinks something's not right and he's in trouble…"

I stared ahead and thought about what she just told me. I no longer believed in coincidences, particularly where Mackenzie was concerned. "Do you want me to see if I can find him?"

Her eyes widened. "You would do that?"

"Sure," I said. I would do anything for her. "We'll at least follow-up with this FBI agent and see what he knows. Maybe if I take what I know and what he knows, I'll be able to figure it out. Don't worry. I'm sure he's fine. I've worked with all kinds of federal agents. The job has a high burn-out rate. It's not uncommon for someone to take a lengthy leave of absence to clear their head and recharge their batteries. I'm sure that's all your friend is doing."

She nodded and reached for my hand, grabbing it. "Thanks, Tyler."

I remained still, praying she wouldn't break the contact. All my focus was devoted solely to the heat of her skin on mine. It was beautiful, perfect, simple, yet more satisfying than I could possibly put into words. Her fingers intertwined with mine and she inched closer to me, the connection growing stronger as a gentle breeze wrapped around us. The silence wasn't awkward like it was when I first came outside. Her anger had subsided and I was able to feel Mackenzie again…her heart, her spirit, her soul.

"Tell me a secret," she murmured.

"A secret?"

"Mmm-hmm." Her voice was sleepy and I could sense she was relaxed. "You know all mine. It's only fair I know some of yours."

"I want you to know *all* of mine," I said gently.

She pulled away from me and searched my eyes. "Really? Even if I may not like them?"

168

"I meant what I said, Mackenzie. I want to start over again. I want you to know everything about me. I want you to know my darkness and my light. Love is all about sharing a piece of yourself with another human and I want to share all of me with you. If you don't like what I've been hiding, well... That's a risk I have to take. My top priority is complete honesty with you."

She studied me as if trying to determine if she could believe my words. Apparently satisfied, she nodded slightly and rearranged her body, lying down and placing her head on my lap. I stroked her hair, gently massaging her scalp, and she closed her eyes.

"So, tell me a secret, Tyler."

"What kind of secret do you want to know?"

"Something you've never told anyone else. Something you swore you would never tell another living soul."

I stared at the sky, my fingers continuing to caress her hair.

"I still have that nightmare," I whispered.

"The one where you're treading water in a well?" She opened her eyes, looking at me. I nodded.

"When I was a little boy, I was scared to fall asleep most nights because of that dream. When it continued, Ma sent me to a shrink. The doctor did everything she could to try and get into my subconscious to figure out what it was."

"But she couldn't, could she?"

"No." I shook my head. "Not right away. It got so bad, I couldn't even take a shower, scared I would drown. We had tried to deal with what was going on without medication but, after a few months, my parents didn't see any other option. Still, the medication didn't take the nightmares away. I was convinced I was being punished for something. For what? I didn't know."

"Did you figure it out?"

Swallowing hard, I said, "Yes…after several years. My therapist tried different and somewhat controversial techniques, convinced there was something in my subconscious that was causing the nightmares and anxiety. It didn't make sense to me. If it was a traumatic event, I would have remembered what it was. People don't just forget things, right? But my dad was a combat vet and had seen stuff like that first-hand."

"What caused it?"

My heart thumped in my chest and I stared down into her eyes, intrigue and compassion covering her expression. She reached up and cupped my cheek in her hand, the contact comforting me.

"It's okay," she said.

"The first few years of my life, I lived in Connecticut. Did I ever tell you that?"

"You may have mentioned it."

I grabbed her hand in mine, finding peace in her support. "We lived in Mystic. It's on the shore, an old seaport. My family was well-off and lived in a beautiful estate on the river that was a captain's house during the nineteenth century. I spent my summer days playing with friends and causing trouble. One day, this green pick-up truck drove up to us. The driver rolled the window down and called out to my friend, Craig. We couldn't have been more than seven or eight at the time. Craig didn't recognize the guy, but the man said he was his uncle, that there was an accident and he had been sent to take him to the hospital to see his parents. When he heard that, Craig jumped in the car without hesitation, although something didn't seem right to me. Growing up, your parents always tell you never talk to strangers, and that's all good in theory, but when you think something horrible has happened to the only family you have, all sense of rationale and reason gets tossed out the window, doesn't it?"

I could feel Mackenzie nod in agreement, although I didn't see it. My eyes were closed, the scene of that moment in time playing out in front of me.

"There was a statewide search for Craig. His photo was flashed on the television, plastered on phone poles, printed in every newspaper. I remember asking my mom where his 'uncle' took him. I could only imagine how difficult it was for her to explain to me that his uncle didn't take him. The weeks went on, the summer ended, and we went back to school. A desk in our classroom was left open for Craig in the hopes he'd come back.

"September in Connecticut could still be warm and, after school on a particularly hot day, a few of us decided to go for a swim in the river. There was a little alcove beneath a bridge we would always go to. I was the first to take a running leap, cannonballing into the water. I remember opening my eyes, swearing I felt a hand grab onto my leg." I paused, needing a moment to collect myself. I had never shared the intricate details of that experience with anyone before, except for my therapist and parents years ago.

"What did you see?" Mackenzie asked softly.

"Craig's body. His face was bloated and there were bruises all over him, but I knew it was him. I tried to get out of the river as fast as possible. In my head, I was treading water for an eternity, calling for help. In reality, it was probably only a matter of seconds. I felt helpless, like if I didn't call someone that second, Craig would die, even though I knew he was already dead. I don't remember what happened after that, but that night was the first time I had the nightmare."

"Did your mother ever tell your therapist about all of that?"

"She did, but my therapist thought it best I remember

what happened on my own instead of someone simply telling me. To be honest, I wouldn't have believed it if she *had* told me. Once I finally worked through what my brain was protecting me from, the nightmare eventually went away."

"When did it come back?" she asked.

"When Melanie died. I felt helpless again. Once I joined the navy, it went away again because my routine helped me cope with the guilt and loss. But then..."

"Yes?"

"Then I lost you." I looked down and met her eyes. "And the helplessness returned, but it was more intense than before. Alexander sent me away because he was concerned for my safety, but that didn't help matters. With each day I didn't see you, I felt myself lose more and more control over everything in my life. I felt like I was drowning, all the lies and deception pulling me down."

"And now?" she asked, running her fingers through my hair.

"Now I'll live with the nightmares. I deserve it for what I did to you."

She closed her eyes, a content expression on her face. Her lips turned up slightly as a breeze blew her hair.

"Say something," I said after several silent moments passed. My admission remained hanging between us, making me uneasy. The guilt I felt for not doing something to protect Craig all those years still ate away at me at times. I wondered where he would be today if I had been smarter and told him not to get in the truck. Would he have listened?

"What do you want me to say?"

"I don't know." I shrugged. "Something. *Anything.* What are you thinking?"

She flung her eyes open. "Do you really want to

172

know?"

"I wouldn't have asked if I didn't."

"I'm thinking..." She paused, studying my face for several intense, protracted moments. Finally, her gaze softened. "I'm thinking it's time to go home." She slowly raised herself up from my lap, taking a minute to steady herself.

"Home?" I asked, deflated, as she brushed her sundress off.

"Yes. Home." She headed toward the house and my shoulders slumped forward. I thought we had turned a corner. Perhaps I was wrong.

As she approached the steps, she halted. Clenching her fists, I could almost sense an internal struggle going on between her head and her heart. Her shoulders rose and fell, and she spun around towards me. "Aren't you coming?"

Chapter Eighteen

Worth The Wait

Mackenzie

"THIS WAY," TYLER SAID to me that evening as we emerged from his company's jet and headed toward the flight operation base at Brownsville airport. "I have a car waiting."

"Wait." I stopped. "I parked my car at one of the long-term lots."

"I'll have Eli arrange to get it to you." He gestured to Eli, who nodded in agreement. It seemed peculiar to be standing between these two men again, as if no time had passed at all, as if things were back to how they were before I found out the truth. Eli's eyes were trained on me, a soft expression on his face. I could almost see the apology etched there, as if he hoped I wouldn't hold a grudge against him for his role in the assignment, and I knew I couldn't. He was simply following orders. I couldn't blame him for that. But wasn't Tyler doing the same thing? Would I be considered a hypocrite if I forgave Eli and not Tyler?

"Mackenzie?" Tyler interrupted my thoughts.

"Fine. It's not the same car, though."

He looked surprised. "You bought a new car?"

I avoided his eyes. "Not exactly."

"Then what?"

I placed my hands on my hips in frustration. I knew I

would have to eventually tell Tyler about what his mother had done for me, but I was dreading it. I was worried he would think everything fell apart when he left, and that I couldn't function without him in my life. That wasn't the case at all.

"Mackenzie, just tell me."

"Fine," I exhaled. "Your mom paid me a visit to apologize for you being a prick. Then she saw you knocked me up and must have seen the huge stack of overdue bills on my kitchen table. So she paid off the loan on the restaurant and my mortgage. She's also covering all my medical expenses, and bought me a new car that could fit a baby seat." Spinning on my heels, I stormed away from him and toward the waiting SUV.

The driver reached for the door, about to open it, when Tyler rushed forward. I was waiting for him to press the issue, to ask questions I didn't feel like answering. Much to my surprise, he simply held the door for me.

"Allow me," he said.

Studying him, I finally stepped back and permitted him to help me into the SUV. As he did, his hand brushed against my stomach. His stature tightened immediately. I met his gaze, a look of unease and bewilderment on his handsome face.

Smiling, I grabbed his hand in mine and placed it against my stomach. "It's okay." Our eyes remained locked as I kept my hands glued to his, hoping he would see I wanted him to be a part of this. Time seemed to stand still and, for that short moment, I was no longer concerned with all the lies he had told me. We were us again...the real us. The us I missed. The us I loved. The us I hoped we could be again.

There was a small flutter in my stomach and I couldn't help but feel as though this was supposed to happen. "I think he knows his daddy's here," I murmured, breaking the perfect silence.

"Really? Why do you say that?"

"I think he's kicking." I removed my hands from on top of his, feeling the sides of my stomach.

"What does it feel like?" he asked, mesmerized. His breathing grew heavier and I knew he was in the moment. I had the same reaction the first time I felt it. Before then, it hadn't really sunk in that this was real, even after seeing the ultrasounds and hearing the heartbeat. But that first flutter… Words were insufficient to properly convey the depth of awe I felt.

"Like a flutter of butterflies," I explained, "but more intense. It's almost like…"

"Yes?" he whispered, bringing his body closer to mine.

I exhaled, a satisfied smile crossing my face at the irony of it all. "Like lightning."

Tyler swallowed hard, his breathing shallow. Our eyes locked and I saw the longing within. Licking his lips, he slowly lowered his head toward mine. My heart raced in my chest and I could have sworn I heard it echoing around us.

His breath on my skin tingled my senses, reminding me how much I craved him. Even the most innocent of touches sent me reeling, never wanting to be separated from him again. I closed my eyes, lost in the moment. I wanted his kiss, but I didn't. I pined for it, but I knew I shouldn't. When his lips brushed against mine, I moaned, my taut stature relaxing.

I had dreamt of this precise moment for months. Hearing his voice in my sleep, imagining his skin on mine… His voice murmuring his deepest and darkest desires had seemed so real. Now it finally was. But was I so weak to let him think he could just waltz back into my life without suffering any ramifications for what he had done to me? It wasn't supposed to be this easy.

Subduing my urges, I pressed my hands against his firm chest and pushed him away.

He flung his eyes open, confused and a bit disoriented. "Mackenzie…"

"Tyler…," I said simultaneously.

"What is it?" he whispered.

"I just… I can't." I sighed, fumbling to explain why I wanted to be us again, but just not yet. "It's too soon. You want to start from the beginning again? I do, too, but it's going to take time for me to forget everything. I need to learn who you are. I don't want to go to bed with the Tyler who broke my heart. I want to go to bed with the Tyler who would walk through fire for me. I need to get to know *that* Tyler. The two weeks we were together were the best of my life…until the bottom dropped. We loved hard and fast. I don't want to make the same mistake again. I don't want to rush this. I need to learn to like you before I can give you my heart again. If you keep kissing me like that, I won't be able to stop at just a kiss. I'll want it all and I can't help but think it won't end well for us."

Despite his apparent disappointment, he pulled away from me, respecting my wishes. Grabbing my hand in his, he placed a chaste kiss on it. "At least you're not saying no."

Pulling my hand from his, I tried to subdue the butterflies flapping in my stomach at the sexy, coy look on his face. "I'm not saying yes, either."

"Not yet, but you will," he murmured against my ear, causing a spine-tingling chill to rush through me.

I had missed those chills.

~~~~~~~~~~

"ELI WILL BE DROPPING your car off within the hour," Tyler said, hanging up his cell phone as the chauffeured SUV pulled into the parking lot of my condo. "He can bring your keys up to you or leave them at the front desk. Whichever you'd prefer."

"The front desk is fine. I'm planning on pouring myself a glass of sparkling water and soaking in the tub."

"Tired?"

"Growing a human is a lot of work." I smiled at him as he leapt out of the SUV, running around to open my door for me.

I held out my hand for him and was caught breathless when he grabbed my waist and lifted me from the back seat. I remained suspended off the ground for several long moments, simply staring down at him, his smile wide. It felt like my first crush all over again…the excitement, the unexpected. I never wanted to stop living in this moment. Earlier this morning, I was furious with him, but his patience and initiative to share even the deepest and darkest parts of his soul spoke to me on another level. With each brush of his skin on mine, each tender word, each caring gesture, I felt my resolve begin to crack. His mother's words continued to play on repeat in my subconscious, urging me to consider forgiving him because he needed it and not because he deserved it.

My feet slowly met the ground, our gaze still locked. "Thanks," I whispered.

"You bet, princess. I need to make sure you have your footing. You are carrying precious cargo, after all." He winked and grabbed my hand, walking beside me toward the building.

Wyatt bolted up from his desk when he saw Tyler and me enter. "Sir," he said curtly, taking purposeful steps across the lobby towards us. "Your brother called and apprised me of the situation. The team is on standby and

178

is happy to stay at their posts."

I tore my hand from Tyler's and took a few steps away from him, a chill washing over me once more. Crossing my arms, I glowered at him. "Team? There's a team? I knew about Wyatt because he told me, but there's more?"

Tyler let out a long breath. "I meant to tell you on the flight home, but I guess I was enjoying our conversation and didn't want to bring up anything that would ruin it."

"Well, now I know, so start talking," I hissed.

"This is Martin," he said, gesturing to the built older man standing next to him who I had known as Wyatt. "He's Alexander's version of Eli."

"We've met, but I thought he was the only one! How many others?"

"Six total on your protection team," he said sheepishly.

"Six?!" I exclaimed in disbelief, wondering how I could have missed *six* people watching my every move and spying on me.

He sighed, apparently unsure of how to handle my outburst. "After everything went down, I didn't know what to do. I wanted to give you space, then Alex came to me with a new assignment. The thought of abandoning you, of not being there to look out for you and ensure your safety... I couldn't stomach it. The only reason I ended up taking the assignment was because Alexander promised you would be better protected than the president. It's been the only thing that's given me some sort of peace of mind over the past few months."

I remained speechless, absorbing his words.

"Like I told you earlier, Mackenzie. I never let you go."

Staring between Tyler and Martin, I straightened my spine. "Who are the others?"

"Three of your new employees at the restaurant,"

179

Tyler admitted, running his hand through his hair.

My eyes widened. "How? I do all the hiring!"

"We made sure their qualifications were such that you couldn't say no," Martin offered.

"Who?"

Tyler hesitated briefly. "Chris, one of your line cooks; Gretchen, a server; and your bar manager, Kevin."

I gasped. "Kevin?"

He nodded.

"Okay. Who else?" I couldn't believe I hadn't seen it all earlier. I thought Kevin was sucking up to me and that's why he always seemed concerned with how I was doing.

"Did you notice the new guy working the front desk at your gym?"

I nodded.

"And I'm sure you noticed a new personal trainer there who tried to hound you?"

I nodded once more.

"That's it, plus Martin."

I stood, dumbfounded, unsure of what to think of Tyler's confession. I knew Wyatt...Martin was keeping an eye on me, but everyone else? I didn't know why it made me feel as if I was being lied to all over again, but it did. And I hated that feeling. I hated wondering what else Tyler was keeping from me.

"I see," I finally said, turning and continuing across the lobby toward the elevator.

"Wait! Mackenzie!" Tyler shouted, running after me. "You're not mad, are you? I just—"

I spun around, my eyes fierce, anger pooling in my veins.

His expression turned pleading as he attempted to reach for my hand. I ripped it from his grasp, refusing to fall under the spell his touch had on me.

"I couldn't let you go, Mackenzie," he said softly. "I needed to make sure *someone* was looking out for you wherever you were."

I glared at him as the elevator dinged, announcing its arrival. His confession hanging in the air, I entered the car.

Just as the doors were about to close, leaving Tyler behind, I huffed. "Well, are you coming or not? I didn't realize you needed a written invitation." I allowed a small smile to cross my face.

"Yes, ma'am!" Tyler beamed back, jumping into the elevator right before the doors closed and it began to ascend to the twelfth floor.

"You're not mad, are you?" he asked softly, breaking the silence.

I sighed, leaning against the wall. "No, Tyler. I'm not mad. Perhaps a little irritated or annoyed, but not mad. You just need to start being open with me. I don't want you to wait to tell me things until you have to and are on the spot. I don't want things to be like that between us. After everything, I need you to be honest with me. No lies. No keeping information from me. I want to learn to trust you again, Tyler, but I can only do that if I know I'm getting full disclosure from you. Okay?"

"Okay," he said, grinning a mischievous grin at me.

I scrunched my eyebrows. "What?"

"Nothing," he replied, shoving his hands in his pockets, his grin growing wider as he rocked on his feet. His dimples popped and I almost heard a whimper escape my mouth at how adorably sexy he looked at that moment.

"Tell me!" I pinched his side. He grabbed my hand and before I knew it, he had me pinned against the wall and was hovering over me. My breath caught, my patience with taking things slow wearing thin.

"Us," he murmured, nuzzling my skin with his nose.

"What?" I breathed.

"You said 'us'. I can't tell you how that makes me feel."

The elevator dinged and I pushed against him, exiting into the corridor. Glancing over my shoulder, I smirked. "Out of that whole conversation, that's the *only* thing you're taking away from it?"

"No," he said. "I get what you're saying. I will be nothing but an open book with you from this moment forward, regardless of the consequences. But that word..." A wide smile crossed his face. I tried to hide my own smile at the excitement that seemed to ooze from every inch of him. "It gives me hope that I didn't fuck up the best thing that's ever happened to me."

"You've got a long way to go, Mr. Burnham."

"I know. But if my memory serves me correctly, something tells me the wait will be worth it." He raised his eyebrows, his eyes raking over my body in a devious way.

His persistence shouldn't have come as a surprise to me. It was one of the things that attracted me to him in the beginning. He saw me as a challenge back then. I could only assume he saw me the same way now. Despite wanting to take things slow, it was oddly comforting to have him here with me, to feel his warmth approach behind me as I unlocked my door. I felt more safe and at ease than I had in months.

I stepped through the foyer and into the living area, clicking on the lights. When I sensed Tyler was no longer behind me, I spun around to see him hesitating just past the doorway, eyeing my security alarm panel.

Crossing his arms in front of his chest, his expression turned concerned. "Please tell me the only reason you didn't arm your system was because you simply forgot."

I continued into the kitchen, grabbing a bottle of water from the refrigerator, and shrugged. "Everything's been fine, Tyler. No break-ins." Taking a sip of my water, I faced him. He took strong, determined steps into my open living area, his presence filling the room in an almost intimidating manner, his gaze unrelenting.

"Anyway…" I sat down on my couch. "It seems you've had someone keeping an eye on me, so I don't really see why it matters."

"It's not just yourself you have to worry about now, Mackenzie." His face softened as his eyes traveled to my stomach. He sat down beside me. "Don't get me wrong." He took my water from me and placed it on the coffee table. Clutching both my hands in his, he continued, "I can't bear the thought of anything happening to you, but there's a lot more at stake now so, please, do me a favor and arm your system. It'll make me feel better. Can you do that?" He furrowed his eyebrows, a pleading look on his face. From the beginning, he had always been fiercely protective of me. It was one of the things that drove me crazy and made me all the more attracted to him at the same time. Still, he had a point. It wasn't just me anymore. What if someone broke in after the baby was born? I didn't even want to think about that possibility.

A look of resignation crossing my face, I nodded. "Okay. I promise I'll use the system again."

"Thank you." He kissed my temple softly, then got up. "Well, everything here appears safe and secure. Good night, Mackenzie." Smiling, he retreated from me, pulling the door open.

"Wait!" I followed him. "When can I see you again?"

"Tomorrow."

"When tomorrow?"

He reached for my hand and brushed his lips against it, reigniting the longing I felt from his absence. "You'll

183

find out." He winked. Just as he was about to close the door and leave me alone with nothing but my thoughts, he popped back into my condo. "I almost forgot." He pulled a black journal out of his cargo shorts and handed it to me. "I want you to have this."

Taking it in my hands, I ran my fingers over the leather, lingering over the gold embossed letters T.J.B. "What's this?"

"Earlier today, you said you thought I forgot about you and that's why I never wrote or called. I knew this wasn't something that could be settled with a phone call or letter. I'm pretty sure you would have hung up on me, or tore up whatever I wrote you. But that didn't stop me from wanting to tell you what I was feeling. That's what's in this journal... Four months of heartache."

I looked up at him, seeing the broken version of Tyler I had seen on occasion, particularly early on in our relationship when he spoke of Melanie. And I knew... I knew the distance between us tore him up more than any other heartache he had suffered in his past.

He grabbed my free hand in his and held it over his heart. "It's yours, Mackenzie. It always has been. And these pages will prove it."

~~~~~~~~~~

Dear Mackenzie,

I guess it's better than writing "Dear diary", as if I were some pre-pubescent girl pouring her heart and soul out to a pretty pink journal. But there are some similarities here, I guess. I am pouring my heart out. It's been two weeks since I last saw you. Fourteen nights I've been forced to fall asleep without listening to your breathing. 336 hours since I last felt your skin on mine. 20,160 minutes since I saw your beautiful, perfect smile.

I don't expect you to ever forgive me for what I did, but I do hope you might understand one day why I did what I did. There's really no excuse for it, other than pride, a desire to be accepted, to prove I wasn't a failure. And you had to pay the ultimate price…as did our love.

It was love, of that I am certain. It was for me anyway. Yes, it was messy, chaotic, and wild, but aren't the best love affairs just that? I loved you without abandon, with every last cell in my body, with every last beat of my heart. And I still love you.

When I first laid eyes on you, I felt as if I already knew you, and it wasn't just because I had studied up on who you were. Watching you walk along the shoreline in the moonlight and look at the stars as if they held all the answers to the questions you were too scared to ask, well… Something sparked inside me. Something I thought I gave up on years ago. Hope. You're my hope, my dream, my light in a world of darkness.

But life isn't supposed to be easy… Love isn't supposed to be easy, but it was for us. I loved you fast and hard. You possessed my heart before you even muttered a single word to me. And the hardest thing I ever had to do was watch you walk away from me because I still love you. I wake up each morning with an ache in my chest, a hole in my heart… A piece that I gave to you and don't want back.

I miss you, Mackenzie. Every hour of every day. I miss you in the morning when I have my coffee. I miss you in the afternoon as I attempt to teach these refugee children how to play one sport or another. I miss you the most at night when the world is quiet, barely a sound to be heard for miles and miles. I stare at the sky, the stars more brilliant than anything I can remember. Silence surrounds me, reminding me you're not here to fall asleep next to me, and my heart aches a little bit more.

I should have treasured each and every moment I had with you. From the beginning, I knew our time was fleeting and I took it for granted. I was so consumed with trying to protect my heart from what I knew would inevitably happen, I squandered what precious time we had together, and I'll never do that again.

I know hearing the words "I'm sorry" won't fix this, but I intend to prove to you that I truly am sorry for what I did. I just pray I eventually have the opportunity to do so.

Until then, I love you, my lightning strike.

Tyler's words consumed me as I lay in bed long into the early morning hours, surrounding myself with his thoughts, his emotions, his love... It was like a blanket wrapped around me, keeping me safe and secure. With each simple gesture...from being patient as I worked through whether I could learn to trust him again, to his beautiful words, to the bewilderment in his eyes when he felt our baby...I was remembering all the reasons I had allowed him into my heart all those months ago.

The realization washed over me like a wave. It wasn't the Tyler I originally thought he was whom I had let into my heart, my soul, my life... It was *this* Tyler. The Tyler who swore he was a broken man. The Tyler who thought he lost me. The Tyler who *did* lose me because I was too blind with anger to see the truth. His love was as real and pure as anything I had ever experienced, as was mine.

Picking up my cell phone, I hastily typed a text to Tyler, punching in the new number he had given me earlier in the day.

I love you.

I waited with bated breath for a response. One arrived almost instantly, causing a brilliant grin to spread across my face.

I know. I loved you even before I truly knew what love was. Love is you. Your smile. Your heart. Your patience. Sleep well. Te queiro, mi cariño.

Chapter Nineteen

Scared

Mackenzie

WITH A RESTORED SENSE of belonging, I drove through the streets of South Padre Friday evening to meet Jenna and Brayden for girls' night. The island again held the promise and magic it did months ago, and I knew it was because Tyler was back. As I went about my routine throughout the day, I did so with him on my mind. I had hoped he would stop by the restaurant, but he didn't. Instead, we sent text after text to each other. With each message that popped up on my phone, my grin grew wider and wider. The butterflies were back after their long absence. His words were sweet, passionate, and even a little hot, reminding me of why I had lowered my walls and allowed him in after years of remaining distant with people.

Pulling up to the tapas bar, I threw the valet the keys to my brand new Audi and entered the restaurant. As I walked through the glass doors, I grew breathless, the scene that greeted me reminding me of that fateful Friday night when I first met Tyler. He sat in the corner, on the same barstool, a dark liquid in a tumbler in front of him, five cherry stems on his napkin. He wore the same green shirt with the sleeves rolled up to his elbows, exposing his muscled forearms.

As I stood admiring him, I noticed his physique had

become more pronounced. His shoulders appeared broader, his leg muscles incredibly defined. His skin was a tad darker than I recalled, and the ends of his dark hair were lighter. I could only assume all that time in the African desert had an effect on his appearance...in a good way. He was more rugged, the slight stubble on his jaw causing a burning need inside me to feel it on my skin.

I approached the bar and sat next to him. He looked at me, an excited smile on his face before his expression flattened. "Mackenzie, you can't sit there."

Straightening my spine, I asked, "Why?"

"I want to go back to the start, where it all began. You say you want to trust me, and I really, *really* want you to trust me, but we need to start over. I need to show you how that first night would have gone if I wasn't on a job. So, please, sit in your normal seat and pretend you don't know me, okay?"

Slowly lowering my legs back to the ground, I slid off the barstool. "Well, you better hurry up. Brayden and Jenna will be here any minute."

"Since when are they on time?" he commented sarcastically, and I shrugged my shoulders in agreement. I loved my friends dearly, but punctuality was not their strong suit. "I have some time to work with." A mischievous grin spread across his face.

A flurry of jitters rushing through me, I retreated from him and took a seat at my usual barstool.

The bartender approached, beaming, asking me what I wanted to drink. I glanced at Tyler, seeing he had ordered the same exact thing he did all those months ago, right down to the number of cherry stems. But I couldn't exactly order a bottle of wine, as I had that night.

"A bottle of sparkling water, please," I said with a

smirk on my face.

She retreated from me momentarily to get my drink. Within seconds, she reappeared with a tall green bottle and a wine glass. Opening the bottle, she poured a bit into the glass and garnished it with a lime.

When she left me alone once more, I took a sip, my body alive with anticipation.

"You gonna drink that whole bottle by yourself?"

Glancing to the far corner of the bar, I couldn't help but laugh. "So what if I am?" I shot back, trying to revert to the cold-hearted, detached woman I was that night. However, that wasn't who I was anymore. I was no longer the girl who would live her life in accordance with her schedule. I was a woman who finally learned to live again, who took risks, who loved, who jumped...who was all in.

"Didn't mean anything by it," he said, toying with the cherry in his drink. "My apologies."

My eyes remained glued to him, waiting for his next move. Looking up from his drink, a brilliant smile crossed his face. "My name's Tyler," he said, scooting down several seats and holding his hand out to me.

I surveyed it skeptically, a nervous tingling spreading through me. I didn't know if I was supposed to shake it or not.

"It's just a hand. See, what happens is—"

"Serafina," I interrupted, allowing him to take my hand in his. "My name is Serafina." My chin began to quiver as the name left my lips. It wasn't until this moment that I realized not only did Tyler cover up his true identity from me, but I did, as well. He wanted me to fall in love with the real Tyler. I wanted him to fall in love with Serafina, even if I wasn't sure who that was anymore. Still, I wanted to find out, and maybe Tyler would help me discover exactly who that was.

"Serafina," he crooned, his voice barely audible. Closing his eyes, his fingers lingered over my hand and traced a delicate pattern on my skin. "That's a beautiful name."

"Thank you," I murmured, lost in the moment. All too soon, he withdrew his hand from mine, leaving me with an empty feeling.

"So...," he began, nervously playing with the ice in his drink. "What do you do?"

"Ummm...," I started, feeling my face flush red with nerves. For some reason, regardless that Tyler already knew all my secrets, I wanted to make a good "first impression". Something about being there with him, getting to know him all over again, made it feel like the first time. "I own a restaurant."

His eyes widened. "Really? You look too young."

I shrugged. "I guess you can say I'm your classic overachiever. When I put my mind to something, nothing will get in my way. So when I said I wanted to open my dream restaurant before I turned thirty, it would have taken a disaster for it not to happen."

He nodded, remaining silent. I took a sip of my sparkling water, my eyes never straying from his for too long. "So what about you?" I finally asked. "What do you do?"

"Oh, a little bit of this, a little bit of that."

I frowned playfully.

He smirked. "Actually, I own a multi-billion dollar private security firm."

"Are you, like, a spy?" I joked.

"No. My brother's the spy."

"Your brother?"

"Yeah," he said. "He runs the company. Up until a few years ago, I was just an owner on paper, then I thought I could help make a difference."

"And did you?"

He tore his gaze from mine, an unsettled expression on his face. "The opposite, actually. I realized that no matter if it's for what you're led to believe is a noble cause or not, there are always some casualties. Not everyone gets out unscathed." He was silent for a moment as I tried to adjust to his sudden change in demeanor. He was troubled, a tortured soul.

"You see, I hurt someone during the last job I was on, and I'll never forgive myself for what I did." He raised his eyes and I saw the torment he had been living with since the day he began the mission. I had seen that look on his face during our time together, and I knew he was struggling early on with his assignment. I had seen it on that first night at this precise restaurant. That knowledge made me relinquish yet another piece of my heart to Tyler.

"I'm sure you didn't mean to," I offered, my voice soft.

"No. I knew all along that I was going to use her, yet I still did it."

"Yes, but once you got to know her, it must have been eating you up inside, knowing the role you had to play." Part of me couldn't believe I was sitting here, rationalizing what Tyler had done to me, but I couldn't help it. I finally understood. I felt his pain, his reluctance, his heartache for the role he played.

"Yet I still continued on in my course of deceit. I made her fall in love with me. I pretended to be someone I'm not." He returned his gaze to his tumbler, toying with the liquid. "I guess part of me doesn't really know who that is anymore..."

"I know who you are," I whispered.

His head shot up and he stared at me. "How could you? We just met."

I turned in my barstool to face him. He mirrored my

movements.

"You like to give off the impression you have everything under control, that nothing really affects you. You've loved and lost before, and you remember how broken you felt afterwards. You vowed to do everything to never feel like that again."

I reached for his hands and it was as if the world disappeared. We weren't sitting at the bar of a bustling restaurant, plates and glasses clinking all around us. We were in our own world, our own universe. A universe that circled around him.

"You love your family and would do anything for them. That's why you took that assignment. You had wandered listlessly through life, unable to figure out what your passion truly was. You tried a little bit of everything, even joined the navy to forget the past. When this assignment was brought to you, you thought it was your chance. You wanted to prove to your brother that you were capable of doing something right. You wanted to make him proud of you, but you never expected to be faced with having to decide between your family and a woman you had just met. Maybe if you had talked to her about it, had been open and honest with her, she would have understood."

"I doubt that," he said, pulling his hands from mine and avoiding my gaze. "Anyway, if I told her, it would have blown my cover." He returned his attention to the drink in front of him, playing with the cherry once more.

"But didn't your cover get blown anyway?" I pushed.

"Yes, but—"

"So you had nothing to lose." Placing my hand on his leg, I tried to comfort him. "If you had been honest with her, if you helped her see everything from where you were standing, she would have said those words you're so desperate to hear right now." A lone tear fell down my cheek, the connection between us more intense than any other interaction we'd had since we met.

"And what's that?"

"That I understand and I forgive you." Raising my hand to his face, I cupped his cheek, reveling in the feeling of his stubble on my hand. I studied the anguish he tried to mask with his forceful demeanor and hesitated. No matter how much I didn't think I could ever forgive him for how he had deceived me, I was wrong. His mother's wise words rang true. We didn't forgive people because they deserved it. We forgave because they needed it, and if anyone was in need of forgiveness so they could move on, the suffering man sitting next to me was. "Tyler…" I took a deep breath. "I understand and forgive you."

"You do?" he asked. I could hear the surprise in his voice. "You don't have to say that for my benefit. I know we have a lot to work through—"

"Yes, we do, but I finally see everything from where you stood, Tyler. For the longest time, I refused to do that, despite everyone telling me I needed to. I was so angry with you and wanted to hate you, as difficult as it was. But listening to your side, finally *listening*, it made me put myself in your shoes. I know this assignment got out of hand for you. You weren't expecting to fall for me."

"No," he agreed. "I certainly wasn't. I hated myself for what I had to do to you, especially once I met you. That first night, when I finally felt you, I couldn't sleep. All I saw whenever I closed my eyes was your face, the tears I would cause when you found out I used you. Then something entirely unexpected happened."

"What was that?"

"I stopped being the Tyler persona I developed to make you fall for me and started to show you the real me."

"I know," I admitted. "I finally realized that last night when I was reading your journal."

He nodded. "I don't know why. I didn't want you to just know the deceptive me. I wanted you to know the *real* me."

"And I do," I said, running my fingers through his hair. Leaning my forehead on his, I closed my eyes. This moment was so much more than I expected. Words couldn't accurately convey the depth of emotion I was feeling from being back in a place that once held painful memories of what I thought to be my biggest mistake. Now I had a new memory...a happier one. I was so grateful Tyler knew enough to realize I needed this.

Lost in the moment, I instantly felt an emptiness. Flinging my eyes open, I saw that Tyler had pulled away from me and was fishing money from his wallet.

"What are you—"

Returning his blazing green eyes to me, he reached for my hand and raised it to his lips. "It was wonderful to meet you, Serafina. I do hope our paths cross again."

With a heated stare, he released my hand. I remained dumbfounded, confused as to why he was so abrupt to leave. I thought we had just made so much progress.

Finally snapping back to reality as his chiseled backside walked out the door, I leapt from the barstool and stormed out of the restaurant, spotting Tyler as he was about to hop into his Jaguar.

"That's it?" I shouted.

He halted and looked over his shoulder, meeting my eyes.

"Seriously? After all that, you're just going to walk away from me?"

Signaling the valet to give him a minute, he strode toward me. Each step he took was slow, determined, his gaze fierce. "I'm not walking away. I'm just..."

"You're what?" I crossed my arms in front of my chest and leaned against the brick of the building, quickly transported back to that night all those months ago once more.

"I had a plan for how tonight was supposed to go, and..." He trailed off, avoiding my eyes. The dominant man I once knew was nowhere, the guilt he was still living with covering his body. I didn't want him to live with that guilt. I wanted him to finally feel like he was in control of his life again. I wanted to give him back that control.

"And what, Tyler?"

"And it hurts, all right, Mackenzie? Looking into your eyes, I can't stop being reminded of your face when you learned the truth. It cuts me open and, no matter how many times you say you forgive me, I will never be deserving of it. I'll never be deserving of *you!*"

"So...what? You put on this whole act, you come back from wherever you were to win back my heart, but now that you have it, you don't want it because of what you did to lose me in the first place?"

"That's not it at all, Mackenzie, and you know it," he growled, catching me by surprise. It was as if he flipped the switch, had become more self-assured, more passionate, more...himself. "You want to know the truth?"

I nodded, unable to find my voice.

"I'm fucking scared, Mackenzie. This," he said, gesturing between our bodies, "scares me more than anything. I'm worried if I make one wrong move, say one wrong thing, you'll leave and not look back. So, yes, I had a plan for tonight, one to try and help you see who I really am, and—"

"And I told you! I *know* who you are! Some things can't be planned!" I exclaimed in complete exasperation,

195

surprised at my own words. "Some things just happen, Tyler." I softened my voice. "Sometimes the best things in life are those that are unplanned, unexpected." I looked down, my hands settling on my stomach. "Please... Let me in. Don't give up on us."

His breath caught and he mouthed *us* as he stared at me. Before I knew what was happening, he had his hands on my hips and lifted me up, forcing my legs around his waist. His eyes met mine, my heart racing at the feel of his body against mine. "Say it again," he growled.

"Us," I whimpered, turned on by his dominance and power.

"Again," he said, his voice still firm, as if the only thing that could chase the demons away was my voice saying that one singular word, assuring him there was hope.

"Us."

His stature relaxed slightly as he leaned in and pressed his mouth against mine. Sighing, I wrapped my arms around his neck, trying to pull him closer. His tongue forcefully met mine, as if my kiss alone could soothe his fears. I knew he needed this, needed this physical connection to me. The truth was, I needed it just as much as he did. I needed to know he was real, he was here, his love was real. It was euphoric, his mouth covering mine, his hands supporting me, letting me know he would never let go.

"Again," he murmured against my lips.

"Us," I whispered.

He groaned. "Again."

"Us. Us. Us."

He exhaled, the unease and torment that had plagued him seconds ago leaving him with each instance of me saying that word. And each time, it gave me the same thing it gave him... Promise.

He trailed soft kisses across my cheek, down my neck,

lingering on my collarbone. I threw my head back, a surge of electricity washing over me with each nip of his lips, each brush of his tongue. With each kiss, he was saying "I love you", "I cherish you", "I treasure you". I didn't need to hear his voice say those words. I just knew. Instead of simply declaring his love to me with mere words, he did what he had always done. He proved it with his benevolence, his passion, his desire.

A loud throat clearing sounded, startling both of us. Reluctantly, Tyler pulled away from me, helping me lower my feet to the ground. He smiled mischievously as he glanced at Brayden and Jenna standing just off to the side.

"Get a room!" Brayden joked.

"Brayden," Tyler said, nodding at him, shaking his hand. "Thanks for going along with everything tonight."

I looked between Tyler and my two best friends, who had guilty, yet satisfied expressions on their faces.

"This was planned?"

Tyler shrugged. "Yeah. I wanted to make sure I had a few minutes alone with you."

"We were a bit hesitant at first," Jenna added, crossing her arms in front of her chest. "After everything, we didn't want to see you get hurt again, but Brayden took care of that."

"How?"

"I told him I have ties to the gay mafia." He winked.

"Gay mafia?" I asked in disbelief.

"Yeah. Seriously, Mack. We've stood by your side through everything, but this schmuck made you happy for those two weeks. Then, when we saw the look of remorse on his face early this morning, well... I couldn't help but get a good feeling about this time around."

Tearing my gaze from my friends, I met Tyler's eyes. "Me, too."

He smiled back at me, planting a soft kiss on my forehead. It was the most innocent of exchanges, but that didn't stop those butterflies from erupting within my stomach at the feel of his warm lips on my skin.

Too soon, he pulled away and retreated toward where the valet attendant still stood next to his Jaguar. "Enjoy your evening, Mackenzie," he crooned, his eyes dark and full of longing.

"You're not going to stay?" I could hear the disappointment in my voice.

"No. It's girls' night." Returning to me, he grabbed my hand in his. "You need time to catch up and you can't do that with me around."

"When am I going to see you again?"

"Why? Missing me already?"

"No." I rolled my eyes in fake irritation.

Brushing a wayward curl behind my ear, he caressed my face.

"Okay, maybe a little," I admitted.

"Can I take you out to dinner tomorrow night?"

"On a date?" I asked coyly.

He nodded. "Yes. A proper date. No expectations for anything more. Just two people getting to know each other."

"I'd like that."

"Does seven work for you?" He raised his eyebrows.

"Yes."

He grinned. Bringing my hand to his lips, he murmured, "Until tomorrow, *mi cariño*." With that, he hopped in his car, leaving me completely satisfied and feeling as if things were going to be okay.

"You were totally eye-fucking him," Jenna commented as she pulled me into the restaurant, Brayden right on our heels.

"It's not eye-fucking if she already knows what the

goods look like," Brayden countered when we all took our normal seats at the bar.

"Says who?" Jenna retorted. "I still eye-fuck Richard and we've been married for a year!"

"Speaking of which," I said, sipping my sparkling water once more, trying to get the focus of the conversation off me. "How's everything going with you two?"

"Good. Better than good." She swirled the liquid in her wine glass that the bartender had just poured for her. "I took your and Brayden's advice and talked to him. He explained everything."

"What did he say about the lack of any record of his previous marriage?"

"Well, it was like you said. He agreed to give his ex-wife a very hefty settlement, but a contingent of doing so was her agreeing to have all records of their marriage and subsequent divorce completely expunged. I had always just assumed she served him with divorce papers, not the other way around."

"Why did he want that?" Brayden interjected.

"He said he didn't want one of the biggest mistakes of his life to always follow him around. He wanted a fresh start, a new beginning, and he didn't think he'd have that if his previous marriage and subsequent divorce were always lurking in the background. It was really kind of sad, listening to him talk about her. I was always hesitant to bring her up because I know all about wanting a fresh start, but…"

"Yeah?" I popped an olive in my mouth. "What is it?"

"I actually felt bad for him. He was more or less conned into marrying her. He was in his early forties when they met. She was in college."

"He's got a thing for younger girls, doesn't he?" Brayden commented, winking.

Jenna smiled, a small laugh leaving her lips. "Yeah, I guess he does. Anyway, they dated, but it wasn't anything serious. He said they were better off as friends, and that's what they remained for a few years. He was tapped to take over the entire hotel chain, and she continued with college. One day, he got a phone call from her and she was sobbing. He said he had never heard her so frightened."

"What happened?"

"She found out she was pregnant. When she confronted her boyfriend at the time, he split, disappearing into nowhere."

I glanced down, placing my hand over my stomach. I could certainly sympathize with how she must have felt. Although the circumstances were different, I knew what it felt like to think you were alone.

"She came from a very strict Irish Catholic family and she couldn't go home as she was unless…"

"She was married," I finished.

Jenna nodded. "And Richard, being who he is, agreed to the marriage. They had a small ceremony a few weeks later. He called it a blessing in disguise. He had been so busy with the hotels and building the brand, he never took a minute for himself or his personal life."

"Sound familiar?" Brayden mumbled under his breath, looking at me.

I shot my eyes to him and slapped him playfully.

"So he settled down with his new bride and began buying baby clothes. He couldn't wait to be a father. He didn't care that the kid wasn't technically his. He said that's not what makes someone a father… It's being there, supporting them, putting their needs above your own. And he was ready and willing to do that."

"But…"

Jenna took a deep breath. "About a month later, she

came home from her doctor's appointment and told him she lost the baby. She was upset, but he told her if she wanted to be a mother, they could try to have a kid themselves. They had trouble conceiving, and Richard became increasingly busy with the hotel. They would argue and Richard would suggest just stopping the whole charade, considering the only reason they married in the first place was because she had gotten pregnant and was worried about telling her parents. She didn't have that problem anymore. However, each time he was ready to walk away, she would tell him she was pregnant, but she kept losing the baby. Finally, after the fourth or fifth time, Richard grew suspicious and called her doctor, then a private investigator. He soon found out there was never a pregnancy, not even at the beginning. He realized this woman, Ariana, was simply after his fortune that was slowly growing as his hotel brand became more and more popular."

"That's why he was able to convince her to sign off on wiping the slate clean," Brayden interjected.

Jenna nodded. "Yes. Instead of facing a very public divorce based on who he was and everyone learning what she had done, he offered her a way out and she took it."

"Well," Brayden said, raising his own wine glass. We both followed suit. "Here's to both my girls being happy with the men they love once again."

"Here, here!" Jenna said.

"I'll drink to that."

Chapter Twenty

New Course

Tyler

EARLY SATURDAY MORNING, I parked my Bronco at the back of the club. I had been back on South Padre for less than forty-eight hours, but it was time to finally get back to work. There were still more questions than answers, even more so now that the CIA handler who had reached out and asked for our help with this case had been missing for several months. Was it connected? I didn't know, but it was a bit too suspicious.

Walking through the back door, I heard voices echoing down the hallway. I headed toward my office and entered, eight men and one woman immediately ceasing their conversation when they saw me. Scanning the room, I made mental notes of who everyone was. I had reviewed their files earlier that morning as I determined who I should keep and who I should send back. Apart from Eli and Martin, they were mostly new faces to me, except one...

Rage washing over me, I stalked toward a tall, muscular man of similar build. "You asshole!" I bellowed out, surprising everyone, Benson included, as I landed a harsh blow to his face.

He stumbled back, attempting to maintain his balance.

"We were on the same training team! We were *friends*!" I spat. "And this is how you repay me? You agree to fuck with her memory? I thought you were better than that!"

Straightening his spine, he wiped at his lip, smearing the bit of blood that was visible. "I did it for you, Tyler. Do you think I *liked* having to do that? I *hated* it. I knew you'd never forgive me for betraying you like that, but it was all about keeping her safe. From day one, everything we've done on this island has been to keep her out of harm's way."

"How?!" I shouted. "Please tell me how you staying at my house and telling her you've lived there for years could possibly keep her safe? If anything, it just confused her more!" I pulled back, about to take another swing when I was swiftly disabled and pushed against the wall.

"No plan is without its faults," Martin growled, restraining me. His eyes met mine as if he was trying to tell me there was no other way.

"My brother said the reason he gave the go-ahead on gaslighting her was to protect the integrity of the mission, to make her think she never met me, to protect *my* ass. He didn't mention anything about trying to protect Mackenzie."

"That was one of the reasons. We had to go through every possible scenario," he explained, releasing his hold on me once he grew confident I was no longer going to do Benson any more harm. "I was the only one who had been made aware of some of the details of the mission and I had to act quickly. My biggest concern was her safety and protecting her true identity. What was one way of putting her on the radar?" Martin asked.

"A police report," I mumbled under my breath. I had done my fair share of interfering with a few police investigations while working the case in order to keep her true identity hidden. I understood all too well.

"Precisely. What if she went to the police with everything? I knew it was a long shot, but I had to

203

consider the possibility. 'Hell hath no fury like a woman scorned.' I had to do everything within my power to ensure her true identity never made it into a public record of any kind. That could have been disastrous. What if, as you believe, her father's *not* behind all of this and someone else is trying to silence anyone and everyone who could prove his innocence? What if they found Mackenzie? I couldn't stand aside and do nothing. The best way for me to protect her was for her to doubt whether any of it happened, that she never met you. So don't blame your brother or Benson. Blame me," he said adamantly, straightening the lines of his dark suit. "He was simply following orders, just like you when you took this assignment."

I stood in place, absorbing Martin's words, as several pairs of eyes stared in nervous anticipation. If I could listen to and trust anyone in this room, other than Eli, it was Martin. He was practically family. He had been my father's right-hand man when he was still alive and running the company. Growing up, I couldn't really remember a day when I didn't see him at my father's side. After my father was killed on an assignment, Martin temporarily ran the company while we figured out what to do. When Alexander requested an honorable discharge and left his SEAL team to come run the company, we were all surprised. Suffice it to say, Martin knew what he was talking about. Despite not wanting to believe there could have been any valid reason to gaslight Mackenzie, maybe there was.

Taking a breath, I ran my hands over my face as I considered his words. He was right. Following orders and chain of command was all we had to make our missions and operations successful. Without it, there would be disorder, chaos. I knew I would do anything to protect Mackenzie. And Martin would, too, despite the effect it had.

"We okay?" Benson asked, slowly approaching me and extending his hand.

Eyeing him, I nodded, shaking it. "Yeah. We're okay."

"Well, good," Eli's voice cut through. "We're all ready to start if you are."

"Right." I took a seat at a large round table, everyone following my lead. "I know you have all been answering to Martin over the past several months." The agents surrounding me nodded. "Not anymore," I said, my voice firm and demanding, trying to demonstrate that I was in a position of authority. This was the first time I was leading a team this size. I had been part of protection teams in the past, but now that I was calling the shots, it was nerve-wracking. I was no longer following my brother's orders. The success or failure fell on my shoulders, and mine alone.

"Eli will be running point here. Everything goes through him. He has been working this assignment with me since day one and is the only one, other than me, who is fully aware of all the intricacies of this case. He'll bring you all up-to-date with what we know, so pay attention." I nodded to him.

Raising himself, Eli stood in front of the assembled team. Pressing a button on his laptop, an image of Mackenzie's father from his army days appeared on the large television monitor on the far wall. "This is Colonel Francis Mackenzie Galloway. He was our original target in this operation."

"Original?" Benson interjected.

Nodding, Eli said, "Yes. Galloway was thought to have been the mastermind behind hundreds of acts of treason against the United States, including selling military arms and secrets to known terror organizations, drug cartels, anyone who would pay top dollar. Allegedly, his defining act was the attack on the U.S. Embassy in Liberia almost seventeen years ago." A still of a charred building with dozens of bodies covered with dark blankets appeared on the screen.

"But you no longer think he's responsible?" Maxwell, an agent with blond hair and medium build, asked. It was apparent he was rather intrigued by what he was learning.

Glancing at me, Eli hesitated briefly, waiting for my permission to proceed. I nodded.

"We're not one hundred percent certain but, based on many suspicious events, we're exploring the possibility that Galloway wasn't the man behind any of these acts and was simply a scapegoat."

"But if he was accused of all those acts in the first place, why is this the first we're hearing about this guy?" Maxwell asked.

"We're not sure of the details, but we *do* know Galloway was presumed to have died in the embassy fire he was accused of setting. A subsequent investigation, led by the team at Army Counterintelligence he had previously commanded, found evidence of his misdeeds. Communications with foreign terror organizations and drug cartels. Wire transfers into off-shore accounts, which they were able to link to Galloway. However, someone issued a gag order. With many unanswered questions still lingering, the case was sealed and all agents who had been working on it were ordered not to discuss what they had found with anyone."

Returning his attention to his laptop, he pressed another button and Mackenzie's photo appeared on the screen. "This, as you all know, is Mackenzie Delano. She was born Serafina Galloway." Another image appeared on the monitor beside that of Mackenzie. "This is her mother, Magdalena Galloway. Shortly after the attack on the embassy, they went missing. A two-year search yielded nothing and it was assumed they were killed. Our theory is perhaps someone knew Galloway was being set up and needed to ensure his wife's and daughter's safety as a precaution."

Pausing, he took a sip from his water bottle and surveyed the members of our team, their eyes glued to him. "Fast forward eight years. During her first year of college, Mackenzie began to date this man." A photo of Charlie in his service uniform appeared on the screen. "This is Charles Patrick Montgomery. At this point, I'm sure you're all aware of who he is."

"Yes," a petite woman with auburn hair I recognized as Gretchen said. "He's wanted in connection with a string of murders."

"Correct," Eli replied. "He was working for Army Cryptology while he was dating Mackenzie and, from what we've been able to ascertain from his file and from Miss Delano, he was asked by an acquaintance to look into a missing person's case – one Serafina Galloway."

"Who was this acquaintance?" Martin asked.

"We don't know. There's certainly more questions than answers in this case and, unfortunately, the two people who could help fill in the blanks are in hiding. Now, it didn't take Montgomery long to figure out Mackenzie was Serafina Galloway and he approached her to verify this. They dated for most of the year until, one day, he was committed to the psych ward at Walter Reed, where he spent the next eight years being treated for schizophrenia. When he was being taken away, he warned Miss Delano of her mother's death. The following day, Miss Delano went home to find her mother was killed in a car crash."

"Have you determined whether there was a connection?" Kevin, an agent who looked more like a

207

playboy than a retired Marine, asked.

"Nothing firm. You'll soon learn that Montgomery's involvement here is open to two different interpretations and we're not entirely sure what to believe about him. So, as far as all things having to do with Charles Montgomery go, exercise an overabundance of caution. Now, back to what we *do* know. During all of this, keep in mind it was assumed Galloway was dead. It wasn't until about two years ago that intel surfaced indicating he was alive."

"And what was that intel?" Martin inquired.

"Unfortunately, we don't know. The CIA handler who had contacted the company to hire us to investigate all of this has now disappeared." Eli pressed another button on his laptop and a photo I had never seen before appeared. There was a distinguished-looking older man in all black staring at the camera, a forced smile on his face. "This is Benjamin Collins. We tried to find as much information about him as we could but, given he was working for the CIA, we were met with several dead ends. I couldn't access any information about his family or whether he has any sort of connection to Galloway. We are unsure of whether his disappearance has anything to do with this case, but we are operating under the theory that it does."

"So, what *is* your working theory then?" Martin asked.

"Well, this isn't set in stone, but here's what we think. Galloway is innocent. We think he was set up to take the fall for someone else, someone with power, either in the military or the government. This is why the investigation was stopped and a gag order was issued. At first, we thought we were getting too close to figuring it all out so Collins was abducted, perhaps by someone thinking they could squeeze him for information, but we don't think that's the case anymore. He's CIA and is trained to withstand days upon days of the most brutal interrogation techniques there are. We think he may have some sort of connection to Galloway and that's why he went missing, although we've been unable to find any link between them. Then there's Montgomery, the loose cannon. We have no idea whether he is responsible for the deaths of which he's accused or whether he's being set up, too."

"Now, the murders Montgomery's accused of...," Gretchen interrupted. "They seem random. Are they, or is that just the police not finding a connection?"

Eli nodded. "A little bit of both. Some were random, but some were connected, although the police could never find what that connection was, considering the file's been sealed. Montgomery was the sole survivor of the attack on the embassy attributed to Galloway. The theory is that he conspired with a man named Justin Whitman, more or less a hired gun, to carry out his plan of revenge against all those who took his family from him. Many of the murders attributed to Whitman and Montgomery were of several men and women who it was thought helped Galloway in his attack on the embassy, although it was never proven. Montgomery had top-level security clearance during his time in Cryptology and used this access and training to eliminate those who killed his family. It is thought his next target is Galloway and he would use Mackenzie to get to him. He escaped Walter Reed a little over four months ago and broke into Mackenzie's place, as did Whitman. Okay, that's one theory.

"The other, as you can probably guess, is that Montgomery stuck his nose somewhere he shouldn't have when he was working for Cryptology and paid with his freedom. Then, when it was discovered he had escaped Walter Reed, whoever is behind all of it wanted to find a way to silence him once more, preferably forever, and planted evidence to set him up for a ring of murders he had nothing to do with."

"But isn't it a bit suspicious that a number of people who helped to kill Mr. Montgomery's family were then killed?" Martin asked.

"This is true, which is why it is important we not settle on any theory when it comes to any of this, particularly in light of new information Tyler has."

All eyes turned to me and I nodded at Eli. He pressed a button, a photo of a man and woman in their sixties appearing on the screen. "These are Mr. Montgomery's alleged latest victims, Mr. and Mrs. Sheperd," I explained. "Emily Sheperd used to be Emily Mills before getting a divorce, then remarrying. At the time of the embassy attack, she lived next door to the Galloways. Incidentally, her former husband, Harrison Mills, disappeared several years ago. He simply never showed up for work one day. He had been estranged from his wife and family for years, so they were no help in finding him. After a year, he was assumed dead.

"Mills was close to Galloway, having served under him in the Rangers, then in Counterintelligence. In fact, after Galloway's disappearance, he was the one who had been tapped to lead the investigation into the embassy attack."

"Have you looked into him?" Benson asked.

"Yes. We believe he's a victim and not involved in any of this. Further, Harrison and his wife had a son together, Damian, who was Mackenzie's best friend growing up. Coincidentally, he hasn't been heard from since the day Montgomery was implicated in all those murders, adding yet another level of *what the hell is going on* to this case. Going forward, what we need to focus on is getting to the bottom of everything, finding out what really happened, including who's responsible. All of these pieces may lead us to the answer."

"Why don't you ask Galloway?" Martin asked, staring at me. "Sir, talk to the girl and convince her to take you to see her father."

I shook my head. "I've thought about it, but I just can't. I need you all to come up with a different course of action."

"I don't think we have one," Martin insisted. "From where I'm sitting, anyone else who may be able to offer help or information is missing, on the run, or dead, which is a bit suspicious, if you ask me. I don't think you have a choice. I think you need to do whatever it takes to finally talk to Galloway."

"But she knows I'm still working this case."

"True...," Eli offered, "but it's not the same case as before, Ty. A lot has changed, including our motive. You're not asking her so you can bring him to justice. You're doing this so you can help clear his name. I'm sure she wants nothing more than for her father to finally be able to come out of hiding."

"He may not know any more than we do."

"Still," Eli responded, "it's worth a shot. He may not think he can help, but maybe he has a missing piece that could bring all of this full circle."

I sat there, surveying my team members, their eyes intense. In truth, I knew this was a way to find out more information, but things had just gotten back to a new sort of normal with Mackenzie. I hated the idea that I had to do this so soon, which would certainly remind her of why I dated her in the first place, reopening old wounds.

Life sometimes forced you to make difficult decisions, and this was another one of those times. But Mackenzie had urged me to be open and honest with her about everything and I knew this was no different. I needed to see her father. I just hoped she understood and didn't think I was using her.

"Okay... I'll see what she says. In the meantime, everyone remain at your posts and keep an eye on Miss Delano," I ordered the six individuals who had been part of her protection detail. "Report anything suspicious to Eli immediately."

"What about us?" Benson asked, gesturing between himself and Maxwell, who had both been living at my house and were charged with convincing Mackenzie her reality was anything but.

"You two will track down everything you can about Charles Montgomery. While you're at it, dig up everything you can about Galloway, as well. I want to know every mission he was on when he was a Ranger, every case he worked in Counterintelligence. No detail is too small. I want to know what he ate. What he drank. How many hours he slept a night. There may be something in his background that could lead us to who's behind all of this."

"And what if he *is* the one behind it all?" Maxwell asked. "What if you're wrong?"

"I don't think I am, but *if* I am, I'm sure you'll find proof to back it up. We'll meet again in a week." I stood up and grabbed my things.

"Sir," they all said in relative unison. As I left my private office in the back of the club, I hoped this was the best course of action to uncover the truth of what really happened all those years ago.

Chapter Twenty-One

My Truth

Mackenzie

I SAT FIDGETING IN the seat of Tyler's Jaguar Saturday evening as he drove through the streets of South Padre. "So, what exactly do you have planned for tonight?" I asked, breaking the silence.

"You'll see," he replied, winking slyly. He grabbed my hand in his and shifted through the gears, a buzz in the air between us as I drank him in. His tan suit fit him perfectly. I was convinced it should be a crime for anyone to look that good in a suit. I couldn't tear my eyes away from him during the drive to wherever we were going.

When he finally pulled into a sandy beach lot, my mouth dropped open as my eyes fell on the same restaurant where we shared that first lunch when I barely knew anything about him.

"What are we doing here?" I asked.

He killed the engine and turned to face me. "We're making new memories."

"What do you—"

"I don't want you to be reminded of my lies whenever you look at certain places."

"I'm not…"

He narrowed his gaze at me. "I know how it is, Mackenzie. I do it, too. I want you to have better memories of us. I need those, too. Every time I drive by this restaurant, I don't want to be reminded of the reason I took you here in the first place. I want to be reminded of new memories that we'll make tonight. Okay?"

Nodding, I smiled. "I'd like that."

Opening the door, he ran around to the passenger side of his car and helped me out. Before I could react, he pulled my body to his, taking me by surprise. "You look amazing, Serafina," he growled, his tongue exploring my neck.

My eyes fluttered closed as I lost myself in the moment, not caring that we were out in public. I wanted nothing more than to go back to my place and finally experience Tyler once more. It had been so long since I had felt his body move in perfect harmony with mine, and I was desperate to be consumed by that mind-blowing high only Tyler could give me.

"I love it when you call me that," I murmured, whimpering as his hands began roaming my body, the silken material of my black dress against my skin only heightening my awareness of him.

"And I like calling you that," he replied.

"Why don't you call me that all the time?"

He exhaled, running his fingers through my hair, forcing me to look into his eyes. "I can't. Not yet. Not until I know that no danger will come to you because of who you truly are. Until then, I only feel safe using your real name in private. Even then, I don't want to use it too much. I don't want to run the risk of getting used to it and slipping up. Okay?"

I remained entranced by his sincere green eyes, the sound of the crashing waves echoing in the distance.

"Okay," I agreed.

"Good. Hungry?"

I laughed. "Always."

He wrapped his arm around me, keeping me close and

steady on my impractical leopard-print stilettos, as we walked up the wooden steps to the restaurant.

We entered the building and I almost didn't recognize the place. Where I expected to be faced with the sound of dishes and lively conversation, I was met with beautiful music being played by a live band... The same band I had hired to play opening night at my restaurant.

Noticing my bewilderment, he placed his hand on my lower back and led me through the empty dining room. "This way, *mi cariño*."

We stepped onto the back deck and I saw that it had been cleared of all the tables except one...a cozy table set for two. I couldn't help but grin at the amount of thought Tyler put into this evening. I didn't want to even think what it cost him to convince the restaurant to close for the night just to accommodate us, but I was grateful he did. I needed this. I needed to be rid of the memory of our first lunch here. Instead, I wanted to look back at this place and this evening as the night we got our second chance.

After helping me into my chair, Tyler sat down opposite me, his eyes glued to mine. His gaze was the perfect combination of endearing and carnal, showing me that he revered me but also wanted me in such a way that he had never craved another human being.

"I hope you don't mind," he began, breaking the silence between us. "Not to sound selfish, but I kind of wanted it to be just us tonight. Is that okay?"

"It's too bad. I was really looking forward to having to talk loud just so you could hear me," I joked.

"I missed that smart mouth of yours," Tyler retorted, winking.

"Is that all you missed?"

He slowly shook his head. "No. Certainly not."

"Well, tell me. What else did you miss? Oh, I'm sorry,"

I added quickly. "I'm breaking the rules." Grinning, I bit my lower lip. "Truth or dare."

Tyler's expression grew wide before his face settled into a brilliant smile. He grabbed a bottle of sparkling water off the table and poured some for me and himself, then placed the bottle back on the table. "Are you sure you want to play this game, Mackenzie?"

"Tyler," I began, grasping his hand, "I don't want to forget *all* the memories I have of you. Do I want to start over? Of course, but I know I saw part of the real Tyler during those two weeks, particularly when you took me here for lunch and we started playing *Truth or Dare*. You've got a playful streak and that lunch was the first time I saw it. So I don't ever want to stop playing *Truth or Dare* with you."

He brushed his fingers across my knuckle just as a gentle breeze blew. There was a light humidity in the air, but it was unseasonably cool for the end of July, making it a pleasant evening to be sitting outside and enjoying a romantic candlelit dinner as we rediscovered us.

"So is that what you like about me? My playful side?"

Freeing my hands from his, I took a sip of water. "I like *all* the sides of you. I love those moments when I don't see the brooding, mystery man who picked me up at a bar back in March. Don't get me wrong. I love your dominance, even though I shouldn't."

"Why not?" he asked, rubbing his hands under his chin.

"I don't know. I swore I would always be the one in charge, that I would keep control over everything in my life…"

"And you do, Mackenzie. Even when I act dominant, as you call it, you still have all the control. You always have. Now, I think you were about to ask me a question." He winked as I considered his words.

He was right. It was the mystery and intrigue as to who Tyler was that first attracted me to him. I couldn't stop thinking about him. Then, it was his power and dominance which flamed my longing for him even more. But I held all the control from the beginning, even during our one night together. I had the power to walk away, but I couldn't, no more than I could now.

"Truth or dare?" I raised my eyebrows at him. Placing an olive on my tongue in a seductive manner, I saw his breathing grow shallow, his eyes glancing to the somewhat voluptuous cleavage of my halter dress.

"Truth," he replied, his gaze intense.

"What else did you miss about me while you were away?"

His expression turned light, clearing the intensity between us for a moment. "Your eyes. I missed peering into them, trying to unwrap all of your layers. There's a depth to you I saw that first night at the bar. I saw all the pain you were trying to bury under the façade you've put on the past few years. The hurt you still feel from having to hide who you truly are is painted in your eyes. I missed staring into them, trying to reassure you with my own eyes that everything would be okay, even if just for a minute."

"What else?" I asked, almost breathless from the unequivocal sincerity etched on his face.

"Your body."

I narrowed my gaze at him. "Oh really?"

He grinned. "Yes, really, but not like you're thinking. I missed the feeling of falling asleep next to you at night, knowing I was there to keep you safe from harm. I was halfway around the world and felt utterly helpless, regardless of all the assurances I had received that you were okay. I hated I wasn't there myself to make sure no one harmed you. It drove me crazy to have to step aside and let someone else take my place. I vowed once I was able to come home, I would do everything I could to return to where I belonged...by your side."

"What else?" I whispered, my throat heavy with the emotion I felt from his words.

"Your love, Mackenzie. I no longer felt it and I hated myself for squandering the most precious gift anyone could give another person... Their love. I didn't deserve your love then, and I'm not sure I deserve it now, but I promise you..." He grabbed my hand in his, his tone sincere, his eyes fierce. "I will do everything in my power to make you believe in me, in my love for you. This is so real for me, and I will spend every day from now until I'm old and gray proving it to you."

"Tyler...," I quivered, struggling to fight back my tears from his impassioned plea. "You broke my heart."

"I know and—"

"But," I interrupted, holding my hand up, "over the past few days, you've slowly put all the pieces back together. Even after all the heartache and tears, I will still choose you each and every time. It's not even a choice for me. Our course was charted, even though the path was one of deception and lies. But through those lies, I found my truth. *You're* my truth. That's all I need." It made no sense that I should be sitting here with him after everything he put me through, especially so soon, but what we had was so much bigger, so much stronger. I felt it from the very beginning. And I still felt it now.

"I was hoping you'd say that," he said, breaking the tension between us. "Eli was getting tired of having to spoon with me."

I laughed just as a server approached our table with two plates, placing them down in front of us. There were three small portions of some sort of meat topped with a gourmet vegetable salsa, a hint of dark gravy drawn in a whimsical pattern on the outskirts of the plate. I had no idea what it was, but it looked delicious. "Roasted duck with leek and fennel salsa, sir." She retreated, leaving us to enjoy our appetizer.

"I don't think I've ever had duck before," I commented, picking up my fork and cutting into it.

"Well, I know you like seafood, but I did my research and found out you're limited to how much and what kind of fish you can have when you're pregnant."

I glanced at him, surprised. "You did research?"

"Of course. I have to admit, I have no idea how you appear so calm about this. If I were a few months away from squeezing a bowling ball through a tiny straw, I'd be shitting bricks."

"That's not even the worst part."

"Then, by all means, tell me what could possibly be worse than that!"

"Are you sure you want to know?" I raised my eyebrows.

"Of course. I'm in this with you, Mackenzie. I want to know everything. I missed the first four months and I plan on making up for that, even if it means running to the store in the middle of the night to get you watermelon and pickles."

"Watermelon and pickles?"

"Don't you have weird cravings?"

"Sometimes," I admitted, taking another bite of the duck. It was absolutely decadent, the texture almost melting in my mouth.

"Like what?"

"Hmmm..." I placed my fork on the table, trying to recall some of my weird cravings over the past few weeks. "Okay, here's one I hate to admit." He stared at me. "Spray cheese."

"Really?" He chuckled.

"Yeah. I always thought the stuff was absolutely revolting, but I was going through Brayden's cabinets one day and found some. I have no idea why he even had any, considering I'm pretty sure possessing that violates some gay code of ethics. But, dammit, that stuff was heaven in an aerosol can."

"And here I am trying to impress you with duck."

"Yeah," I said, shrugging my shoulders. "I'm a cheap date."

"Mackenzie, *mi cariño*, there is absolutely nothing cheap about you. And that's why I love being around you, even if you eat spray cheese."

We shared a look, the longing in his eyes causing my stomach to do somersaults. No man had ever gazed at me with the admiration and yearning Tyler did, and I doubted whether any other man ever would.

"So," he began, breaking his eyes from me and finishing off his appetizer. "Tell me what the worst part of being pregnant really is, like you were about to before we started talking about watermelon, pickles, and spray cheese."

"Six weeks," I said, observing his response.

"What do you mean?"

"Well, after I push this kid out of me, no sex for six weeks *at all*...like, nothing going on down there."

His jaw dropped and he was speechless for a moment before he recovered and swallowed hard. "I have a feeling that may just be the longest six weeks of my life."

"Mine, too."

~~~~~~~~~~

"DID YOU ENJOY YOUR dinner?" Tyler asked as I devoured the final spoonful of the strawberry cheesecake he had arranged for dessert.

I nodded, rubbing my stomach. "Yup. Baby boy is happy in there."

"How about Mama? Is she happy?"

"I am. Of all the first dates I've been on…"

Tyler scowled playfully in response.

"This is certainly one of the best."

"One of?"

"Well, I don't want to say it's *the* best just yet. It's still not over, is it?"

"It certainly isn't, *mi cariño*. This is just the beginning." As if on cue, the band faded out of the song they were playing and, after a brief pause, launched into a tune that would always make me think of my mystery man.

Raising himself from his chair, Tyler held his hand out to me. "Do me the honor of dancing with me?"

"Of course," I murmured, allowing him to lead me away from our table.

He placed his hand on my lower back, keeping his other one wrapped around mine. His warmth and comfort surrounded me as we sauntered to the melody of "Every Time We Say Goodbye".

"New memories?" I whispered.

"Better memories."

"Definitely better."

I stared into his eyes as he led me across the wooden deck. Just a week ago, this song made me want to scream with rage. Now it sparked a renewed sense of devotion, which was what I saw when I looked into Tyler's eyes. Reverence. Passion. Love. It was all there, just as it had been all those months ago. Despite the initial reason for him approaching me, it changed for him. At some point, he fell in love. He muttered those three words to me not to get me to share my deepest and darkest secrets with him, but because he couldn't go another second without sharing his feelings with me. I saw it all there in those

221

brilliant green eyes. I sensed it in the way he held me in his arms as if he would never let go. Most importantly, I felt it in my heart.

The song came to an end, silence engulfing us, but that didn't matter. We continued to sway to the music in our heads, just as we did that night all those months ago. Our bodies were perfectly in tune to each other, as if our souls were singing a song only we could hear.

"Mackenzie," Tyler said as the band began to play a classic Frank Sinatra tune.

"Yes?" I pulled away from him and noticed an uneasy expression on his face.

"You said you wanted me to be completely open and honest with you, right?"

I nodded, swallowing hard, nervous.

"I wanted to wait to talk to you about all this, but it's important that you know. I need to ask a favor of you. I just need you to know that, regardless, nothing will change between us."

"Is everything okay?" I asked, my voice cautious.

"Yes, I suppose." He looked out to the darkened ocean illuminated by the moon.

"Then tell me. As long as you're honest with me, I promise I won't get upset. That's all I need from you."

He returned his eyes to me, smiling a small smile. "Do you think you're up for a walk on the beach?"

"With you?" I scowled playfully. "Always."

I slid my shoes off and took Tyler's hand, allowing him to lead me down the wooden steps of the back deck and onto the white sand of the beach. Apart from a few other couples going for a moonlight stroll, the shoreline was nearly empty.

"So what do you want to talk to me about?" I asked after several long moments had passed as we walked along the beach. I tilted my head toward Tyler as the ocean wind picked up. I attempted to tame my hair, but it was useless.

"I like this look on you," he commented, fondly looking at me.

"What look?"

"I don't know. I can't quite put my finger on it. When we first met, you had this wall around you, and I was always curious as to who you really were. Over time, I started to see more and more, but even after you let go with me, you still didn't let me all the way in. But now I see such a carefree version of you, and I'll do anything to keep this look on your face."

I nudged him. "You're procrastinating."

"You caught me." He nervously met my gaze. "Maybe I'm just worried I'll lose you again, and I'm not willing to do that."

I halted and turned to face him. "Tyler, as long as you're honest with me, that's all I care about. Everything else, we can work through. I may yell and become irrational, but that's why I keep Jenna and Brayden around. They're really good at smacking some sense into me."

"Okay." He took a deep breath and I prepared myself for him to drop some sort of bomb that would make me question everything I thought I knew about him. "I just need you to know the only reason I'm doing this is because I care about you...deeply. Probably more than you can even begin to fathom."

"Tyler, just spit it out."

He paused briefly before releasing a breath. "I've ordered Martin and everyone else to remain on their protection detail."

"Why?" I asked, confused.

"Because, Mackenzie. I need to do everything I can to ensure your safety and my top priority right now is to figure out what the fuck is really going on here. Between your father, our mysteriously disappearing CIA handler, your friend, Damian, and Charlie—"

I inhaled quickly at the mention of that name and Tyler noticed my reaction.

"What is it?" He raised his brows.

"Nothing," I replied, turning from him and continuing along the shore.

"It wasn't nothing," Tyler said, catching up to me. "You want me to be open and honest with you? This is a two-way street, Mackenzie. I can only keep you safe if I know what's going on."

"I've told you, Tyler. Charlie isn't a threat to me. He knows where I am. If he really wanted to hurt me, he's had plenty of opportunities to do so. Am I certain he didn't kill all those people? I don't know. But I'm not ready to believe he's got a vendetta out against my father or me."

"Let me be the judge of that." Crossing his arms in front of his chest, making him look formidable, he glared down at me. A chill enveloped me, part of me irritated with his inability to accept I was an adult capable of taking care of myself, the other part becoming increasingly turned on with the dominance and power that covered his appearance as he stood in that stance, his suit making him even more attractive than I thought possible.

"You know," I began, "you make it nearly impossible for me to be upset with you. You're using your suit against me."

He scrunched his eyebrows briefly before his stern expression melted into one of amusement. Chuckling loudly, he pulled my body into his and I got lost in his strong arms, the sound of his laugh vibrating through him and warming me with adoration for him...my strong, protective mystery man.

"You know, a man in a suit to a woman is like lingerie to men. There's nothing hotter."

"I'm glad you think so, Mackenzie."

"I do," I admitted, pulling my head from his chest and peering into his eyes, the stars and ocean causing them to shimmer. Forgetting my former irritation with him, I reached up and ran my hands through his hair, playing with it.

"Kiss me," I begged, pulling his face toward mine. Our lips met, the kiss soft and tender. He took his time exploring my mouth, his hand running over the contours of my body as if it were the first time. *Everything* with Tyler felt like the first time. It was always new and exhilarating, the high I continued to feel whenever he swept his tongue with mine or brushed his fingers on my skin more vibrant than the previous time. We were still chasing the dragon together and I never wanted to stop.

I dropped my shoes, pulling his body closer, our kiss growing fevered and intense. Growling, Tyler lifted me and I wrapped my legs around his waist, but it still wasn't enough. At first, I appreciated the effort Tyler was making to take things slow, giving me the opportunity to learn to trust him again, but I didn't care about any of that right now. I needed to feel him on each and every inch of my skin.

"Tyler...," I exhaled, trying to catch my breath.

"Yes?"

"Take me home. We'll talk about whatever you want later."

"Mackenzie...," he began, and I could see him struggling.

"I know you want me. I can feel it. I need you right now. We need to make up for lost time. So, please, take me home and make love to me."

225

Staring at me with hunger, his expression carnal and animalistic, he closed his eyes. When he opened them, the thirst was gone.

"We need to talk first, Mackenzie," he said, helping me lower my legs back to the sand.

"We already did," I replied, my voice bordering on being a bit whiny. I ran my finger down his shirt, settling on his belt buckle as I pulled him back toward me. "You're keeping your team of trained mercenaries on board to look after me. You know how much I get turned on when you go all protective. We talked, so let's go do something else now." I began to unbuckle his belt, but his hands caught mine before I could go any further.

"That's not all I need to talk to you about. There's more."

"More?" I raised my eyebrows.

He simply nodded in response, swallowing hard.

"What is it?"

"Besides us needing to talk about what you're keeping from me regarding Charlie…"

"I'm not—"

He raised his finger to my mouth, hushing me. "You *are*, Mackenzie, and I get it. You're learning to trust me all over again. You're not sure where my loyalties lie right now. You're worried I may use what you tell me to hurt Charlie. And you're right to think that, especially if I find out he's a danger to you. That's where my loyalties lie. With you and only you. Okay?"

I nodded slightly and he removed his finger from my mouth.

"It's about your father…," Tyler reluctantly said.

"What about him?"

Sighing, he rubbed his temples, his shoulders shrinking. "If I thought there was any other option, I wouldn't be asking this of you."

"Asking what?" I countered, crossing my arms in front of me, suddenly feeling exposed and vulnerable.

"I need to talk to him," he said, his voice soft.

I stared at him, not expecting him to ask so much of me. For most, meeting the parents was a rite of passage, something all couples did. But this wasn't a simple dinner to make sure I wasn't dating a complete asshole. This was a man who had approached me for the sole purpose of finding and turning my father in, and was now asking that I bring him to meet the man he may still be hunting.

"Tyler..." I sighed, unsure of what to say to him.

"I know what must be going through your head right now," he said, grabbing my hands. "I understand your reluctance, but I'm not going to stop working this case until I know you're safe from harm. That means finding out what really happened all those years ago. There's been too many suspicious things happening, giving rise to more questions than answers, and I think your father may be able to give us some insight that could help put this puzzle together."

"Tyler, I just..." I paused, collecting my thoughts. "I spent eight years of my life thinking he was dead. Having to disappear and change everything about me, including my name, was the hardest thing I ever had to do. It broke me and, the day I saw my father step into the living room at my mother's house, I vowed to do everything I could so I'd never have to lose my family again." I tore away from him, a chill washing over me as I recalled how lost I felt all those years when I thought I had no father.

"But what about your mother?" Tyler shouted, catching up to me.

"What?" I hissed, spinning around to face him. "Don't you *dare* bring her up! She has nothing to do with this, not anymore!"

"Don't you want the person responsible for her death

behind bars?"

"Who? Charlie?! Last I checked, you seemed to be hell-bent on blaming him for all this!"

"Don't you think your mother would want you to finally be able to let her go?!"

"Why don't you think—"

Tyler reached into his pocket and pulled out a long velvet box, holding it out to me.

"What is that?"

"It's something that belongs to you," he said softly.

Taking the box from him, I opened it, my eyes settling on my mother's ornate rosary. I had felt so empty and alone without it over the past few months. It was the only thing of my mother's I had left, and when I left it in Boston, I felt as if I had left a piece of my soul there.

"You'll never be able to let her go until you have closure," he said as I ran my fingers over the soft beads. "I can give you that closure, Mackenzie, but I think the only way I can get on the right path is if I talk to your father."

"He may not be able to help," I insisted. "If he knew what happened all those years ago, don't you think this would have been over already?"

"Not if there's a reason he's keeping quiet." His eyes were urgent as he tried with everything in him to persuade me to agree.

Studying him, I pulled my lower lip between my teeth, an old nervous tick. "My relationship with my father is built on mutual trust. I can't blindside him like that."

"I get it," Tyler said, rubbing his hand up and down my arms. "Can you just talk to him about it? About why it's necessary? See if he's willing to meet with me?"

"I can't make any promises about what he'll say…"

"Just talk to him. Please."

Reluctant to agree, I knew he had a point. Perhaps my

father knew more than he was letting on and Tyler could find out what. Nodding, I relented. "Okay. I'll talk to him, but I can't make any promises."

Letting out a long breath, Tyler smiled as his tense stature relaxed. "Let me see that." He grabbed the velvet box back from me, taking out the cross. Opening the clasp, he hung it around my neck, his fingers brushing my skin, sending a chill through me.

"There. That's better," he crooned, pulling me into the crook of his arm as we stared at the soft ocean waves. "Everything's back where it belongs."

Chapter Twenty-Two

With You

Tyler

"WANT TO COME IN?" Mackenzie turned to me, giving me a demure look as we stood outside her condo. I had been uneasy about this precise moment all night long, even more so than asking about her father. I wanted to spend every minute with this woman, but I didn't want to move so fast that our lust clouded our minds.

"I'm not sure that's a good idea, Mackenzie," I replied.

Her face dropped, her expression turning to stone. She spun around and unlocked her door. The silence between us could be cut with a knife. I didn't know what I wanted her to say, but I wanted her to say *something*...how she understood why it was important that we take things slow. Hell, just a few days ago, she was turning down my advances for the same reason.

Angrily turning the knob, she threw her front door open and stomped toward the panel, disarming the system. As I was about to step into the foyer, she slammed the door in my face.

"Mackenzie!" I bellowed. "Don't be like this." Refusing to have a screaming match through the door, I gingerly turned the knob and entered her condo.

"Like what?" she hissed, whirling around. "You keep saying you want to take things slow, and I get it, Tyler. But you have no problem making out with me, feeling me up, making me straddle you as you push your cock against me! Then when I invite you in, you suddenly want nothing to do with me!"

I stared at her in shock as tears streamed down her face.

"It's because you don't find me attractive anymore, isn't it?" she whimpered, avoiding my eyes. "I don't know what I was thinking. Of course you don't. I mean, you disappear from my life and come back to see me like this." She gestured to her stomach. "You don't have to pretend you like me just to get information about my father. We've already played that game, Tyler. It's tired and old. So just get out and leave me alone."

"Mackenzie..." I had no idea what I could say to her that would assuage her fears. Maybe that I thought she was the most beautiful woman on the planet? And even more so when I found out she was carrying our child? But they were just words, insufficient to properly convey how I felt about her. I needed her to see, to *feel*, how much I needed her in my life. She needed to know it was her, that it was *always* her. Everything that had happened in my life, from my triumphs to my failures, all led me to her.

"Don't, Tyler. Just don't." With heavy footsteps, she stormed down the hallway.

Running after her, I grabbed her arm and pinned her against the wall. Her mouth fell open as she gave me an incredulous look. Before she could say anything, I crushed my lips to hers and thrust against her. Finding her hands, I raised her arms over her head, trapping her in place. "Is this what you want?" I growled, my eyes hooded as I looked down at her.

"No," she hissed, shaking her head. "I don't want a pity fuck." Her chest heaved as she glared at me, her eyes on fire in the darkened hallway. I ran my tongue down

231

her neckline, tracing circles as I inhaled her alluring scent. A barely audible whimper escaped as she craned her neck, giving me easier access to her perfect skin.

"But you *do* want to fuck?" I murmured. Releasing my hold on her arms, I ran my fingers across her collarbone, tracing the line of her halter top dress.

"You know the answer to that, but it's obvious you're not attracted to me. Not like you used to be..." She pushed against me and I stumbled back, keeping my distance from her. We stood in the hallway and stared at each other, both of our chests heaving.

"Mackenzie, I don't know what you want me to say. I can tell you I thought you were the most beautiful woman I'd ever seen from the first moment I saw you, but I'd be lying."

She frowned.

"When I saw you at my mother's house and saw this..." I stepped toward her and placed my hand on her stomach. "Well, I had never been so stunned before, so speechless that any woman could capture my heart with her beauty and radiance. I'm just worried if we move too fast, we won't make it."

"Tyler..." She wrapped her arms around my neck and stood on her toes, placing a soft kiss on my lips. "I want us to make it, too, but did you ever think that maybe I *need* this. I need to feel you, feel the connection I've missed. I need to know you again..."

"You *do* know me."

"We've agreed to get to know each other again, but I'm not just interested in your favorite color and your most memorable childhood vacation, Tyler. I want to know you intimately. I want nothing more than to open up my heart to you again, but I can't do that unless I know you...all of you."

Tracing circles on my neck, she ran her hand down my

chest, a renewed hunger washing over me. Passion flooding my veins, I drew her body close and covered her mouth with mine, my kiss ravenous and unyielding as I pushed her down the hall toward her bedroom. It had been ages since I had walked these steps, but it was so familiar, so natural, as if I had walked this path every day of my life.

Approaching her bed, I tore my lips from hers, desperately trying to catch my breath.

"What do you want?" she whispered, eyeing me with part confusion, part lust.

"You," I replied in a low groan. "Always you." I thrust my hand in her hair, gripping it hard and forcing her head back so she had no choice but to stare into my eyes. Her chest rose and fell, and it took everything in me to not throw her onto the bed at that instant. I hadn't been with her in months and I wanted to make up for lost time. For all the lost kisses, lost embraces, lost I love you's, lost moans... I wanted to remember each and every shiver, every taste of her skin, every waft of her sweet cinnamon aroma. This was the start of our new beginning, and I wanted to give her everything. I wanted to give her all of me.

"Take me." She swallowed hard. "Feel me, Tyler."

Hooking my arm around her waist, I pulled her into me, our two bodies molding together. I ran my hands through her hair, brushing a tendril behind her ear as I gently caressed her face.

Sighing, she covered my hand with hers. "There you are," she said softly.

"What do you mean?"

"My Tyler. My loving, powerful mystery man. The man who is fierce, in control, and full of fervor one minute, then is sweet, caring, and loving the next. I like how it's never boring with you, how it's always..."

"Unexpected?" I said, finishing her thought.

"Yes. You were unexpected, but the most wonderful unexpected thing that ever happened to me. And I wouldn't change one minute of it. Not the lies or the heartache because it led us to where we are."

She reached toward the nape of her neck and pulled at the strings of her halter dress. Stepping back, she allowed it to pool at her feet and stood in front of me wearing a red strapless bra and matching panties.

The room was dark, the only light coming from the moon as it filtered through her windows. It was serene, tranquil, still, in complete contradiction to the frenzied beating of my heart that I was certain was reverberating against the walls.

Slowly, she unclasped her bra and it fell to the ground before sensually lowering her panties down her legs. Her eyes met mine as she stood in front of me...exposed, bare, vulnerable.

Taking several determined steps toward her, I kissed her again, our exchange soft, momentarily lacking the ravenous characteristic most of our previous kisses had. She tugged at my hair, pulling me into her as a small moan escaped her mouth. Clutching onto her hips, I deepened the kiss.

I lifted her up and walked across the room, pushing her back against the wall. It was a mixture of hands and legs as we fused into each other, feeling each other, *experiencing* each other. I needed her. I needed to feel her. To taste her. To consume her.

With one arm, I held her, using the other to brush all the bottles off her vanity, and lowered her to the mahogany surface. Before she could utter anything, I kneeled before her. Spreading her legs, I placed them over my shoulders and traced my tongue against her calf.

"Tyler," she moaned, reaching for me as I remained

just slightly out of reach of her touch.

"Yes, *mi cariño?* Something I can help you with?"

"I need you." She threw her head back, overwhelmed with the sensuous torture of my tongue's slow journey up her leg.

"And you will have me. Don't rush to the finish," I murmured, growing closer to the spot I was sure she wanted me to touch...to taste. "Enjoy the moment. Don't you want to live in the present instead of looking forward?" I squeezed her thighs, my thumb brushing over her center. She took a quick inhale of air, her body growing taut around me. "Don't you, Serafina?"

"Yes, Tyler. I do." She ran her hands through my hair, gripping it as she tried to force my head between her legs, but I resisted momentarily.

"Serafina..."

"Yes...?" She squirmed against me, telling me with her body what she needed.

"Eyes on me," I said, just as I had during our first time. "I need to know you're with me."

She flung her eyes open, meeting mine. There was an intensity, an awareness of something bigger than either one of us could have imagined growing at that moment. I thought I loved her before, and maybe I did. But this love, this strange emotion flowing through me right now, was bigger and more vibrant than anything I'd felt before.

"I'm with you, Tyler," she whimpered through the lump forming in her throat. "I've always been with you."

I brought my tongue to her, wanting to savor each lick, each swirl. Her tense body relaxed, our eyes remaining locked, the connection between us deep and unwavering. "God, I love the way you taste," I growled, increasing my speed, tightening my grasp on her thighs. "Does this feel good?"

She simply nodded, her mouth slightly agape as she tried to subdue the orgasm that was on the verge of washing over her.

"Say it, Mackenzie. Tell me you've been craving my touch, that no one else can ever satisfy you like I do."

"It's only you, Tyler," she moaned, tugging at my hair, pushing my head further into her. "I'm an addict and you're the only one who can satisfy me."

Her breathing increased, her body clenched and I knew she was on the brink. I quickly pulled back, leaving her breathless.

"Tyler!" she exclaimed, frustrated.

"What?" I asked coyly.

"Why did you stop? I..."

"You...?"

"I need you," she said softly.

I raised myself to my feet and hovered over her, placing a gentle kiss on her lips. "I know," I murmured.

"Then why did you stop?" she asked once more.

"I want you to ask me." I tilted her chin back and stared into her eyes. She was unable to escape me.

"Please, Tyler," she whispered, dragging her finger up my chest, pulling at my tie and tugging me closer. "Please make me come."

In one swift motion, I picked her up and strode across the room toward her bed. I hurriedly removed all my clothes and slithered up her legs. She moaned loudly when I swirled my tongue around the spot she wanted me to touch, her body beginning to tremble beneath me. Instantly, she screamed out my name, yanking on my hair as she rode the waves of what I hoped to be one of the most intense orgasms of her life. By the way she was responding to me, I had a feeling it was.

Her tremors subsiding, I crawled up her body and placed my hand protectively over her stomach, kissing her softly. "How was that?"

"Better than I remember." She crushed her lips back to mine, plunging her tongue in my mouth before pulling back, nibbling on my lip in such a way that made me want to feel her even more. She raked her fingernails up and down my back, digging into my skin a little harder each time. I kissed her once more as I gently thrust against her, being careful to put all my weight on my arms.

Tearing from her lips, I stared deep into her hazel eyes, a look of peace and contentment in her gaze. I delicately ran my fingers through her hair, drinking in her face. I studied each dip and valley, each dimple, each freckle. I never thought I'd be here and I wanted to cherish this moment, a beautiful memory that would stay with me if the lonely ever found me again.

Grabbing the back of my neck, she found my lips once more. "Tyler, make love to me," she murmured in a sultry voice.

Without saying a word, I nodded, keeping my eyes glued to hers. I carefully held onto her hips and rolled onto my back, bringing her to settle on top of me. Her gaze widened, showing her surprise.

"You're in charge."

Before I could say anything else, she leaned back and took me inside of her, her motions slow as she acclimated herself to me once more.

"Fuck," I hissed through a clenched jaw, a tidal wave of carnal thirst surging through me. After our first time together, I craved her more than I thought possible, the way my body responded to her filling a void in my life. Each and every time we were intimate after that was more thrilling, more electrifying than the time before. But now, as Mackenzie moved sensually and slowly on top of me, her lips almost touching mine, her breath dancing on my skin, it was different. Lies no longer hung heavy between us. We could finally be us, the us I hoped we would eventually be, and my heart filled with more love and hunger for her.

My fingers clawing into her skin, I pushed into her with greater intensity, guiding her on top of me, wanting to feel every inch of her. No matter how fast and deep I went, it still wasn't enough. I could make love to her for days on end, explore every crevice and dip in her body, and still need more. I was greedy with desire, the months apart making my appetite more voracious. Her skin flush with mine, our two bodies connected, was ecstasy and I could no longer control myself.

Uttering a low moan, I closed my eyes, grunting her name as I released inside her, my orgasm gratifying and intense.

Slowing our movements, we stared at each other and basked in the moment. "I love you, Serafina," I whispered, my voice barely audible as I cupped her face in my hands.

"And I love you, Tyler, lies and all." She climbed off of me and snuggled up beside me. I pulled the duvet over our sweaty bodies and placed a soft kiss on her head.

"I'm glad you finally found it in your heart to forgive me."

She sighed, her body relaxing as she toyed with the little tendrils of hair on my chest. "I needed to forgive you," she replied, her voice light. "Do you have any idea how horny being pregnant makes you?"

"Really?" I stared down at her and she met my eyes.

"Yup. So you better rest up. If you thought my sex drive was something before, you haven't seen anything."

"As I've said in the past, Miss Delano..." I adjusted my position and hovered over her, rubbing myself against her. "I'm always up for a challenge."

Chapter Twenty-Three

A Decision

Mackenzie

A LOW HUM FILLED the comfort of my bedroom, a vibration on my neck sending a shiver through my body. My eyelids fluttered open, the autumn sun streaming into the room on this last Friday in September. The weeks had passed quicker than I expected as I settled into my new normal. Tyler and I saw each other practically every spare moment we had. He worked long days as he investigated what was going on with my father and everything else, in addition to running his club once more. I had asked why he was back there when it was just supposed to be a front. He told me it took his mind off everything and gave him a bit of clarity. I could certainly understand that.

With Tyler back on the island and in my life, I fell into a new routine with surprising ease. He spent every night at my condo...except for Fridays. That was reserved for girls' night, and I appreciated his understanding that I still needed time with my two best friends, even though he was practically living with me.

Tyler had taken on the role of soon-to-be dad with an excitement I wasn't expecting. He accompanied me to all my doctor's appointments, which had become slightly more frequent now that I was in my third trimester. The look of awe on his face the first time he saw our little boy on the ultrasound, hearing his fast little heartbeat, made me fall in love with him a little bit more.

As September came to an end, the humidity that had become almost unbearable finally began to subside. The summer vacationers started to leave the island, and things were beginning to slow down, finally giving me time to prepare for the arrival of Baby Boy Burnham...or Triple B, as we had been calling him...in less than three months.

A hand splayed on my stomach, caressing me, loving me, supporting me as a low moan escaped Tyler's mouth. I sighed, losing myself in his warmth. He pulled me closer, his lips feathering kisses across my shoulder blades.

"Morning, Mr. Burnham," I whispered, not wanting to break our moment. Each day I woke in his arms, I fell for my duplicitous mystery man even more. I fell in love with every inch of him all over again. With his eyes. With his mouth. With his arms. With his heart. It was all mine to possess, and he gave me his love freely with no restraints. Our love was pure, perfect, and finally honest.

"Morning, Miss Delano." He nuzzled his nose into my hair and inhaled. "Mmmm," he groaned and I felt him grow rigid against me. "I will never tire of waking up next to you."

"And I will never tire of feeling your hands on my skin."

"Is that right?" he asked.

"That's right."

He leaned in, his lips roaming my heated flesh. I couldn't seem to get my fill of him. I wanted him every hour of every day. When we were apart, I ached for him in such a way I didn't think I would ever survive without his touch.

"Tell me, Mackenzie," he murmured, his voice husky.

"Where do you want my hands?" He clenched his teeth on my neck, sucking lightly. My eyes rolled back into my head, lost in the combination of pain and pleasure. A rush of electricity ran through me, my skin even more sensitive than I imagined. I was in tune to what his simple presence did to me, an ache between my legs growing more and more pronounced with each passing second.

"All over," I breathed, squirming as I continued to lay on my side. "I need your touch everywhere."

His fingers grazed across my collarbone, his touch light and perfect. "Tell me where," he growled and my breath caught at his tone. It was demanding, forceful, harsh, at complete odds with the reverent way he ran his hands over my body, his thumb barely grazing my nipples. I inhaled at the almost contact, my skin on alert. My body was an instrument and he had mastered it. He knew exactly where to touch me to make me hum, vibrate, or sing.

"There," I whimpered, still feeling the heat of his fingers just shy of where I needed to feel him. This was torture, pure and simple. Waterboarding had nothing on what I was enduring at the moment.

"Where?" He pulled me against him, my back to his front, his motion forceful.

"My nipple," I answered, exhaling when I finally felt his fingers linger on my breast, gently taking my erect nipple between them.

"Is this how you want it?" His voice was heavy with amusement.

I shook my head. "No. Harder, Tyler," I begged, writhing against the sheets.

"What was that?"

"You heard me," I shot back in a firm voice. "Stop teasing me. I want your teeth on me, on my nipples."

Groaning, he flipped me onto my back and, in a flash,

his mouth was clenching onto my nipple, which had become even more sensitive since I became pregnant. I could only explain the sensation streaming through me as a bolt of lightning, an electric current running through my veins. The combination of biting and sucking overwhelmed me and I arched my back, needing more, but not knowing how much more I could take.

He pulled back and his eyes met mine, a wild and untamed look about them. The room was eerily silent, the only sound that of my racing heart and uneven breathing.

"More," I murmured.

"What?" he asked coyly.

"Tyler…" I ran my hand up and down his arm softly at first before wrapping my fingers around his nape, tugging him down toward me. "I said I want more. Don't hold back. Give me all of you. Every side of you. I want them all right now."

"Mackenzie, I…" He tore his eyes from mine, his gaze settling on my stomach.

"Tyler," I continued, cupping his face in my hands. "I'm not going to break. Just because I'm pregnant doesn't mean you have to be gentle with me." Running my fingers through his dark, messy hair, I craned my neck and nibbled on his earlobe. "Sometimes I want it rough. And Tyler?"

He pulled back, staring at me with his mouth slightly agape.

"Right now, I want it rough."

A small smile spread across my lips when I felt him harden between my legs. He swallowed hard before prying himself from the trap my legs had ensnared him in.

"Flip over," he ordered, his harsh tone making me almost breathless. "Get on your hands and knees."

Without a moment's hesitation, I followed his demand, adjusting my body into the position he requested. His hand traveled across my shoulder blades, his touch light. I shivered, ready to fall apart from the anticipation.

"You said you wanted it rough?"

"Yes, Tyler."

Before I could wrap my head around what was happening, he was behind me, slamming into me. I screamed out as he groaned, his tempo relentless.

"Is this what you want?" he ground out through his labored breaths.

My legs were already jelly. I leaned my head on the pillow, attempting to steady myself when it felt as if the world was spinning in the most amazing, mind-blowing way.

"Harder," I bellowed, meeting his pace thrust for thrust. A hard slap resonated against my ass and I screamed out in unyielding pleasure, confident I was going to come from the sharp contact alone.

"Again," I begged. The combination of intense euphoria from him inside me and that roughness in which he loved me lit me on fire. I needed more, so much more. I needed all of him in ways I never thought possible, my world spinning as I tried to make sense of what was going through my head. I wanted to cry, scream, laugh, yell.

Grunting, Tyler reeled back and landed another blow on my other cheek. I continued to meet his rhythm, my pace only increasing with each punishing slap of his hand. I couldn't remember ever being so turned on, so ready to fall over the edge with another person. I never let anyone see this side of me before. I never knew I *had* this side to me before. And that was what love should be. Love was finding that one person who made you laugh, cry, smile, hope, crave, want, lust, and grow. I had that with Tyler and I refused to let it go. I knew I would do everything to keep this man at my side... My beautiful, caring, selfless mystery man.

Sweat prickled my brow as I was lost in the sensation of Tyler's body giving me exactly what I wanted and needed. Gasping, I fought for air, knowing I was about to unravel. Tyler sensed it, as well, and found my nipple, squeezing it between his fingers, delicately nibbling on my shoulder blade.

"I love you, Serafina," he whispered in his raspy morning voice, his declaration setting me off.

My screams echoed through the bedroom and I didn't know how even the thickest of soundproofing could muffle them. Waves of intense pleasure continued to roll through me, my body clenching as Tyler moaned through his own release.

Wrapping his arm around me to support me, he kept me upright when I felt as if I was ready to fall. He trailed a finger down my spine and I giggled.

"Rough is fun," I commented.

He helped lower me back onto the bed and pulled my body against his. I settled into the crook of his embrace, running my fingers through his chest hair. This moment was perfect as he caressed me, wiping the sweat off my forehead.

"I'm a big fan," he agreed.

"Oh, yeah?"

"Oh, yeah," he responded, a devilish grin on his face. "Let's do more of that."

"Right now?" I asked in disbelief, shooting out of his embrace to see he was already hard again. He began stroking himself and I shook my head. "You're an animal." I leaned in and softly placed my lips on his.

"Only for you."

Gently, he positioned me on my back and took his time

entering me, flexing toward me and withdrawing with an air of absolute reverence. I wrapped my arms around his neck and stared into his eyes as he made love to me, giving me all of him once more.

~~~~~~~~~~

"HAVE YOU HEARD ANYTHING yet?" Tyler asked after I sat down at the kitchen island. Seeing his eager eyes, I hated giving him the same answer I had for the past several weeks.

At my last meeting with my dad back in August, I had asked him to meet with Tyler. I wasn't sure how he would react, whether he would think Tyler was using me again, but that wasn't it at all. He seemed torn. Part of him wanted to jump at the opportunity to finally put this chapter of his life behind him. The other part of him was cautious, worrying whether this was a trap we were both blind to. In the end, he told me he would think about it and asked for time to look into a few things of his own before making up his mind. I had no idea what he needed to look into, but Tyler was optimistic he hadn't turned him down flat.

But now that a month had gone by with no communication, both of us were a bit on edge. This was the most time that had ever passed with no mention in the weekly bulletin I received of a mass being said in honor of a member of my family.

"Not yet," I responded, trying to remain cheerful as I raised the cup of decaf to my lips. "But I'm sure I'll hear something from him any day now."

"You're positive he hasn't sent anything?" he asked, crossing his arms, stretching the fabric of his gray t-shirt. His eyes bore into mine, as if trying to figure out whether I was telling him the truth.

"Yes, I'm sure," I spat out, irritated at his insinuation. "Unlike *some* people in this room, I'm actually truthful with those I care about."

A vein on his neck became engorged and his face reddened a bit, one of the tell-tale signs he wasn't happy. Then a defeated look washed over him and he sighed, his stature dropping. "I deserve that."

He turned back around to finish cooking breakfast, making me feel guilty. Over the last few months, he had tried so hard to do everything to bury the past and only look toward our future, but every time he questioned my own truthfulness, I threw it back in his face, reopening the wound I was sure he wanted to heal.

In truth, I *hadn't* been entirely honest with him. He had brought up Charlie on countless occasions, asking me if I knew anything else, and I denied having spoken to him. I never told him about that phone call back in July when he told me his side of what happened the night of the embassy attack. I didn't know why. It wasn't like it would be helpful in figuring out what was really going on, but that conversation was the real Charlie and I wanted to protect it.

Sliding off my barstool, I went to Tyler and wrapped my arms around his chest from behind. "No, you don't deserve it, and I should stop bringing it up every time I'm not getting my way. I said I had forgiven you, and I have, yet I still remind you at least once a week. I've learned to trust you all over again, Tyler, but I also need you to trust me. I have nothing to gain by keeping my father from you. In fact, I tend to think I only have something to lose if I prevented you from picking his brain. I want this as much as you do. Should I have heard from him at this point? Probably, but I'm certain he has a very good reason for not arranging a meeting yet."

"Do you think something happened?" Tyler asked

urgently, tearing out of my embrace, a frenzied air about him. From what he'd told me of the case, just when they were about to uncover something that may put the pieces together, there would be a setback. It had been a constant battle of two steps forward and three steps back, and I felt for him.

"Tyler..." I wanted to assure him everything was okay, but did I know for certain nothing had happened? No, but I knew my father. He had survived on the run for over fifteen years. He wasn't going to do something stupid now, not when freedom and the truth were potentially within arm's reach. "You don't know my father like I do. He's a brilliant man. He's probably taking his time to do some research on *you* to determine whether you're trustworthy. From where I'm standing, the fact that he's taken this long to get back to me is a good sign. It means he's most likely going to agree to talk to you. So just be patient and trust that when I get notice of a meeting, I will let you know immediately."

"Okay," he said, kissing the top of my head before turning off the stove and dishing out scrambled eggs, bacon, and toast onto two plates. I followed him back to the island and returned to my seat, my stomach rumbling. Triple B was a bit of a parasite. I could eat a feast, only to be starving again ten minutes later. Thankfully Tyler was more than aware of my increased appetite and always cooked extra eggs for me...and the baby.

"So what's on your plate for today?" he asked as I chewed on a piece of bacon.

"I'm going into the restaurant for a bit, then Jenna's dragging me into Brownsville."

"For what?"

"She's insisting I finally go buy some furniture for the nursery. She's worried I'm not taking this seriously and

247

the kid will be forced to sleep in one of my dresser drawers when he's born."

"Do you want me to come with you?" He glanced at me.

"No, that's okay. We kind of decided to make a girls' day out of it. Brayden works in town so we're supposed to be at his office around noon to grab lunch, then go shopping. I have a feeling he's more excited about this than I am. You're still coming to the baby shower tomorrow, right?" I placed my hand on his leg. "It really means a lot that you'll be there with me."

"Of course." He gave me a small smile. "I wouldn't miss it for the world."

He broke his gaze from me and turned his attention back to his food. I glanced at him, hoping he wasn't upset that I wanted to have a day with my friends. He didn't seem like he was, but the way he was pushing his eggs all over his plate, barely touching them, made me grow concerned something else was bothering him.

Taking a deep breath, he looked at me. "Have you thought about which room you want to make into the nursery?"

I took a sip of my coffee and considered his question. The truth was, I had been avoiding making a decision. I lived in a three-bedroom condo, but there wasn't much space. The master bedroom was adequate, the two guest bedrooms being nothing more than a room in which you could fit a bed and not much else. I kept walking by each of them, hoping inspiration would strike, but it never did. I simply couldn't imagine raising a child here. His clothes alone would take up the entire room.

"A bit, but I haven't decided yet. There's not much space."

"I think I might have a solution to the space problem," he offered.

"Oh, yeah? What is it?"

He took a deep breath, and I couldn't help but think that whatever the solution was, I may not like it.

"I want you to move in with me..."

My heart dropped to the pit of my stomach. I had known this day would come, especially now that the baby was almost here, but I guess I didn't want to acknowledge it. I liked having my space. I liked knowing if things went to shit with Tyler, I still had my home. It gave me control.

Before I could open my mouth to respond, he added, "At my house in Boston."

"Boston?!" I exclaimed, unsure whether I had heard him correctly.

"Of course, we'll wait until after the baby is born and you're both able to travel. You can keep the condo and use it as a vacation rental, but I'd really like for you to think about this, Mackenzie. I want you to be a part of my life and family, and I'd like that with you back in Boston."

He reached for my hand, but I ripped it from him, storming away from the island. My hands shaking, I scraped all the eggs off my plate and into the trash, my ravenous appetite gone. I tried to ignore the warmth approaching behind me, but I was unable to. I could feel Tyler from miles away.

"Mackenzie," he said, running his hand up and down my arm in an attempt to placate me. "Don't get upset about this. I've been thinking about it for a while, but I knew you'd react this way so I kept putting it off. I just want you to consider this as an option."

"But what about my friends?" I asked, spinning around to face him. "My family? This place has been my home for the past five years! I've built a life here! A business! You're asking me to just walk away from all of that and move somewhere completely new and foreign to me. I don't know if I can do that!" I threw the dish in the sink and grabbed my purse.

"Mackenzie, just—"

"No!" I whirled around as I approached the front door. Tyler reeled back, his eyes studying me as if my reaction was completely unexpected. "The truth is," I continued in a low voice, "I've seen this coming, but maybe I'm just not ready to do this…" I gestured between our bodies. "Not like I thought I was."

Not wanting him to see my tears, I stormed out of the condo and jumped into the elevator. I knew my reaction wasn't entirely reasonable, but the idea of moving to Boston confirmed an aspect of our relationship I had been content to ignore the past several months. Now, it had brought itself to the forefront of my mind.

The elevator doors opened and I dashed through the lobby, ignoring Paul, and toward my SUV.

"Mackenzie, please!" Tyler bellowed as I was about to hop in. "I understand. I get it." He grabbed my hand, spinning me around to face him. "I know it's going to sound cheesy, but when I bought my house in Beacon Hill, I always imagined eventually raising a family there. For years, it's been so empty, so cold. There was no life to those four walls…until you walked inside. Even back then, I imagined how life would be if you lived there with me." I listened to his plea, trying to put myself in his shoes.

He reached out and brushed a tendril of hair behind my ear, his expression softening. "We can wake up each morning and have coffee together, like we do now. In the summers, we can watch the sunrise from the rooftop deck. We can watch the leaves on the trees change colors in the fall and take in the beautiful scenery. During those snowy nights, we can snuggle in front of the fireplace and

250

watch the city get covered in a coat of white. In the spring, we can soak in the blooming flowers as they bring new life to the city around us."

"I…"

I stared into his eyes that were begging me to at least consider it. South Padre wasn't an ideal location to be raising a child, not with all the alcohol and partying that happened here almost year round. Most of the condos in this building were used as vacation rentals. I wanted to live where my son could play with friends when he was a little older, and he certainly couldn't do that here. But Boston? Away from Jenna and Brayden? Away from my father? I didn't know if I was ready to take such a big risk.

Worse, it made me come to terms with the fact that Tyler and I came from two separate worlds, despite what I had told myself time and time again. His world was up in Boston, while mine was down here. I didn't know if we'd ever truly be able to coexist, not when we wanted two different things.

"I can't do this right now," I quivered, pulling my hand from his and jumping into my car. He stepped back, allowing me to leave, much to my surprise. I expected him to stop me, to want to push the conversation, but he didn't. He simply let me leave him standing there, a hurt expression on his face. I didn't know if I'd ever forgive myself for causing that look, but that still didn't mean I could give up my life so he could live his.

Chapter Twenty-Four

Tripwire

Tyler

I PULLED MY BRONCO into the driveway of my house, wishing I had pushed Mackenzie to tell me what was really holding her back from agreeing to move to Boston with me. I knew asking her was risky, which was why I had been putting it off for the past month, but I didn't want to go any longer with our current living arrangement. I wanted to come home to her every night to a house we shared. I wanted to be there to rock our son to sleep. I wanted to read him bedtime stories. I wanted him to be surrounded by a family who loved him.

And I wanted all of that back in Boston, not down here where we would both be reminded of our past. We had been given a chance to have a new beginning, and I didn't want to squander that opportunity.

Entering my code into the keypad on my front door, I walked through the house, hearing animated voices coming from down the hall. I headed toward the study, surprised to see Martin, Eli, Benson, and Maxwell sitting around the table. The remainder of the team had stayed on, but I decided to only use them in a purely protective role, not investigative. I liked keeping my inner circle small, and everyone present had proved to be trustworthy, even Benson.

"What's this all about?" I asked, sensing there must

have been some sort of new development if all these people were here.

"Sir," Eli began, shooting up from his chair. "We think we may have something. Benson and Maxwell found some questionable information about one of the missions Galloway was on while a Ranger."

"Really?" I perked up. Over the past few months, we had hit nothing but dead ends. Just when we thought we were getting closer to figuring out who was behind everything, it turned out to be nothing. We had dug and dug into Galloway's background...his time in the Rangers, his investigations while in Counterintelligence, even his home and family life. We had come up mostly empty-handed, which was frustrating and made me start to think that maybe he wasn't being set up. Maybe he just wanted us to *believe* he was.

"What did you find out?" I asked, eyeing Benson and Maxwell as they sat at the table.

"Well, it took a while to put the pieces together, but we were finally able to access field reports from when Galloway's unit was in Bosnia in the early nineties."

Eyeing him skeptically, I grabbed a file off my desk and flipped through it. "I think you're mistaken. There's no record of him going to Bosnia. Not to mention, according to all the information we received from the CIA, Galloway had already transferred to Counterintelligence by the time of the conflict in Bosnia." I had practically memorized the entire dossier of the missions he was involved in when a Ranger, and Bosnia wasn't on the list. I would have certainly remembered that.

"Precisely," Maxwell said, his excitement growing. "We always thought perhaps this guy was hiding something. He was Special Forces, then in Counterintelligence. It's obvious he's got some skeletons in his closet. Skeletons he had the skills and training to hide."

Closing the file in front of me, I nodded, giving my full attention to Benson and Maxwell. "Tell me about this supposed mission he was on in Bosnia."

"Well, his Ranger unit was sent there during the crisis in the early nineties," Benson began. "As you know, the United States didn't want to get involved in the civil war, but that didn't mean we didn't have some troops in the area. We did, and Galloway's team was one of the units sent over there."

"And what was their mission?"

"We don't know," Maxwell said, "but we found a copy of the only field report Galloway filed during his time over there, accounting for the casualty of two of his unit members. No details were given, just their names."

"But if they weren't involved in active combat...?"

"We had the same concerns," Benson agreed. "So we took the initiative to look into the remaining members of Galloway's team. We found it particularly disconcerting to learn that all of them, except for Galloway and two others, are now deceased."

"Or missing," Maxwell added.

"Missing?" I scrunched my eyebrows.

"Yes. Harrison Mills, Galloway's neighbor, was on the mission and, as we know, he's been missing for several years."

"So it looks like we should go talk to someone who was in Bosnia with Galloway and see if there's a connection. It may not clear anything up, but maybe we can find out a little bit more."

"We're one step ahead of you," Eli said. "Maxwell and Benson are heading to Oklahoma to talk to one of them...Peter Carlyle. You and I are going to head to Florida to see if we can get some answers out of Bruce McDonough."

"Perfect. See if you can get these guys on the phone and make plans to go talk to them on Monday—"

"Sir," Martin interrupted. "We've all discussed this and think time is of the essence here. If someone has been killing the members of the unit, there's a possibility they're after Carlyle and McDonough. It took Maxwell weeks to even track these two down. They've been living completely off the grid for years, making me believe that perhaps they knew someone was after them. Granted, it's been several years since the others died, but I'm not sure this is a risk worth taking."

Sighing, I ran my hand over my face. I knew I needed to go talk to at least one of them, but I had promised Mackenzie I'd be there for her baby shower tomorrow. I glanced at my watch, noting it was just eleven in the morning. If we hurried and got a flight plan in place, we could be in Florida by two or three. That gave us a little wiggle room. Even if we had to track him down, as long as we were back by tomorrow morning, I'd be able to make Mackenzie's shower.

"Fine. Let's go. Benson. Maxwell." I nodded at them. "You'll most likely be getting to your target's house first. I want a full report after you've spoken to him. It may help us when we're interviewing our guy. Understand?"

"Sir," they said in unison.

~~~~~~~~~~

"WHAT DO YOU THINK Galloway's time in Bosnia has to do with all of this?" Eli asked as we drove from Tampa airport and out to St. Pete Beach. My thoughts had been elsewhere, thinking of Mackenzie and the argument we'd had earlier. I had tried calling her to let her know what was going on and assure her I would be back in plenty of time for the baby shower, but my calls went right to voicemail, so I knew she hadn't cooled off yet. I just hoped she would come around so we could at least discuss this like two rational people.

"Tyler?" Eli said, snapping me out of my thoughts.

"Which makes more sense, or which do I want to believe?"

"Let me guess. It's not the same."

I sighed, leaning my head on the window of the rental SUV, soaking in the warm Florida sun. "I wish it were. Am I a horrible person for beginning to think maybe I was wrong before? That maybe, with everything going on, it makes more sense Galloway really *is* the one behind all of it? Everyone associated with him seems to be dead or missing, and I can't help but think he's the cause. The only evidence I have that he's not is my girlfriend's assurance he couldn't be, even though she barely knows him. Does this make me a horrible person?"

"No," Eli agreed, keeping his eyes on the road as we drove across a bridge toward the island. "You're looking at everything rationally, like any good investigator should. But sometimes circumstances are such that we want to believe one thing, blinding us to the truth."

"I know... I just wish there were some sort of tangible evidence out there other than word of mouth to go on! We have no idea who to trust or believe here. Anyone could be lying. Hell, being here could just be one giant wild goose chase."

"Could be, but it might give you the answers you've been looking for. Don't forget that."

Nodding, I closed my eyes, wishing I had some sort of clarity about this case. I had been so convinced Galloway wasn't behind it because Mackenzie believed it, but I wasn't so sure now. As with everything else in this case, the more we found out, the less certain I was about what was really going on.

"We're here," Eli announced twenty minutes later as he pulled up to a beach house on the Gulf of Mexico. It was a cream-colored home on stilts. A flight of stairs led up to a large wrap-around deck overlooking the ocean. A vintage BMW motorcycle and a pick-up truck sat beneath the house. "Ready?" He glanced at me.

"Yeah. Let's do this." I opened the car door and started up the dozen or so steps to the deck. I rang the doorbell and waited, expecting to hear some sort of movement from within, considering the television was audible, but I heard nothing. No sign of life at all.

"Mr. McDonough?" I called, hoping he could hear me over the television. I knocked loudly and called his name once more. When there was still no response, I walked around the deck and peered through a window into the kitchen. I saw vegetables chopped on a cutting board, along with a pot of water boiling on the stove. "He's got to be here," I mumbled, heading back to the front door just as my cell phone began to ring.

"Want me to pick the lock?" Eli asked.

I looked down at the caller ID, not really liking the idea of breaking into the house of the guy we were here to get information from, but what choice did I have? I needed answers. "Yeah. Do it," I ordered, bringing my cell to my ear. "Benson, how did it go?"

"It didn't," he replied, practically yelling. I heard sirens and a commotion in the background, a sense of urgency washing over me.

"What do you mean? What happened?"

"I don't know, but when we got here, our guy's house was fully engulfed in flames. The entire street was blocked off, but we were able to sneak in. Apparently, there was evidence of some sort of bomb. There was a tripwire that triggered an explosion when the front door was opened."

My eyes immediately went to Eli using his lock pick set to pry open the front door and my stomach dropped. I hung up on Benson in mid-sentence as Eli turned the knob and I heard a click. Everything after that was in slow motion as I felt a rush of heat. Meeting Eli's terrified eyes, we escaped the scorching flames the only way we could. Placing one arm on the railing of the deck, we hoisted our bodies up and over, an explosion sending us flying onto the sand of the beach before darkness washed over me.

Chapter Twenty-Five

Change

Mackenzie

"HOW DO YOU LIKE this one?" Jenna asked, pointing to a rustic-looking crib made of reclaimed wood. "Oh, and it will transform to a toddler bed, then a twin bed, too. What do you think, Mack?"

I shrugged, indifferent about the whole process. Now that I wasn't sure about anything in my life, the excitement of buying nursery furniture had faded. In its place was an overwhelming feeling of unease in the pit of my stomach. "It's nice," I said, my voice soft.

"And how about this mobile for over it?" Brayden interjected. "This whole setup is perfect, don't you think?"

"Yeah," I agreed, not even looking. I just wanted to get out of here and be alone. "It is. I'll get it."

"Really, Mack?" Brayden said. "Really? You really think it's perfect? You didn't even look at it! You've been out of it all day, and now you just agreed to give your baby *boy* a Disney princess themed crib."

I finally looked at the nursery set and cringed at all the pink and purple surrounding me. "Sorry," I offered. "It's pregnancy brain, I suppose."

I continued past them, running my hand against another crib that was a darker wood. Glancing up the aisle, every crib looked nearly identical. Did the kid really care what the furniture in his room looked like?

"No," Jenna said, catching up to me. "It's something else. You can't fool us, Mack. We know you. What's *really* going on?"

Sighing, I stepped into another nursery setup and plopped down on the glider, rocking back and forth. "It's Tyler."

"What about him?" Brayden asked. "I thought things were good between you two."

"They were…until this morning when he asked me to move in with him…"

Brayden's and Jenna's faces lit up, displaying a level of excitement I hadn't seen in a while.

"In Boston," I finished. Their expressions fell just slightly, but not nearly as much as I had thought they would.

"Let me guess," Brayden began, walking toward me. "You said no."

"I didn't really *say* anything. I yelled at him for even thinking I was willing to move somewhere I had only spent a few days just so he could be close to his friends and family. What about *my* friends? What about *my* life? Doesn't he understand I worked my ass off for years to make the restaurant as successful as it is? How can he expect me to just walk away from all of it?"

"You said you were planning on taking a few months off from work after the baby was born anyway," Jenna said. "The restaurant has been practically running itself for a while now. Not to mention we've been talking about expanding the brand into newer markets, Boston being one of the places we discussed. If you lived there, you'd be in a perfect position to manage the opening of that restaurant!"

"That's beside the point!" I exclaimed, my face flaming. "His life is up there. Mine is down here. With everything going on, I can't leave my dad. And I can't leave you two! We've been practically attached at the hip for the past eight years! How can he expect me to pick up and leave the only family I have?" Tears began to well in my eyes at the thought of not being able to have my traditional Friday girls' night, of not waking up some mornings to see Brayden lying in bed beside me, of not walking into the kitchen at the restaurant to another one of Jenna's culinary experiments. When I was younger, I dreamed of finally going back to North Carolina, to the only home I thought I had. I finally had a new home, a new family that I loved more than I thought possible. I couldn't abandon that again, not when the memory of what it was like to be forced from the only home I had was still fresh in my mind, despite the passing years.

"But we'll only be a quick flight away," Brayden assured me, rubbing his hand up and down my arms. "We'll come visit as much as we can. And when you're able, you can come see us, especially in those cold winter months." He shivered in a dramatic manner, bringing a smile to my face. "I'm not a fan of snow, unless I'm watching it fall with a hot guy keeping me warm…if you know what I mean." He winked.

"You moving won't change our relationship," Jenna added. "A few thousand miles can't come between us, and you know it."

"It's just…" I took a deep breath, trying to compose my thoughts. All day, I had been trying to figure out what it was about Tyler's proposition that I didn't like. The truth was, it scared me. I would be in a new place, with a new family, with no support system like I had here. "Who will I run to when things get bad?" I asked with a quiver in my voice.

Brayden sighed dramatically. "You're such a pessimist."

"No, I'm not!" I insisted. "I'm a realist. Big difference."

He rolled his eyes. "Who says things are going to get bad? How have things been lately?"

"Great. Better than great. Perfect...which is exactly why I'm worried. I'm just scared I'll get there and will see a different Tyler than the one who's been down here with me. I won't be able to run to you guys for advice..."

"Of course you will! We're always just a phone call away," he interjected.

"Mackenzie," Jenna said, her voice low. "You know as well as I do that this isn't a place where you can raise a child. Don't you want Triple B to be near children his own age he can play with? He won't have that here, not when the population of this island changes each week."

"I know." I sank further into the glider, feeling defeated. "I guess I'm just scared of all this change at once. Not only am I going to have to completely rearrange everything because of the baby, but now I have to uproot my life? I just—"

"Do you love him?" Jenna interrupted.

I nodded without hesitation.

"And you know he loves you. If you don't want to move to Boston, you know damn well he will stay wherever you *do* want to live. I think you owe it to him to at least consider Boston as an option."

I sighed, knowing she was right. It was selfish of me to not at least start the discussion with Tyler. Yes, the idea of having to move to a completely new city scared me, but wasn't that part of being in a relationship? Making sacrifices? Stepping out of your comfort zone? I would have been lying if the thought of Triple B growing up in Tyler's gorgeous house hadn't crossed my mind once or twice over the past few months. And maybe that was what was most important. Not what was best for me or Tyler, but what was best for our baby.

"I'm not saying yes, but I'll think about it."

"That's my girl," Brayden said, helping me up from the glider.

"But you promise you'll both come visit every chance you get?"

"Of course! We can't have Friday girls' night without you!" He nudged me.

I wrapped my arms around both of them, pulling them in close. "Thanks, guys. I love you wholes."

"And we love you, too, Mack," Brayden said, kissing my forehead.

Chapter Twenty-Six

Regret

Mackenzie

SATURDAY WAS A PERFECT day. The air was crisp and warm, the sun was shining, a few clouds adding a beautiful texture to the sky, and the summer tourist season was over, leaving the island calm and peaceful for a change. On the outside, it appeared as though everything was just as it should be. But inside, I struggled to fight back the uneasy feeling growing stronger with each passing second.

As I stood on the sidewalk outside my restaurant, listening to Tyler's voicemail pick up for the seventh time that morning, I struggled to control my anger. I had tried to reach him yesterday evening before girls' night, but got no answer. At the time, I shook it off, knowing he'd be at my baby shower today. But now that it was thirty minutes past the time the shower was scheduled to begin, I questioned my entire relationship with him. I had told him how important it was to me that he be at my side today. I didn't know what to think anymore.

"Mack," Jenna's voice cut through. I spun around to see her stepping outside.

"Hey," I said, my expression dropping.

"I'm sorry, Mack, but it's time."

She placed her hand on my arm in a consoling manner and led me toward the front doors. "I'm sure there's a very good reason he's not here," she offered. "He wouldn't just not show up. That's not like him."

"Apparently, he's not the man I thought he was," I hissed. Pausing, I put a fake smile on my face, not wanting all my friends, who had traveled from far away, to see how upset I was about Tyler's absence, especially Colleen and Olivia.

"There she is!" Brayden exclaimed, wrapping his arms around me as I entered the dining room of the restaurant that had been decorated in pastel blues and yellows. I blindly followed him as I approached each table, thanking everyone for coming. I tried to put on a smile, but my brain was elsewhere.

"Is everything okay, Mackenzie, dear?" Colleen asked, placing her hand on my arm as we sat eating lunch. I had barely touched the food in front of me.

"Hmm? What?" I responded, trying to snap out of my thoughts. I could feel the eyes of everyone sitting at our table, Olivia and Melanie included, on me.

"Are you okay?" she asked in a hushed tone.

"I'm fine. Just tired." I continued to move my salad around my plate, a lump beginning to form in my throat.

"Does this have something to do with the reason my son's not here?" she whispered.

I tore my eyes from my food and sighed. "I suppose." I lowered my voice. "He asked me to move to Boston with him…"

"He did?" she replied in shock, her voice rising in pitch before she lowered it. "I had no idea he was thinking that. I thought he'd want to stay here."

"Join the club," I responded flatly.

"It threw you for a bit of a surprise, didn't it?"

"Yes, but Brayden and Jenna smacked some sense into me after I told them I may have overreacted when he asked me. Now he's just ignoring me."

"Well, don't worry. When I see him next, I'll give him hell for missing this. He's already missed so much of your pregnancy. Even if he *is* upset, he has no reason not to be here today."

I placed a bit of lettuce in my mouth, a sick feeling in my stomach as I tried to swallow. I couldn't shake what Jenna had said earlier. Tyler *wouldn't* simply miss this. I never considered anything could be wrong, but I was now consumed with the idea that something had happened.

Our lunch plates were cleared and I proceeded through the spectacle of opening gifts in front of grown men and women, as if I were still ten and celebrating my birthday. Clothes, diapers, wipes, strollers, car seats… It was all there, and then some.

Finally, the guests began to trickle out. As grateful as I was to everyone for coming, all I really wanted was to go home, crawl into bed, and forget about the last two days.

"We may need a truck for all of this," Brayden joked after the last guest had left and it was just him, Jenna, and me. I looked at the overflowing gift table. I had no idea where I was going to put it all.

"Do you want to keep all of it here for now?" Jenna asked. We shared a look and I knew she could tell I was having trouble reconciling why Tyler had missed today. "That way, you won't be tripping over all this stuff at your place. The back storage room is empty, so we can just put it in there."

"Do you mind?"

"Not at all," she said, grabbing my hand and pulling me toward the exit. "Now, go home and relax."

"But the gifts… I can help move them."

"Not a chance in hell," Brayden said. "The only lifting you need to be doing is that of your feet and a spoon as you gorge on ice cream."

I stared at him, wondering how he knew what I intended to do when I got home.

"I know you, Kenzie," he explained. "Since you can't seek comfort in a bottle of wine right now, it's our other best friends to the rescue."

"At least Ben and Jerry have never stood me up," I mumbled, grabbing my purse.

"I'm sorry, Mack," Brayden said, planting a kiss on my forehead. "But don't worry. When Tyler shows his face again, he's going to regret missing today. You can count on that."

"Thanks, boo." I stood on my toes and kissed his cheek.

After making plans to get together at my place tomorrow to watch football, which was just an excuse to order pizza and check out built men with nice asses, I said my goodbyes and drove the short distance back to my condo.

As I walked into the lobby, I paused briefly when I saw Martin sitting at the security desk. I should have known he'd be there. He was there when I left earlier. However, at that time, I was under the impression Tyler would be attending my baby shower. Now, I needed answers.

"Where is he?" I asked, my eyes fierce.

"Who?" Martin replied in an uncertain tone. He tilted his head, his lips pursing as he studied me with a furrowed brow.

"Tyler. He was supposed to be at the baby shower today and he never showed up. What do you know? Is he still upset I didn't agree to move to Boston with him? If that's the case, I tried calling late last night and early this morning to talk about it, but he refused to pick up!"

"Wait. Slow down, Miss Delano," Martin said, getting up from the desk and pulling me to a corner that led down to a back hallway. "You haven't heard from him?"

His eyes were intense, his grip on my arm harsh.

"No," I replied, my voice softening. "The last time I saw or spoke to him was yesterday morning. Why? What's going on?"

He released me from his grasp, his gaze intense. "All I know is he and Eli went to Florida yesterday to chase down a lead."

My heart sank, a horrible premonition forming. "Do you think something happened?"

"I'm sure he's fine," he replied, his voice distant. Snapping his eyes back to me, he led me toward the bank of elevators and pressed the call button, the doors opening immediately. "Go upstairs and relax. I'll do what I can to get in touch with him and make sure he contacts you immediately."

"But—"

"Please, Miss Delano. Don't stress about this. I assure you. I will let you know when I find out anything. Okay?"

I nodded just as the doors closed and the elevator whisked me to the twelfth floor of my building.

A thousand scenarios ran through my brain as I walked down the hall and into my condo, disarming the alarm. I fell onto the couch and closed my eyes, keeping my phone clutched in my hands, praying Tyler's phone call would come.

~~~~~~~~~~

A LOUD KNOCKING ON my door startled me and I flung my eyes open, staring at my darkened living room. Slightly disoriented, I sat up on the couch, wondering for how long I had fallen asleep. The last thing I remembered was talking to Martin about Tyler, then going to my condo. I had planned to relax and watch some mindless television while I waited to hear from Tyler...

Tyler.

I snatched my phone off the couch, hopeful to see a missed call or text. When I looked at the screen and saw nothing, I grew more worried. The knocking at my door continued and I jumped up. I took several determined steps into the foyer and pulled open the front door.

"Did you find...?" I stopped short when I saw Martin standing there, panic in his eyes. My heart dropped to the pit of my stomach, the fear that something had happened returning. I didn't know Martin well, but I knew enough to sense that something had to be amiss.

"What is it?" I asked in a small voice.

He unexpectedly reached for my hand and clasped it in his, his expression soft as he looked down at my small hand enclosed in his.

"Martin, please...," I begged.

He cleared his throat and met my eyes once more. "There's been an accident."

"An accident?" I shrieked, my hands beginning to shake as a chill ran through me. "What kind of accident?"

"It took a great deal of digging to find out what I could. Tyler and Eli went to Florida yesterday to question someone who may have been able to help with the case, someone who had apparently served with your father. I don't know the details, but the house exploded."

I gasped, letting out a loud sob as I clutched onto Martin's arms, unable to stand.

"Where is he?" I asked through the ache in my throat. There were a million things I had left unsaid with Tyler and I had no idea if I would ever be able to tell him everything.

"He's in the trauma unit at Tampa General Hospital. I

269

don't know the status of either his or Eli's condition, but I've been in contact with Alexander and he's informed his mother and wife what's going on. You'll be heading to Florida with them to meet up with Mr. Burnham. Everything's been arranged. I just need you to pack a bag, then I'll take you to the airport."

He ushered me inside my condo as I remained in a relative daze, still not truly comprehending what I just learned. All I knew was it sounded like Tyler was still alive... I hoped.

The entire drive to the airport was filled with thousands of scenarios of what really happened. I absently heard Martin on the phone, obviously irate with whomever he was speaking with, still unable to get any concrete answers about what was going on. This made me even more unsettled about what would greet me when I stepped off that plane in Florida.

I remained in a trance as Martin helped me onto the jet. The pilots and flight attendants introduced themselves to me, but their words went in one ear and out the other. Within minutes, both Colleen and Olivia climbed onto the plane, Melanie in tow. Olivia attempted to hide her emotions by keeping little Melanie occupied, constantly assuring her that her Uncle Tyler would be fine. Colleen was struggling to hold it together, her usual vibrant eyes full of the same emotion I was feeling...confusion, unease, dread.

I walked over to her and sat as we taxied toward the runway. Without saying a word, I took her hand in mine and we sat in heavy silence during the short flight to Florida.

Trying to fight back my tears, I feared I wouldn't make it in time to tell Tyler what I should have said to him the last time I saw him. I vowed to never say goodbye to him again without uttering those three words that too many people took for granted... *I love you.*

Chapter Twenty-Seven

Apologies

Mackenzie

"HOW COULD THAT EVEN be possible?" a familiar voice bellowed through the lobby of the flight operations base in Tampa. I trailed behind Colleen and Olivia, little Melanie clutching her mother's hand, while someone dealt with all of our bags. We all stopped dead in our tracks as Alexander paced the comfortable lobby, other passengers who were getting ready to take off in their own private planes staring at him in awe.

Melanie looked back at me and grinned. "Daddy's working. That's his work voice."

I smiled for the first time all day, thankful for the break in the tension that had permeated the flight across the Gulf of Mexico.

"Hush, Melanie," Olivia said. "Daddy's just trying to figure out what's going on. That's all."

"What happened, Mama?" she asked.

Olivia looked down at Melanie, then at me, then back at her daughter once more. Her little green eyes were alive with eagerness as she stared at her mother, waiting. "I don't know, sweet pea," Olivia finally said, caressing her daughter's face in such a caring and doting manner. I instinctively placed my hand over my stomach, hoping I'd have that same bond with my son...and that Tyler would, as well. "But Uncle Tyler is hurt and we're all

272

here to make sure he gets better."

"Like when I scraped my knee?" she asked.

"Exactly. Remember how Daddy kissed your boo-boo and made it all better after you had to get those stitches?"

She nodded.

"Well, that's why we're here."

"Olivia, love," Alexander's voice cut through, but it wasn't the same demanding, irate voice that was bellowing through the lobby just minutes ago. It was calm and serene, as if her presence was the only thing that could assuage his anxiety about what had happened to his brother.

"Alex..." She sighed into his embrace. I couldn't help but feel a hint of jealousy at their exchange. He placed an affectionate kiss on her lips before turning his attention to Melanie. He swooped her up in his arms and spun her around, her infectious giggles lightening the mood.

"Did you miss me?" Melanie asked through her laughs.

"What kind of silly question is that? Is the sky blue?"

"Yes!"

"Then I missed you more than words can say, peanut." He lowered her back to the ground, kissing her head in a loving manner.

"I'm going to kiss Uncle Tyler's boo-boo to make it all better."

Alexander's solemn expression immediately returned, causing a rush of nerves to course through me. Despite everything I thought about who he was as a person, that one look conveyed his love for his brother, how distraught he was over the fact he was lying in a hospital bed with severe injuries.

"I've called the hospital," he said in a firm voice, addressing all of us. "They wouldn't give me details regarding his condition."

"Is he conscious?" Colleen asked quickly, desperate for

any sort of news that her son was okay.

"They wouldn't say. Our best bet is to go over there and make someone give us some answers. There are two SUVs out front to escort us to the hospital." He turned to Olivia. "Why don't you and Ma take one. I'll go in the other with Miss Delano."

I immediately tensed up and shot my eyes to Colleen, silently begging her to volunteer to ride with me. I didn't know how far the hospital was from where we were, but the idea of being alone with a man who, just months ago, did everything he could to keep Tyler away from me made me edgy.

"I think Mackenzie may be able to help me figure out what happened to Tyler." He turned to me, his green eyes imploring. Those green eyes that were so similar to Tyler's. "I know I'm probably the last person you want to sit in a car with…," he said quietly as Colleen and Olivia began heading toward the front doors.

"You've got that right," I hissed, my voice barely audible.

"But I think if I tell you what I know, you may be able to fill in the blanks."

"I don't know anything. All I know is he was supposed to be at my baby shower today and he never showed. I assumed it was because of the fight we had yesterday, then Martin told me…" I bit my lip, trying to hide my tears from Alexander at the thought that the last words I would ever say to Tyler were during a fight.

"It's okay. Let's talk." He placed his hand on my back and escorted me to an idling SUV. After helping me in, he ran around to the other side and got in beside me.

The driver pulled the car out of the parking lot and onto the road. I kept my eyes glued outside, watching as streetlights zoomed by. My back remained straight, my posture taut as to not show weakness.

"I guess I should start by apologizing," Alexander finally said.

I shot my eyes to him, somewhat surprised. I didn't know what I expected him to say to me, but it certainly wasn't that.

"I thought I was doing what was best for Tyler by keeping him out of the country," he continued. "You have to look at things from where I'm sitting. Tyler's my brother and all this shit kept happening. I didn't know what to think, and until I knew what was going on, I needed to do everything I could to make sure nothing happened to him."

"But he's an adult!" I shot back. "You took advantage of the way he looks up to and admires you, and used that against him! Not to mention you tried to fuck with my memory! Do you have any idea how horrible it is to wake up every morning and question your own reality? To wonder if something finally snapped in your mind and you made everything up?"

"I can only imagine…"

"And *you* did that to me! *You!* And why? To make me think I never met Tyler? What could you possibly gain from that?"

"Sometimes in the field, no matter how much training you have, you make bad tactical decisions, particularly where a loved one is concerned. I'm sorry you were the collateral damage of that. I'll be the first to admit I never considered anything from your perspective. If I could rewind the clock, I would handle everything differently, but I don't have that luxury. What I do have is the present, and I hope you'll find it in your heart to give me the opportunity to start over with you. You're one of the most important people in Tyler's life, and that makes you one of the most important people in *my* life."

"You two are pretty close, aren't you?" I asked, shifting

gears. I wasn't sure I could forgive Alexander for everything he did to me, but I could at least try to get to know him as a person and the brother of the man with whom I was in love.

He sighed, a troubled look crossing his brow. "We were. While he was going to college, we used to get together at least once a week for a drink. Then..." He sighed. "Then it was awkward between us. He left to join the navy, and I had a family of my own, so we kind of grew apart. When he came back and started to work at the security company, things were still tense between us. It wasn't until he came back from Sudan a few months ago that we finally started to *talk* again. He was absolutely livid at me over what I had done. He even got a few punches in."

I gasped, giggling a little. "He did?"

Alexander nodded, caressing his jaw. "Yeah. So I actually have you to thank. If he never met you, I don't know if we'd be back to having the normal relationship we did all those years ago. Granted, now he's a few thousand miles away so that makes being able to go grab a drink together a bit cumbersome..."

I bowed my head, starting to realize why moving back to Boston was so important to Tyler. He had been away from home for so long, and not just because of this assignment. Even when he was home, it didn't seem like home, not if his relationship with his family was strained. But now that it was back to normal, according to Alexander, I could understand his desire to return there and have that connection once more. I regretted being so selfish as to not even consider his side.

"So," I said, clearing the air a bit. "What did you want to talk to me about?"

Alexander shrugged. "Actually, that was it. I just wanted to get you alone so I could properly apologize to you."

"So you don't know anything about Tyler? You sounded quite upset on the phone when we landed."

"Well, yes, but I'm not sure you have any answers that will help us."

"Try me," I said, leaning against the window of the car. "You never know. Maybe I know someone who can give us some insight about what happened." I raised my eyebrows at him, hoping he'd take the bait. I was desperate to know what he knew about Tyler's condition and would promise him anything, regardless of how empty those promises were.

"You know Tyler was looking into who could have set up your father, correct?"

I nodded. "Yeah. The last time I met with my father, I asked if he'd speak with Tyler and give him his side. Tyler hoped maybe there was something he was missing and my dad would have that missing piece."

"He mentioned that," Alexander said. "Tyler had some of his guys digging into your father's past...his time in the Rangers, then Counterintelligence, all of it...hoping to see if they could uncover something that would tell us who was behind everything. Two of Tyler's team members uncovered a classified mission your father led in Bosnia."

An unsettled feeling formed in the pit of my stomach at his words. My father didn't speak much of his time on deployment, but he did talk about all the places he had been. He had never mentioned Bosnia, and I knew something must have happened there that he'd rather leave forgotten and buried. I just prayed it wasn't something that would paint him as a monster.

"There was no record of it anywhere," he continued, "apart from your father filing a report that two of his team members had died. It could have been nothing, but they decided to check it out."

Sighing, he ran his hand over his face, his unease returning. "Upon closer inspection, it was discovered that only two members of your father's team are still alive. Everyone else is dead or missing. So Benson and Maxwell, two of Tyler's team members, went to go question one of them. Tyler and Eli went to question the other. When Benson and Maxwell got to the guy's house, it was in flames. The door was wired to trigger an explosion when it was opened. The subject in question was not in the house at the time, but his housekeeper triggered the explosion and died. Subsequently, *his* body was found in his car at a casino parking lot in Oklahoma, the cause of death an apparent heart attack."

"And Tyler...?" I asked with a quiver in my voice.

"Well, Benson said he spoke with Tyler to apprise him of the situation. He and Maxwell decided to stay in Oklahoma to follow-up on any information they may find. It wasn't until Martin touched base with them earlier today that they grew concerned something was wrong. They called around and found that Tyler and Eli were discovered unconscious on the beach below a stilt house that was engulfed in flames. As you would have guessed, the individual they were sent to question was found in the parking lot of a bar, having also died of an apparent heart attack."

"It's suspicious though, isn't it?" I said softly.

He nodded. "Someone must have known Tyler's team was looking into your father and wanted to put a stop to it."

"But how? Who else knew about what they were doing?"

"Well, that's the million dollar question. One I intend to get to the bottom of."

Chapter Twenty-Eight

Forever

Mackenzie

I SAT IN A sterile white waiting room on an uncomfortable chair, doctors and nurses rushing past us every few minutes. The sound of various monitors and the automatic doors surrounded me. It wasn't until now that the reality sank in. Even after Martin told me there was an accident, it didn't seem real. Now, as I waited for some news, my hand clutched in Colleen's, the truth was impossible to ignore.

"Mrs. Burnham," a gentle voice said and we all shot our heads up to see a short, blonde doctor dressed in scrubs standing with a clipboard.

"Yes?" Colleen replied as we all eagerly awaited news.

"I'm Doctor Pell. I've been in charge of your son's treatment over the past twenty-four hours."

"No one would tell us anything," Colleen began. "How is he?"

"He's in a lot of pain," she explained. "He's suffered some burns on his arms, but they're relatively minor and will fully heal in time. He must have taken a pretty nasty fall, which resulted in three cracked ribs."

"Can we see him?" I asked, desperate to see his chest rise and fall so I knew he was still alive.

"Yes, but we've been keeping him relatively sedated to ease the pain a bit. I'm hopeful he'll make a full recovery, but he has a few weeks until he'll be able to walk out of here."

"I still need to see him," I insisted, raising myself from my chair and placing my hand over my stomach.

The doctor surveyed me and her lips turned into a gentle smile. "Of course. Follow me."

I started out of the waiting room, then glanced over my shoulder to see Colleen, Alexander, Olivia, and Melanie remaining behind. "Aren't you coming?" I asked.

Colleen shook her head. "No, you go ahead. Now that we know he's okay, in a manner of speaking, we'll go check into the hotel and give you some time alone with him. Just call one of us when you're ready to leave and we'll send the car to come get you."

"Are you sure?"

"Of course, dear," she replied in a reassuring manner. "Now, go see my baby."

Smiling appreciatively, I turned and followed the doctor down several corridors toward the recovery suites. She paused outside one of the doors and slowly pushed it open, allowing me to enter, then left me alone.

The sound of monitors surrounded me, the decibel level seeming to get increasingly louder and higher as I put one foot in front of the other. With each step, Tyler's tall, built body, drained of all color, came more into focus. Bruises covered his face, stitches stretching across his chin and brow. His arms were covered in bandages, as was his midsection. Everything made him look frail, as if he were teetering on the brink of living and dying. Seeing Tyler in this state, confirming with my own eyes that he had narrowly escaped death, brought forward all the emotions I had been suppressing all evening.

I fell to the chair beside him and grabbed his hand in mine. Burying my face against him, I shivered as a chill flew through me. "I'm so sorry, Tyler," I sobbed into his chest. "I was so stubborn the other day. You just want to share your life with me and, being who I am, I completely blew it out of proportion. I get it now. I promise I'll stop being a pain in the ass. I want a new beginning with you. I want to start over again where we can watch our son play in the leaves and make snow angels. I want my new start with you...in Boston."

I glanced up to see his eyes still closed, his breathing light and even. I soaked in his face, memorizing everything about it. My tears continued to fall as I thought how different tonight could have gone, how it was a possibility I could have been sitting in a morgue instead of next to Tyler's unconscious body. Life was fragile, and I vowed to never take it for granted again.

Lowering my lips to his, I kissed him, his mouth unmoving against mine. "I love you, Tyler Burnham." I rested my head on his chest and listened to the drumming of his heart, the rhythm soothing me.

"So is that all it takes to get you to agree to move in with me?" a husky voice commented. My eyes widening, I pulled back and gazed into a pair of tired green eyes. "Surviving an explosion and a two-story fall?"

"Tyler!" I exclaimed, wrapping my arms around him. I was breathless, a tingling spreading through me.

He yelped softly and I immediately drew back.

"Sorry." I bit my lip. "I got carried away."

"You're worth the pain," he replied, clutching my hand in his.

"I thought I lost you," I choked out as he closed his eyes once more, obviously trying to fight off the drugs.

"Impossible, Serafina," he crooned. "You think a small little fire can keep me from you? It'll take a lot more than a few burns and some cracked ribs."

I laughed at how nonchalant he was over nearly dying, allowing the warmth of his presence and heart to surround me as I rested my head next to his.

"I love you, Tyler."

"Even with my stank ass hospital breath?" he joked.

"*Especially* with your stank ass hospital breath."

He let out a content sigh as a small smile crossed his face. "Stay," he murmured in a lazy voice.

"For how long?"

"Forever."

I took a satisfied breath and held onto his hand, remaining by his side throughout the night. Forever sounded like a good plan to me.

~~~~~~~~~~

LOW VOICES ECHOED AROUND me, but I tried to tune them out. A sort of glow filled me and I didn't want to wake up only to find out it had all just been a dream.

"You can't really think it was someone on the inside," a voice said softly.

Tyler.

"I don't know what to think," Alexander whispered in response. "Who knew what you were doing?"

"Just Benson, Maxwell, Eli, Martin, and me. Hell, Benson and Maxwell had just tracked down the lead. We hadn't even contacted either subject to let them know we were coming."

"And Martin already did a sweep of your house for bugs." He sighed loudly. I could sense his frustration.

It was silent for a moment before anyone spoke again. "You said Maxwell hacked into some army database and that's how he found out about the mission in Bosnia, right?" Tyler asked, his tone growing urgent.

"Yes. You don't think...?"

"What other explanation is there? Maybe whoever did this is just as talented, or more so, than Maxwell is.

Mackenzie's friend, Damian, has been missing for months now, and he just happens to be one of my most skilled hackers out there. Maybe he was taken, like his FBI colleagues think, and is being forced to do this guy's dirty work. From what I've read about him, he's more than capable of putting a trace on the file, and maybe when Maxwell hacked into it, he could have stirred up something that had been left dormant for years. Think about it... The members of the team who had died or gone missing did so years ago. And now, all of a sudden, the remaining two, who had been practically impossible to even track down, end up dead, their houses wired to explode. I think we may have found out the link as to why Galloway was set up. I have a feeling it has something to do with the mission in Bosnia and how two of his men ended up not coming home from that mission."

"Well, in light of recent events, there's an unfortunate reality we need to face," Alexander said.

"That Galloway is the only remaining member of his Ranger team still alive," Tyler responded, dejected.

"Precisely... Suspicious or just a coincidence?"

"I know. I just..."

I began to stir, not wanting to listen to any more. I didn't want to hear anything else that could taint the picture of my father I had in my head.

"There you are," Tyler crooned, meeting my eyes as they adjusted to the light in the room. "I hope we didn't wake you."

"No, you didn't." I sat up in the chair, rubbing my sore neck, my entire body aching from whatever position I had fallen asleep in.

"Well," Alexander said, eyeing both Tyler and me. "I'll give you two a bit of privacy. I'll be back sometime this afternoon with Olivia and Melanie." He placed his hand on Tyler's shoulder, squeezing gently. "I'm glad you're okay, Ty."

Tyler met his brother's eyes, placing his hand over his. "Me, too. See you in a bit."

"You bet." Alexander released his hold on him and retreated from the room, closing the door behind him.

"Good morning," I said, grabbing his hand in mine. "How are you feeling?"

"Like I jumped off a deck."

I smiled warmly at his ability to make light of what he had been through.

"How's Eli doing? Have you heard?" I asked. I had been so concerned with Tyler's well-being, I had completely forgotten about Eli.

"He's actually doing a lot better than I am. From what they said, they figure I pushed him out of the way and took the brunt of the explosion. He dislocated his shoulder and has a mild concussion, but he's up and walking today."

"What happened?" I asked now that he seemed much more coherent than he did just twelve hours earlier.

He sighed. I could tell he was tired of repeating the story over and over. I had heard the basics from Alexander, but I wanted Tyler's point of view.

"Friday, Benson came to me with a potential lead," he began, repeating what I already knew about a link between my father and a classified mission in Bosnia. "When we got to the guy's house, there was no answer. We peeked in and saw signs that struck us as odd, so we decided to break in, just in case something was amiss. That's when I got the phone call from Benson about the explosion at the house of the guy they were supposed to question. Just as Eli turned the knob, I heard a click and pushed him out of the way. Everything after that was kind of a blur. I remember hoisting myself over the railing of the deck and landing on the beach below. The last thing I could recall before waking up here was seeing your eyes."

"My eyes?"

He nodded. "I was so worried I wasn't going to make it and you'd have to raise our son without me. I began to regret so many things, Mackenzie...missed opportunities, missed moments, missed kisses. And I swore, if I survived, I'd do everything to make up for all of that lost time with you. I've been so focused on finally figuring out what happened with your father all those years ago. I lost sight of what's really important." His voice had an urgent and demanding quality to it. I was lost in his words and eyes as his hand caressed my knuckles, a yearning coursing through me.

"And what's that?" I murmured.

"You," he exhaled, a peaceful smile on his face. "The doctor said I'm stuck here for at least two weeks while they treat my burns. After that, let's go somewhere and get away from everything for a while. I want to go somewhere different, somewhere fresh, somewhere we can get the new beginning we both need. We're already in Florida. We'll go rent a house in Palm Beach for a few weeks. We can wake up every morning and watch the sunrise. We'll spend our days watching the relaxing waves. Every night, we can make love like it's the first time. Hell, we can even get married while we're there."

"What?!" I exclaimed, pulling away and staring at him, wide-eyed.

He reached for my hand, caressing it once more as my spine remained taut. I wondered if this was simply the pain meds talking. "I know it may not be entirely conventional, but since when have we really followed any rule book?"

"Never," I replied, laughing through my nerves.

Everything about this was completely unexpected. But, then again, everything about my relationship with Tyler had been that way from the very beginning.

"Serafina Galloway," he began, surprising me with the ease he spoke my real name, "I know things haven't always been easy between us, not to mention the fact our entire relationship early on was based on lies. But I'd rather be completely exasperated by your thick-headedness than have it easy with someone else. I'd rather fight my way through every jungle, desert, and stormy ocean to hold you than to never feel my heart race with adrenaline like it does when I think of you. I'd rather wake up to an empty bed without you in it than wake up next to the wrong person every day for the rest of my life. You are it for me. You're my turtledove, my lightning strike."

I remained speechless, holding my breath. This proposal seemed different than his first one. That one was tainted with his lies and deception. I had been hesitant to consider marrying him back then, concerned with the fact that it was too soon, that people didn't just meet and get engaged a few weeks later. But now, after everything that had transpired between us, there was no hesitation on my part. I knew what my answer had to be.

"Tyler, I…"

Before I could finish what I wanted to say, he reached into the neck of his hospital gown and pulled out his dog tags.

"Since when do you wear those?" I asked.

Shrugging, he lifted them over his head, cringing a bit from the pain in his ribs. "Usually only when I go somewhere that could be dangerous. It's always good to have them as a form of identification, just in case. I wore them every day while I was over in Sudan."

"Was it dangerous there?"

He shook his head, toying with the chain a bit before breaking it open. "No. I wore these to keep a reminder of what I lost close to my heart."

I followed his hands and saw him slide off a brilliant diamond solitaire, the stone easily at least three carats, surrounded by a double band of smaller stones. "Serafina Galloway," he said, his voice steady, his expression serene, "I've lived every day with the pain I caused you. I know we still have a long way to go, but I promise I will do everything I can to make you smile more than you frown. I promise to love you and our son more than words can even express. I promise to always be honest with you. Please, marry me." He raised the ring to my finger, his eyes eagerly awaiting my answer.

Ever since I was a little girl, I had dreamed of what my proposal would be like. I had envisioned a handsome man clad in a suit kneeling before me, asking me to spend the rest of my life with him. I never imagined sitting in a hospital room, my Prince Charming covered with burns and scars, holding a stunning ring up to me, begging me to give him a chance to prove his words were true. But I wouldn't trade this moment for anything. It was perfect. It was meaningful. More importantly, it was us.

"Yes, Tyler. Of course I'll marry you!" I exclaimed, throwing my arms around him and kissing him fully on the mouth.

He let out a low groan and I pulled back to see a look of discomfort on his face.

"Sorry," I said, cupping his cheek. "I keep forgetting."

"It's okay. Feeling your lips on mine is certainly worth the pain. Don't worry. Doc said I'll be back to my fighting shape in a few weeks, and I plan on making up for lost time, if you know what I mean." He raised his eyebrows in a lascivious manner, and a heat radiated through me from his intense gaze.

"Oh, really? And how do you intend to go about that?" I asked, my mouth hovering over his.

"It's a surprise."

I shook my head. "You don't get off that easily, mister. I want a sneak peek at your hand." I tugged at his hair, running my tongue across the stubble that had grown on his cheek.

"You don't play fair. If a nurse came in right now, do you know how hard it would be to hide what you're doing to me?"

I glanced down and saw his excitement through the hospital sheets. "Good. I want them to be jealous of what's mine," I murmured in a sultry voice.

"Yours?" he raised his eyebrows.

"Yes. Mine."

"Mine," he repeated, running his tongue across my lips. "I would start slow," he breathed, caving in to my request that he give me a sneak peek. His chest began to rise and fall faster, his tone becoming more raspy with each word he spoke. "And by slow, I don't mean gentle. I know you, Serafina, and I know you like it just like I do."

"And how's that?" I asked, my voice seductive.

"Rough, hard. You like to feel every thrust and push. And I like the way you feel around me when I bring you closer and closer to the brink."

I moaned, my body on fire. Just picturing how he wanted to seduce me was setting me off, every nerve in my body sensitive. "More," I exhaled. "I want more."

"I'll push you against the wall and make you feel how much I want you. You'll plead with me to get on with it already, but I'll make you wait for it, beg for it. I won't even kiss you, not yet. I'll be so close, yet just far enough away that you'll be on edge, ready to fall apart the first time I touch you…and I *will* touch you."

"Where?" I moved toward the edge of my chair, wishing I could crawl into the hospital bed beside him and feel his skin on mine. The next few weeks would be torture.

"I'll start by running my fingers through your hair," he said as he grabbed my ponytail, forcing my head back. "I'll have you trapped, unable to see anything I don't want you to. Then I'll take my time exploring the rest of your body. Your lips. Your neck. Your chest. Your stomach. Your nipples. I'll push against you as I take them in my mouth, sucking on them. Your entire body will be on edge, your mind a blank slate as you fight against coming from that alone."

I kept my eyes closed, moisture pooling between my legs. I squeezed them together, praying for some sort of release. I didn't care that we were in a hospital where his nurses or doctor could walk in at any minute. I needed *something* to ease the tension.

"Then, just when you're about to let go, I'll release my hold on you, leaving you a panting mess. This is when I'll ask you one question."

"Yes?" I breathed. "What's that?"

"Do you want more, Serafina?"

"Yes," I responded almost immediately. I lowered my head to his and nibbled on his earlobe. "I need more."

"That's my girl," he crooned in a sly voice. "I'll lift you onto the desk and tell you to spread your legs, and you'll obey like the good girl you are."

My legs were on autopilot, obeying his demand as if we were acting out the words he spoke.

"Good." He ran his hand through my hair before traveling the length of my body, down my torso, over my hip, stopping at my thigh. My stomach clenched, anticipation rushing through me. I felt light-headed, my skin tingling with each passing moment.

"I'll run my tongue up and down your inner thighs, keeping my eyes glued to that perfect pussy of yours, and I'll get so fucking hard when I see how wet you are. I won't be able to take it anymore. I'll need to taste you, to feel you, to watch you come." Instantly, his fingers found their way beneath my skirt, pushing my panties to the side, and he began to circle me. I bit on his neck, trying to muffle my screams.

"We wouldn't care that we were in front of the window where anyone could see us. We would only get louder and louder as we put on a show for all the miserable couples outside. And we would vow to never become one of those people. We would promise to never let life and commitments come between us. I couldn't imagine going more than a day where I couldn't listen to your moans, where I couldn't watch you move against me, where I couldn't feel this beautiful pussy as it comes around me."

His motions grew more frenzied and before I could stop it, I was reenacting his words, releasing around his fingers, the orgasm ravaging through me as I fought to contain my screams. It was euphoric, the fierceness of the pleasure never seeming to end.

Finally, my tremors began to subside, but I remained in place, keeping my head snuggled against his chest. The room was still, except for our breathing.

"I hope that all sounds good to you," he said, breaking the silence.

All I could do was nod, desperately trying to get my heart rate under control as I heard a familiar thump echoing, thinking it was simply Tyler's heart. Then it grew louder, slowing to a stop in front of the door. I shot up and quickly readjusted myself, my mind racing.

"What is it, Mackenzie?" Tyler asked in a low voice.

Before I could respond, the door opened and I snapped my head in that direction, unsure of what to say.

Chapter Twenty-Nine

No Guarantee

Tyler

"DAD...?" MACKENZIE SHOT UP from her chair and rushed toward the older man limping into the hospital room, his eyes studying me in an unnerving manner. This wasn't the first time I was meeting the parents but, considering I had only started dating his daughter to get close to him and he knew about it, I couldn't help but be on edge. Not to mention, I had a million questions I needed answered, the most important being whether it was merely a coincidence he was now the only remaining team member alive.

"What are you doing here? It's not safe for you!" She ushered him toward the chair she was just sitting in, glancing over her shoulder for any perceptive hospital staff members. "And how did you find out where I was?"

"Serafina, dear, don't be rude," he said. His voice was raspy, weathered, but even-tempered with a hint of amusement. "We'll get to all of that in due time, *mi bichito*. First, don't you think you should introduce me to this young man, whom it appears you're going to marry?"

She followed his line of sight to see him staring at her ring, a warm smile crossing his face.

"Of course." She appeared to be a bit on edge at the surprising turn of events. "Dad, this is Tyler Burnham," she said hesitantly, looking between the two of us, almost unsure of how this was going to play out. "Tyler, this is my father." She took a deep breath. "Francis Galloway."

"Tyler," he began, taking my hand with enthusiasm. "It's a pleasure to finally meet you."

"Likewise, Colonel," I responded, wanting to show him the respect he deserved at one point in his life. The respect he may *still* deserve.

He sat back in the chair, his stature relaxing. "Please, call me Francis."

I smiled slightly. "Very well, Francis."

A heavy silence fell and I looked at Mackenzie. I had no idea what was going on, but that seemed to be par for the course lately.

"Well… I guess I'll go to the ladies room and allow you two to get to know each other better," Mackenzie said, practically running toward the door.

"*Mi bichito?*" Francis called as she was about to leave.

"Yes?"

"I think it best you stay. I have a feeling Tyler has many questions for me, and I'd like you to hear all the answers, as well. We promised each other full disclosure. I kept you in the dark for years, and I can't do that anymore. It's time I stop hiding and finally confront the past. Too many people have gotten hurt, your mother and Tyler included, trying to find out the truth of what really happened. There's too much blood on my hands and it needs to stop, even if I can't save myself."

Her brow furrowed as she listened to his words. She slowly returned to the bed and pulled up another chair, sitting down. They both looked at me with eager eyes and I could see the resemblance. Even through the burns that had scarred the entire left side of Galloway's body, there was no mistaking the similarity between the two.

"I'm not exactly prepared," I said, breaking the

tension.

"It's okay. I suppose it's best we start at the beginning."

"The embassy fire..."

He shook his head and grinned mischievously. "No. That's the end...more or less. The beginning was Bosnia."

I settled in for what I knew had to be a story unlike any I could have anticipated.

"The U.S. didn't want to get involved in the civil war, but that didn't mean troops weren't sent over there. There were thousands of troops deployed who were stationed in a safe zone, ready to intervene if need be. And there were some of us there on intelligence gathering missions. What you need to understand is that things were so fucked up over there. The carnage was unlike anything anyone should ever have to see and it gets to you. Our unit's sole purpose was to try to get intel on Serbian and Croatian movements, plans, et cetera, and that meant turning someone on the inside. We went through thousands of dossiers, looking for someone who would have some motive to help us. We stumbled on a man name Viktor Popovic. Granted, there was nothing too suspicious about him on paper, but when I looked at family history, something struck me as odd."

"What was that?" I asked, intrigued.

"He was only twenty-three at the time of Bosnia and Herzegovina's declaration of independence. At which time, he also filed for and was granted a very quick divorce. Upon further inspection, I realized his father was very influential in the Bosnian Serbs. It all could have turned out to be nothing, but something didn't sit right with me about this. I looked into his former wife and learned she was Muslim. It made me very suspicious. Maybe this guy's father forced him to divorce her. Maybe he had privileged information regarding the forthcoming ethnic cleansing of the Muslims and wanted to save his son from that. So we took our chances and made our approach to learn more."

"And what did you learn?" I asked, taking a sip of water.

"That my instincts were right. It took some time to get this guy to open up and talk about everything, but he eventually admitted he tried to fight his father on the matter, but his father promised him his wife would not meet any harm if he agreed to divorce her. So he did. Of course, this wasn't what I wanted to hear. I was hoping to use his ex-wife as leverage to get him to be my man on the inside. So I did what I could to look into his ex-wife's whereabouts. We found that she was being held at a sort of concentration camp just over the border from the safe zone. At first, Viktor didn't want to believe us. He insisted he had been secretly seeing her up until about a month prior when his father put her on a flight to Greece, but I had planted that seed of doubt. Days later, he came to me, furious. He had confronted his father and found out that his wife, Irena, had been taken to a camp. He agreed to help us with any information we wanted, as long as we agreed to bring Irena to safety."

He shook his head and took a deep breath, briefly looking away as he composed himself. When he looked back up, his eyes were worn, the weariness etched on his face. "I'm not proud of it, but I agreed, although I had no intention of following through. An operation like that could take months to plan and, by that time, I hoped to be long gone with enough information that could help our country should we have to become involved in the conflict."

"But that didn't happen, did it?" Mackenzie asked, grabbing her father's hand, comforting him.

"No, it didn't. The more I learned about what was

going on over there, the harder following my directive to not get involved became. When I learned exactly what was happening in those camps, I knew I couldn't sit by and do nothing. Based solely on my promise that I would deliver his wife to safety, Viktor had put his own life at risk to help me and my country. And I knew I had to make it right.

"When I approached my team with my plan, I gave them an out. Going in and doing an extraction at the camp would be dangerous. Lives could be lost, but I needed to be true to my word. I couldn't live with myself if I didn't. Surprisingly, my entire unit was with me. Since we didn't have the backing of the U.S. government, we would need to go in, do the extraction, and get back across the border and into the safe zone without being detected or firing a single shot. It was a smaller camp set up at a hotel, but it was still risky, especially without having the luxury of time to properly plan. We were pretty much going in blind, hoping his wife was still alive."

"You didn't even know whether she was alive?" Mackenzie asked.

He slowly shook his head. "No, but I knew I would regret it if we didn't at least *try* to go in. The following night, we made our way the few kilometers from our base camp and into Bosnian territory. As we approached the hotel, the screams I heard were chilling. The cries..." He shuddered.

"I wished I couldn't speak their language. That way, I wouldn't understand their words, begging for their abuser to stop, saying they'd rather die than have to suffer through any more brutality."

He buried his head in his hands and tugged at the little hair he had. The room was still as we were on the edge of our proverbial seats to find out how the mission went.

Francis slowly raised his head and, with a furrowed brow, met my eyes. "I had seen a lot of things during my time with the Rangers," he started, his voice strained. "And I have seen a lot of things since. But nothing compares to what I witnessed that evening. It's stayed with me always, and I have a feeling it will until my dying day."

He stared into the distance as a lone tear trickled down his cheek. I barely saw any combat during my time in the navy, so I had no idea how I would react to the sights and sounds he was describing, albeit vaguely. I knew enough about the conflict in Bosnia to fill in the blanks, though.

"Viktor went in first and made small talk with the Serbian guard stationed at the front, giving us an opportunity to sneak in. Once inside, we broke into teams of two to search for our target. Harrison and I were pretty lucky, finding her in the first room we swept."

"Harrison Mills?" I asked.

"Yes."

"Wait a minute," Mackenzie interjected. "Is that...?" She raised her eyebrows, her father simply nodding in response. "How did I not know that?" She leaned back in her chair as she rubbed her temples.

"Not know what?" I asked, feeling like I was missing something.

"That one of the members of my unit eventually moved in next door to us when he transferred to Counterintelligence."

"Damian's father?" I looked at Mackenzie.

"Yes."

"So, besides you, he's the only one from your team who's still alive, although he's supposedly been missing for years."

He shook his head. "He's not missing, but we'll get to

296

that."

"Okay," I agreed, curious as to what the story with Mills was.

"Like I was saying, Harrison and I found Viktor's wife and did a quick extraction. She was in a room with roughly twenty other women, all of them chained to the wall. They were pleading with us to be set free, to take them with us, but I couldn't. We weren't even supposed to be there, and I needed to do everything to minimize the potential backlash of causing what could be viewed as an international incident. I hated what I did, but I simply shook my head without giving them so much as an explanation. Later, when I found out that only about twenty women ever made it out of that camp alive..." He let out a breath. "Well, I don't have to tell you how much that guilt still eats at me to this day."

"I can imagine," I commented.

"We were lucky to have even been able to get in and find our target with no issues. But luck eventually runs out, and I knew ours would, too. As we were approaching the lobby, where Viktor was still distracting the guard, I heard two gunshots come from down the hall, followed by frantic shouting from some guards. I knew I shouldn't have looked back, that I should have kept going, but I needed to know. I saw two of my guys, Ian McKay and Michael Cranston, lying on the floor, each with a bullet hole in their heads. They were both married with children, but their families never got to bury their loved ones. We never got to hand over a body to them so they could properly say their goodbyes. They never got the closure they needed."

"You can't blame yourself, Dad," Mackenzie said, clutching his hand in hers. "You gave them an opportunity to stay back, but they did what they thought was right, regardless of the consequences."

"They weren't the only casualties that night," he continued, as if he didn't even hear Mackenzie. He was in a trance, telling the story he had probably wanted to share for decades. "As we approached the border, a small group of Serbian guards gained on us, haphazardly firing their weapons. It was every man for himself, all of us trying to cross the border into the safe zone as quickly as possible.

"It was chaotic as my team members followed me across the border and concealed ourselves in the heavy forest, all of us letting out a collective sigh. I looked at Harrison, thinking he had Viktor's wife with him, and grew confused when I saw he didn't. Several more shots were fired and there was a loud scream. I snapped my head in the direction of the commotion, still trying to hide myself, and saw Irena fall to the ground, clutching her leg.

"The Serbs grabbed her and tied her to a tree. Viktor began firing on the guards, who returned fire. It was ten men against one and, just shy of the border, he fell. He looked at me as blood poured from his chest. His eyes are still permanently ingrained in my memory, pleading with me to finally fire my weapon. I remember feeling the metal of my gun in my hand as I raised it, knowing I was at a crossroads. We were easily outnumbered. The mission was a failure. If I engaged, I risked losing more team members. If we walked away, at least I could ensure the rest of my men would make it home to their families. So I lowered my weapon, refusing to fire. There was one final gunshot and Irena's body went limp as she remained tied to the tree. I remember being transfixed by the sight of blood pouring from the bullet wound in her head.

"Before we returned to camp, standing with Viktor's and Irena's dying bodies just feet from us, we swore to each other that we would never speak about that night. According to us, McKay and Cranston died due to a friendly fire accident during a training session. Harrison even went so far as to forge body transport documents so as not to raise a question about why we were unable to produce their bodies. It wasn't our fault if they were misplaced. We left Viktor's and Irena's bodies because we couldn't bring them with us."

"Why didn't you carry them back to camp with you? Maybe you could have saved them?" Mackenzie asked.

"I wanted to, but I had probably already caused a bigger mess than I could even sweep up. If I brought two bodies, two *Serbians*, to the closest army medic, there would be an investigation, an inquisition, and I knew it could lead to all of us receiving a dishonorable discharge for disobeying direct orders."

"What happened after?" I asked, still absorbing his story and failing to see a connection to the embassy fire. "Did you return home?"

"Not right away. The army still wanted intel. Sources come and go all the time in the intelligence world. Just because we lost one contact on the inside didn't mean our mission was over. We had to keep at it, confronting and bribing any known member of the Serbian forces, at least those we determined could be bought."

"Bought? How?" My mind started racing, recalling how this man had been accused of selling military secrets and arms to enemy forces. Was this where he got his start in betraying his country?

"We had more weapons than we knew what to do with, and some of these Serbs were more than eager to get their hands on them. So we did a trade. Their information for some guns."

I narrowed my gaze at him, questioning him.

"I know how it sounds." He put his hands up

299

defensively. "But if you let me continue, I can tell you who is responsible for the misdeeds of which I am being accused, okay?"

"You mean, you know who did all of those things?" Mackenzie blurted out, her eyes growing wide.

"Yes, little bug," he responded, his voice soft and pacifying.

"Why didn't you come forward if you knew who was responsible?" I asked. "Why stay hidden for all those years and take the blame?"

"I didn't put the pieces together right away. Now, looking back, it was all so obvious, but maybe I didn't want to see it. Maybe I didn't want to think that someone I had grown so close to could do something so spiteful as to set me up for treason, which carries the penalty of death."

"Who?" Mackenzie asked.

Francis sighed. "Harrison Mills."

"Mr. Mills?" She stared in shock at her father, her mouth open as she tried to process that piece of information. "How? Why?"

"It's probably my fault he got into everything like he did. During our time in Bosnia, I realized he was remarkably good at the art of persuasion, so he became our man on the ground. He was young, charismatic, just an all-around great person. He was the type of guy you'd drop everything to be around, and this personality even drew the enemy to him. He'd make the deals, while the rest of us worked different angles or tried to determine movements based on intel and coded messages he received. Nearly every day, we'd send him on his way with a truck full of weapons. He'd come back with an empty truck and pages upon pages of his notebook filled with intel. Some of it was good. Some turned out to be false leads.

"After two months, we were pulled out of Bosnia, all of us given an award of distinction for our service to our country while there. We never uttered a word about our one failed mission. To everyone, the operation was a complete success. However, I couldn't help but think that I was at a turning point in my life so I decided to put in for a transfer to the Army Criminal Investigative Command. I thought with all my special ops and investigative training from the Rangers, it would be a good alternative. Plus, I found out there was a baby on the way." He looked at Mackenzie and grabbed her hand in his. "I hated the idea of having to spend weeks or months away from my wife and daughter. I was given a role as a special agent before being transferred into Counterintelligence as a supervisory special agent, where I spent the next ten years of my life putting some really horrible people behind bars."

"But something must have happened toward the end, right?" I asked, knowing there had to be more.

He nodded, releasing his hold on Mackenzie's hand. "Roughly seven or eight years after I started working in Counterintelligence, I received notice of a new agent who would be part of my team. No information had been given to me, but my superior officer assured me he'd be a great fit since he had just spent the past fifteen years as a Ranger. I was thrilled about having another Ranger under my supervision. That evening, I went home and you could imagine my surprise when I saw Harrison and his family moving into the house next to mine. I hadn't seen him since the debriefing after Bosnia. When he told me he was my new special agent, I couldn't have been happier. I took him under my wing, showing him the ropes at Counterintelligence. I trusted him blindly, but I shouldn't have."

"When did everything start to spiral out of control?"

Mackenzie asked. "Toward the end, I remember you were barely ever home."

"I thought I was on to something. The clues were all there. Arms shipment going missing overseas, the weapons eventually ending up involved in some big shoot-out between notorious drug cartels and the DEA, among other incidents. I remember thinking about Harrison and his knack for making these kind of deals while we were in Bosnia. I even brought him into my office to question him, especially when I caught wind of an arrangement between someone on the inside and the U.S. ambassador to Liberia. The ambassador had agreed to turn a blind eye and provide tactical support to a large weapons trade that was about to happen with the rebels in Sierra Leone. In exchange, he'd get a percentage of the diamonds for which the weapons were being sold. Harrison swore to me the only time he sold military weapons was under my guidance. I believed him, but I couldn't let this lead slip through my fingertips." He shook his head in frustration. "I should have seen it all before, but I blindly requested and was granted permission to go to Liberia and investigate."

"Let me guess. You got there and there was someone already at the embassy, shouting about a circle of trust." I knew enough that I could fill in the blanks at this point.

"He burned those people alive. I did all I could to save one of them." He looked at Mackenzie. "Charlie."

"But why would Mills want to set you up like that?"

"At first, I thought he was purely motivated by greed. He could continue to make arms deals, but I had confronted him about it and spooked him. The Liberian deal was already in place, so what better way to silence me than to go over there and kill me in the fire, all the while making it look like I was the one responsible for all those deals. But that didn't sit right with me. I needed to

302

know more.

"By the time I had figured out this much, I had been presumed dead, my name dragged through the mud. Hell, Harrison had done such a thorough job, all the compelling physical evidence pointed to me as the man behind those arms deals...including bank accounts. I had nothing to go on, but I just knew it *had* to be him. It was my word against his, so I would need something more. Thankfully, Chaplain Slattery still had some contacts who could access information for me. For years, I had Harrison followed, had access to information in his accounts, his emails, monitored his phone calls... I hoped we'd find something, but we couldn't. Nothing at all. And it was eating me up to see him simply living his life while I had to remain in hiding. So I thought maybe if I sent him a message that I was still alive and knew what he had done..."

"How? I thought he went missing?" I inquired.

Francis nodded. "He did. It was shortly after Magdalena's death." He closed his eyes, taking a deep breath. "I stalled, always thinking I was missing something, that maybe he wasn't the one behind it all. Hell, all I had to go on was my gut that he set me up. For years, I continued searching for a needle in a haystack when I should have trusted my gut from the beginning and confronted Harrison when I had the chance. If I had, I can't help but wonder if things would have turned out differently. If my Magdalena wouldn't..." His voice trailed off.

"Dad, you can't blame yourself–"

"But I do, Serafina! Every day, I wake up wondering if I had opened my eyes sooner, had pressed the issue, had come out of hiding and followed my gut, maybe things wouldn't have spiraled out of control. I know Charlie confronted Harrison about his investigation into the embassy attacks. This was just weeks before he was institutionalized. Then Charlie spoke with your mother. She told me about it, asking me whether she should tell him what she knew. I told her it was her decision but to be safe and meet in a neutral place. She never made it to that meeting. I know in my heart she didn't have an accident. Someone didn't want her to go to that meeting and give Charlie any information that could lead him on the right path. And now he's on the chopping block, too."

"So you think Charlie's being set up?" I asked. From the beginning, Charlie had been a loose cannon to me, his intentions always confusing and open to several interpretations.

"I think this guy is ready to do anything, including killing, to silence anyone who could point a finger at him."

"Like my mother?"

He nodded. "And Harrison."

"Wait. What are you talking about?" Mackenzie asked loudly before lowering her voice. "So he's not the one behind it all?"

"It would appear not. I think Harrison was just a puppet, doing what he had to in order to survive, including silencing anyone who could potentially incriminate him…until now."

"So he *is* dead," I stated.

"Possibly. He went missing back in March, so—"

"Wait a minute," I interjected. "I thought you said he went missing shortly after your wife's death."

"That's what I thought, as well," Galloway said. "I was beside myself with remorse, thinking my only shot at some real answers was gone. I didn't even consider the possibility that he *made* himself disappear."

"How did you figure out he was still alive?"

"I didn't. Father Slattery has been by my side since day one. He knew me probably better than anyone else at Fort Bragg. I grew up Catholic, but didn't really follow the religion much until I met your mother, Serafina. She went to confession regularly on the base and grew close to Slattery. And so did I. He had been just as involved in trying to put the pieces together, although he still had connections at the base who could access the information needed. I didn't have that luxury. I couldn't stick my nose out too much for fear of being found."

"So how did he find out Mills was still alive?" I asked.

"Charlie."

"Charlie?!" Mackenzie exclaimed. "How?"

"I have no idea how he figured it out, considering he was locked up at Walter Reed at the time, but he did. He always was able to see things no one else could. Charlie's therapist was a friend of Slattery's and before Charlie escaped Walter Reed, he shared things. Notebooks full of what would appear to anyone else to be the scribblings of a mad man. But to a man trained in special ops, it was more than that. Charlie was suspicious of Mills and had been tracking him, probably because of the timing of his disappearance and Magdalena's death. He had always seen patterns where no one else could and he saw this. He found that Mills was alive and had been recruited by the CIA to work a deep cover mission. The CIA made Mills disappear on paper and gave him a completely new identity. Even his family assumed he had died. He walked away from all of it. Why? He loved his family, so there must have been something going on to make him accept that mission and give up his life and family."

"Doesn't sound like it was too deep of a cover if you know who he is," Mackenzie argued.

"And I would never have found out if it wasn't for Charlie. He knew. I don't know how, but he found out that Harrison disappeared for a year, reappearing as Benjamin Collins..."

My eyes flung to Francis, shock apparent at the mention of the man who had contacted our company to find Galloway in the first place. "What did you just say?"

"Name sounds familiar, doesn't it?" he asked smugly.

All I could do was nod.

"Benjamin Collins is Harrison Mills, and he has done a damn good job of hiding his true identity. I watched him for weeks, in awe at how he had adapted to a new life. Hell, he must have even gone so far as to get plastic surgery on his face to hide his true identity. I've tried to figure out what his mission was, but his cover is so deep, it's been nearly impossible to determine what it is. Finally, after months, I sent him an unmarked package with something in it that would tell him, without question, I was still on to him, I was alive, and I knew who he was. You could imagine his surprise when he opened it."

"What was it?" Mackenzie asked.

"A package of Beeman's bubble gum."

"And what was the significance of that?" I asked.

"You know how in the field, rank is sometimes forgotten? Especially at night when you're sleeping in shifts or you're all eating, faced with the reality that no one is immune from a bullet, regardless of the number of stripes on your sleeves?"

I nodded.

"Well, one night, we were somewhere in the Middle East, staring at a cloudless desert sky. As we listened to shells being fired in the distance, he told me a story. He was a little kid, and he and a friend had shoplifted a pack of gum. He was caught and, instead of owning up to it, he told the shop owner his best friend said he had paid for it. He thought nothing would happen, that all the shop owner would want is for his friend to apologize. Well, the following day, his friend wasn't in school. He had been detained for stealing a pack of gum. Apparently, his father was the police chief and wanted to make an example out of him. He told me how horrible he felt for betraying his best friend. The Beeman's gum was a message saying I knew he was alive and I knew he had betrayed me. I didn't know what I hoped to get out of it. Maybe I wanted him to come clean and finally grow the balls to name who had scared him to the point that he ruined his life, but that didn't happen."

"How long ago was this?"

"About two years."

I nodded. "I can finish the story. Collins, or Mills, not knowing what else to do, eventually contacted my security company with the directive to find you and bring you to justice, knowing you could claim you weren't responsible all you wanted, but all the physical evidence still pointed to you."

"If he even *wanted* to bring me to justice," Galloway said. "A desperate man will do whatever he needs to save his neck, and saving his neck may just mean slitting mine. Not to mention, this case was deemed closed years ago. I have a feeling he used his position in the CIA to get you to do his dirty work, then silence me."

"You really think he would have killed you over this?" Mackenzie asked.

"I don't think, little bug. I'm fairly certain of it. And that's where we still are today. Unless I find who's really pulling the strings here, it's my word against what everyone's been led to believe."

"And where is Mills now?" I asked.

"That's the million dollar question, son. His ex-wife and her husband have been murdered, their deaths attributed to Charlie. His son took a leave of absence from his job back in March…around the same time you lost contact with the man you knew to be Benjamin Collins, I presume."

"Sounds about right," I muttered.

"I just think there's something fishy going on here, and that Mills isn't the one ultimately responsible for all of this. I could be wrong, but I've learned to always trust my gut. Whenever I haven't, I've regretted it. So if my gut tells me to look for someone other than Mills, we look for someone other than Mills, someone with tremendous resources to pull something like this off."

"Who do you think it is?" I asked.

"I don't know, but it must have some sort of connection to my time in Bosnia. I plan on going through my notes of everyone I ever came into contact with over there, every asset we had, to get to the bottom of this."

"So what do we do?" Mackenzie pushed.

"*We* don't do anything. Tyler needs to focus on getting better after that nasty accident, and you need to focus on that baby."

"I have a whole team of people who can help track this guy down," I offered.

"And I appreciate that," he replied calmly. "But I don't think it's necessary."

"It isn't? Why?" Mackenzie interjected.

"Because he's looking for one person, and one person alone."

"No," she breathed, covering her mouth to hide her quivering chin.

"He wants me? Well, he can have me. I'm not going to remain hidden away and put anyone's life at risk anymore." He brought her hand to his lips and kissed it softly. "You know I love you very much, don't you?"

"And I love you, too," she choked out. "I don't want anything to happen to you, Dad."

"And I'll do everything in my power to make sure it doesn't, but nothing's a guarantee. Just do your old man one favor first."

"Anything."

"Let me walk you down the aisle and see you get married."

She nodded, wiping at her tears. "Of course."

Chapter Thirty

Us

Mackenzie

I STOOD JUST INSIDE the foyer of the ridiculously opulent house in Palm Beach that Tyler and I had been staying at for the past several weeks. After he was discharged from the hospital, Eli returned to Texas to try and make sense of the story my father had told us. We, on the other hand, stayed away from home, away from any reminder of the bigger problems that we would soon have to face head-on.

"Is it time?" Melanie asked, looking back at me, her green eyes wide and rounded. Her dark hair was curled and styled for the occasion. She had been so excited when we asked her to fill this role for us today and had spent most of the morning practicing.

"It is. Go ahead, sweetie." I smiled at her in her frilly white sundress with pink and yellow flowers adorning it.

She flashed her adorable smile, showing where she was missing a tooth, and walked out the front door and onto the picture-perfect white sand beach. Despite the jitters in my stomach, a sense of serenity washed over me as I glanced out the large floor-to-ceiling windows and absorbed the scene in front of me. The sun was setting behind the extravagant house on that late November day, casting the beach in a beautiful pinkish glow. There was barely a person in sight...except for the small group of friends and family who had dropped everything and flew out here to be with us.

"Are you ready, *mi bichito*?" a scruff voice asked, startling me.

I turned to him and smiled. "As ready as I'm going to be."

Looking at me affectionately, moisture pooled in my father's eyes. He placed his hands on my arms and surveyed me, his eyes growing bright. "For years, I didn't think I'd ever see you again, let alone be able to stand by your side during one of the most important days of your life." Reaching up, he cupped my cheek. I leaned into his warmth, recalling all the times he would push me on a swing when I was a little girl. I didn't remember much about my childhood, but that memory was strong.

"You look so much like your mother." He let out a shallow sigh. "You always have, but today, it's unmistakable that you are your mother's daughter."

"I'm your daughter, too, Dad."

"I know, but I really see her in you today. She would have been so proud of the woman you've become. *I'm* so proud of the woman you've become."

"Thanks, Dad." I squeezed his hand gently as our eyes remained locked. It was taking everything I had not to break into tears, my emotions on overdrive.

"I want you to have this," he said, breaking the tension. Reaching into the pocket of his linen pants, he pulled out a small box and handed it to me.

"What is it?" I asked, caressing the black velvet.

"If you open it, you'll find out." He winked.

Letting out a small laugh, I shook my head. "I know where I got my sarcasm from, I guess," I retorted, opening the box to see a beautiful turquoise bracelet. It looked to be an antique, the gold holding the turquoise stones together almost tarnished. I picked it up and felt its weight, wondering how he had come to own such a remarkable piece of jewelry. I looked up at my dad, my brows furrowed.

"Your mother wore that on the day we got married, as did her mother, and her mother, and so on. It's been in your family for centuries, its roots dating all the way back to the Guaymi tribe in Panama. Ages ago, I promised her you would wear it on your wedding day, as well." He reached for the bracelet and unclasped it.

"I'd be honored." A lump formed in my throat as I held my arm toward my father and allowed him to secure the bracelet around my wrist. His fingers lingered on my skin and our eyes met. I had gone years without my father's touch, and all I could do was pray that this wasn't the last time I'd ever feel it. This moment was bittersweet for me, the reminder of all the troubles I had tried to ignore the past several weeks rushing forward. I didn't want this to be goodbye between us, but I couldn't help but shake the feeling it would be.

"Well..." My dad cleared his throat and I snapped out of it, adjusting my composure as best I could. "We better get going. We don't want to keep the groom waiting." He held out his elbow for me to grab on to. "Ready, *mi bichito?*"

I nodded. "Always, Papa." I placed my hand in his arm and he escorted me out the front door and onto the large deck of the beach house. I lifted my floor length champagne-colored dress so as to not trip on it and made my way down the short steps onto the beach, trying to savor the moment of feeling my father's warmth next to me.

With each step I took past the handful of people we invited, I grew more at ease. The nervous jitters that overwhelmed me just moments ago were absent, and I knew this was where I was meant to be...making this journey with my father at my side, my eyes glued to Tyler's, the sea breeze blowing his white linen shirt just slightly.

"Hey," Tyler said as I approached him.

"Hey," I replied.

"Hey…," he said once more, his eyes roaming to my cleavage that the halter top of my dress made more voluptuous.

"Hey," I repeated.

"Hey," Jenna said, giggling as she and Brayden stood next to Father Slattery, both of them grinning.

My father grabbed my hand, snapping me out of my daze, and placed it in Tyler's.

"Take care of my girl," he said with a slight quiver in his voice. "You're her family now. Treat her like the princess she is."

"Always, sir," Tyler responded as my father leaned down and kissed me gently on my temple.

"*Te quiero, mi bichito. Siempre.*"

"*Siempre,*" I replied, wiping at the tear that had fallen down my cheek.

My father retreated from me, taking his place among our few guests, and I faced Tyler, unable to comprehend that we were finally here. Every little girl dreamt of the big extravagant wedding with the Cinderella gown and the posh reception, and I was no different, but I wouldn't give this moment up for anything. Instead of a room full of distant relatives I only saw during weddings and funerals, I was surrounded by the handful of people I cared about the most. It was perfect.

"Now, it's my understanding you two have written your own vows, correct?" Father Slattery said, breaking into my thoughts.

"Yes," we responded in unison.

"Well, then, I'll give you the floor. Age before beauty,

313

so Tyler first." He nodded at him to proceed, a low chuckle echoing around us.

With eager eyes, Tyler took a deep breath, his smile perfect, showing his brilliant white teeth. His bruises and scars had mostly healed over the past several weeks that he spent in the hospital and then recuperating here, soaking up the late autumn rays. His skin was tanned, his dark hair disheveled in the way that had attracted me to him from the very beginning.

"Mackenzie," he began before leaning in and whispering, his voice barely audible, "Serafina..."

I warmed when my name rolled off his tongue in such a delicate manner.

"The last thing I was looking for when I took an assignment a little over a year ago was to fall in love, especially with the woman who was supposed to be the asset."

Polite laughter sounded around us.

"And I am certain I was the last person you wanted to infiltrate your perfectly ordered life, but then something magical happened. We both let down our guard. I stopped caring about my job, and you finally threw out that blasted timetable. We finally did something we both thought we'd never do again. We loved... And that love has only grown stronger through the truth, lies, tears, miles, and heartache. And I know it will only continue to grow with every day that passes.

"I'm not perfect. I make mistakes. I can be stubborn as hell. I have good days and bad. I lose my temper. I can be completely irrational at times. However, you chose to look past all my faults and love me anyway. Every day from this day forward, I promise to do everything I can to make you fall in love with me all over again. You deserve the fairytale, princess, and that's what I intend to give you each and every day until I'm turned into dust."

He closed the distance between us once more. "Serafina Galloway," he whispered so no one else could hear him, "I love you."

He pulled back and I met his eyes, nodding. *I love you, too*, I mouthed as I tried to maintain my composure, but it was impossible.

"How do you expect me to follow that?" I said through my tears.

Everyone laughed politely.

Closing my eyes, I took a deep breath before focusing them on Tyler, the one man who had seen my demons and had embraced the darkness within. And he would always be at my side. With him, I could get through everything, no matter what the future held.

"Once upon a time," I began, my eyes remaining glued to Tyler, "there was a little girl. She dreamed of men in black tuxes, dancing in the moonlight, and falling in love. Then her world was ripped apart and she lost everything. Her friends, her family, her life. Worst of all, she lost hope. She stopped dreaming and believing in the fairytale because her life had turned into a nightmare, and she lived that nightmare for years. Then, one day, a charming and annoyingly persistent man woke her up from the spell that had been cast over her. She finally experienced what she dreamed about for years. Love.

"Tyler, you may not think you're perfect, but you are in my eyes. I've loved you since I felt your soul. When you just wouldn't take no for an answer, I fell in love with you a little bit more. When you thought you lost me and I saw the look of terror on your face, I gave you another piece of my heart. Even when I walked away from you after finding out the truth, I still loved you. Through all our ups and downs, my heart has been and will always be yours. From this day forward, I promise to hold you when you're having a bad day or memory. I promise to love you even when you don't think you deserve it. And I promise to give you everything I have...my heart, my soul, my love...because there's no one more deserving of it than you are, Tyler Joseph Burnham."

A look of serenity washed over his face and he leaned down, his lips hovering over mine. "I don't deserve you, but I'm glad you think I do."

"You do," I murmured as he kissed me softly.

"Hey!" Brayden interjected. "Not yet, kids. There's still a few more things to get through, isn't that right, Padre?" He winked at Father Slattery.

"He's right. The rings please," he said, looking at Jenna, then Alexander, who stood beside Tyler. They both handed over the rings.

"Tyler, repeat after me," Father Slattery said, handing him my wedding band. I lost myself in Tyler's eyes as he made his vow to me, promising to remain true and honor me for the rest of my life. I barely made it through my own vows, the emotion overwhelming me as I thought back to the roller coaster ride our relationship had taken over the months. Regardless of the lows, the heartache of finding out the truth was worth it as I stood here, marrying my own Prince Charming.

"By the power vested in me," Father Slattery said after I finished my vows, "I am happy to call you husband and wife."

I grinned excitedly, looking down at the diamond band that now sat above my engagement ring.

"You can now kiss your bride," he said, and before I knew what was happening, Tyler pulled me into his arms, his lips on mine, our kiss passionate and intense as the world disappeared around us. And that was what life with Tyler was like. My troubles vanished. I could live in the moment with him and our love. It was exactly what being in love was supposed to be like. He shielded me from everything, protecting me and keeping me safe.

"Thank you," he murmured against my lips.

"For what?"

"For chasing away the lonely, once and for all."

~~~~~~~~~~

"WELL, SINCE I'M THE man of honor," Brayden's boisterous voice broke through the chatter at the large table set on the upper deck of the house overlooking the beach. "I suppose I should say a few words." He stood up, his tall and lean stature poised. A dapper smile on his face, he looked at all the important people in both Tyler's and my life. He finally met my eyes, and his expression warmed. It brought me back to the day he moved in with Jenna and me.

"I'm beat from all that unpacking." He plopped down on the couch in our living room, surprising me with the ease in which he made himself at home, even though he barely knew us. "I think I deserve a drink. You girls game?" He raised his eyebrows, looking between Jenna and me.

"You know what?" Jenna exclaimed excitedly. "I think a drink is exactly what we all need."

"You two go ahead without me," I mumbled, not looking up from the book I was barely reading. I had spent the past few months of our summer break moping around the apartment, having just lost my mother and finding out that my boyfriend wasn't the man I thought he was. "I'm not in the mood."

Huffing dramatically, Jenna grabbed the book out of my hand and threw it on the coffee table. "You're never in the mood. I've put up with your excuses all summer, but I'm not going to do it anymore, Mack. It's our sophomore year and it's time to bring back the old Mack. That includes going out and meeting some hotties with our fake IDs. I can't make you have a good time, but I can try my damnedest to at least get you out of this apartment. Especially now that we have a tall, strong man as a roommate who can probably carry you out of here." She looked over her shoulder and winked at Brayden.

"*Damn straight I can,*" he replied jovially. "*Just look at these guns!*" He pushed back the sleeves of his t-shirt and began to flex. "*Feel 'em,*" he said, coming up to me. "*I know you want to.*"

"*Nope. No desire.*"

"*Feel 'em,*" he repeated, shoving his arms directly in front of my line of sight.

I tried to pretend I was irritated, but it was useless. A small smile cracked my lips and I reached out to squeeze his toned bicep.

"*See,*" he said, heading down the narrow hallway toward his bedroom. "*Told you I'd be able to get you to smile.*"

"*Thank god you came into our lives, Brayden. I've been trying to get a smile out of her for months.*"

"*You were just looking for your missing piece, that's all. Now that I'm here, there's nothing else to worry about.*" He winked and disappeared into his room. "*We're leaving in forty-five minutes, so you both better get a move on!*"

That was the first night I finally began to feel normal again after all the loss and heartache I had suffered months earlier. From that moment on, I knew Brayden was my soul mate, the only man I had ever met who knew exactly what I needed, even if I didn't. We spent that night bar hopping around campus, all of us checking out the same guys, although what we were attracted to in the opposite sex, or the same sex for Brayden, vastly differed. Still, on that Friday night over eight years ago, we had our first girls' night, and barely a Friday night had passed since then that we didn't have our girls' night.

"I've known Mackenzie for nearly a decade." Hearing his familiar voice broke me away from my memories. "And, during that time, I've seen many men come and go in her hunt for Mr. Right, but she was convinced they were all Mr. Wrong, mainly because she said it wasn't the right time for her to date. Mackenzie's always had a plan for how her life should go. She's always been driven, and it's been this drive that has helped her achieve the professional success she has. But that drive inhibited any long-term relationships. Maybe that's because she was waiting for the right person to come along...her turtledove, as she always called him...and that's exactly what she's found in Tyler Burnham." He gestured to Tyler as he sat beside me, clutching my hand.

"You two are all wrong for each other. You barely know each other but, like I've always said, the heart wants what it wants. You have given each other a piece of your heart. That's a magical, beautiful thing. *Love* is a magical, beautiful thing. Listen to each other. Love each other with everything you've got to give because, without love, we are nothing. Without each other's love, *you* are nothing. Mackenzie, Tyler, I wish you years of happiness. To Mackenzie and Tyler!" He raised his champagne glass, everyone at the table joining in and toasting.

"I'm nothing without you," I murmured into Tyler's ear, kissing his neck.

"Now that's over, let's kick this party up a notch," Brayden exclaimed as he grabbed his smart phone, pressed a few buttons, and music began to blare from the speakers he had set up. Leading the way, as always, Brayden grabbed his beau, James, and dragged him toward the makeshift dance floor. His enthusiasm was contagious and, in seconds, everyone else had followed his lead and migrated away from the table.

The hours passed while everyone danced, my friends mingling with Tyler's family as if they had known each other most of their lives. It particularly made me laugh to watch Brayden swing dance with Colleen. I think even he was surprised at how easily she kept up with him. It left

319

no doubt in my mind where Tyler had learned to dance. He had his mother's ease and grace.

Needing a break while Tyler danced with little Melanie, I looked around the crowd and noticed Richard off in the corner. I hated that he seemed to appear left out at a celebration of what should have been two families becoming one…and Richard was family to me. Excusing myself from my conversation with Eli, I made my way across the large deck toward where Richard stood next to the bar, a glass of scotch in his hand.

"Hey, Richard," I said, sidling up next to him, savoring the cool ocean breeze. After dancing for hours, it felt refreshing.

"Hey, Kenzie," he replied, his speech slurred. "Got married just in the nick of time." He raised his eyebrows as he glanced to my stomach, a smile bordering between playful and snide crossing his lips. I didn't read too much into it, though. Jenna had mentioned how stressed he had been with work. One of his newer hotels wasn't doing nearly as well as he had expected and was in the red by close to a billion dollars. That would cause me to be somewhat irritable, as well.

"I guess so." I placed my hand over my stomach, feeling the baby move around as he tried to get comfortable. "How's everything going?" I asked, breaking the awkward silence that settled between us.

"As good as can be expected, I suppose," he responded, his gaze and attention elsewhere…on my father. I was certain he had a thousand questions about how, almost overnight, I had a father when, from the beginning, I had told Richard he was dead. I was waiting for him to ask me what the story was, but I didn't know if I was ready to tell him everything just yet. I had spent the last several weeks living in a state of blissful ignorance, able to momentarily forget about my past and the questionable future that lay ahead of me. I didn't want my wedding night to be tainted by anything but happy memories.

The music changed to a slower number, Ella Fitzgerald's sultry voice crooning the opening lines of "Bewitched, Bothered, and Bewildered" filling the air. "Come on, Richard. Let's dance, like old times." I winked and held my hand out to him.

For the first time all night, a genuine smile crossed his face and I saw the Richard I knew all those months ago before his job began to take control of his life. Jenna didn't talk much about how their relationship was doing, but I couldn't help but feel for her a little. No wonder she had been practically ignoring him most of the night, preferring to spend time with Brayden and James instead.

He escorted me out to the dance floor, other bodies swaying to the tune, and grabbed my hand in his, leading me with ease.

"It's funny how things work out, isn't it?" he commented after we had moved in silence to the classic tune for a while. Things felt awkward around him when, just months ago, I had been incredibly comfortable in his presence. Now he was aloof, standoffish, unreadable.

"What do you mean?"

"Nothing, really. Just how sometimes when you lose all hope of things going your way, of finally getting everything you've dreamed of and wanted for so long, something happens to bring the light back into your life, giving you that renewed drive."

"Jenna told you about why I left Tyler, didn't she?"

"Not the details, just that he wasn't the man you thought he was, yet you learned to look past all that. It must have been difficult."

"Actually," I began, "it wasn't. I realized that, despite the lies he told me, his love was still true." I paused for a moment, trying to find a way to put into words how I felt. My eyes met Tyler's from several feet away, a hammering starting in my chest from that one look. It told me everything I ever needed. How he loved me, craved me, cherished me, worshiped me. That he would walk through fire to keep me at his side, just as I would for him.

A warmth filled me as I tore my eyes from Tyler's and back to Richard's. "Have you ever loved someone so much that, even though you knew the two of you didn't make sense together, you couldn't stay away? Even when those around you said it would never work out, you couldn't help but hold on to that small kernel of hope that it would?"

I looked up to see Richard staring off into the distance, his face relaxed, as if recalling some rather pleasant memories. Swallowing hard, he said, "Yes, I have." His eyes glimmered from the reflection of the moon on the water and I could almost see the forming of unshed tears.

"Richard, is everything–"

"Jenna..." He cleared his throat, returning his attention to me. "Hell, look at the two of us. We're not exactly your traditional couple, are we? I'm twice her age."

I eyed him skeptically, trying to figure out if I caught him in a lie or whether he was really thinking about Jenna. I couldn't shake the feeling that something wasn't right about Richard. Maybe Jenna was on to something when she thought he had been cheating on her.

"Richard, are you–"

"I'm sorry to interrupt," my father's voice cut through as the music changed to a Spanish-influenced tune, the sound of drums and a guitar filling the air.

"Dad," I said, tearing away from Richard's arms. "This is Jenna's husband, Richard. Richard, this is my father, Francis."

Richard tentatively held his hand out to my father, studying him, lingering on the scars on the left side of his face. He probably had questions about what happened to him, and whether it had something to do with me lying about his existence. "Nice to meet you," he said, his voice and motions guarded as he cautiously took my father's hand in his.

"You, as well, Richard," my father responded, returning his curious gaze, as if he had seen him somewhere before and was trying to place him. I knew exactly where he had seen him... Richard's face was practically everywhere due to the success of his hotels. That was why he liked living in South Padre so much. No one there made a big deal about who he was. Most of the tourists were too drunk to focus on his face, and none of the locals cared.

"Well, you two enjoy your dance," Richard said, pulling his hand away from my father's. "Congratulations, Mackenzie." He placed a soft kiss on my temple. "And congratulations to you, as well, sir." He took my father's hand once more and whispered something in his ear. A brilliant smile crossed my father's face as he slapped Richard jovially on the back, his laughter echoing in the crisp night air. Then Richard walked toward Jenna, slinking his arm around her waist and kissing her affectionately. It helped settle my unease about his faithfulness toward her.

"Promise to take it easy on your old man?" my father asked with a twinkle in his eye.

"Are you sure you're up to it?" I countered, giving him a playful grin. "If I remember Mom's stories correctly, she said you couldn't dance the Flamenco to save your life."

"And she was right, but that doesn't mean I don't want

to dance with you."

"Okay," I said, placing my hand in his. "You asked for it. It's a good thing I'm pregnant and ready to pop, or I'm pretty sure I'd be wiping the dance floor with you."

"I have no doubt about that." He led me a few steps toward the center of the now empty dance floor, the eyes of my friends and family on us. I hadn't done this exact dance in years, but I settled back into it as if no time had passed at all, as if it were permanently ingrained in my muscle memory.

Glancing at my father, I noticed him almost in a trance, his eyes focused straight ahead.

"You're not *that* bad," I joked, trying to bring his attention back to me.

Slowly returning his gaze to mine, a small smile crossed his face as he continued to go through the intricate steps with a slight limp, forgoing his cane for the first time I could recall.

"Ah, *mi bichito*. Your mother was the picture of grace when she danced, much like you. I'm just an Irish bloke lucky enough to stumble across her one day and she changed my life for the better. Much like Tyler did for you."

"You think he changed my life for the better?" I asked as the rhythm of the drums grew more intense and frenzied.

"I think you both changed each other's lives for the better," he said warmly. "And that's something worth holding on to."

"Mind if I cut in?" Tyler's voice sounded and I stopped my motions to see his hand held out.

"Not at all," my father said, releasing his hold on me.

"You know how to dance the Flamenco?" I asked in surprise.

"A wise woman once said that any man who learned to

dance the Flamenco for her was a man worth marrying."

My eyes went to my dad, a look of nostalgia on his face as he recalled my mother saying those words to him.

"So I figured it was only fitting that I learned this dance to prove to you that I was a man worth marrying."

"You've already proven that, and then some," my father said, placing his hand on Tyler's shoulder. "You take care of my little girl, okay?"

"Of course, sir."

A satisfied smile crossing his face, my dad leaned down and softly kissed me on my temple. "Goodbye, *mi bichito*," he whispered. "I'll be seeing you."

"Wait!" I shouted as he turned to walk away from me. "You're leaving?"

He nodded. "You enjoy your night. We'll see each other again."

"When?" I asked.

"At this point, I do believe it's out of my hands."

My chin quivered, a lump in my throat. I knew he wasn't expecting to see me again, not in this world anyway. I refused to consider that to be a reality. My father had survived this long and I knew he would get through whatever other challenges he was about to face.

"Shall we?" Tyler said, breaking through my thoughts. I nodded, still distant as I tried to put on a smile and pretend everything was okay. I held my hand to him and he pulled me into his body, both of us pausing for a beat before moving to the rhythm of the music that had filled my soul for years.

My life had always been a strange series of tragic events, the memories of the happier times I spent with my family always painful. But as I stared into Tyler's brilliant green eyes – those green eyes that wouldn't leave my dreams from the first time I saw them – I no longer felt that pain. I finally had everything of which I had ever dreamed. I was living proof that fairytales did come true.

But even in a fairytale, there was always a struggle to overcome, and I knew mine could potentially destroy everything I held dear.

Chapter Thirty-One

Goodbye

Mackenzie

I TOSSED AND TURNED, sleep evading me as the sky began to turn from black to a deep blue. Giving up on getting any rest, I extracted myself from Tyler's warm arms and pulled a silk robe around my naked body, sliding open the glass door and emerging onto the balcony overlooking the ocean below. Our time here on the beach was coming to an end, and I was both excited and apprehensive about returning to South Padre to get ready for the next stage of my life...moving to Boston.

As I sat contemplating whether I made the right decision in agreeing to give up my life in South Padre in favor of Tyler's family in Boston, my cell phone vibrated in my robe, startling me. I looked at the caller ID to see the call was coming from a Texas number. My curiosity getting the better of me, I answered.

"Hello?"

"Kenzie...," a familiar voice said.

"Charlie," I whispered softly. "Why did you call me on this phone? And from an unblocked number? Someone could be tracing this call and can find you! Is everything okay?"

"Do you want the truth or just an empty reassurance?"

"The truth scares me," I admitted.

"Me, too," he said, his voice muted.

Silence fell between us as I listened to the combination of his gentle breathing and the ocean waves. "Why are you calling, Charlie?"

"To say congratulations. You looked beautiful last night."

I bolted off the lounge chair, my eyes scanning the barely illuminated beach. "You're here?"

"Yes. Well, I was."

"Why?" I asked, frantic, pacing the balcony. "What if someone saw you?"

"Still worried about me even after everything?"

"Of course, I am," I answered quickly. "I'll always care about you, Charlie. No matter what."

He took a deep breath. "I wish you wouldn't. I don't want to cause you any pain."

"What do you mean by that?" I pulled my robe closer, a sudden chill washing over me.

"Like you told me once, my luck's eventually going to run out. I can't keep running forever. And the longer I run, the more people will get hurt. Maybe it's time I stopped…"

"You're giving up?" My voice was trembling. This didn't sound like the Charlie I knew. He sounded defeated, as if he knew it was useless to continue on the path he had been on. It made me lose hope that we would ever get to the bottom of what happened all those years ago…and what was still happening now.

"You know me better than that, Kenzie. You know I'll never go down without a fight, no matter what. I just have a bad feeling that if I don't do something to put an end to all of it, it never *will* end. If it takes me throwing in the towel to finally open people's eyes to what's really going on, that's a sacrifice I'm willing to make. I made an oath years ago, the same oath I still repeat each and every morning… 'I, Charles Patrick Montgomery, do solemnly swear that I will support and defend the Constitution of the United States against all enemies, foreign and domestic; that I will bear true faith and allegiance to the same; and that I will obey the orders of the President of the United States and the orders of the officers appointed over me. So help me God.' I know it may not look as though I've followed that oath every day, but I have. And I've come to the point where I need to stop running in order to continue fulfilling that oath."

I tried to fight back the tears. Not only was my father willing to give up his fight, but now Charlie was, too? "What do you know?"

"More than I probably should. That's what has gotten me into this mess. I just want you to know that if anything happens to me, no matter what anyone tries to make you believe, I am a good person. I've always done what I thought was right, and I've done everything to defend our country against any threat. So has your father."

"My father?" I asked in surprise.

"I'm glad he was able to see you get married. It's good you now have the memory of this day. Never take advantage of the importance of family. They can be taken from you too soon."

"But he *will* be taken from me. He's sick with the amount of blood on his hands from the years of hiding. He's ready to use himself as bait to put an end to all this."

"I figured as much," Charlie said.

"You did? How?"

He chuckled slightly. "You forget that I can see things most people can't. Your father wouldn't come out of hiding if he didn't have an end game in the works. But I promise you, Kenzie. I will do everything in my power to make sure it doesn't come to that, that you will always have a family. Okay?"

"What do you mean by that, Charlie?"

"Sometimes we have to change our course to keep those we love happy."

"Charlie," I urged, panic in my voice. "Promise me you won't do anything stupid."

"I've made that promise to you in the past, but I'm not going to do it this time." His voice was solemn and I couldn't help but let out a low sob at the idea of something happening to him. Last year at this time, I never anticipated seeing him again but, over the months, something changed in our relationship. I knew he was the caring, compassionate, loving man I was convinced he was when we dated all those years ago.

"Nothing's going to happen to you, Charlie," I said through my tears, unable to shake the feeling that this was his way of saying goodbye. I didn't know how many more goodbyes I could go through.

"I know I've never done anything to win back your trust, but I'm glad you saw it in your heart to forgive me. Goodbye, Kenzie…"

"Charlie, wait!" I shouted, hoping he hadn't hung up just yet.

"Yes?"

"That friend of a friend," I began. "The one who asked you to look for me… Was it Damian?"

I heard a loud exhale. "Yes. It had been years since you disappeared, but he never gave up hope he'd find you. Even got himself arrested doing so."

"They have him, don't they?" I asked hesitantly, remembering everything my father had told Tyler and me at the hospital all those weeks ago.

"It appears so, but I don't want you to worry, Kenzie. I've been doing everything I can to locate him. I'm doing this all for you. Please remember that."

"You don't have to…," I wept.

330

"Yes, I do. You have a chance to have the life I never could. Don't waste it. Promise me you won't."

I shook my head, refusing to say the words.

"Kenzie, please…"

"I promise," I squeaked out, wiping at my cheeks.

"Enjoy the sunrise. It's sure to be a beautiful one. Goodbye, Serafina."

"Goodbye, Charlie," I murmured, remaining on the line until I no longer heard any background noise and I knew he had hung up.

"What did Charlie have to say?" Tyler asked, startling me. I spun around to see him standing in the doorway, his arms crossed in front of his chest, his stature slightly intimidating.

"Nothing." I shrugged him off. "Just wanted to offer his congratulations and…"

"And…?" Tyler pushed, stalking toward me as I leaned against the railing of the balcony.

"And I think he's going to do something stupid. Something that may cost him his life."

He saw the tears reforming behind my eyes once more and pulled my body into his, trying to calm me. "Don't worry. Remember what you've always said… Charlie's a brilliant man. If he's gone this long without anything happening to him, who's to say anything will happen now?"

"Because he's Charlie and is too noble for his own good. Maybe I'm wrong, but I can't help but shake the feeling that something horrible is about to happen to him, and he knows it."

"Mackenzie, look at me," Tyler said and I pulled my head out of his chest to see a look of concern on his face. "I may not have always been the biggest Charlie supporter…even now, I'm still not certain of his motives…but I promise to do everything I can to make

331

sure nothing happens to him. I'll have my guys work harder at finding him and try to figure out what he knows. We'll do everything we can to uncover the truth here. That way, no one else gets hurt. Okay?"

"Okay," I whispered, the intensity in his gaze burning into me as the sound of early morning on the shore echoed around us. The wind was calm, the waves light, and we welcomed our first day as a married couple.

Safe and secure in Tyler's arms, despite the unease I couldn't shake from my phone call with Charlie, I turned around to watch the sun peek over the horizon. Wasn't that what love was supposed to do? Help you forget your problems? Make you feel that everything would work out? Shelter you from the heartache? Uplift you when you were at your lowest?

Splaying his hands across my stomach, he inhaled deeply. "Mmmm...," he groaned, the huskiness in his voice making me want to melt into him, our two bodies to become one and never separate again. "Cinnamon." He gently pushed against me and I could feel how aroused he was.

"You're a fiend, Mr. Burnham."

"Only for you, Mrs. Burnham."

My heart warmed at the sound of that rolling off his tongue and I spun around, wrapping my arms around him as he pinned me to the railing of the balcony, his devilish eyes causing a burning excitement to stir in my stomach. "I like the sound of that," I whispered, tilting my head toward his, desperate to feel his lips on mine. But every time I drew closer to his mouth, he pulled back, keeping me on edge.

"As do I. Want to know why?"

Biting my lower lip, I nodded, keeping my eyes on his, the green vibrant on that chilly November morning.

"Because it means I belong to you, and you to me."

Running my fingers through his hair, trying with everything in me to pull his lips against mine, I said, "How very Neanderthal of you."

"I've never heard you complain about my caveman tactics before. In fact, if I remember correctly, you get turned on when I go all, and I quote, 'protective ape man' on you."

"That was months ago." I smirked. "I may have changed my mind since then."

"Oh, really?" He raised his eyebrows in a flirtatious manner.

"Yes, really."

"We'll see about that," he growled, grabbing my hips and hoisting me onto the balcony railing. Looking over my shoulder, I was thankful the railing was quite wide, at least several feet, making it nearly impossible for anyone to lose their balance.

I yanked at his boxer briefs, pulling him toward me. Wrapping my legs around him, I locked him in place. His eyes grew even more hooded, his chest heaving, his stare carnal and full of lust.

"Kiss me." I closed my eyes, desperate to feel his lips on mine. Since that first kiss all those months ago, I had grown addicted to them, each kiss different and unexpected.

"Not yet."

"Why?" I whined playfully, loosening the grip my legs had around him. This was all part of his game and I loved every exhilarating moment. The anticipation was almost as fulfilling as the catch. The longer we waited, the more I burned for him, and he knew it. My body gave me away by the way it reacted to his nearness, my nipples alert, my skin flush, my breathing uneven.

"Because I want my lips on other parts of your body first," he explained, yanking at the tie around my robe, allowing it to fall open.

I shrugged the robe off my shoulders, leaving me totally exposed. Tyler's eyes remained fixed and calm as he surveyed my body. He took his time, raking over me as if trying to memorize every dimple and curve. Without warning, he grabbed my hair, forcing my head back as he ran his tongue down my neck. My skin flamed, despite the chilly temperature.

"Do you like that we're outside where anyone could walk by and see us?"

"Yes," I said quickly, feeling as if I was about to fall over the metaphorical edge the second he touched me. It didn't matter that he had given me too many orgasms to count throughout the night as we made love over and over again. This was different. Another unexpected side of Tyler.

"Do you remember the night we met?" he whispered, his tongue traveling down my body.

I nodded, not uttering a sound.

"Do you remember what you told me? How you tried to convince me that your body was flushed because you had been drinking?"

A finger trailed over my protruding stomach, finding its way to the spot I needed him to touch.

"I was able to read your body that night, Mackenzie. You wanted me. God, you wanted me so fucking bad, but you refused to admit it."

Kneeling in front of me, his hands clutched onto my thighs, spreading them, and the warmth of his breath between my legs made my chest rise and fall. The promise of what was about to happen would be my undoing.

"Do you want to know what I thought about all night long?"

"Yes," I responded, although I knew it was a rhetorical

question.

"Your pink lips and how they would taste."

I moaned as his breath grew closer to my center.

"And I thought about doing this to you all night long, how much I wanted to hear you scream my name."

Finally, his mouth was on me, his tongue circling me, exploring as if it were the first time.

"But you played hard to get," he said, pulling away. I cried in frustration and opened my eyes to see a frisky smirk on Tyler's face. "There was a moment when I considered throwing in the towel, thinking no woman was worth this amount of effort, mission be damned."

Grabbing onto the balcony railing, he slithered up my body, his tongue roaming over every dip and crevice as he stepped out of his boxer briefs.

"I tried to stay away," he admitted, his lips hovering over mine. His eyes burned into me, his formerly lascivious gaze replaced by one of yearning and idolization. "I didn't want to do anything to hurt you and I knew being with me would destroy you. But I couldn't stop thinking about you. We had barely spoken ten words to each other, Serafina, but the thought of letting you walk away crushed me. I couldn't breathe. I couldn't think. I couldn't *exist*. So I let down my walls. I let you see the real Tyler. I wanted you to fall in love with the real me, not the person I was supposed to be for my job, not the person I had been for years. You brought the real Tyler back. You breathed life into this dead heart with your kiss..."

Pressing his lips to mine, he caressed my tongue with his. I wrapped my legs around his waist, the space between us too much. He was a part of me and I never wanted to be separated from him again.

"With your touch..." He traced the outline of my neck, his tongue following, lighting me on fire.

"With your love…" His voice was serene as he pushed into me, filling me and withdrawing in quick forceful movements. His motions were at odds with his calm voice and gentle eyes. I tried to hold back my screams, but was unable, both of our voices rebounding in the air on that perfect November morning.

I grasped his hips as they continued their relentless motion, my fingernails digging into his skin. His rhythm grew more frenzied and punishing, a guttural moan escaping his lips as sweat dotted his forehead.

"Harder," I murmured, a surge of electricity running from my toes and everywhere in between. My mind was blank, all my decisions motivated by that unmistakable sensation of euphoria and bliss only Tyler Burnham could give me.

He grabbed my hair, forcing my head back once more and clamped onto my neck, causing me to yelp and moan, the pain only heightening the pleasure coursing through me. I had never felt as alive as I did at that moment, Tyler's teeth digging into my skin, forcing an orgasm to ravage through my body. He picked up his pace even more, finally letting out a low grunt, signaling his own release.

Cupping my face with his strong hands, he pressed his lips to mine, his kiss tender as we attempted to control our breathing. Our gaze held and we shared our love through our eyes, our flesh, our bodies. It was fitting. Our first declaration of love wasn't said with words. One look was all it took. With one look at the bar the night we met, I knew I had met my match. With one look on the dance floor during opening night of the restaurant, I knew I never wanted to be apart from this man. With one look when I found out the truth, I knew his love was true, despite being surrounded in a myriad of lies. And not a day had passed when I didn't feel his love for me.

Chapter Thirty-Two

Grief

Tyler

"FEELS GOOD TO BE home, doesn't it?" I asked Mackenzie as we walked down the hallway toward her condo. After spending a final few days in Palm Beach, we arrived back on South Padre the day before Thanksgiving. I was anxious to get back into the swing of things, but knew a lot of that would have to be put on the back burner to what was now becoming the more important issue... The arrival of our baby in just a few weeks. I still couldn't believe I would become a father in less than a month.

"It sure does. At least we won't have to live out of a suitcase anymore. And I'm sure Meatball missed me."

"Did Jenna look after him?"

I nodded. "Yeah. Between her, Richard, Brayden, and one of the girls at the restaurant, he's been well taken care of."

"You could have just had Martin arrange for one of my team members to make sure he had food and clean litter, ya know?" I said, trying to hide my unease about anyone I hadn't done a thorough check on being in her condo unsupervised.

"Tyler...," she cautioned. "You have nothing to worry about with any of my friends. And Mia, my hostess, only came to watch Meatball when everyone else so graciously dropped everything they were doing to be there when we got married. And look," she said smugly, sticking her key in the knob and pushing the door open, her eyes still trained on mine. "Everything's just fine."

My attention focused straight ahead at her kitchen table. My adrenaline spiking, I reacted quickly and grabbed her arm, pulling her back into the hallway and away from the door.

"What the hell, Tyler?!" she exclaimed. "What's gotten into you?" She narrowed her eyes at me. "Are you still freaked out about what happened...?" She raised her eyebrows, giving me a knowing look.

"That's not it, Mackenzie." I glanced back into her apartment, bile rising in my throat. Swallowing it down, I hoped she couldn't see how unnerved I really was.

"Then what is it? I can handle it."

Shaking my head, I pulled her close to me, trying to do everything I could to protect her from the knowledge I now had. "I don't think you can handle this one."

"It's *my* condo," she insisted. "I have a right to know what's got your panties in a bunch."

"I know. I promise to tell you exactly what's in there, but please don't go inside. No one should have to see this. I'm begging you."

She glanced up at me, her eyes glistening with worry. "What is it?" she whispered. "Is it Meatball?"

"No, Mackenzie. It's not Meatball."

"Then what is it?"

I took a deep breath. "It's Charlie, Mackenzie. He's..." I hesitated and ran my hand over my face.

"He's what, Tyler?" she asked in an unsteady tone, trying to fight against me.

I remained silent and peeked at her open door once more, unsure of how I could even explain what was in there without her wanting to see it for herself.

"He's what, Tyler?" she asked again, her voice louder and growing irate.

Letting out a long sigh, my shoulders slumped forward. "He's dead, Mackenzie."

She violently shook her head and pushed against me, bolting into the condo before I could stop her.

"Mackenzie, don't!"

Stumbling, I tried to pull her away, but it was too late. Her scream echoed against the barren walls and she threw herself onto Charlie as he sat hunched over at her kitchen table, a Beretta M9 loosely held in his hand. His face was almost indistinguishable from the gunshot to his head, and I hesitated to get any closer to see the wound.

At first glance, it appeared Charlie had committed suicide, the blood spray pattern on the light gray walls of Mackenzie's condo confirming my suspicions. She had feared that Charlie's last phone call was to say goodbye. I hated that she was right. I hated that she had to see this. Most of all, I hated that I had no idea what to say to comfort her right now.

"Wake up, Charlie!" she begged, shaking his body, obviously uncaring that she was covering herself with his blood. "Please," she cried out, her plight heartbreaking to watch.

I went to her and placed my hand on her shoulder. She snapped her head to look at me, her mascara streaking down her cheeks. She heaved through her sobs, almost unable to breathe. Over the months, I had seen her highs and lows, convinced I had been there for the lowest of her lows, but I was wrong. This woman in front of me was torn in two, heartbroken, confused, bitter, angry, and a thousand other emotions I couldn't even label. This was a woman who had forgiven Charlie, who chose to see beyond the image everyone else wanted to paint him as, and my heart went out to her. With each tear that streamed down her face, I could almost sense her starting to lose hope in finally getting the happy ending she deserved. And I began to feel it, too.

Instead of pulling her away so she didn't contaminate what could be a crime scene, I squeezed her shoulder in a compassionate manner. "I'll give you a minute."

She nodded and mouthed, *Thank you,* her chin trembling. She returned her attention to Charlie, resting her head on his knee, her sobs rolling through her body once more. Retreating from her, I couldn't help but think that something about this didn't sit right with me. Was Charlie really the type of person who would kill himself? I didn't know much about him, but I couldn't shake the feeling that this wasn't what it seemed. Nothing in this case was.

As I looked back at Charlie's body, I surveyed the pattern of the blood on the wall from where he had supposedly shot himself in the head. It seemed off. It was low...too low, as if someone was standing over him and pulled the trigger.

Disarming the alarm that was now going off, I grabbed my cell out of the pocket of my cargo pants. "Eli, I need you to come over to Mackenzie's condo as quickly as possible. Charlie's dead." I hung up, not wanting to say anything else, unsure of what the truth was.

The next several hours were a flurry of activity as law enforcement officers and forensic analysts swarmed the scene, asking question after question... Questions we couldn't answer. Mackenzie simply remained sitting on the floor, refusing to look away as the coroner removed Charlie from the kitchen table and wheeled him out on a gurney, a white sheet covering his body.

"Wait a minute," she said just as they were about to leave with him. Springing to life, she bolted down the hallway toward her bedroom, rummaging through the chest where she kept her father's Victoria Cross. She came back carrying a folded American flag. Eli and I responded quickly, helping her unfold it and place it over his body.

As they began pushing the gurney down the hallway once more, Eli and I stepped back, snapping to attention and saluting, giving him the hero's goodbye I knew, deep down, he deserved.

~~~~~~~~~~

THAT EVENING, I BROUGHT Mackenzie back to my house. I had Eli and Martin collect as many of her belongings as they could so she never had to step foot in that condo again. Meatball was a little unsure of his surroundings, but once he realized Griffin was more scared of him than he was of the dog, they got along famously, even within the span of just a few hours.

"Why don't you get some rest?" I told Mackenzie after I got out of the shower and saw her in the same exact position she had been in since we had gotten here…sitting in the bay window, overlooking the channel behind the house.

"No," she said evenly, still in shock. "I need to call his aunt and uncle, let them know what's happened."

"I'll do it. Just get me their information and I'll make all the phone calls you need me to. You need to try to think about something else for a minute…"

"Think about something else?" she sobbed, tilting her head to look at me. "How? How can I possibly be expected to think about *anything* else right now? He warned me this was going to happen and what did I do?"

"Mackenzie, you can't—"

"*Nothing!*" she exclaimed. "I told him to be smart, and that's it. I should have pushed him harder to stay hidden…"

"Don't do this to yourself," I urged, pulling her body into mine. "Don't bury yourself in that guilt. You didn't pull the trigger. I burdened myself with guilt after Melanie died, despite telling my friends and family that the only person to blame was behind bars. But for the longest time, I went to bed thinking I could have done something to prevent it. It took me years to realize I couldn't. I forced myself to live with that guilt and I wouldn't wish that upon anyone, so don't you *dare* do that to yourself. There's nothing you could have done to stop this. I promise you, we will find the bastard responsible and he will pay. Okay?"

"But what if Agent Suarez rules it a suicide? That's the way he was leaning when he examined the crime scene. No one seems to believe that Charlie just wouldn't kill himself. They keep bringing up his record at Walter Reed, not even examining the evidence because he was a schizophrenic who had been off his meds for too long. What if they don't look harder?"

"They will," I assured her, having doubts myself, but I didn't let on. "And if they don't, we will."

She studied me for a protracted moment, then nodded and returned her attention to the window, staring outside once more. I wished there was something I could do or say to make her feel better about all this.

Grief is like a storm. It can be calm and refreshing, a way to finally close one chapter of your life. Or it can be as unforgiving as a hurricane. It can bring our world into the abyss of darkness and turmoil. But just like with the most perilous of storms, it will soon pass. We never truly forget the helplessness and fear we felt during the eye of the storm, but we learn to move on and rebuild our lives. We never forget the loss, but the loss no longer consumes us.

We all grieve in our own way, and Mackenzie was grieving how she needed so she could finally move past this chapter in her life.

"I need to go brief Eli and the team about what's going on," I said, running my hand up and down her arm. "Do you need anything? Tea? Water?"

She shook her head. "No. Just promise you won't let Charlie's death be for nothing." She looked at me once more, her eyes wide and pleading. "That his blood is the last that has to be spilled. I... I can't lose anyone else."

Nodding, I leaned down and placed a soft kiss on her head. "I promise, *mi cariño*."

Her lips turned up just slightly in the corners, a weak smile crossing her face, then she stared out the window once more.

Taking that as my cue to leave, I retreated from the master bedroom, unsure of whether I'd be able to fulfill my promise to her. I entered my office, ignoring the multiple sets of eager eyes sitting around the conference table, and headed straight to the wet bar, pouring myself a scotch. After downing a much needed sip, I took my seat at the table and just stared. Silence surrounded us and I had no idea what to say to everyone.

"Someone say something," I finally said.

"I made contact with the medical examiner's office," Eli began quickly, "and they refused to tell me whether this would be ruled a homicide or suicide. The M.E. seemed a bit annoyed, so that makes me think the agent in charge is leaning toward suicide."

"Have you done any research on this Agent Suarez who seemed to be at the scene alarmingly fast for an FBI agent? I would have expected local police to call the FBI in *after* they realized who the victim was, but he was there almost immediately."

"I've looked into him. He's been the agent in charge of

finding and apprehending Mr. Montgomery since he was linked to all those murders months ago. When I asked how he arrived so quickly, he said he was in the area chasing down a lead."

"And did you believe him?"

"Not one bit," Eli answered. "Maybe I'm wrong, but I've been around cops my entire life. I get a feeling he's dirty. He's working without a partner, which seems suspicious enough, and when I called his office in Washington, his secretary told me he's on vacation overseas for the next month."

Soaking in what Eli had just told me, I simply nodded. "Okay. Thanks. Just keep on it."

"Yes, sir."

"What else?"

Martin cleared his throat. "On a possibly unrelated note—"

"Nothing is unrelated anymore," I interrupted.

He nodded. "We have a lead on who may have killed McDonough and Carlyle, and who may have rigged their houses to explode."

"Go on…"

"Maxwell called in a few favors with some of his contacts involved in running guns and explosives. They put us on to a contact in the area. He confirmed that he sold the same explosives found in both houses to a Serbian drug runner."

"Serbian?" I asked, making sure I had heard correctly. It seemed like too much of a coincidence.

"Exactly. His name is Boris Ranko. We're trying to locate him and ascertain his known associates."

"Good. Benson, Maxwell, stay on it. The fact that a Serbian national nearly tried to kill us makes me pretty certain there's a connection between what's been going on with this case and Galloway's time in Bosnia. I need you to find that connection. Let's put an end to this."

"Sir," they both said in unison.

"Martin, Eli, I want you both to follow the investigation into Charlie's death. There's no question in my mind it is related. We've got to nip this in the bud."

"And what about Colonel Galloway?" Eli asked, looking up from his file. "Do we know of his whereabouts?"

I took another sip of my scotch. "At this point, no. Unfortunately, he disappeared after the wedding. He had insinuated he was ready to use himself to put an end to all of this, but I want to avoid that at all costs. Mackenzie's already lost enough people. We don't need to add to that number. Got it?"

"Yes, sir," Eli said.

"That's it for now. Keep me updated with anything else you find out." I raised myself from my chair and retreated from my team. Immediately, they started whispering amongst themselves, already devising some sort of plan. Even though it was the night before Thanksgiving, none of them had complained about having to spend it away from whatever family they had. Hesitating as I reached the door, I turned around. "Thank you," I said, "for being here and doing everything you can to put an end to this."

They all looked up and met my gaze. "Of course," Eli said. "We want to catch this bastard just as much as you do."

Nodding, I spun on my heels and bolted upstairs to check on how Mackenzie was doing. Based on her fragile state, I didn't want to leave her alone for too long. When I opened the door, the sun was setting, a glow spreading through the room and illuminating her body as she lay on the bed.

With light steps, I went to her and sat down beside her.

Brushing her hair behind her ear so I could look at her face, I placed a kiss on her temple. She sighed, her eyes remaining closed. "I'll make this right. I promise."

Chapter Thirty-Three

Giving Up

Mackenzie

"HE DIDN'T KILL HIMSELF," I insisted as I sat in a cold room of the South Padre police department the following day. I was going on hour number two of their inane questions, and we hadn't gotten anywhere. All they wanted to talk about was Charlie's attack on me during my freshman year of college, which resulted in his eventual institutionalization. But he didn't kill himself and I knew it. I just wondered why this so-called FBI agent refused to look at the actual evidence, dwelling instead on Charlie's institutionalization as the most poignant piece of information to prove it was suicide.

The longer I sat, Tyler beside me, the more irritated I became. This was *not* how I expected to be spending our first Thanksgiving together. I had hoped to be sitting with a stomach full of turkey, watching football as I snuggled next to Tyler. Instead, we were stuck at the police department, an incompetent FBI agent hell-bent on trying to convince me Charlie killed himself.

"If he didn't kill himself, who did?" the overweight agent asked in a thick Spanish accent.

"*No lo se.* Why don't you get off your ass and figure it out instead of sitting here asking *me* who did it? If I knew who killed him, don't you think I'd tell you?"

"Not if you're trying to cover for him."

347

"For whom?" I asked, my voice growing louder.

"For this man," the detective said, opening up the manila folder that sat in front of him. He pushed a photo of my father in front of me. On one hand, I was relieved he had finally admitted that Charlie was murdered. On the other, the insinuation my father was the one responsible for his murder was ludicrous. "You are Serafina Galloway, aren't you?"

I maintained eye contact with Agent Suarez, wondering how he knew who I really was.

"I know all about how you and your mother disappeared after your father attacked the U.S. Embassy in Liberia all those years ago."

Tyler bolted up from his chair, the fury on his face visible. "Mackenzie, you don't have to answer any more of these questions. I'll call my lawyer immediately."

"No," I insisted, grabbing Tyler's hand. When I had gotten the phone call earlier this morning asking if I'd come down to answer a few questions, he begged me to tell them no, that we'd reschedule when he could arrange for his lawyer to be there with me. But I had nothing to hide and I wanted to do everything I could to finally move on from this chapter of my life.

Looking up at him, I said, "I've done nothing wrong." I faced Agent Suarez. "Yes, after my father's *alleged* attack on the embassy, my mother and I disappeared. I didn't know why. All I knew was that I left the only life I had ever known and was forced to hide for years."

He nodded smugly, pulling another photo out of the file. "And how about these three individuals? Do you know who they are?"

He slid a photo of a happy family across the table. I stared at the old photo of my former neighbors. Emily was enclosed in Harrison's embrace, when I still knew him as Harrison Mills and before he became Benjamin

Collins. In front of them was my best friend, Damian. I traced the contours of his youthful face, wishing I could rewind the clock and go back to that time, that I could warn my father not to go to Liberia.

"Yes. They were my old neighbors. The Mills," I said finally, shoving the photo back at him.

"And do you know what happened to Emily Mills?"

"It's Sheperd now, I guess," I responded. "And she was murdered a few months ago, along with her current husband. I saw it on the news."

"So you didn't discuss this with Mr. Montgomery? If you saw it on the news, you must have known the prime suspect in that case was one Charles Patrick Montgomery."

Tyler slammed his fist on the table, his face red with anger. "Don't answer that, Mackenzie. This prick has no idea what he's talking about."

"Tyler," I said calmly. "I have nothing to hide. I haven't done anything wrong, so this prick, as you so aptly called him, can ask me all the questions he wants. He's not going to find anything, but if he wants to waste his time, so be it." I returned my attention to Suarez. "Now, you want to know if I discussed the Sheperd's murder with Charlie... Yes, I did. He called me the night I learned about it and I accused him of the murder."

"And what did he say?"

"He said he was innocent, just as he did with all the other murders of which he was accused. He said he was being set up."

"And did you believe him?"

"Truthfully, I didn't know what to believe. I remember analyzing everything in my head, thinking if the only connection between Charlie and Whitman, the supposed hitman he had hired to kill all those people, was just a web blog and visitor records from Walter Reed, the FBI should work harder at finding some concrete evidence. But when I learned a hair fiber was found, I didn't know what to believe. I didn't want to think he was a killer, and I'm still not quite convinced he is...or was."

"Why?"

"Because I know Charlie," I insisted through clenched teeth.

"Sometimes the most hardened criminals are those we never suspect, but you do have a point, Miss Galloway."

"It's *Mrs.* Burnham," I corrected.

"I apologize," Suarez said. "Mrs. Burnham. As you mentioned, we found a hair fiber of Charlie's around the bodies of Emily and Lucian Sheperd back in Lafayette. We also found several prints on the door frame and windows, but we disregarded them because it was *your* old house."

"Whose prints?" Tyler demanded, his patience waning even more.

"Francis Mackenzie Galloway," the agent said, a satisfied smile on his face. "Considering that house has sat empty since he was assumed to have died in the attack on the embassy, we didn't think much of it...until the initial forensics on Charlie's death came back this morning."

"And what did you find?" I asked softly.

"Well, it seems your father didn't really die in that fire, did he? According to our source in Counterintelligence..." He shoved a one-page document across the table. It was the results of the classified investigation into the embassy attack, which named Colonel Francis Mackenzie Galloway as the perpetrator behind that and dozens of other acts of treason. "He's the one responsible for it. Charlie was the lone survivor, wasn't he?"

I nodded.

"So doesn't it make more sense that all those people Charlie's accused of killing were actually your *father's* victims?"

"What?!" I exclaimed, my voice rising. "That's ridiculous! My father was set up, just like Charlie was!"

"You keep saying that, but you've yet to offer any solid proof of who set him up, Mrs. Burnham! I'm just looking at the facts. Proof... Your father traded U.S. military weapons for money, secrets, diamonds." He became angrier with each word he spoke. "Proof... He's had an off-shore account for years, and the dates of dozens of large deposits coincide all too conveniently with dates of known deals he made."

I continued shaking my head, trying to tune out what he was saying. I didn't want to believe it. I couldn't.

"Proof... He killed everyone who could have revealed he was still alive, including your mother, his own wife!"

"No, no, no, no, no," I said, burying my head in my hands.

"Proof... He killed Charlie!"

I shot my head up. "What?"

"Proof, Mrs. Burnham!" he shouted, pushing a report across the table. My eyes scanned the words printed on it, but my brain couldn't comprehend what I was reading. "Proof... Your father's gun was used to kill Charlie. Proof... A fingerprint was lifted from the trigger and it matched your father's. Proof... The same weapon was used to kill Harrison Mills, or Benjamin Collins, whose body was found yesterday by fishermen out in the Gulf of Mexico. Proof... Your father's prints, along with signs of an intense struggle, were found all over the apartment of Damian Mills, who's been missing since April! Proof... Your father is a criminal, a traitor! He's put on an act so long, he may have even begun to believe he's not the man he truly is, but you don't have to. You

351

can put a stop to all of this. You keep saying he's been set up, that you're trying to find out who did this. Stop fooling yourself, Mrs. Burnham! Your father did it! He did all of it!"

"*Stop!*" I cried, covering my ears.

"*That's enough!*" Tyler roared, shooting out of his chair, sending it flying across the room. "We're done here. If you want to talk to my wife or me, you can go through my lawyer."

He wrapped his arms around my trembling body as tears streamed down my face, the agent's words hitting me to my core. And it hit me hard because it made complete sense.

"Don't cover for him, Mrs. Burnham!" he yelled down the hallway as Tyler escorted me out of the police department. "Just tell us where he is and you can end this! If you don't, you may just be giving birth in prison. You need to decide if he's worth it!"

I tried to shake off everything Agent Suarez had just told me as Tyler drove me back to his house, but I couldn't. "Please don't give up hope," he whispered as I stared at the ocean waves, wishing they would give me the clarity to separate the truth from the lies.

Chapter Thirty-Four

Set Up

Mackenzie

"WHY DON'T YOU TAKE a break from going through all that?" Tyler said to me as I sat surrounded by boxes in the living room of his house. The lights on the Christmas tree illuminated the room on that early December afternoon. A little less than a week had passed since Charlie had died and Tyler's attorney had put the fear of God into Agent Suarez. I didn't know what he had said to him, but we hadn't heard from him since the day he questioned me.

The day after Thanksgiving, Tyler's team had somehow tracked down a storage unit Charlie had been renting the past several months. There were photo albums, yearbooks, cards... All things Charlie thought important enough to hold onto. I had been spending the past few days reading through his journals. Tyler and his team had looked through them, hoping they would find something that could help clear my father's name, but they turned out to just be journals of his thoughts, nothing more. And I found that, over the years, I hadn't left Charlie's thoughts for more than a day, and neither had the family he had lost.

I was consumed with his words, the passion and heartache he had been enduring pouring through the pages. For years after the fire, Charlie suffered from survivor's guilt, and I wondered if he ever truly recovered from it. But he was a brilliant man, a man who had learned to read people and put on an act, which was what he did in order to enlist in the army and eventually become a Ranger. He made everyone think his life was perfect, that he was a model soldier, ready to give his life for his country. And he did just that, although his downward spiral was one no one could have seen coming.

"No," I insisted, meeting Tyler's eyes. "I like doing this."

"I just don't want to see you upset," he said, sitting next to me on the floor. He ran his hands across my back, comforting me.

"I'm not. I know he's gone, but reading his journals… It's like he's here with me."

He took a deep breath, kissing me on the cheek before raising himself off the floor. "Okay. If you're sure."

I smiled at him. "I am."

"I hate to leave you, but Eli wants to go over everything again to see if we're missing something."

"Like what?"

He shrugged. "I don't know. I keep holding out hope we'll stumble across something we missed that will make everything clear."

"Then you should go."

"Are you sure you'll be okay on your own?"

"I'm fine. Jenna texted earlier and I promised I'd meet her for a coffee this afternoon, so that will force me away from all of this." I waved at the boxes scattered around me. "I think she misses having me at the restaurant, but she'll never actually admit it."

He narrowed his eyes at me, apprehension covering his face. I had been cooped up inside his house since returning from Florida. While it certainly gave me time to rest and prepare for the birth of Triple B, I was starting to go a little stir crazy.

"I know what you're thinking and I want you to stop, Tyler. I've barely seen Brayden or Jenna since I got back from Florida, except for the day after Thanksgiving when they found out about Charlie. Not to mention, I won't be seeing them at all once we move to Boston. I want all the time I can get with them."

He rubbed his hand over his face. "I don't feel comfortable with you leaving."

"Duly noted." I smirked. "What can possibly happen? If it makes you feel better, I'll text Jenna and see if she's okay with getting together at her place instead."

He cupped my cheek, a relieved expression washing over him. "That *would* make me feel better. Thank you." He poised his lips over mine and I couldn't help but smile at his closeness.

"You're welcome," I murmured as we shared a soft, beautiful kiss.

"Will you do something else for me?" he asked, pulling away.

"What is it?"

Spinning on his heels, he retreated down the hallway, disappearing into his office momentarily. When he returned, he was carrying a familiar small, black case. Opening it, I saw the pistol he bought for me all those months ago when he taught me how to shoot.

"Really?" I raised my eyebrows at him. "A bit of overkill, don't you think?"

"Probably, but will you bring it with you when you leave here, just to be on the safe side?" His eyes were pleading with me and I could sense a hint of vulnerability about him. It seemed completely unnecessary, but if it eased Tyler's troubled mind, there was no reason for me not to agree to his request.

"Okay." I took the pistol out of its case, made sure the round wasn't chambered, and placed it in my purse.

"Thank you," he said, planting one final kiss on my lips. Pulling back, he headed toward the front door allowing me to admire his backside, just as I had that first night all those months ago. He glanced over his shoulder, a brilliant smile on his face. "I love you, Mrs. Burnham."

"And I love you, Mr. Burnham."

He winked and disappeared outside, leaving me alone with just my thoughts and the background sound of Christmas carols. I lost myself in Charlie's words once more, flipping through the pages, as if I was desperate to find out the anticipated ending of some spellbinding story. However, I already knew how the tale would end. This wasn't about that. It was about keeping a piece of Charlie with me.

My phone buzzed, tearing me away from Charlie's words for the first time in what seemed like hours. I saw a text from Jenna saying she was leaving the restaurant in about ten minutes. I replied, asking if we could just get together at her place instead and she agreed.

Reluctantly, I pried myself away from Charlie's journals and grabbed my bag, leaving the house. The air was crisp and a bit cool, a nice breeze coming in from the ocean. Taking a calming breath of the salty sea air, I jumped into the SUV and turned toward the main strip of South Padre. It was relatively quiet for just a few weeks before Christmas. Soon, I knew I would treasure the tranquility, especially once Triple B decided to make his entrance into the world.

As I sat at a stoplight, I thought how I'd soon be saying goodbye to this town and starting my new life in Boston. It was bittersweet, but it was fitting that Tyler and I were set to start over again somewhere far away from here. I didn't want our son around any of the troubles of my past. He needed a clean start just as much as I did.

I was still lost in my thoughts as I parked my car in the lot of Richard's hotel and strolled through the lobby. It was adorned with stunning Christmas decorations, a thirty-foot tree filling the large atrium-like space. A pianist sat by the tree, playing Christmas carols, and vacationers came and went...some in shorts and flip-flops, others in long pants and sweatshirts.

Smiling at a group of tourists, I entered the elevator and took it all the way to the top floor. Exiting when it came to a stop, I walked down the long corridor and approached the door to Richard's and Jenna's condo. As I was about to knock, I noticed it was slightly ajar. It could have been nothing, but after recent events, I no longer believed in coincidences.

"Hello?" I yelled out, knocking on the opened door. I waited for an answer but none came. Alarm bells went off, but my curiosity got the better of me, driving me forward when everything else told me to turn back and go home.

Retrieving the pistol from my purse and chambering a round, I pushed the door open and stepped inside. "Jenna? Are you in here? It's Mack."

Still no answer. Their condo appeared as it always had. The living room was practically immaculate with a beautifully decorated tree just in front of the large floor-to-ceiling windows overlooking the Gulf of Mexico. Walking further into the condo, my weapon at my side, I noticed Jenna's purse sitting on the kitchen island, the contents spilled as if she had been looking for something rather hastily.

"Jenna?" I called out again. Tiptoeing down the corridor off the living room to see if she was in her office, I halted in my steps when I heard an angry voice speaking in a foreign language. It sounded Russian, but I couldn't be sure.

Frozen in place, I didn't realize when the conversation had ended...until a light flooded the hallway and I snapped my head up, trying to make sense of why this person I thought I knew had a gun aimed at me.

With shaky hands, I raised my own weapon. Before I could get off a shot, I felt a sharp pain in my head and my world went dark.

Chapter Thirty-Five

Puzzle Pieces

Tyler

I SAT IN THE office of the club, anxiously waiting for Eli to show up. He had said he was on his way from Brownsville with what he thought was a possible connection between Galloway and this Boris Ranko, who had tried to blow us up. I prayed it was one that would finally put an end to all of this. The more time that passed without any new information, the more uneasy I became that everything would fall out from underneath me. I needed answers, and I needed them now.

Focusing on my laptop, my eyes glossed over the massive amount of information we had accumulated since the beginning of this case over a year ago. I tried to separate what I knew to be fact from what I knew was clearly fiction. Unfortunately, what I knew to be true and backed up by physical evidence was lacking. For the most part, all we had was one person's story against another's, all of it contradictory. The little physical evidence we *did* have, from an FBI agent I still wasn't sure was reliable, supported a story I didn't necessarily want to believe, although it was the theory I had bought into when I first began to work this assignment. Now, I wasn't so sure. All I did know was that I desperately needed answers, and I hoped Eli would give me some when he got here.

A figure standing in the doorway caught my attention

and I swung my head up, trying to hide my surprise.

"Francis…," I muttered under my breath, confused about what he was doing here, particularly now that the FBI seemed to know of his existence and had plastered his face all over the national news. I quickly ushered him into my office, hoping none of my staff members had arrived for their shift just yet, and closed the door behind him.

"What are you doing here?" I asked in a low voice as I gestured for him to have a seat across from my desk.

He briefly closed his eyes as he dropped into the chair. "Saying goodbye." There was something different about his demeanor. He was no longer the collected former army colonel I had grown to know over the past few months or so. His eyes were dull, his expression blank. His stature was slumped, no longer exhibiting the confidence I saw in him when he nonchalantly strolled into my hospital room as if he didn't have a care in the world. I could tell this was it. He was finally giving up.

"What do you mean?"

"I know it may not make sense, but I can't go on like this anymore, not now that the FBI has decided to broadcast my face and identity across the country. If I don't do this, they'll never leave Serafina alone. I'm doing this for her."

"Doing what?" I demanded.

"I contacted Agent Suarez of the Federal Bureau of Investigation. I understand you've had the pleasure of meeting him recently."

I nodded.

"I've agreed to surrender myself into his custody, effective this afternoon."

"Francis, you can't—"

He held up his hand. "I understand the ramifications of what I'm doing. I don't need you to lecture me about

360

it."

"But what about Mackenzie?" I urged, my voice growing louder.

"I'm doing this *for* her. She's the *only* reason I'm doing this!" he insisted, the life and passion returning to him as his eyes lit on fire. "To save her from a life of always having to look over her shoulder, never knowing when something I've done will come back to haunt her. By doing this, I can take full responsibility for everything, and finally let Serafina live the life she's been meant to live!" He paused, looking past me at a photograph sitting on a small chest. I followed his line of sight to see him gazing affectionately at a framed picture of the two of us kissing on the beach just after we were married.

"There has to be another—"

"By doing this," he interrupted, his voice barely audible, "she can finally forget about me, like she should have all those years ago."

"Did you go see her?" I asked.

Meeting my eyes, he shook his head slowly, remaining silent.

"Why not?!" My body tensed as I struggled to maintain my temper. I had trouble wrapping my head around what I was hearing. "You're just going to turn yourself in and not even do the decent thing and tell your own daughter about it?!"

"I *am* doing the decent thing," he replied harshly, slamming his fist on the desk. "I've been sick with this decision since I heard about how she had been interrogated regarding Charlie's murder! I knew I'd have to do this without saying goodbye. It's the only way to save her from any more heartache!"

"You left once without telling her!" I bellowed out. "For years, she was convinced you were dead! And now, when it appears as if you *are* the monster you swore you

weren't, you just get to cut your losses and walk away?!
Without giving her an explanation?! What about the rest
of us who have agreed to stand by your side and put our
own necks on the line, regardless of what the physical
evidence actually says?!"

"Cut my losses?!" he shouted, his face flaming red, his
nostrils flaring as he jumped up from his chair. His face
was mere inches from mine, both of our breathing
intense. "I'm losing *everything* by this decision, but I don't
care! By doing this, I'm giving Serafina her life back! A
life that was better without me in it in the first place! But
that doesn't mean I'm ready to tarnish the few memories
of me she has left! And I don't want her last one to be of
me saying goodbye!"

He took a protracted breath and ran his hand over his
face. Pulling back, he turned his gaze away from mine.
His chin quivered as he struggled to fight back the tears
that had formed in his eyes. "I want her to remember her
father, the man who would do anything for her…not her
father, the criminal. And I want my last memory of her
to be one of joy, of smiles…not of tears and sorrow.
Please, Tyler, I beg you to understand."

"But she'll want to see you," I said, lowering my voice.
"Even after you turn yourself in, do you think she won't
do everything she can to visit you?"

"She can't. Please, keep her away. I can't bear the
thought of my little girl seeing me locked up in some
prison. She doesn't belong there. I can't put her through
that."

"You're her family," I offered, grasping at straws. "The
only family she has left."

He shook his head and began to retreat toward the
door. I wanted to stop him, to figure out some way to
prove he wasn't the man the world, maybe even he,
thought he was.

"I'm not her family. Maybe I was once upon a time, but not anymore. She has a new family now, but she'll never be able to enjoy that new family if she's still hung up on the last." He pulled open the door, pausing briefly. Glancing over his shoulder, he said, "We *will* see each other again. I have faith the good Lord knows the truth and will make sure we eventually find our way back to each other."

He disappeared, leaving me stunned. I sank back into my chair, wondering how I was not only going to tell Mackenzie that her father had turned himself in, but also how I was going to keep her from visiting him. I knew it was impossible. Mackenzie was one of the most stubborn women I'd ever met, and she would do everything she could to see her father. I could just picture her eyes when she went to wherever he was being held to visit and he refused to see her. I hated to admit it, but I understood. If I were in his shoes, I would have done the same thing for the exact same reasons.

"I've got something." Eli came barreling into the office, breathless, snapping me out of my thoughts.

"What is it?" I waved him in, trying to adjust my composure so he couldn't see I was unnerved.

"Boris Ranko... I tracked him down. He was up in Brownsville, which I found to be suspicious, considering how close it is to us. Anyway, I did a bit of research on him and found out he's not exactly a Serbian drug runner anymore. He was, but fell out of his boss' good graces. Seeing as he's not here legally, I *may* have threatened deportation. Once I did that, he began to sing like a fucking canary in a coal mine." He leaned back, a satisfied smile on his face.

"What did you find out?" I asked, on the edge of my seat.

"Viktor Popovic... That's our man."

I furrowed my brow, confused. "It can't be. I heard Galloway's story about what happened in Bosnia. He said Viktor and his wife both died the night they tried to rescue her."

Eli shook his head, his smile growing wider. "It appears he didn't. Yes, he was shot, but he survived. Several months later, Popovic entered the United States and was granted asylum. After that, he disappeared. No credit cards. No bank accounts. Nothing."

"So he's still alive?"

Eli nodded. "Ranko insisted he was, said he was supposed to meet him at an address in South Padre later this afternoon. I tried to see if Popovic changed his name when he arrived here and that's why I couldn't find any information about him when I ran it, but Ranko insisted his name was Viktor."

"And where is Ranko now?"

"Handcuffed in the back of the car."

I sighed, leaning back in my chair. "I wish there was something more. This doesn't really prove anything. It's just another piece in this convoluted puzzle that keeps getting bigger and more confusing the deeper we dig. We still have nothing conclusive to prove that anyone other than Mackenzie's father was responsible for everything. Hell, I don't even see a motive for this Viktor to want to set Galloway up!"

"I do," Eli insisted.

"What?"

"Revenge."

"I don't know," I said, getting up and pacing my office. "It's a stretch. Do you have a photo of what this Viktor looks like so we know who we're dealing with?"

He scrolled through his cell phone. "The only photo was from when he first came here nearly thirty years ago, so you'll need to use your imagination and picture him as a man in his fifties."

I took the phone from him and scanned the grainy photo from the immigration database, imagining what this man would look like after having aged several decades. He had dark hair and gray eyes. They were haunting and I couldn't help but feel as if I knew those eyes. I continued to study the photo, mentally adding a few wrinkles on his face, graying his hair...

Time stood still as the photo transitioned from a man in his twenties to one in his fifties. It all became clear and dread coursed through me.

"Fuck," I hissed, shoving Eli's phone back at him.

"What is it?" he yelled after me as I ran out of the office.

"I know exactly who that is!" I responded, my phone up to my ear, anxious for Mackenzie to pick up.

Chapter Thirty-Six

Vindication

Mackenzie

MY EYES FLUTTERED OPEN, scanning my surroundings. I was somewhere I didn't recognize. It looked like a beach rental that hadn't been used in months, maybe years. A thin layer of dust had settled on the modest furniture in the living room, the only light coming from the setting sun filtering through the rips in the curtains. And sitting across from me in that musty living room was the man I thought I trusted, sharpening a long blade.

"Richard," I hissed, my eyes narrowing on him as I fought against the rope he had tied around my hands, securing me to an uncomfortable chair. I tried to ignore the pain in my head from where he had knocked me out with the barrel of his gun. Everything about him seemed different. His gray eyes that once made him seem distinguished and prominent now made him appear malevolent and sinister.

"Ah, look who's finally awake," he said in an Eastern European accent, taking me by surprise. My pulse raced, venom pooling in my veins at how easily I had fallen into his trap... How easily we *all* had.

"What are you doing?"

"What does it look like I'm doing?" he asked maliciously, his hooded eyes staring at me.

"Sharpening a knife," I quietly responded, a chill

spreading through me.

"What a rather astute observation."

"What are you planning on doing with that?" I asked, even though I already knew the answer.

"I wouldn't want to ruin the surprise." His lips turned up at the corners. "One of my biggest pet peeves is when someone tells me how a movie's going to end, completely ruining it for me. It makes me..." He shook his head, a wild look about him. "Hell, it makes me really just want to...*kill* someone." The vein in his neck engorged, he pressed the blade into his finger and blood seeped out of it.

I swallowed hard, trying to fight back the bile forming in my throat.

"Well, I think it's sharp enough, don't you, Serafina?"

I cringed at his use of my real name, feeling utterly stupid for not seeing all the signs earlier. Now that he was sitting here, it all made sense. I flashed back to the night of the wedding, remembering how brooding and quiet Richard had been. It was in stark contrast to the man I knew him to be. The entire night, he had been studying my father, his eyes trained on him.

"So it was you all along, wasn't it? You killed my mother and Charlie? You're the one who set my father up to take the fall for all those crimes?"

"Yes...and no," he said, getting up and stalking toward where I sat with my arms tied behind my back. "Yes, I killed your mother, Charlie, and quite a few other people. However, I didn't set your father up."

"So Mr. Mills did that?" I asked, wishing it wasn't true. I didn't want to believe the man who had been like a second father to me would do something so hateful to his neighbor and best friend.

"More or less, with a little bit of my urging."

"Why?"

"Because your father had it coming to him!" he growled. I flinched, the fierceness in his eyes and voice making my hands grow clammy. "He was no hero. He didn't deserve to live when so many other people...true heroes, people who didn't cower in the face of death...had been taken. I was simply correcting the natural order of things!"

"What do you mean?" I asked, wanting to keep him talking for as long as possible.

"He did *nothing*! My wife, Irena, was tied to a fucking tree!"

I gasped, remembering the story my father had told me about his time in Bosnia, and a man named Viktor Popovic. Now I knew... Richard was Viktor and he wanted revenge.

"Your father was there and he did *nothing*! He stood aside like a fucking coward and watched as she was shot in the fucking head. Then he left *me* for dead, too. He is no saint. He is no hero. And he deserves to die for what he did!"

"He told me that story, how torn up he—"

"*No!*" He rushed toward me, his eyes on fire, holding a knife up to my throat. "You do *not* get to sit there and say he felt guilty. Guilty doesn't bring my wife back!"

Resolving to stay strong, I took a deep breath. "How does Mr. Mills fit into this?" I hoped by changing the subject, he would calm down.

He glared at me, his eyes dark and sinister. Seconds passed even though it felt like hours, as he kept the knife pressed to my throat. Convinced he was going to cut me with the blade, I began to say the prayers my mother had taught me all those years ago. Finally, he loosened his grip on me and retreated to the couch, sharpening the blade once more.

"Harrison Mills... Let's see. He had been rather useful

to me over the years. Once I was granted asylum here, just months after your father returned from Bosnia, I changed my identity so Viktor Popovic no longer existed. I tried to leave that person behind, not wanting to be reminded of my past...but my past would not leave me alone. Years later, I watched as your father received some commendation from the president for solving a large case for Counterintelligence. I was enraged. Something inside me snapped and I knew I couldn't move on until I finally righted that wrong.

"I spent my days keeping tabs on the members of your father's team from Bosnia. That's when I discovered what your friend's father had been doing. Selling military secrets, weapons, et cetera, to terror organizations, drug cartels, anybody who would pay. Since I had no desire to go to prison or be sent back to Bosnia, I knew I could blackmail him into doing my dirty work for me. I sent him photos I had amassed of all the deals he had been involved in, telling him if he didn't want me to leak them, he had to dispose of Galloway. I do have to admit, his method was quite ingenious. Set a trap for your father to investigate a certain deal, kill him in a fire, then leave enough evidence to attribute said fire to him, along with all the weapons and secret deals Mills had made. I couldn't have done it better if I had planned it myself.

"When I saw the newscasts reporting what happened, something changed in me. I can't explain it. It was a rush, a high unlike anything I had ever experienced, knowing that *I* was the reason Galloway was dead."

"But you didn't exactly get what you wanted, did you?"

"I suppose not, although I didn't know it at the time. I saw the footage of the fire and Mills said it was done. I suppose he thought it was, as did I."

"How did you find out he was still alive?"

He got up and walked into the kitchen, returning with an apple. Bringing the blade up to the fruit, he peeled it, his eyes trained on me. A shiver traveled down my spine at the menacing look he was giving me, coupled with him running the knife against the skin of the apple, peeling it off in one carefully orchestrated movement.

"I hadn't heard from Mills in years. Now that your father was supposedly dead, we had agreed to go our separate ways. I actually got on with my life. I had been working at this up-and-coming hotel. I started as an engineer, fixing things that needed to be fixed. Soon, I found myself running the hotel. Then another. Then I had been tapped to take over the entire chain. Things were good. I even married a girl, although it was purely a business arrangement and nothing more. But as the years wore on, there was this kind of nagging sensation deep inside of me. I had been riding that high from being responsible for Galloway's fall, but it was starting to wane. I needed to feel that rush again. You can imagine my excitement one day when Mills called saying some schmuck was looking into your father, convinced he wasn't guilty of the fire or any of the other deals. We learned he worked in Cryptology and had been the lone survivor of that fire. Then he told me a bit of news I wasn't anticipating... That this guy had found your mother and she was still alive. We both grew concerned everything would crumble on top of us if they spoke and began to put the pieces together. I saw this as a golden opportunity to chase that high again, so we took matters into our own hands."

"You killed my mother and had Charlie institutionalized."

"More or less, although I didn't pull the metaphorical trigger myself."

"No. Whitman did, didn't he?"

"He was a very reliable employee of the hotel. He got the job done, so to speak."

"Why are you telling me all of this?" I asked.

He gave me an ominous look as he sliced into the apple. "You're a bright young girl, Serafina. I think you can figure out why I'm telling you everything." He popped the apple into his mouth and took a bite, the juices flowing down his chin.

"Well, what happened next?" I asked. It was readily apparent he had no intention of allowing me to walk out of that house so my only saving grace was to try to stall him as long as possible in the hopes that someone would figure out where I was. Or for me to come up with some sort of plan. I wasn't putting too many eggs in that basket, though.

"Killing your mother wasn't enough. I was addicted to this now, desperate to recreate that high I felt when your father was killed. There was something lacking and it drove me crazy so I did the only thing I could think of. I knew it would only be a matter of time until someone else came out of the woodwork, throwing Mills' and my world into a tailspin once again, so we decided to take preemptive action this time. Everyone on Mills' team at the embassy fire... Gone. The Ranger unit in Bosnia... Gone. Anyone who could potentially leak the truth... Disposed of. Of course, law enforcement never put the pieces together, the incompetent fools they are. For the most part, Whitman made everything seem like an accident and no one ever thought it odd that nearly an entire Ranger unit had died. And with each new kill, that rush came back, but it still wasn't enough. Then, roughly two years ago, I got a phone call from a frantic Mills, telling me something I never expected to hear."

"That my father was alive."

He nodded. "Yes, and he was convinced your father

371

knew everything. It was only a matter of time until he ruined it all. The only thing we had on our side was that Galloway was deemed a treasonous bastard, although some higher-ups of the U.S. military issued a gag order on his alleged misdeeds so the public never knew about it."

"But I'm sure it would have all come out if there was evidence that he was still alive and had committed a crime…say, murder."

He winked. "Smart girl, but you're skipping ahead. We'll get to that. I saw this as the perfect opportunity to finally… What is the phrase you use to refer to recreating that first high?"

"Chase the dragon," I muttered.

"Precisely! That's the one. So, yes, with the news that your father was alive, this was my opportunity to feel that same rush again. Mills promised he would take care of Galloway once and for all and I grew antsy as I waited for news. Months had passed and I heard nothing. *Nothing!* Mills had forsaken his old life years ago, leaving behind his family for a deep cover assignment with the CIA, and I had become uneasy that this whole thing was a ticking time bomb. That's when I found out the infamous daughter of Colonel Galloway, now parading around as Mackenzie Delano, was living on South Padre. And I knew this was the perfect spot to open up a new hotel."

"So you came here and…what? Married Jenna to get close to me? Seems like a lot of effort, if you ask me."

"I soon found getting close to you to be next to impossible, so the next best option was to get close to someone you trusted. Jenna. She was so desperate to fall in love with someone, it was perfect. While I was working you from one angle, Mills…or Collins, as he was now going by…had hired a private security company to work you from another, no questions asked."

"Tyler..."

He nodded, devoting his attention to sharpening his knife again. The sound of metal against metal was like nails on a chalkboard, each drawn out motion unnerving me a little bit more.

"Everything was going great. I did everything I could to convince you to finally lower your guard and let this guy in, knowing if it worked between you two, you may just lead him, and me, to your father. Then it all started to spiral out of control. Charlie had escaped from Walter Reed, then Elizabeth overheard me talking to Whitman on the phone while I was at the Chamber of Commerce's office, ordering him to do everything he could to spook you...so she had to be dealt with."

"What was the point of having Whitman make those phone calls to me?"

"Charlie had escaped and I was certain his first stop would be to pay you a visit. I wanted you to think he was the one responsible for the phone calls so you wouldn't trust him. The last thing I wanted was for you to put the pieces together before we could find your father."

"And you didn't think of just using me to get to him?"

"What do you think we were doing? Hell, I had people following you almost everywhere. Whitman had broken into your place on countless occasions to go through your mail, your cell phone, everything. And we got nothing! If you were communicating with him, we couldn't figure it out."

"Because my father is much smarter than you are," I sneered.

"I'll just let you believe that for now. We'll soon see what kind of a man your father truly is."

"What do you mean by—"

"All in due time."

I studied him, hoping I could figure out what he meant by that, but he gave nothing away.

"Well, I can pretty much figure out the rest," I said, breaking the heavy silence, trying to drown out the sound of him continually sharpening the blade. "Tyler ran the footage of Whitman breaking in. You freaked out that there was an ID of Whitman and a possible investigation, which could lead back to you, so you killed him. Then you were able to somehow hack into the database at Walter Reed and alter visitor records to make it appear as if Charlie had hired Whitman to commit all those murders Whitman had, in fact, committed at your instruction."

"I particularly liked the special touch of leaving a photo of you and your mother at the crime scene."

"Why did you do that?"

"So the police would reopen the investigation into her death and certain things may come out about your father. I knew he was still alive, and perhaps an open criminal investigation in which you were a possible victim would force you to finally divulge where he was hiding."

"But Tyler beat you there and was smart enough to make sure law enforcement didn't find those photos."

"I certainly did underestimate his abilities. It was a mistake, but one I didn't intend to repeat. After Charlie had been named as a suspect in all those murders, Mills, or Collins, came to me and said he was done, that he was ready to put an end to it and finally come clean. I had sensed his loyalty to me waning over the months, so I made sure I had a little insurance against that happening."

"What did you do?"

"This…" He stalked toward me, revealing his iPad. I tried to make sense of what I was seeing… It was a live feed of what appeared to be surveillance footage. On the screen was a man about my age, chained to a wall of what I could only imagine to be a cold, cement cell. Surrounding him were several monitors and computers.

"What is—"

"Oh, of course you wouldn't recognize him. It has been...what? Sixteen or seventeen years since you've seen each other?"

"Damian...?" I exhaled, a tear forming in my eye at the bruises and scars dotting his face, hands, and legs.

"Did you know he's quite skilled with computers and hacking? So he had a dual purpose for me. Not only did he serve as insurance that dear old dad wouldn't go to the police, but he's done everything to make sure Charlie, and your father, have taken the fall for what some other bastard has done. It's a good thing he's remained useful to me, or he would have gone the way of his father and mother a long time ago."

"It was you who tried to have Tyler killed when he decided to look into a possible connection with Bosnia, wasn't it? And you killed those last few remaining team members of my father's Ranger unit, right?"

"Guilty," he said playfully. "Well, technically, I hired an old acquaintance from back home to do all that. I'm rubbish when it comes to explosives, but he has what I would call a very unique talent."

"How did you know Tyler and his team would be going to question them?"

"Remember how I had mentioned your buddy, Damian, had remained useful? Well, I had him flag certain files in various government databases, particularly any of them having to deal with your father's Ranger unit. I had eliminated most of his team members, except for two who had apparently gone underground. One day, we saw there was some activity on them. Then there was nothing for weeks, but I still couldn't shake it off.

Thankfully, Damian was able to find out the IP address of who hacked into the government database, who just happened to be one of Tyler's guys, then broke through his firewall to see what information he had. Luckily for us, he had been able to locate the two missing team members. When I saw flight plans, one to somewhere in Oklahoma and another to Florida, I knew something was up. We had about an eighteen hour head start, but we still had to act fast. So we made sure both men suffered an unfortunate 'heart attack', then rigged the houses to explode when someone tried to enter. Of course, my man was smart enough to leave clues out in the open that would indicate someone was home so your boy would break in. And when he did... Boom."

"Why? You killed the guys in the Ranger unit. What did you have to gain by trying to kill Tyler and his team?"

"Everything!" he growled, his face growing red. "He was determined to find who was responsible for everything and I knew he wouldn't stop. I couldn't have that happen, not until I finally got my hands on your father!" The vein in his neck flared and the wild look in his eyes reminded me of an addict desperate for his next fix. And that was precisely what Richard was. He had become so addicted to how powerful and in control he felt when he thought he was responsible for taking my father's life that he had been trying to recreate that high over the past several years, but nothing topped it. This man in front of me was desperate and crazed, completely irrational.

"But if you were so anxious to get your hands on my father," I said, snapping out of my thoughts, "why didn't you do anything at the wedding? He was there. You were there."

"It's not just about your father. I need retribution, an

eye for an eye, and just killing your father isn't enough anymore. However, I did make sure he knew who I was, that I was still alive and not dead as I'm sure he hoped."

My mind raced, wondering why my dad hadn't said anything to any of us.

"And Charlie? That was you?"

"I still don't know why he made it so easy for us to find him. After all those months of him on the run, he just called you on your cell phone, allowing Damian to trace the call. Imagine my surprise when we found out it was from your condo. I called a favor into my buddy, the agent who had been leading the investigation into all of Charlie's murders, and gave him a lead on the location. It's not a coincidence he was assigned that case and, like most low-paid government workers, he was more than willing to help me stage a suicide in exchange for a heavy payoff."

"Agent Suarez?" I asked.

"I met him years ago during a fundraiser at one of my hotels in Washington. I heard he had a certain talent and knew he may end up being useful to me one day. He was more than willing to put an end to Charlie, then try to pin his death, and a whole slew of others, on your father...particularly when I showed him classified documents naming him as the man behind dozens of acts of treason, including the embassy fire. Agent Suarez has a very twisted sense of patriotism."

"Didn't quite work out for you, though, did it?" a loud booming voice bellowed out. We both snapped our heads toward the front door, surprised to see my father standing there, holding a pistol.

Richard rushed toward me and cut my restraints, lifting me out of the chair and holding me against him, the knife to my throat. "I'll kill her!" he hissed, pressing the cold metal against my skin. I whimpered, feeling as if

I was staring death in the face.

"Why? What do you want with her? She didn't do anything!" my father argued, taking slow steps toward us. "You want your revenge against me for not saving your wife, then take it but Serafina has nothing to do with this and you know it."

"See, that's where you're wrong, Frankie! She has *everything* to do with this. I've been looking forward to this day for years. I thought I'd be happy knowing you were dead, and I was, but it faded. I've tried recreating that high for years now. *Years!* Nothing's worked. And I know there's only one thing that will! Finally killing you isn't enough. I need something more! An eye for a fucking eye, Frankie!" he screeched out in a shrill voice.

"You already killed my wife! Let Serafina go and take me! Then we're even!"

"No! As long as she's still alive, we'll never be even! Did I forget to mention that my wife, the love of my *fucking* life, was pregnant? I will never have peace in this world unless I do this," he said, the blade pushing into me even harder, drawing blood.

"You won't be able to walk away from this," my dad said, trying to rationalize with him, but I knew it was useless. Richard was mad, completely irrational.

"I don't care about that! I don't want to walk away from this! I should have died in that forest, but I was sentenced to live a life without my soul mate instead! I welcome death at this point. But, first, I need to make this right! I need to restore the natural order of things!"

Out of the corner of my eye, I saw him raise the knife. Fear washed over me as it closed in on me once more. Time passed in slow motion and my entire body trembled, the blade growing closer with each drawn-out second.

I met my father's eyes, wanting the last thing I saw to

be one of love. "*Lo siento*," he whispered as a loud gunshot echoed.

Stunned, I looked down to see blood streaming down my chest as I fell to the ground.

Chapter Thirty-Seven
Every Time We Say Goodbye

Tyler

"WHERE IS HE?" I hissed, pressing my gun against Ranko's throat as Eli drove through the streets toward the hotel Richard ran. I still couldn't believe he was behind it. I had done background checks on the guy and came up empty. He was clean... A little too clean, which should have been a giant red flag. Instead, I chose to believe he was simply a man who had never done anything to bring attention to himself. It was eating me up that this had gone on for months when the answer was right under our noses.

"What makes you think I'm going to tell you?" he spat out in a thick accent, his blue eyes narrowed on me in a malicious way. "Go ahead and report me to immigration! I know people who have been waiting for their hearing for years! You don't scare me!"

"You're absolutely right. Deportation is one thing. You could sit in a holding cell for months, maybe even years, while your removal hearing is pending. So threatening deportation won't really work, will it? But imagine if you get a visit from Emil Kovac, your old boss, who you stole... How much was it, Eli?" I asked, glancing over my shoulder as Eli continued to drive.

"My sources say it was over a hundred million."

I whistled, smiling coyly at Ranko. "That's a lot of

green. I'm sure Kovac is just itching to get his hands on you. From what I've heard, he's a bit of a sadistic fuck, isn't he, Eli?"

"Sure is. I heard he hooks up electrodes to his victims' testicles. He likes to watch them suffer, usually for days, before finally killing them."

"Days..." I shook my head. "That's a long time to have to suffer through that kind of torture, don't you think?" I sighed. "So, what's it going to be? You can tell me where your buddy, Viktor, is. Or you get to enjoy a few hundred volts of electricity running through your balls. Your choice."

Sweat dotted his brow and his body began to quiver. "Hibiscus," he said softly.

"What was that?"

"He owns a vacation rental on Hibiscus. He asked me to meet him there this afternoon, said it was very important."

"Why?"

"I don't know," he answered quickly. "He doesn't fill me in on any of the details. He just tells me where I need to be and when, and what he expects me to do. All I know is he was planning something big today."

"Something big? Like what?"

"He said this was the end game."

"Shit," I muttered just as my phone vibrated in my pocket. "Eli. Step on it."

"Yes, sir."

Keeping my gun trained on Ranko, I fished my cell out of my pocket, a number I didn't recognize flashing on the screen.

"Burnham here," I answered curtly.

"Tyler?" Jenna's small voice sobbed out. My face immediately paled, knowing Mackenzie was supposed to be having coffee with her at this precise moment. I hated that I had insisted they get together at her place, the home she shared with Richard, instead of somewhere else. I convinced her to go right into the lion's den.

"Jenna, are you okay?"

"No! Richard, he…"

"What happened? Where is he?"

"I don't know," she choked out. "I was getting ready to go into the restaurant this afternoon, and he was crazed. Manic. I had never seen him like that before. I tried to get away, but…" Her voice became strained, her cries growing louder. "He attacked me. I thought he was going to kill me. The last thing I remember was him slamming me against the wall in our bedroom. The next thing I knew, I was being woken up by the head of housekeeping. It's Wednesday, and she cleans our condo every Wednesday. God knows how long I would have been locked in there if she didn't come. I didn't know where else to go so I went to Brayden's, but he's still at work. I'm just really scared to be alone right now."

"Jenna, did you text Mackenzie today and ask her to meet you for coffee?"

"What?" she asked, sounding confused. "No. Why?"

I let out a long breath and tried to control my nerves. "Don't worry about it. Have you gone to the police?"

"Not yet. I didn't know what to do so I called you first."

"Good. I'm going to text Martin to come get you. He'll bring you to my place and make sure nothing happens to you."

"What's going on? Is everything okay?"

"No," I said dejectedly. "I don't think so."

Eli turned onto Hibiscus and Richard's car, as well as a dark sedan, came into view, parked a block ahead of us.

"I'll be in touch," I said quickly, then hung up.

Pinning my gun against Ranko's temple one more

time, I growled, "Stay here!" Jumping out of the car, Eli following, I tread carefully on the gravel driveway leading up to the simple one-story beach house Ranko said he was to meet Richard this afternoon.

Every crunch of rock seemed to be amplified ten-fold as I listened to two distinct male voices reverberating from inside the house, one with a thick eastern European accent that had to be Richard. I chambered a round and gingerly walked up the wooden steps and onto the porch, my feet light.

I peered into the window and my heart dropped when I saw Richard holding Mackenzie, a knife at her throat. I tried to see who Richard was talking to, but was unable. I feared the worst would happen if we went in through the front door. Richard would be able to see us and react before we could even get off a shot. Meeting Eli's eyes, I signaled that we would head around the wrap-around porch and enter through the back door. Nodding, he followed.

My heart echoed in my ears as I turned the knob of the door, hoping the low click didn't alert anyone to our presence. Before I could make sense of what was going on, a gunshot sounded and I snapped my head up to see Colonel Francis Galloway, Mackenzie's flesh and blood, holding a smoking gun, both Mackenzie and Richard falling to the ground in a heap.

"No!" I bellowed, firing at Francis before I had time to figure out what just happened.

"Hold your fire!" Eli shouted when Francis fell from the two shots I was able to get off to his shoulder and chest.

"He killed her! It was him all along!" I ran to Mackenzie, cradling her in my arms, blood pouring from a through-and-through bullet wound to her upper chest.

"No," she squeaked out, her breathing strained as her

eyes met mine. "He killed Richard."

"What?" I studied her, looking for an answer.

"He's not a monster. He slew the real dragon. If he didn't, Richard would have…" She swallowed hard, her breathing uneven as she shivered.

"I'm so sorry, Serafina," I whimpered, her body growing limp in my arms. "I should have gotten here sooner."

"No," she breathed, grabbing my arm with her cold hand. "You have nothing to be sorry about. You gave me something I never thought I'd ever have."

"What?" I asked, barely able to see through my tears.

"A home."

I let out a loud sob, not caring that anyone saw me cry. I wanted them to see me like this, to see that I was human, that I couldn't bear the thought of history repeating itself.

"Promise me one thing," she said, her voice growing softer.

"What's that?"

"Save our baby."

"What do you mean?"

"Our baby comes first. Do you understand what I'm saying to you?"

I shook my head, refusing to listen. "Stop talking like that. You're going to be fine. It's just a shot to your shoulder. People survive those wounds all the time. It barely grazed you," I choked out, staring at the blood covering my hands. I was more than aware that even typically non-fatal bullet wounds could become fatal if not treated in time.

A slight smile crossed her mouth. "You're a horrible liar."

"I'm not lying. I've waited my entire life for you. Do you think I'm just going to let you give up?"

"Please, Tyler. Promise me. If it comes to having to decide, you'll choose our son."

I continued to shake my head, the reality of having to make that decision gutting me.

"Please…" Her breathing grew shallow and I knew she was on the brink of losing consciousness.

Sighing, I nodded, although the thought of losing her ripped me apart. A content smile crossing her face, she closed her eyes as she struggled to breathe. Sirens grew closer and closer, but they still sounded like they were miles away.

"Chase the demons away, Tyler," she whispered, opening her eyes once more, a lone tear falling down her cheek.

I lowered my lips to hers, wishing I could breathe life back into her. Kissing her softly, I sang the words to "Every Time We Say Goodbye", barely able to get through the lyrics, praying this wasn't the last time we would ever say goodbye.

Chapter Thirty-Eight

Over

Tyler

IT WAS A FRANTIC scene as I followed the paramedics out of the ambulance and into the emergency room, nurses and doctors meeting us before we could even take two steps. They spoke in medical terms I couldn't understand, and I had no idea what anything meant.

"Sir."

I snapped my head up to see a woman with green scrubs addressing me.

"How far along is your wife?"

"Almost thirty-eight weeks," I answered.

"Okay. She's lost a lot of blood. If there's any chance of us saving the baby, we need to perform a C-section, but that means we have to delay operating on her own wounds."

I nodded solemnly, taking a deep breath as I remembered the promise I made to Mackenzie. "I understand. I promised her I'd save the baby."

She gave me a sympathetic smile before following the stretcher through a pair of swinging doors, one of the nurses staying behind to ensure I didn't follow. I retreated down the hallway, watching as the second ambulance arrived carrying Mackenzie's father, the paramedics pumping oxygen into him as they ran him down the same corridor.

I paced the empty sitting area, time seeming to crawl as I desperately waited for someone to come to me with good news to put my concerns at ease. But I had a feeling that wasn't going to happen.

Falling into a chair, I buried my head in my hands, trying to figure everything out. I had no idea how everything went down. How had Richard, or Viktor, gotten away with what he did for years? I feared the only people who could answer those questions wouldn't survive, leaving the rest of us with more questions than answers.

"Tyler!" Eli shouted, snapping me out of my thoughts as he barreled into the waiting room.

I stood up and hugged him briefly before noticing the crazed look on his face. "What is it?"

"This," he said, shoving an iPad at me.

I scrunched my eyebrows, unsure of what I was supposed to be looking at. All I knew was it appeared to be a camera feed of a man chained to a wall and surrounded by a bank of monitors and computers.

"Looks like Richard has this guy locked away somewhere," he explained.

"Who?"

A satisfied smile crossed his face. "I ran a facial scan on him and we got a hit. That is Damian Mills."

"Damian?!" I exclaimed. "Mackenzie's Damian?" I had all but given up hope we'd ever find him alive.

He nodded. "Benson and Maxwell are doing their best to trace the source of this feed right now."

I exhaled and collapsed into a chair. "That's a relief. I was so worried with everything that just happened, we'd all have more questions than answers. Maybe Damian can fill in some of the blanks we're left with right now."

Eli placed his hand on my arm in a comforting manner. "Don't think that way. She's a fighter. She'll get through this. I'm sure she has all the answers you need."

"I hope you're right," I said solemnly.

Over the next few hours, people began to trickle into the waiting room...other members of my team anxious for any news about what happened this evening; Mackenzie's co-workers at the restaurant; Brayden and Jenna, who seemed to be in a daze as she was now faced with the reality of who the man she married truly was. Despite the scratches and bruises on her face, she remained strong, vowing to stay at the hospital until Mackenzie was well enough to walk out of here with her. I knew she saw the truth in my eyes, that there was a strong possibility that would not happen, but I didn't want to dampen her spirit. In fact, it was her positive attitude that gave me hope everything would be okay.

I had no idea how much time had passed and I was getting anxious for some kind of news about Mackenzie and the baby...good or bad. The waiting was eating me up. Finally, the doctor who had met the paramedics when we arrived appeared in the waiting room, her expression blank.

"Mr. Burnham," she said, looking at me. "Will you come with me, please?"

Standing up, I hesitated briefly, glancing at the full waiting room, everyone else just as anxious for news as I was.

"Go," Eli said, gesturing. "We'll be here if you need us."

I nodded and followed the doctor. "How is she?" I asked quickly as she led me toward an elevator.

"She's in surgery right now," she replied, getting into the elevator and pressing a button for the fourth floor. I scanned the directory, seeing that the fourth floor was the labor and delivery unit. "We had to be careful when we delivered the baby, but he made it. We gave him a thorough exam because of all the trauma he had endured, but he's doing wonderfully."

I remained somewhat in shock as I followed the doctor down a hallway and into a room, a nurse sitting on a chair in the corner and rocking a little blue bundle. I'd had months to prepare for this moment, but it wasn't supposed to happen like this. Mackenzie was supposed to be here so we could celebrate the birth of our child together. Instead, she was undergoing surgery to save her life.

The nurse heard us enter and looked in our direction, a warm smile crossing her face. "You must be the father."

I remained still, in awe. Even though I felt our baby kick and move around in Mackenzie's stomach on a daily basis, it was still just an abstract thing. But as the nurse raised herself from the chair and walked toward me with the little bundle, it dawned on me... I was a father.

As I stood there and held my son for the first time, I knew why Mackenzie made me make that promise to her. This moment was what life was all about. A year ago, I never saw myself settling down for long enough to even have a wife, let alone actually want to have kids. Now, as I stared into his hazel eyes dotted with speckles of gold and green, I got it. He was only hours old, yet I saw so much of myself and Mackenzie in him.

Too mesmerized by my son, I barely noticed when the doctor left, promising to come find me when she had any news of Mackenzie's status.

Throughout the evening, nurses came in to check on us at least once an hour, offering to show me how to put him down in the crib so I could give my arm a rest, but I refused to let go. I wanted him to feel all the love he deserved.

A million thoughts swam through my head as time

crept by with no word on Mackenzie… How was I supposed to do this without her? How was I going to explain to our son that his mother gave her life for his? I didn't know the first thing about raising a child. My mother had assured me we would figure it out as we went along. But I wondered if I could possibly be a good father without Mackenzie at my side.

As the clock neared midnight, I finally relented and allowed one of the nurses to put him in a crib, but I couldn't stop looking at him. I wanted to remember this moment…a moment when, in my mind, we were still a family. At any minute, the door to this room could open and a doctor could give me the news I had been dreading all night long. Then I would finally have to face the reality that we would never be a family, that Mackenzie would never be given the opportunity to hold her son.

Reaching into the crib, I grabbed our son's hand, holding it tight. "Don't worry," I whispered. "I'll never let anything happen to you."

~~~~~~~~~~

"Mr. Burnham," a soft voice said and I felt someone nudge me. I opened my eyes, taking in the serene surroundings of the hospital room in the maternity ward. I looked at the crib to my left, my hand still wrapped around my son's as he slept without a care in the world.

"Yes?" I answered groggily. Trying to snap out of it, I wiped at my face and straightened myself. I met the doctor's flat expression, a sinking feeling forming in the pit of my stomach that there was no way I'd receive good news twice in one night. Then her mouth turned into a warm smile and my eyes widened, hope washing over me.

"She's going to be just fine. The bullet missed any vital

organs. She did lose quite a bit of blood, but we were able to stop the flow and stitch her back up."

Letting out a huge breath, I sagged into my chair, closing my eyes. All the tension that had been building up over the hours was immediately gone, gratitude filling my heart. I was a bundle of a thousand emotions, unable to properly convey how thankful I truly was that Mackenzie was okay. Part of me thought this was all a dream, that I would wake up to find out she didn't make it.

"Can I see her?"

"You may, but she hasn't woken up just yet. Between the C-section and the surgery on her shoulder, she's been through a lot. We're keeping her as comfortable as we can. When she does wake up, it may only be for a few minutes, and she will most likely be out of it."

"I understand. I just need to see her."

"Understood," the doctor said, beginning to walk out of the room.

Hesitating, I looked back at the crib and our son.

"Don't worry," the doctor said as a petite blonde woman entered the room. "I called for a nurse to come look after him for a while."

I still didn't like the idea of leaving him, but I knew I couldn't bring him with me. Reluctantly leaving his side, I followed the doctor back toward the bank of elevators. We rode in silence to the second floor, the journey seeming to take forever. Finally, it slowed to a stop and we exited into the bustling lobby of the trauma unit. After navigating through a few hallways, she stopped in front of a door and pushed it open.

Entering, I was surrounded by the sound of beeping machines as I shuffled toward where Mackenzie lay, a soft smile on her face. Seeing her chest rising and falling in a gentle rhythm, I couldn't remember ever being so relieved. It still didn't seem real to me. I had hoped and prayed for this outcome, but I didn't think it was in the cards, not the way my luck had usually gone.

All of a sudden, it dawned on me that Mackenzie wasn't the only one injured this evening. Spinning around, I called, "Doctor?"

"Yes?" She met my eyes.

"The man who came in with her... Francis Galloway..." I swallowed hard, worried that I had acted impulsively and would now be faced with having to tell Mackenzie I had killed her father. "How is he doing?"

"Mr. Galloway lost a lot of blood and one of the bullets lodged in his chest cavity. You need to understand the survival rate of that kind of wound has a tendency to be rather low."

I rubbed my temples, the guilt I felt making me sick.

"But...," she continued and I snapped my head up, meeting her eyes once more. "We were able to extract the bullet and stopped the flow of blood. He's in the room next door and is also expected to make a full recovery."

My shoulders relaxed as I blew out a breath. "Thank you, Doctor. I appreciate it."

"Of course." She turned from me and I started back toward Mackenzie, marveling at how much had happened in the span of just six hours. It had been the longest and most trying time of my life and I wouldn't wish anyone to have to suffer through what I had.

"One more thing," the doctor said. I faced her and waited for her to speak. "Those burns on Mr. Galloway... How did he get them?"

A small smile crossed my mouth. "It's a *very* long story."

The doctor nodded. "Understood. Have a nice evening, Mr. Burnham."

"You, too," I replied. "And thanks again."

The doctor closed the door and I turned my attention back to Mackenzie, pulling up a chair and sitting next to her. I reached for her hand and took it in mine, toying with her wedding band and engagement ring.

Her face was serene, her lips turned up just slightly as she slept. The demons of her past no longer haunted her. She was finally at peace.

"I'm so glad you're okay," I said to her sleeping form. "I don't know what I would have done if I lost you, Serafina. I don't think..." I trailed off, composing myself. Despite the fact she was okay, I was still choked up thinking about what almost was. "I wouldn't have been able to go on if I lost you. You're a part of me." A small smile crossed my face as I recalled how far we had come since our first meeting.

"I knew the first day I met you that I was never going to let you go. You were the first woman who ever challenged me, and in that instant, I could tell you were the one for me. Sure, we've had more than our fair share of disagreements, but I wouldn't trade one of those for anything. You made me finally feel like I found my place in the world, and that's by your side, with our beautiful son."

Mackenzie began to shift in her bed and her eyes fluttered open, meeting mine. "Hey," she croaked out.

"Hey," I responded.

A small smile crossed her lips. "Hey."

"Hey." I pushed a strand of hair behind her ear, savoring in the warmth of her skin, a warmth I didn't think I'd ever feel again.

"Our son..." She looked at me with worry in her eyes.

My gaze softened. "He's perfect. He's a healthy seven pound, six ounce boy and already has a full head of dark hair."

She sighed, closing her eyes as if thanking someone from up above for answering her silent prayers.

"Can I see him?" she asked, her voice growing lazy as she struggled to keep her eyes open.

"You will," I promised. "But you need your rest. Everything's going to be okay." I planted a soft kiss on her forehead. "You won't have to pretend to be someone you're not ever again. It's finally over."

Chapter Thirty-Nine

New Orders

Mackenzie

A WEEK AFTER BEING shot by my father to save my life, I lay in the hospital bed, surrounded by all my friends and family as they fussed over the little bundle I held in my arms. It took me a few days to finally be able to stay awake for longer than five minutes at a time, and once I felt the pain all over my body, I knew why the doctors had been keeping me drugged. It would still be a few weeks until I could comfortably walk around, but I didn't care. I was here and so was my son.

I looked to my right, Tyler standing there with a wide grin on his face. He had spent nearly every minute at my side, vowing to stay with me until I was strong enough to leave which, according to the doctors who had checked on me this morning, could be tomorrow. I was itching to finally leave this hospital...as a family.

"Have you picked out a name yet?" Jenna asked.

I met her brilliant blue eyes and smiled warmly. Over the past few days, she had apologized over and over again about what Richard had done, how she should have seen the signs, how she should have known there was something off about him. But there was no way for her to know any of that. I had trusted him, too, thinking he was the perfect catch for someone like Jenna. He was charming, smart, debonair, always knew what to say and when to say it. He had put on the perfect act and we all fell for it. Brayden had been doing his best to keep her mind off of everything. He even went to the hotel, packed all her belongings, and relocated her to my old condo, which had been released and was no longer considered a crime scene.

"Yes," I said. "Francis Charles Burnham… Charlie for short," I said with a slight lump in my throat.

"He looks like a Charlie," Brayden commented.

"Well," Colleen said, leaning down to kiss her grandson on the forehead. "Welcome to the family, little man. You better give your father as hard a time as he gave me when *he* was growing up."

"Hey!" Tyler exclaimed. "I was a complete angel. At least compared to him, I was." He gestured to Alexander.

"Oh, really?" Alexander said, rushing his brother and putting him in a headlock.

"Boys!" a small voice shouted. We all turned our heads to see little Melanie standing next to Olivia, her hand on her hip in mock irritation. "Play nice! Or Grandma's going to take away your toys. Isn't that right?" she asked, looking toward Colleen.

Shrugging, she responded, "That usually *is* the punishment." She winked.

"Well, I'm sure you're tired," Jenna said, squeezing my arm. "Why don't you get some rest? We'll stop by in the next few days when you're all settled back at home, okay?"

I nodded. "I'd like that."

Everyone said their goodbyes and began to file out of the room. "Dad, wait," I said, grabbing his hand as he was about to follow everyone else.

"Yes, *mi bichito?*" he asked, his eyes brimming with love and affection.

Once the last person had left and it was just Tyler and

us, I faced him. His shoulder was in a sling, but other than that, it didn't appear as if he had suffered a gunshot wound to the chest just a week ago. "How did you know?" I asked. The question had been eating me up for days.

"Know what?"

"Where I would be?"

A smile crossed his face as he kept my hand clasped in his. "I knew Agent Suarez was dirty, particularly when I made arrangements to turn myself in and he asked me to surrender at a location other than the local police department. When he took me into 'custody', he didn't really search me too well, so as he was driving around the island with me handcuffed in the back seat, I put one of my old skills to use. It's amazing what a bobby pin can get you out of these days." He winked.

"So you got out of your handcuffs, then what?"

"Suarez stopped in front of the house, saying it would be his big pay day. When he opened the back door to let me out, I easily overtook him and snatched his weapon from him. Then I made him call 911 and confess to everything. How do you think the police arrived so quickly?"

He raised his eyebrows at me, a satisfied look crossing his face. "It's a good thing, too, because during the internal investigation, they found a video file Suarez must have confiscated when looking into Charlie's death. Charlie hid a camera in your condo and got his murder on video, including Richard's confession beforehand. He always was a smart guy." He squeezed my arm and I fought the lump in my throat now that I had confirmation Charlie had sacrificed himself in his quest for the truth. Kissing me on the temple, my dad walked away, leaving Tyler and me alone.

"So he knew all along...," Tyler mused.

"What do you mean by that?"

"He came to me that day and said he was going to turn himself in. He must have known it was a setup and that he would finally be able to put everything to rest." He slouched into his chair. "Damn. He's good."

A small laugh escaped my mouth. "He *was* in Counterintelligence, after all. What did you expect? The truth?"

I tore my eyes from Tyler's as little Charlie began to stir. I still couldn't believe we had created this adorable little man in my arms. I never saw myself being a mother, but now I couldn't imagine my life without him in it, even though he was only a week old. For the first time, I got it. I understood why my father had done what he did all those years ago. I knew I would do everything I could to keep Charlie safe, and that was exactly what my father had done.

Over the past week, I had begun to process everything that had happened. All of the questions I had been searching for were answered. I finally had the closure I had looked for throughout the years. Now that Richard was dead and the truth was revealed, I no longer had to hide who I was. I could finally be me again. The only thing that was missing was Damian. I was desperate to know if anyone had found him, but Tyler only said he was waiting on news. I didn't know if that meant he was still looking into it or he was trying to shield me from the truth.

Tyler's cell buzzed, bringing me out of my thoughts. He grabbed it off the side table and looked at the screen before turning to me.

"I need to step out for a minute. Want me to put him down?"

I nodded, my arm growing tired.

I gave Charlie a kiss on the forehead and allowed Tyler

to place him in his crib beside me.

"I'll be right back," Tyler said as he headed toward the door. Just as he was about to walk outside, he glanced over his shoulder. "I love you, Mrs. Burnham."

I smiled. "And I love you. Now hurry back. I miss you already." I closed my eyes and enjoyed the momentary break from visitors.

What seemed like seconds later, the door opened once more and Tyler walked in, a man who was about six-foot with dark scraggly hair and medium build following. I met his eyes through his glasses and gasped, wishing I could get out of my hospital bed and run. But I was still sore, and probably couldn't make it more than a few steps without needing to take a break.

"Damian?" I said in bewilderment, almost not believing my eyes. For years after I was forced to leave North Carolina, I had dreamt of the day we would be reunited. He was my best friend, my first love. It had been nearly two decades. We had both grown and matured, but I saw the same little boy who used to look at the stars with me.

"Hey, Fi," he said, gently wrapping his arms around me.

"How did you know I'd be—"

"I told him," Tyler interrupted and we both turned to him. "The night you were..." He trailed off, taking a deep breath. "Well, Eli found the iPad Richard had at the scene. Maxwell was able to run a trace on where the camera feed was coming from and, although it was being bounced off a dozen different satellites, he finally isolated it and we found him."

Damian looked down on me and grabbed my hand in his. "I'm so sorry, Fi. You have to understand. I didn't want anything to do with what that sick bastard was planning, but I didn't have a choice. He threatened to kill

399

everyone close to me, including you. After I saw what he did to my parents and how they set Charlie up, I just couldn't take that risk. I never meant for all of those people to get hurt, but I just couldn't let anything happen to you."

"How did you know Charlie?"

"Through a mutual acquaintance. I had confided in a friend about you and how I couldn't shake the feeling you were still alive, but even after using my access at the FBI to locate you, I was coming up empty. He put me in touch with Charlie, saying he could usually see between the lines and find things that aren't there. In no time at all, he found you. I was thrilled, but Charlie warned me it could be disastrous if I approached you because someone could put the pieces together. I didn't know what he was talking about, but he made me promise to be patient while he tried to figure things out. Then he was locked up and I couldn't shake the feeling it had something to do with what I had asked him to look into, so I kept my distance, not wanting anything to happen to you."

I nodded. "But it all caught up to you, didn't it?"

"I wasn't tracked down because I asked Charlie to help."

"It was your father," I muttered, recalling Richard's confession.

"I suppose this guy wanted to make sure my dad didn't stray too far from the plan and he used me as a guarantee. I don't know how he figured it out, but he knew about my...computer skills."

"You mean hacking?" I raised my eyebrows.

He shrugged. "More or less. One day, as I was leaving work and heading to the gym, my car was pushed off the road and into a ditch. The next thing I remember was waking up in a cold cement room, chained to the wall. Two days later, my father joined me. I hadn't seen him in years and, at first, I didn't believe it was him. He didn't look like the man I remembered him to be. Hell, I thought he was dead. When I heard his voice, I knew it was him, despite how he had changed his appearance for whatever deep cover job he was on. He told me everything... How he had been blackmailed into killing your father. How he planned the embassy attack to do just that, never expecting him to make it out of the fire. How he planted evidence to cover up all the deals so no one caught on. How relieved he was when his superiors signed off on the results of his investigation that your dad was responsible. How things started spinning out of control once Charlie began to ask questions. How he followed him one night, saw him with your mother, and grew concerned all over again that someone would figure it all out. How he had Charlie locked up and did nothing when Richard planned to kill your mother.

"He told me he jumped at the opportunity the CIA gave him to go under deep cover. He was scared for us, and for himself. This gave him an out and he took it, disappearing from my life and leaving me with a thousand questions...and a thousand more when he showed up that day in that cold cement room. He said he had tried to make amends, had told Richard he was done and was going to turn himself in. Apparently, that didn't go over too well." He swallowed hard, closing his eyes. "Two days later, my father was gone, and I knew he was..."

"Damian, I'm—"

"This guy kept me down there for what seemed like an eternity," he interrupted. "I was under constant surveillance. He had me use what I knew to look into anything and everything, to use my skills to plant evidence, incriminating certain people in crimes I'm certain *he* committed. Sick of being there, I tried to send a message to someone one day about where I was and what was going on. Hell, I had all these computers in front of me. I was done living in fear."

"Who did you try to send a message to?"

"My mother."

I nodded, briefly closing my eyes.

"It's my fault she's gone," he admitted, a quiver in his voice. "I was stupid and didn't think about the repercussions. I was valuable to this guy. He needed me, but that didn't mean he was willing for me to get away with what I had done. So, the following day, he placed a newspaper on the floor in front of me. The headline announced my mother's and her new husband's death. From that day forward, I did everything asked of me, not wanting this guy to get to anyone else I cared about, including you."

"It's okay," Tyler said, giving Damian a sympathetic look. "No one here could have done anything to stop this. You did what you had to in order to survive."

He nodded, squeezing my hand. "I'm just glad you're okay."

"And I'm glad you never stopped trying to find me."

"Never," he said. "Like I told you all those years ago, it would take a hell of a lot more than just new orders to tear us apart."

He wrapped his arms around me and I relished in his embrace for the first time in nearly two decades. I met Tyler's eyes, a satisfied smile on his face. Everything had come full circle. All my prayers had finally been answered. That was the moment I learned to never give up hope. I had shielded myself for years, remembering how alone I felt when I was younger, wishing upon a star and praying to whomever would listen. I thought all those prayers and wishes had gone unanswered, but that wasn't the case at all. They were just waiting until I *needed* them to be answered.

Epilogue

Two Years Later

Tyler

SNOW FELL AGAINST THE windows of our house in Beacon Hill, the streets of Boston sporting a fluffy white coat.

"I have no idea how you suffer through this, Mack," Brayden's boisterous voice cut through all the laughter and frivolity surrounding us as we celebrated Charlie's second birthday. I couldn't believe two years had passed since he entered this world in what I thought would be the worst night of my life. Instead, it ended up being the night I received the two greatest gifts a man could ask for...a son and a second chance – or third, depending on how you looked at it – with the woman of my dreams, my lightning strike.

About three months after Charlie was born, Mackenzie was finally cleared to travel and she couldn't wait to get to Boston. We finally got the new start we both needed and left the past in the past. True, everything Mackenzie had endured made her into the person she was today, but she stopped living in the shadows.

For the first time in her life, Mackenzie finally had everything she ever wanted. Her father was back in her life. In fact, he had been recruited by one of the top private security firms in the country...mine. Now that his name was cleared, he was more than eager to get back into investigations. Plus, he was close by so he could spend as much time as he wanted with Mackenzie and Charlie.

Even better, Mackenzie finally had Damian back in her life, who came up to visit as much as he could. The sound of her laughter echoing through the house as they reminisced about their childhood always brought a smile to my face, knowing I was able to give that to her.

Jenna and Brayden remained in South Padre, where she continued looking after the restaurant operations, although she had been spending quite a bit of time in Boston to prepare for the opening of a second location of their restaurant in the Financial District. She seemed to have forgotten all about Richard, although it was hard to tell with her.

"Daddy!" a small voice called to me, breaking me away from the snow and my thoughts. Charlie ran into my arms and I swung him around, making him squeal with delight. "Presents?" he asked.

"Did you ask Mommy if it was time yet?" I replied, glancing up to see Mackenzie laughing with Jenna and Olivia. A warmth spread through me as I caught sight of the little bump on her that was starting to show. I missed the early stages of her first pregnancy and was thrilled that I would be here every day of this one, morning sickness and all.

"She said to ask you."

I chuckled at what had become our parenting style. "Do you want to open presents?" I asked in hushed tones.

He nodded, his eyes growing wide.

"Then you can open your presents."

When he squirmed, I put him down and he darted from me, shouting, "Daddy said it's time!"

Meeting my eyes, Mackenzie smiled and sauntered

across the room toward me. "You're incorrigible, you know that? You *do* understand you'll be up all night long assembling all the toys, right?"

I pulled her against me, raising my eyebrows. "Well, if I'll be up all night, I'm sure we can find *something* more constructive to fill our time, rather than putting together a bunch of toys that will just be destroyed in two days."

"Oh, really?" she replied, pulling on my blazer jacket, leading me toward the bay window in the formal sitting room of our house.

"Mmm-hmm…"

"And what would that be?" she asked as I folded my arms around her, both of us staring at the snow falling at a steady pace.

"I have a few ideas," I murmured, kissing her neck.

"I don't know. I'm exhausted from growing a human inside of me. You could rub my feet and tell me a bedtime story."

"What kind of story?"

"A good one." She raised her eyebrows.

"Anything for you," I said, savoring the warmth of her body next to mine. "Once upon a time," I began, planting a kiss on her forehead, "there was a little girl who stopped believing in fairytales. She had been hidden away for years, always holding out hope her Prince Charming would come and rescue her from her self-imposed prison. Then, one day, a man appeared. He was a little rough around the edges and may not have had the purest of intentions to begin with, but he fell in love with the woman that little girl had turned into."

I glanced down to see her eyes closed, a look of serenity on her face. I began to rock her back-and-forth, almost swaying to the music in both our heads. "But there was an evil dragon who tried to keep the prince from his love. The prince knew he had to protect this woman from the monstrous beast who was trying to tear them apart, so he set upon a quest to slay the dragon and free his love."

"And did he?" she asked, turning to me.

Grabbing both her hands in mine, I simply nodded. "Yes, with a bit of help. And he used his powers to return all the people who had ever been taken from the princess to her so she could finally have the family she had been yearning for her entire life."

"How did it end?"

"Like all fairytales should," I said, raising her hand to meet my lips. "They lived happily ever after."

The End.

Playlist

Losing Your Memory - Ryan Star
Cannonball - Damian Rice
This Woman's Work - Greg Laswell
Sideways - Citizen Cope
The Space Between - Dave Matthews Band
Your Ghost - Greg Laswell
If You Love Me Let Me Go - Colbie Caillat
Gone Away - Lucy Schwartz
Between The Lines - Sara Bareilles
I'm Through - Ingrid Michaelson
Over You - Ingrid Michaelson, featuring A Great Big World
Everything's Not Lost - Coldplay
The Lonely - Christina Perri
Cold Blooded - The Pretty Reckless
1000 Times - Sara Bareilles
Awake My Soul - Mumford & Sons
You Make It Real - James Morrison
All Of Me - John Legend
Boston - Augustana
Breathe Me - Sia
Apologies - Grace Potter & The Nocturnals
I Do - Susie Suh
Bewitched, Bothered, And Bewildered - Ella Fitzgerald
Tamacún - Rodrigo y Gabriela
Magic - Colbie Caillat
In The Embers - Sleeping At Last
Nothing But The Water (I) - Grace Potter & The Nocturnals
Weapon For Saturday - LOLO

By My Side - William Fitzsimmons
Future Days - Pearl Jam
The One - Kodaline
The Luckiest - Ben Folds

Books By T.K. Leigh

The Beautiful Mess Series
A Beautiful Mess
A Tragic Wreck
Gorgeous Chaos

Heart Of Light
(Cam's Story)

Heart Of Marley
(A stand-alone Heart of Light prequel)

The Deception Duet (Tyler's Story)
Chasing The Dragon
Slaying The Dragon

For more information about these titles, please visit T.K.'s
website:
www.tkleighathor.com

Vanished

It's not over yet...
A new Beautiful Mess series novel coming your way in 2016!

Rayne Kilpatrick has everything. A job she's dreamed of since she was a little girl. The perfect house. And a man she loves and is about to marry... Until he never returns from a humanitarian mission.

Gone. Disappeared. Vanished.

When footage of his gruesome murder by a Muslim extremist group is shown across the country and around the globe, she wants the person responsible for the disappearance of the man she loves to pay. She wants him to lose the one person who means the world to him, too, and she won't stop until he does.

Alexander Burnham has everything... Finally. A job he enjoys where he can actually make a difference in the world. The perfect woman who he's loved his entire life. And the most beautiful daughter a father could ask for... Until he wakes up one morning and her bedroom is empty.

Gone. Disappeared. Vanished.

It's a race against the clock for Alexander to put the pieces together and find out who has taken his daughter and what they want from him. As information comes to light, he is forced to bury the guilt he feels after losing his fellow team member and focus instead on finding and saving his daughter... Before it's too late.

The Other Side Of *Someday*

A brand new Romantic Comedy coming from T.K. Leigh in 2016!

You know how you always say someday I will?
Well, I've hit my someday.
Someday begins today.

Baylee Morgan is at a crossroads of her life. Leaving her marriage of ten years and the only life she's ever known, she starts over in a penthouse ocean-front condo in Santa Monica, California. She soon finds herself immersed, albeit reluctantly, in the daunting and perilous world of dating as an almost thirty-something in Los Angeles, unsure of how to act, what to do, or whether that hot guy she meets in yoga class is straight.

Sebby Powers' dream has always been to work in the film industry. At the age of thirty-five, he's one of the youngest up-and-coming producers in Hollywood. His life is perfect. Perfect apartment. Perfect girlfriend. Perfect dog. Until a friendship with a beautiful new neighbor with vibrant red hair and a similar taste in cheesy movies throws his perfect life into a tailspin.

The Other Side Of Someday is a fun, sexy story of looking for Mr. Right in a world full of Mr. Wrongs, when Mr. Right could be just next door.

Acknowledgements

These books in my Deception Duet have probably been the most difficult for me to write, from a technical perspective. There are so many puzzle pieces that make up this story and the amount of read-throughs I've done to make sure everything made sense, that nothing was too confusing far surpassed the number I've done on any of my previous books. Of course, I had a lot of help from my wonderful beta readers who read this story and were brutally honest with me regarding whether everything made sense.

So, first and foremost, a big thank you to these wonderful women... Lynn Ayling, Sylvia Chavarin, Melissa Crump, Karen Emery, Stacy Hahn, Natalie Naranjo, Victoria Stolte, and Stacy Stoops... Thanks so much, and I can't wait to finally start working on something *completely* different!

To my wonderful editor, Kim Young, the only woman I'll ever trust with any of my manuscripts... Thank you for always working your magic and treating my baby as if it were your own.

To my admins that keep me sane and manage my social media so I can spend more time writing and less time on Facebook, Twitter, etc... Lea, Victoria, and Melissa... Thanks for everything you do to keep me offline and writing! And a very special thanks to Joelle for helping these girls keep the street team organized!

On that note, to my fantastic street team, thank you for all your tireless efforts in helping to spread the word about my books. If it weren't for all your time that you so selflessly volunteer, I would never have even imagined I'd be where I am now, so I thank you.

To my amazing husband, Stan. Thanks for all your support from day one. I still can't believe all the authors I speak to whose husbands don't support their wives' writing ventures and I'm truly grateful that you have been from the beginning.

To all you amazing bloggers who help spread the word about my work, thank you, thank you, thank you! It still blows my mind that you all do what you do out of the kindness of your heart. Your dedication to reading and promoting authors has made my decision to remain independent a very easy one.

Last but not least, thank you to my readers for loving my characters and stories as much as I do. We're not done yet.

About The Author

T.K. Leigh, otherwise known as Tracy Leigh Kellam, is the *USA Today* Bestselling author of the Beautiful Mess series. Originally from New England, she now resides in sunny Southern California with her husband, dog and three cats, all of which she has rescued (including the husband). When she's not planted in front of her computer, writing away, she can be found running and training for her next marathon (of which she has run over fifteen fulls and far too many halfs to recall). Unlike Olivia, the main character in her Beautiful Mess series, she has yet to qualify for the Boston Marathon.

T.K. Leigh is represented by Jane Dystel of Dystel & Goderich Literary Management. All publishing inquiries, including audio, foreign, and film rights, should be directed to her.